SERPENT ASCENDING

JENNA KINKADE

InkVane

Print editions published by InkVane Press

Paperback ISBN: 979-8-9891728-1-8
Hardcover ISBN: 979-8-9891728-2-5

Digital edition published by InkVane Portal

Digital ISBN: 979-8-9891728-0-1

Cover art by Reza Afshar and Miblart.com
Interior layout by Miblart.com

This book is dedicated to those whom I've had the privilege of serving as dungeon master, and to the amazing stories we stitched together with snarky comments, childish antics, and poor choices.

THE REALMS HUMANI

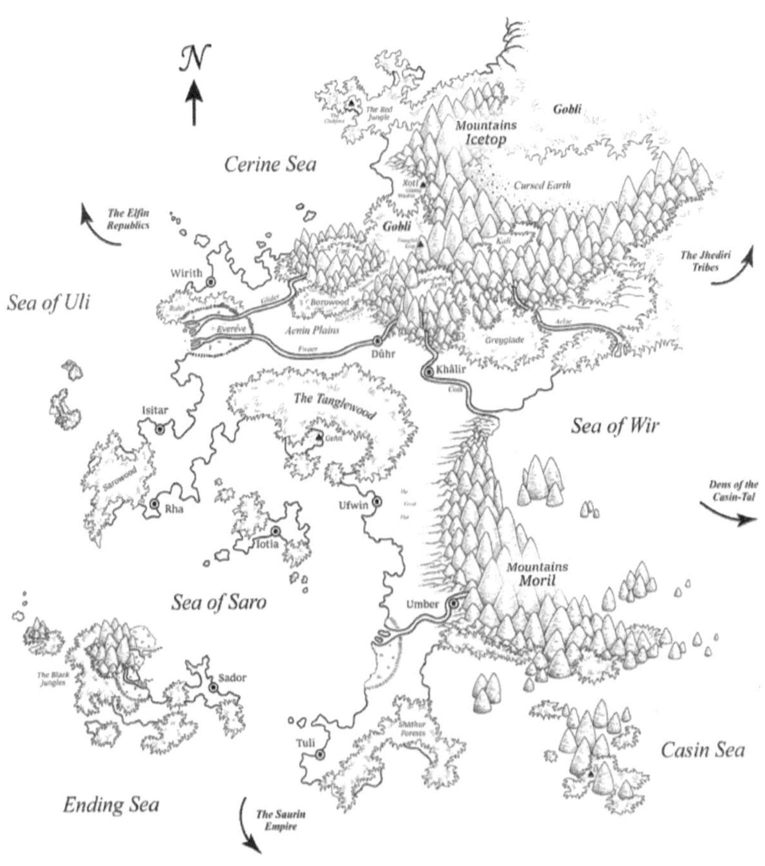

HOUSE BLACKHAND

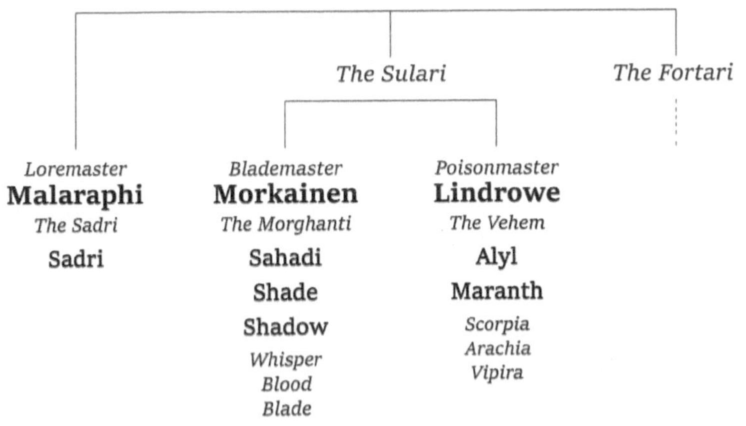

THE CHURCHES OF SATHIIS AND ELEM

The Church of Sathiis

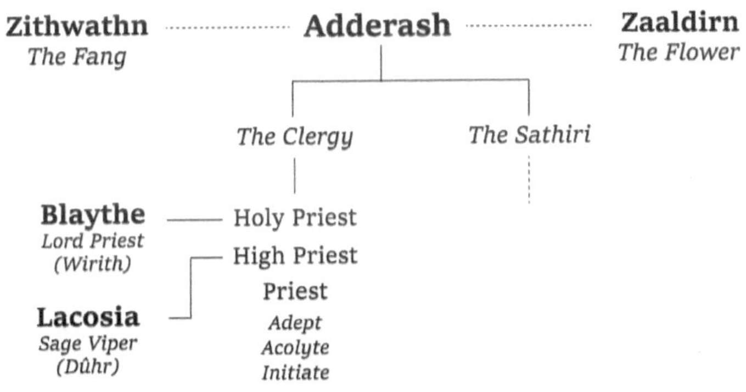

The Churches of Elem

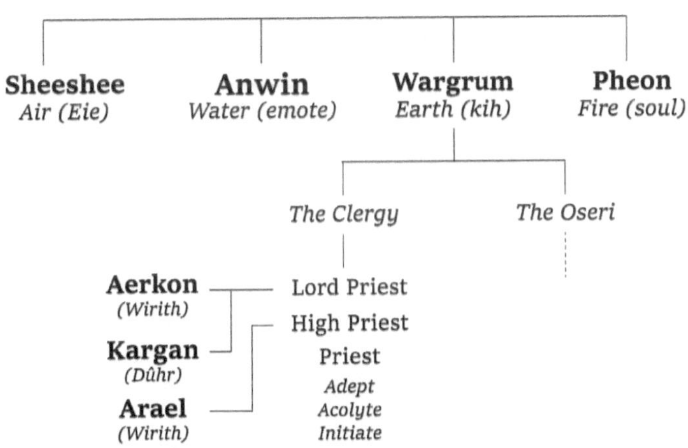

PROLOGUE

THE SERPENT AND THE FROG

The two men faced each other across a wide expanse of scorched land, purple robes and colored sashes flapping in the breeze.

The man in the green sash was young, beautiful. His skin was golden and taut over wiry muscles, as smooth and unscarred as virgin marble. His hair was soft and delicate and flowed black in the breeze. His eyes, too, were black. Haunting.

The man in the blue sash was old, ugly. His body was ravaged by time, cadaverous and gaunt. His hair was red straw that grew in irregular patches about his mottled head and spotty arms. His eyes were white and cloudy.

"Well," croaked the ugly man. "Now what?"

"Now," called the other, "I want you to strike me down."

PART ONE

ASSOCIATIONS

*In which the Church of Sathiis forms a covenant
with House Blackhand of Dûhr
and both parties begin their plans for betrayal.*

CHAPTER 1

THE MASTER AND THE MESSENGER

The assassin sat calmly behind his desk, his posture calculated to project an illusion of indifference. His tall chair and wide desk were cut from heavy wood and braced with thick strips of black iron. The desk was clear but for an oblong silver tray upon which rested two empty drinking glasses, a pitcher of water, and a small wooden box inlaid with delicate gold tracings. With its metal shutters closed, the room's dim lighting came from a few recessed sunstones and two fat red candles that melted unevenly at either side of the desk. The only visible door was at the chamber's far end. It was flanked by two marble hauhantu, deceptively inanimate and fully alert.

The assassin was humani, not young but short of middle age. His flesh was unblemished and bronzed, lending warm contrast to his gray eyes and inky hair. His nose was angular. His lips were thin and framed by a short and meticulously trimmed mustache and beard. He wore no regalia, just a simple black tunic unadorned by heraldry, and no jewelry, save a modest band of red crystal on the third finger of his left hand. He drummed the fingers of that hand lightly on the desktop while he observed the messenger seated before him, careful to allow his eyes to wander periodically to convey false distraction. With the greased thumb and forefinger of his right hand, he stroked his mustache and gently tugged at his lower lip.

The messenger was also humani, a formal representative of the Church of Sathiis. He wore a hooded robe of purple cloth tied about his waist with a thick cord of braided white silk. His bald head and hairless face appeared leaden and waxy despite the warm glow of the candles and sunstones. His nose was bent, his lips were full. His eyes were flat and lusterless. Green, perhaps.

When the messenger finally spoke, his voice was low and dry.

"Arwynn Blackhand," he said, bowing his head mechanically as he addressed the assassin. "Lord Priest Welbley Blaythe of Wirith sends his greetings and congratulates you on your triumph over Hotath."

Arwynn accepted the greeting with a slight nod.

He leads with Hotath?

The recent spate of gobli raids in the Aenin had greatly hampered communication between Wirith and Dûhr. The lord priest clearly maintained an impressive network to know of Hotath's demise, but why would he make his knowledge known?

Is Blaythe playing my own game? Is he hoping that I will underestimate him if he presents himself as careless? If so, it will not work.

Arwynn dismissed the matter of House Hotath with a small wave.

"I am concerned with the business of today, not yesterday," he said.

His fingers resumed their gentle tapping.

The messenger offered no reply. He simply waited, silent and expressionless.

He's good, Arwynn noted. *He won't be baited. He's memorized his part and is waiting for the drug.*

Arwynn straightened in his chair. He carefully took the gilded box of wood and gold from its silver tray and slid it across his desk to face the messenger. As he lifted the lid, his tacky fingers collected traces of powder that clung to its edge.

Dûhrani Houses Assassin used the tehelu ceremony to formally open negotiations with prospective patrons of notable status. When used by both parties, the heightened awareness granted by the drug assured a candid and truthful exchange. One small pinch of tehelu powder diluted in a glass of water delivered honesty, whether embraced or eschewed.

"Tehelu reveals," Arwynn said.

The messenger looked at the powder in the box, then at Arwynn.

"Truth obscures," he said, declining the drug.

Odd.

As master of House Blackhand, it was Arwynn's right to partake despite the messenger's refusal. Doing so, however, would be taken as an insult. Arwynn acknowledged the messenger's refusal, carefully closed the box, and returned it to the silver tray. He offered the messenger a sliver of a smile and settled back into his chair.

"How may I be of service to the lord priest of Wirith?" he asked.

The messenger answered in soft words.

"The Church of Sathiis has formed a covenant with your prince and is building a temple in the Gardens of Twilight. Supplies from Wirith will soon begin to arrive in Dûhr by way of the River Fwaer. It is here that Lord Blaythe seeks your service."

Arwynn casually stroked his mustache again as the messenger spoke. His thumb and forefinger left traces of tehelu tingling where they touched his lip. Very slowly, he drew a deep breath and braced himself for the drug's onrush. Though tiny in measure, the drug on his lip was undiluted and pure.

"Surely the lord priest's covenant with House Kythidûhr provides transit assurances," Arwynn said.

The tingling on Arwynn's lip became a burning. Random patches of his visual field began to snap in and out of disorientingly sharp focus. His blood felt hot. His pulse banged in his ears, and his clothes felt rough and heavy. The soft glow of the sunstones burned his eyes. The candlelight grew brighter with each flicker until it lanced through the chamber like lightning to bring out every nuance, every detail. The scent of flowers and polishing oils thickened the air.

"The gobli have overrun the Borowood and the Tameron," the messenger said, "and now raid the Aenin Plains. It will not be long before they threaten Dûhr's outer reaches and draw away the prince's attention. This will compromise his ability to deliver on his promises. Your House is Assassin. Gobli hostilities will not affect you directly."

Arwynn felt the sickly sweet scents of unknown flowers settle on him like a sticky film. The smells clung to him, pushed against him, into him…

"You will be well compensated for your services," the messenger finished.

… filled his lungs, bored into his skin.

Arwynn felt his control begin to slip under the oppressive redolence. He set his jaw, held his breath, then tensed his torso and pressed his thigh against the short needle fixed to his desk's inner kneehole. The shallow prick flooded him with pain, providing a glaring and crystallizing cynosure. Arwynn welcomed the pain, focused on it, dissected it—its taste, its color, its sound, its smell—and used its characteristics to recalibrate his senses.

Though he'd shown no outward sign of distress, Arwynn took a moment to compose himself before speaking, relaxing his torso and slowly releasing his breath. He casually wiped a faint smudge from his desktop with his finger, examined that finger briefly, then wiped it clean with his thumb.

"Why this House?" he asked. "There are several other entries into Dûhr, all controlled by Houses that would serve your master at less expense."

"The River Fwaer is the only reliable trade lane between Wirith and Dûhr," the messenger replied. "The Fwaer enters Dûhr through Westgate. You control Westgate. You can guarantee secure passage of cargo from Westgate to the Gardens of Twilight."

Arwynn scowled at the courier and searched for deception: uneasiness about the eyes, faint facial twitches, subtle shifts in posture. He listened for any sharp intake of breath, sniffed the air for a hint of fresh sweat.

Nothing. Just dust and polishing oil.

And flowers, sweetly pungent.

Arwynn leaned forward in his chair and clasped his hands together on the desktop.

The lord priest's needs are too plain to warrant the involvement of a House Assassin. I am missing something.

"What compensation does Lord Blaythe offer?"

"Kalypshia vine and achaelos root for your poisoners," the messenger answered. "For your swordsmen, saurin steel. For yourself, elfin laef, the rarest of currencies."

And there it was.

So subtle. I almost missed it.

Arwynn heard the messenger's words yet perceived no breath. The messenger's chest swelled and shrank, but not in time with his speech. Almost, but not quite.

It's not what's there, he thought. *It's what's missing.*

Arwynn smelled no perspiration but his own and felt warmth only from the candles. He saw no wetness in the messenger's eyes, just a glassy sheen. The same with the man's teeth and tongue. Dry. Glassy.

The assassin leaned back in his chair and stroked his mustache over pursed lips. His fingers returned to their gentle drumming.

You have succeeded, Welbley Blaythe, he thought. *I am intrigued by this creature of yours. So much like a man and yet not a man at all. Very well. I will play your game, for a while at least, if only to see what scheme merits such deception.*

"I think," Arwynn said, "that something might be arranged."

CHAPTER 2

POSTULATES AND PORTENTS

Arwynn summoned his lieutenants to his conference chamber on the eve of the messenger's departure. The four men sat around a great oaken table, the remnants of their meal lost amid a clutter of papers, maps, and colored tiles. For some time, they discussed their affairs in Dûhr, and each apprised the others of developments within their sphere of control. Then their conversation shifted to Welbley Blaythe's mysterious emissary.

"What does this mean, a man that does not breathe?" the fat man grunted as he poured himself wine. "I'll tell you what it means. If there is no breath, there is no man. It's as simple as that."

Arwynn eyed his poisonmaster. The man's short-cropped hair and languid eyes conspired with his corpulence and torpid demeanor to make him appear oafish and indolent. He was neither. Arwynn was one of the few who knew that Urath Lindrowe's bulk was born of not gluttony but the interaction of dozens of poisons he'd carefully introduced to his system over the years. Poisons that were now a part of him.

Arwynn stroked his bare chin with a pale hand.

"Your reasoning, Urath?" he asked.

The fat man smiled.

"My friends," Lindrowe said to the others at the table, "bear with me as I recount what we know."

He breathed noisily and counted on his pudgy fingers as he spoke.

"The messenger did not perspire. Not at all. Despite the heat of the day and a brisk walk from the White Raven Inn. He had no breath. His tongue was dry. His eyes—"

He glanced at Arwynn.

"Dry," Arwynn said.

"Dry," Lindrowe repeated. "No scent of food or drink spilled from his mouth, nor any hint of oil from his hair or sweat from his skin. Yet he moved, he spoke! I must draw the obvious conclusion—the messenger was not a man. At least, not in the living sense."

Opposite Lindrowe, Malaraphi (*Cognition, Flame, Fortitude, Animus*) leaned forward on old and frail arms. Fine gray hair tumbled over his bony shoulders. The loremaster's red eyes narrowed at the suggestion of Unlife.

"You would consider a liche, Lindrowe?" he asked, voice uneven.

The fat man scowled at the timeworn elfi wizard for a moment, then fell back in his chair and blew out a heavy breath. "Beya. It does seem unlikely." He reached for his goblet, adding, "Besides, we'd suss a liche long before it reached our gate."

"Usually," Malaraphi muttered, then again more quietly. "Usually."

Lindrowe frowned and swirled the wine in his goblet, watching it smoothly coat the inside of the vessel as he allowed the cup to turn it in his hand, then looked back at the loremaster.

"Besides," Lindrowe said, "a fleshy liche would stink on such a hot day, no? After all, the flesh goes first, beya? Yes, indeed—the flesh goes first."

"After the eyes," the elfi mumbled.

Lindrowe shrugged and drank his wine.

Arwynn watched the wizard and waited.

You know something, he thought. *Say it…*

"Unless masked," the elfi said softly.

"Uh?" Lindrowe raised a thick eyebrow.

"Masked," Malaraphi repeated, loud enough for all to hear. "Masked. Magickally shrouded."

"A liche, you mean? Disguised to be taken for a living thing?"

The wizard nodded.

"By flowers?" Arwynn asked.

"Why not?" Malaraphi shrugged. "It's possible… though the Aethic requirements would be… immense. Even the least of liches, a simple bone soldier or puppet corpse, requires two infusions of Aethic energy: one to enchant the dead form and another to control it. But to mask the rotting and give it voice?" Malaraphi shook his head slowly. "If Blaythe's messenger was an unliving thing, it's of a kind I've not encountered before."

"Even in Xotl?" Arwynn asked.

Malaraphi stiffened. He tightened his lips and narrowed his eyes into an indignant glare.

"Yes," he said to Arwynn. "Even in Xotl."

Arwynn held the wizard's eyes for a heartbeat, then another. Then he smiled evasively and reached for a carafe. Speaking to the table as he poured, Arwynn said, "If this courier was indeed unliving, then it will not have been fooled by so unsophisticated a disguise as painted skin and a false beard. Even my talents at deception cannot fool the dead."

Lindrowe grunted.

Malaraphi muttered under his breath, "No. I suppose not."

Arwynn took a drink and wiped his mouth carefully with a linen napkin, then turned to his blademaster.

"You've been more quiet than usual tonight, Rahain," he said. "What do you think of the Sathiian messenger?"

Rahain Morkainen was a tall man, lean and strong like his humani father, with silver eyes and silken white hair like his elfin mother. He was also a hollow man, long ago deprived of his capacity for empathy and compassion. Spurned by the elfi and mocked by the humani for his mixed blood, it was only in Arwynn's service that he'd found acceptance and a sense of worth.

Morkainen frowned and shook his head. He disliked dealing with mages and priests, even Malaraphi to some degree, and the talk of unliving creatures soured his stomach.

"A liche?" he asked, letting the words hang for a moment. "Perhaps. For myself, I saw no signs and felt no portents. But if it was a liche, it would have detonated several glyphs before reaching your door. At the very least, it would have activated one of the hauhantu."

He thrust his chin toward one of Arwynn's macabre statues.

"Yes, yes, yes," Lindrowe agreed. "Quite true, quite true." He shot a glance at Malaraphi and added, "Unless masked."

Malaraphi nodded. "Unless masked."

Morkainen shook his head.

"You, my friends," he said, "are men of philosophy and magick. I am not. My expertise is bound to flesh and steel and what can be killed by the two. I saw nothing, and my Whispers have reported nothing that would mark Blaythe's man a liche."

"And what have they reported, your Whispers?" Arwynn asked.

"Nothing not already known," Morkainen said. "Blaythe's courier approached from the White Raven Inn by the appointed route at the appointed time, met with you, and left by the same path. He took no food or drink and spoke only to you."

Morkainen glanced at Lindrowe and Malaraphi. "This is unusual, but not unnatural."

Lindrowe did not reply. Neither did Malaraphi.

Morkainen continued, "Ciridan Lothloran took up the messenger's shadow as he left the keep. Her orders were to follow him until relieved by Morgru Murgwei at Westgate Market, then return here. Morgru will shadow the messenger and send back word of his doings through our agents in the west. With luck, he will lead us to Blaythe."

"You still have not located him?" Lindrowe asked.

Morkainen shook his head.

"He's elusive. He's the Sathiian lord priest of Wirith but doesn't reside in the temple there—nor anywhere within the city proper, as far as I can tell. My Morghanti began searching for him well before Arwynn accepted his emissary and have yet to determine his whereabouts. The man is a snake in tall grass."

"So speaks his reputation," Arwynn said. "Perhaps his calling to the Church of Sathiis is more apt than he realizes. In any event, let us hope that Morgru succeeds, but plan against it. As for Ciridan, she is the Shade we discussed earlier, yes?"

"She is," Morkainen confirmed. "But my needs will soon call for a Sahadi."

"Loquay?"

Morkainen nodded. "Her House is stronger than we believed, and she's been recruiting."

"Recruiting?" Lindrowe raised an eyebrow. "Her outward numbers haven't changed. Is she bolstering her House reserves?"

"She is," Morkainen said. "And in a very concerning way. Her visible cadres haven't changed, but their composition has. More novices and fewer veterans. She's moving experienced sulari to her reserves and replacing them with fledglings. The only reason she'd do that is to train fresh recruits she keeps hidden. Her existing reserves are already trained."

"How many newcomers?" Lindrowe asked.

"Several hundred at least."

"Beya."

"That's only half the problem," Morkainen said. "Openly deploying so many inexperienced sulari is a risk Loquay would never take unless she could mitigate her downside. She must have something, or someone, very powerful tucked away."

They considered possibilities and implications for a long moment before Arwynn broke the silence.

"Lacosia," he said softly. "Loquay struck a deal with Lacosia."

All eyes turned to the master.

"Blaythe oversees Wirith, but Lacosia manages the Black Church's interests in Dûhr," Arwynn said. "He needs someone local to provide protection for the new Sathiian temple until construction is complete. Loquay holds a large section of the sewers under the Gardens of Twilight, so she'd be a logical choice. The Sathiians could house Loquay's new recruits in the temple basements and conceal adepts among her cadres to misrepresent their numbers."

"It plays," Lindrowe said. "Blaythe forms a covenant to move supplies into Dûhr; Lacosia forms a second to protect it once it's here. Using rival Houses Assassin prevents graft at the transfer."

Lindrowe looked at Malaraphi.

"If there are liches on the transport side...?"

The loremaster's face darkened as the poisonmaster's voice trailed off.

"There will be worse in the temple," Malaraphi finished. He looked at Morkainen, then Arwynn. "Barring our personal involvement, it may require a Sahadi to deal with these snakes."

"And you believe Ciridan could be Sahadi?" Arwynn asked Morkainen.

"I do," the blademaster said. "I propose testing by season's end and training in illusory weaves under Mirithwin Mirroreye."

Arwynn folded his hands before his face and considered Morkainen's proposal. Although the idea of a Sahadi appealed to him, he was reluctant to grant his blademaster's request. Lyete had been the last of their Sahadi, and the reverberations of her unraveling still echoed in the psyche of his House.

"Her test would call for the maddram," Arwynn said.

Lindrowe placed his heavy hands on the table and spoke slowly, his voice low and even.

"The test of maddram has killed more than one Sahadi hopeful, Rahain."

Malaraphi chuckled. "And a few Alyl, as I recall."

"Beya." Lindrowe brushed aside the old wizard's wheedling, his attention on Morkainen.

"Ciridan is a valuable asset to this House," the poisonmaster said. "You are certain she can survive the maddram?"

Morkainen hesitated, then firmly nodded.

"Ciridan Lothloran is an extraordinary talent. As one of her teachers, I'm sure you'll agree."

"Hmm… yes." Lindrowe licked his heavy lips and weighed his response. "She is aware, I'll give her that. Perhaps more so than we yet appreciate. And illusory training under old Mirroreye, you say? Interesting. Quite."

Morkainen nodded. "The Mindbender's weaves are well suited to manipulation and deception."

Lindrowe smirked. "And currently lacking amongst our Sadri, no?"

"With reason," Malaraphi chided. "There is no telling what you'll unleash when you open a mind."

"Or what remains trapped when you keep it closed," Lindrowe scoffed.

Morkainen ignored them and addressed Arwynn.

"Ciridan has served me well as Shade. Her value will only increase as Sahadi. More so if Loquay has indeed allied herself with the Black Church."

He paused a moment, then added: "She will survive the maddram."

But you are not sure, Arwynn thought. *I can see it in your eyes. I can hear it in your voice. A Sahadi would prove most useful... but is she truly ready?*

"Very well," Arwynn declared. "She will be tested tonight. Upon her arrival."

Morkainen stiffened.

"Tonight?"

Arwynn leaned forward in his chair and fixed his eyes on Morkainen's.

"Yes, Rahain, tonight." His voice was soft, stern.

"You are my blademaster, but this is my House and its needs must come first. You claim that a Sahadi is warranted. I agree. You tell me Ciridan Lothloran is a worthy candidate. Again, I agree. But I see the way you look at her, the pride you take in her success. Is it possible that your desire clouds your judgment?"

Morkainen set his jaw and lowered his eyes.

Arwynn leveled his gaze on Lindrowe and Malaraphi in turn. Like Morkainen, they had pupils of merit in whom they found delight. He lingered long enough on each to silently pose the same question.

When his eyes returned to Morkainen, Arwynn said, "Your payment to me for this service will be your silence until she has passed her test or lies dead. If she is as good as you claim, she will survive this night as well as any other."

He thought a moment, then added: "And be warned, Rahain—one word from you, one hint from you, and I will kill her myself."

CHAPTER 3

THE PRIEST AND THE SPY

Welbley Blaythe's keep was hidden deep in Evereve Marsh, reclaimed from the ruins of an ancient fortress by magickal prowess and botanical skill. Over the years, it had become his sanctum, a place of quiet beauty where he could escape his clerical obligations. Welbley (*Transmutation, Flux*) preferred to walk his garden alone at night with the silver light of his staff granting color and vibrancy only to areas of his choosing. Tonight, he was accompanied by a squat humani with a large nose and small eyes. The man's name was Tehru Shaddoht, and he was one of many spies in Welbley's employ.

The two men walked in silence from the east hall of Welbley's keep to the old well in the middle of the garden. Welbley drew aside his vestments and sat gently upon a patch of clover. He closed his eyes and sighed at the pungent smell of achaelos blossoms drifting on the breeze.

The spy rolled his eyes and shifted his weight nervously from leg to leg before dropping to the ground near the priest.

"Does something trouble you, Tehru?" Welbley asked, eyes still closed.

"No, m'lord."

"You are comfortable in my garden?"

"Yes, m'lord," the spy lied. "It's lovely."

"Mmm."

They were silent for a time.

Welbley calmed himself and carefully composed his questions.

Tehru considered what he'd discovered and debated what to withhold.

Tehru had learned enough about House Blackhand to earn himself a great deal of wealth if he played his hand wisely. His task tonight was to deliver just enough information to satisfy Blaythe—what he did not tell could be sold to others. Loquay Yellowhand, perhaps, or the Crimson Witch. Both would pay handsomely for information they could use against Blackhand.

Tehru appraised the priest as he waited. Welbley Blaythe was humani of uncertain descent, dark haired, fair skinned, and unremarkable in size or stature. He was dressed in clerical vestments of black and green. He wore a serpentine torque of braided silver about his neck and a green crystal ring on his right thumb. His features were neither homely nor handsome, and pudgy in a way that bespoke a pampered life. His eyes were small. Green. His lips were thick. His age was unclear.

"Tell me, Tehru," the priest asked, "what have you learned?"

The spy cleared his throat and licked his lips.

"This man, Arwynn Blackhand," he began, "is as crafty as a daemon. His methods are brutal an' precise, but he honors his contracts t'the letter."

"This I already know," Welbley said as he ran his fingers lightly over the clover. "You would do well to provide me with new information, Tehru."

"So, let's talk about why House Blackhand's so strong, beya?"

"Sulari and silver?"

Tehru shook his head and wet his lips again.

"No," the spy replied. "Structure."

"Houses Assassin are typically divided inta two divisions."

Tehru held out his hands, palms up, and extended his left.

"The fortari are support. Planning, investing, collections, graft, forgery, that sorta thing. The sulari—"

He extended his right hand.

"—do the actual stalking, hunting, an' killing. Blackhand's fortari an' sulari are separate divisions with separate leadership, same's the other Houses Assassin. But Arwynn's House has a third component division called the Sadri, and his sulari—"

Tehru curled three fingers into his palm.

"—are split into two separate orders: Vehem an' Morghanti."

Interest played like sparks in Blaythe's eyes.

"That's the key to Blackhand's strength," Tehru explained. "Autonomy and specialization. Each order functions independently, under the control of lieutenants."

"How does he benefit from giving up direct control?" Blaythe asked.

"Three ways," the spy replied. "First, he leaks off internal pressure by giving his lieutenants independence—under his oversight, o'course. Keeps 'em all happy. Second, by puttin' the orders under his lieutenants' command, he reduces his costs. He doesn't have to maintain a bureaucracy separate from the fortari, so it's less costly t'operate compared to other Houses. That means more profit, much of which he funnels t'his lieutenants. Third, the orders are divided by discipline: poison an' weaponry. This gives Blackhand distinct talent pools he can mix an' match, depending on the contract."

"Smart."

"Beya."

"What keeps his lieutenants from banding together to overthrow him?"

Tehru shrugged.

"What keeps your adepts from banding together to overthrow you?"

The priest raised an eyebrow.

Fear, he thought. *Absolute terror at the consequences of failure. Something you would do well to think about, Tehru.*

"Point," he said.

Blaythe thought a moment. "Clearly, Blackhand could not have survived for so long without having some checks and balances in place, yes? We will have to look into that."

"Yes, m'lord."

"I assume you have more detailed information on these groups?"

"Of course, m'lord."

Tehru withheld only minor details as he reported his findings.

"The Vehem are poisoners. They're trained in brewing, neutralizing, an' delivering poisons, toxins, an' venoms. Their boss is Urath Lindrowe, a pig of a man always on a bounce between brilliance an' recklessness. He's a good strategist, though. No question. But erratic—more risk than asset, if you ask me."

Welbley nodded.

You miss the point, Tehru. It does not matter what this man appears to be. What matters is that he is still alive, therefore must be of great value to Blackhand.

"The Morghanti are swords mostly," Tehru continued, "but they're also trained in the favored weapons of rival Houses: rakesi, slipknives, spraydarts, flingblades—that sorta thing. Their boss is Rahain Morkainen. He's a half-elfi who—"

"Half-elfi?"

Tehru nodded.

"Yeah. Half-elfi. Don't see many of them with status. The elfi hate mixed blood an' the humani treat 'em like trash. Call 'em 'drossi.' As you'd expect, Morkainen's pretty bitter—he's also cold, heartless, an' brutal. But I've seen him fight an' watched him train some of his sulari. He's amazing with a blade, an' he's fast. Very, very fast."

"An elfin trait," Welbley commented offhandedly. "To be expected."

"No," Tehru corrected. "It's more th'n just elfin reflexes. There's a flow to his movements... I dunno what it is, but it's more 'an just speed an' agility. I wouldn't underestimate him. He's one dangerous skokker."

Your base pejorative demeans the man, Welbley thought. *The drossi is a lieutenant in a Great House Assassin. He deserves more respect.*

"You may have a point," the priest conceded.

He idly picked a piece of clover and sniffed it.

"And the Sadri?" Welbley asked.

Tehru shrugged.

"They're weavers. Notoriously secretive an' rarely seen outside Arwynn's keep. All I managed to find was a name: Malaraphi."

Welbley brought the clover to his mouth and rubbed it gently against his lips.

Malaraphi.

The name was familiar, but Welbley could not associate it with a face or an event. He decided to think about it later. Right now, he was more interested in squeezing out every drop of information that Tehru tried to hide.

CHAPTER 4

THE TEST OF MADDRAM

Ciridan Lothloran had been a member of Arwynn's House for a little over eleven years, distinguishing herself as a keen observer and extraordinary tracker. Her natural talents, dedication to discipline, and adherence to protocol brought her to the attention of Rahain Morkainen, who promptly recruited her for his esteemed Shadows.

Under Morkainen's direct tutelage, Ciridan's talents flourished. She proved an ardent pupil, eager to devour what knowledge Morkainen chose to share, and was quick to apply it in practice. When her perceptive powers and mastery of traplore were matched only by her uncanny resourcefulness, Morkainen elevated her to the rank of Shade and assigned a cadre of Shadows to her command. But it was not until this night, as she prepared to report to Arwynn himself, that she appreciated just how far she'd come.

From a frightened child to a stalker of men.

From a scrawny runaway to a Shade among Shadows.

And now I am summoned by my master.

Ciridan steeled herself, adjusted her dark cloaks, and strode purposefully down the long corridor that led to Blackhand's conference chamber. She moved with a predatory ease belied by her round face and sturdy frame. Her short, flaxen hair bobbed gently as she walked. Her eyes were alert, light violet fading to purple in the dim light.

Black torches in skeletal iron sconces cast a flickering light over the smooth stone beneath her feet. Uncast shadows seemed to congeal from nowhere to writhe about her, move with her, and match her stride as she approached her destination.

Two guards in plate armor stood silent before the massive doors to Arwynn's conference chamber. Their armor was unnaturally black and embossed with vivid red highlights. Shimmers of glass marked the hollows of their scabbards.

High Crystal, Ciridan noted. *Sharper than a razor, stronger than steel.*

As Ciridan approached, one of the guards stepped forward. Despite their heavy armor, they made no sound as they moved to block her path. The torchlight threw down no shadow but her own.

Ciridan felt her stomach tighten.

"Who approaches?" the sentry demanded in a hollow voice.

"I am Ciridan Lothloran," she replied.

She traced a pass sign in the air before her left breast.

"I am expected."

"You are expected," the guard echoed, withdrawing.

Ciridan stepped forward. She raised the knocker, an iron ring set in the nostrils of a dragon, and let it fall. A loud clang echoed beyond the door. She waited a moment, then raised the heavy ring again.

An armored hand snatched the ring.

In one fluid motion, Ciridan pivoted to face the sentry—a poisoned dagger in her left hand inches from the sentry's groin, her right at defense before her face and throat, palm out and fingers slightly curled. But the sentry made no move to attack.

"You are expected," the hollow voice said.

Ciridan peered into the eye slits of the sentinel's visor as she slowly lowered her guard. No eyes met hers, only blackness and a glimmer of a glacial blue light.

Without sound or effort, the sentry opened the enormous door and returned to its station.

Ciridan stepped through the doorway into a small anteroom. Its L-shaped design required her to move away from the door and turn to the right before she could see into the conference room.

An excellent place for an ambush.

The conference chamber was circular and some forty feet across. The walls were the same smooth gray stone as the rest of the keep, scantily dressed with curious tapestries and mysterious trophies. The floor was red-mottled Ufwinian marble, adorned with numerous colorful rugs. A fire burned in a circular hearth in the center of the room, adding light and heat to the black metal torches along the chamber walls. Intricate symbols were etched deeply into the hearth, about the bases of the wall sconces, and along every seam that joined a wall to the ceiling or floor.

Glyphs. Weaves stored in symbols.

Four large oval windows were sealed against the night with heavy shutters carved and painted in the likeness of ogreish faces. Cabinets, crates, and chests lay scattered about the room in no apparent pattern. Four marble statues of winged daemin hunched at equidistant points about the room's perimeter.

Hauhantu. Those who wait.

As the heavy door eased closed behind her, Ciridan faced the four men seated at a large oaken table on the far side of the room. She lowered her eyes respectfully as she spoke.

"My lords, how may I serve?"

"Enter and sit, Shade," Arwynn said cordially, pointing to a chair opposite his own. "We have much to discuss."

Ciridan glanced at the others at the table as she approached. Two accepted her presence with a silent nod. One ignored her completely.

As she settled into a chair between Lindrowe and Morkainen, Ciridan scanned the table: a patchwork of papers and maps, the stains of a recent meal, three silver carafes with matching goblets, several ceramic tiles in black, red, and purple. Two weapons, a dagger clearly displayed and another—*Poisoned?*—under some papers. The barest hint of asmein swam below a lingering incense. *Spice from the meal, certainly.* Yet it seemed fresh against so many other scents. And localized, or she would have smelled it as she approached the table.

Curious.

Rahain Morkainen's long white hair was tousled, and his characteristic green tunic was unwashed. It barely concealed his leather armor beneath. He looked long without sleep, yet his silver eyes held their edge.

Malaraphi, old and feeble, sat hunched in crimson robes, intent upon his scribblings and muttering to himself. He paid her no heed. This was his trap. While his eyes and ears were away, his magicks touched her, caressed her, penetrated her. There was nothing he could not know.

Urath Lindrowe reclined in his chair, his gray and yellow cloaks loosely wrapped about his great bulk. He steepled his pudgy fingers before his heavily lidded eyes and watched her like a reptile might eye its prey. He looked indolent. That was his lie.

Then there was Arwynn Blackhand.

The Chameleon.

He sat directly before Ciridan, relaxed and confident, dressed in a white tunic with thin blue sleeve garters. The fire lent a soft glow to his milky skin and an oily gleam to his fine black hair. He rested his head on his left hand, thumb to chin, two fingers to temple, and watched her with calculating eyes.

He's watching me watch him, Ciridan noted, *observing my methods of observation.*

"I trust all went well at Westgate," Arwynn said, motioning for Morkainen to pour wine for her.

"It did, Master Blackhand."

Morkainen poured as bid and casually passed a silver goblet to Ciridan.

Arwynn smiled. "Excellent."

He nodded at the goblet.

"You must be thirsty. Refresh yourself, then we can talk. The night is not so old that we must forsake hospitality for expedience."

Ciridan took the goblet and instinctively swirled the liquid in the cup, allowing it to turn in her hand as she did so.

One was expected to observe a wine's streaking, Lindrowe had taught her years ago. *As you perturb the fluid, allow the glass to slide so that you might drink from the side opposite the one given you, should the cup, and not the drink, be poisoned.* A simple defense against a common method of murder that allows a killer to drink from the same glass as the victim, thereby allaying the victim's fear of a poisoned drink.

Ciridan watched the wine slide gracefully down the inside of the goblet. She sniffed it, discerned nothing.

The others were silent.

Watching.

They are waiting for me to drink.

She glanced at the table. The second—*Poisoned!*—weapon was gone.

Then she understood. She was expected to drink from a poisoned cup and survive.

It's a test.

Ciridan raised the goblet in a silent salute to Arwynn, nodded deferentially to the others, then brought up the cup and touched it gently to her mouth. As the cool metal touched her lips, she frantically racked her brain for a poison that would leave wine clear and fluid without tainting its bouquet. She could think of none. There was no contaminant that—

The asmein!

The spice wasn't part of the meal. That's why it was so fresh and localized. It was a blockscent, a deliberately placed aroma intended to mask a similar smell.

Ciridan quickly considered possible poisons and immediately settled on one of two: maddram or xiim. Both effused hints of asmein, but one warmed and the other did not.

She tilted the cup. Cool wine spilled into her mouth.

Maddram.

Ciridan bit hard into her inner lip. Warm blood spilled into her mouth and mixed with the poisoned wine as she swallowed. The blood would denature the maddram. She would become ill—very ill—but she would survive.

She let a small amount of blood and wine trickle from the corner of her mouth, proof that she had both drunk from the cup and identified the poison.

"Bravo, child! Bravo!"

Lindrowe clapped his fat hands together at the sight of the blood and shot a knowing glance in Malaraphi's direction.

"Did I not tell you that this one was aware? Eh? Did I not? And did you see her twist that goblet?" He made a sweeping circular motion with his right hand. "Wonderful! Wonderful! Simply marvelous!"

Malaraphi snorted. "You only say that because it's your favorite technique."

"Who cares whose favorite technique it is, you goat!" Lindrowe rumbled. His great bulk quaked with excitement. "It worked, didn't it? By Anwin's Heart, she'd have escaped any poison on the rim of that goblet, I can tell you that."

Morkainen said nothing. Were he to speak, he would be charged with misleading the Shade and breaking down her guard. He clenched his fists beneath the table and drove his fingernails into his palms.

Arwynn smiled.

"Congratulations, Ciridan Lothloran," he said, rising from his seat. "You have done well."

Arwynn walked across the chamber to a glass-faced cabinet. From it, he removed a blue crystal decanter and a single long-stemmed glass. He returned to the table, to Ciridan's left side, and silently poured a thin amber fluid from the decanter into the glass, which he then offered her.

"Drink up, child." Lindrowe patted her hand. "It's one of mine. Quite tasty. Undoes maddram."

Ciridan accepted the glass but waited to drink until Arwynn put the decanter back in the cabinet and returned to his seat at the table.

Something's wrong.

Ciridan glanced at the men seated around the table, recalling their teachings and specialties. As her eyes fell upon Morkainen, she remembered a frosty day during the war with House Savarat, winters past. They'd been setting traps, a near-invisible slicelace backed up by pressure plates over spraydart arrays. The slicelace was never meant to be more than a distraction. A wise assassin sets two traps, Morkainen had taught her that day. Once the first is discovered and removed, few search for a second. The more elaborate the first, the more deadly the second.

She looked at the amber fluid in the delicate crystal glass.

Does the same rule not apply to poison?

Ciridan poured the contents of the glass onto the floor. It hissed and fizzled in a bubbly froth.

Acid!

Ciridan was shocked—as much by how close she came to drinking the acid as by the gusto with which it ate through the marble at her feet. Yet she did not reveal her surprise, just held her breath, set her jaw, and gently placed the empty glass on the table. Her hand barely trembled.

Malaraphi looked up from his scratching for a moment and sniffed the air. He chuckled, muttered something unintelligible to himself, then shrugged bony shoulders and bent back to his scribbling.

Lindrowe smiled and nodded his head approvingly.

Morkainen sighed and fell back in his chair, wiping hair and sweat from his brow with a sweep of his hand, leaving a trail of blood.

Arwynn showed no emotion. He bade Ciridan to remain seated as he and his lieutenants rose from their chairs and raised their cups.

"Well done," Arwynn said. Then, he proclaimed: "Ciridan Lothloran the Shade is dead, poisoned by the maddram. Ciridan Lothloran the Sahadi now stands in her stead, strengthened by poison and tempered by acid. Her triumph is our triumph, and ours is hers."

Arwynn and his officers formally initiated Ciridan into her new station within House Blackhand with congratulations and warm words. Fine wine was poured, fresh bread was broken, and Malaraphi supplied her with an elixir to lessen the effects of the maddram. Ciridan accepted the potion skeptically and downed its contents only after Malaraphi first sipped from it himself. When at last it came time to return to business, it was Lindrowe who spoke.

"Tell me, child," he said, wiping his mouth daintily. "The Sathiian messenger you followed today. What was he like? Hmm?"

Ciridan set her goblet down on the table and scowled thoughtfully.

"He was an odd sort," she said. "Overly dedicated, perhaps. When he left the keep, he walked straight to the western docks, apparently unconcerned over any attention he might attract along the way. No, that's not quite right—he was more oblivious than unconcerned. He made no attempt to conceal his affiliations."

"None?"

Ciridan shook her head. "None."

"Strange," Morkainen said. "Most keep secret their dealings with a House Assassin. At least initially."

"Indeed." Lindrowe frowned and tapped his chin. "This disregard for secrecy is disturbing. Most disturbing. The messenger would be able to send any number of signals to accomplices as he left our premises, beya? Even the way he held his head could speak volumes if properly encoded. And worse, any spy watching the compound—Loquay's operatives and Kaleena's familiars, at the very least—would surely find the presence of a Sathiian envoy intriguing enough to merit further scrutiny. Hmm? Yes. Yes, indeed… why, I wouldn't be at all surprised to find that several of the Great Houses already know of today's meeting, if not the particulars."

Lindrowe grunted and tossed his napkin onto his plate.

"I'd count on it," Malaraphi said.

Lindrowe shot him a quizzical look.

"The Sathiians wanted the other Houses Assassin to be aware of today's meeting with Arwynn," Malaraphi said.

"Why?"

"Implied affiliation. Houses Assassin are conservative by nature. They will assume an accord was reached. It would be too risky for them not to."

Arwynn shook his head.

"There is too much speculation here and not enough fact," he said. "It is becoming clear that Welbley Blaythe is a cunning man. He is not, however, our primary concern. The most immediate threats to this House remain Loquay and the Crimson Witch. For the time being, we must continue to focus our energies there. Unless, of course"—he eyed Ciridan—"our Sahadi has information which would cause us to reconsider."

Like Morkainen, Ciridan had remained silent, intently following the conversation. She knit her brow and forced herself to remember more details of her encounter with Blaythe's messenger. Somewhere in the pit of her stomach she felt a stab of pain. *The maddram, no doubt.*

"I have nothing unusual to report, my lord," she said to Arwynn. "The messenger took a direct path to the western docks and boarded a laden barge bearing the markings of the Church of Sathiis. The barge's cargo was listed as foodstuffs, textiles, stave wood, and a dozen silver ingots. These listings could have been falsified, but the dockmaster on duty assured me that they were not."

"And you believed them?" Lindrowe asked.

"Yes," Ciridan said. "There was no reason not to after I confirmed it myself. It seems the Sathiians use river trade along their route to offset the cost of operating their barges."

She paused a moment. "Morgru Murgwei and Fedahi Hasraheed took up the messenger's shadow at Westgate. I came directly here to make my report."

"Fedahi?" Lindrowe frowned. "I thought Morgru alone was to follow him. Two men are thrice as likely to be detected."

"That is true, my lord," Ciridan agreed, "however, I felt that the additional risk was warranted."

"How so?"

Ciridan felt a warm flush in her cheeks and neck: the maddram fever beginning to build. She ignored her discomfort and focused on Lindrowe.

"Once his business with Lord Arwynn was concluded, the messenger proceeded swiftly and directly to Westgate, stopping for neither food nor rest," she explained. "It occurred to me that his training might include longfasting, which would allow him more travel time per day than a typical courier. At first, that seemed of little advantage since the messenger was traveling by water rather than land. Then it struck me that there was no reason to assume that his journey would be completed by barge alone, especially if the Sathiians intended to carry out trade along the route. Trade takes time—time that most couriers cannot afford to sacrifice. It made more sense for the messenger to take to land rather than stay on the barge."

"You sent a tracker along," Morkainen said.

"Yes, my lord," she replied, turning.

The burning in her stomach grew more persistent, and her fever mounted.

"Fedahi's talents are unparalleled," Ciridan explained. "I thought it best that he accompany Morgru in case the messenger took to land. It seemed a prudent course of action."

Lindrowe frowned, but slowly nodded his assent. "It was."

Ciridan heard him only faintly, as though he were suddenly far away. The dim echo of her pulse became a rhythmic hiss in her ears, and a strange tingling began to spread over her fingers and toes. Her eyes felt hot and dry. The pain in her belly grew more intense and radiated outward.

It was then she realized just how close her brush with death had been. In her excitement and triumph, the true consequence of failing her master's test had been lost. Her failure would not have simply lessened her rank or postponed her promotion; it would have killed her. Though she'd known the price of failure since joining Arwynn's House, she never really believed that it would be levied upon her.

Until tonight.

Ciridan turned to Arwynn, concern on her face.

"Lord Arwynn," she said, voice now strained and unsteady. "If I had died tonight, all of this information would have been lost to you. You took a great chance on me."

Before Arwynn could respond, Malaraphi placed his bony hands flat on the table and raised himself from his chair, frail arms threatening to buckle under his weight. He leaned forward and locked his eyes on Ciridan's.

"Such naivete." He chuckled.

He held her gaze with magick and will.

"You think death is the end, don't you, hmm? Of course you do. And why shouldn't you? It isn't. Never forget that, Sahadi. Your enemies won't. There are many ways to touch the beyond. Many ways to glean information. None are pleasant."

The old wizard waited until he was certain that his meaning was clear; then he released her and went back to his doodling and mumbling.

Ciridan was visibly shaken, as much by the poison in her system as the elfi's magicks. She'd been caught and held, unable to turn away.

And those eyes.

Then she passed out.

CHAPTER 5

SERPENTS IN THE GARDEN

Welbley Blaythe conferred with Tehru Shaddoht for a long time. For the most part, his questions revolved around the structure and interaction of House Blackhand's three orders. Tehru was pleased to answer, though he suspected the priest already knew much of what he relayed. Eventually, the conversation turned from generalities to specifics.

"What about Blackhand's sulari?" the priest asked. "Not his lieutenants. His common thugs. The lower rank and file. What can you tell me about them?"

"Smart. Skilled. Fiercely loyal. More t'their order than the House, I'd wager."

He screwed up his face, recalled the pertinent information, and gave the most general to Blaythe.

"All new recruits are required to undergo training in the basics: climbing, dancing, shadowing, trapping, an' such. After that, they rotate through Vehem, Morghanti, and Sadri. Short stints. They study with each order for a few months to learn some advanced techniques an' gain exposure to diff'rent kinds of warfare, so they're better trained an' more capable than most sulari."

He tapped his chin, added: "After that, they're either assigned to fortari, recruited inta one of the sulari orders, or initiated inta the Sadri. Or retired."

"Retired?"

"Shhhhkt." Tehru drew his thumb sharply across his neck.

"Houses Assassin never *murder* anyone, they *retire* 'em. By the end of their initial training, new recruits know too much about Blackhand's affairs to be allowed t'leave the House."

"Of course," Welbley said. "Severe, but judicious."

The spy nodded but said nothing.

"These orders, Tehru. You have more detailed information on them, yes? More than just their primary functions?"

Tehru felt his fortune dwindling away.

"Some," Tehru said. "Each order's divided inta three ranks. The titles vary with the order. The Morghanti use Blade, Blood, an' Whisper. The Vehem use Vipira, Arachia, an' Scorpia. Sadri are the exception. They have only one rank: Sadri."

"Analogous to other Houses," Welbley said. "Soldier, Captain, Commander."

"Pretty much, but distinct enough t'give Arwynn's sulari more defined identity."

There, Tehru thought. *That ought t'do it.*

"Special suborders?" the priest asked. "Splinter groups?"

Damn.

Tehru nodded. "One for each order."

"Elite forces, I assume?"

"Yeah," Tehru said.

Now comes the tricky part. Tehru had to give the priest enough to satisfy him without giving him everything.

"The Morghanti promote their best to Shadow. From there, they can advance t' Shade an' command a small group of Shadows. There's talk of a position beyond Shade, but I haven't been able to confirm it. Likely just be a rumor t' keep the other Houses guessing. By my count, Arwynn has fourteen Shadows and four Shades."

A lie.

Tehru continued quickly before Welbley could ask more questions.

"The Vehem promote their best to Maranth an' from there to Alyl."

"After the poisonous orchid?"

Tehru nodded.

"The Vehem are harder t'count. Arwynn has maybe seven or eight Alyl an' maybe three times as many Maranth."

Another lie.

"Of the Sadri... no one could say."

Welbley steepled his fingers before his face and freed his thoughts to slither over this wealth of new information. Tehru knew more than he was telling, otherwise he would have mentioned Blackhand's special forces when he described his orders. Even so, what the spy had chosen to divulge lent weight to many of Welbley's suspicions and raised several new concerns. Along with a name that his other agents had failed to provide.

Malaraphi.

Welbley squinted and pursed his lips.

I have heard that name before.

He closed his eyes and dredged up a distant recollection.

It had been during his youth, long before he'd found the Truth of Sathiis, during a time of upheaval in Isitar. The king of Isitar had mysteriously disappeared without naming an heir, bringing the realm to the brink of civil war. During the turmoil, the Mad Mage, Zithwathn the Blue, brazenly decreed his lordship over Isitar's domains. The opposing factions immediately discredited Zithwathn's claim and ridiculed him for his temerity.

And Zithwathn turned them all into frogs…

Despite the years, Welbley remembered the details with disgusting clarity.

… three myriadi, eighteen hundred humani, all transformed into blue frogs.

After that, every twisted weaver from the neighboring realms flocked to Zithwathn's banner and hailed him as lord and king. They rallied about a standard of a great blue frog on a field of black and made a game of crushing once-men underfoot and stringing their remains into sashes and belts. It was in the wake of this lunacy that a young elfi named Malara-phi stepped forward to challenge Zithwathn. Zithwathn could not refuse and maintain authority over his depraved disciples.

Welbley once again felt the unsettling mixture of fear and exuberance he'd experienced those decades past.

He'd been part of the crowd that followed the young elfi and the Mad Mage to a clearing outside the city. Not a word was spoken by either magickan until they reached a barren knoll and turned to face each other. Tension spilled into the crowd with a palpable chill as their eyes locked.

Suddenly, Zithwathn dropped to his knees, snapped his head back, and let loose a hideous scream. The crowd shrank back as the terrible cry coalesced into a black cloud that bore down upon the elfi.

Malaraphi's shields shattered in a spray of Aethic shards. The cloud entangled him with an inky web of vaporous tendrils and drew him into its seething blackness.

And he was gone.

And then he wasn't.

On a chorus of anguished cries, the blackness thinned and roiled. Jagged streaks of blue lightning slashed through its inky mass and seared across the elfi's convulsing body. Louder and louder Malaraphi's cries erupted from the writhing cloud, until the lightning burned crimson and he again vanished from sight.

Then there was laughter.

Wild, insane laughter.

It took the crowd a moment to realize that the laughter was not Zithwathn's. They turned and saw Malaraphi, again visible in the twisting blackness, cackling and gibbering and jerking about like a puppet on tangled strings. He aged decades with each spasm until he was finally hurled from the cloud, withered and broken. Then the cloud lurched and churned… and turned upon Zithwathn.

And consumed him.

Welbley shuddered at the memory.

No remains of Zithwathn were found, save a single scrap of burned blue cloth. Malaraphi, horribly enfeebled, disappeared into the eastern wilds. The Brotherhood of the Blue Frog disintegrated, its remnants driven from Isitar under genocide.

Welbley opened his eyes slowly.

Can it be the same elfi?

It was no secret that the Great Houses enlisted the services of weavers; however, the measure of their power was assumed to be relatively minor. Powerful magickai were loath to demean themselves to subservient roles: they gravitated to religious institutions, aligned themselves with the Families Royal, or operated independently. But if this Malaraphi was indeed the same magickan that brought down the Brotherhood of the Blue Frog, then all the Church's carefully laid plans might come undone.

For the first time in many years, Welbley felt uncertain. Nervous.

I must know more.

The priest turned his attention back to Tehru.

"What more have you to tell me, Tehru?"

"Nothing, m'lord," Tehru said. "That's the extent of my knowledge."

"You are certain?"

"Yeah. I'm certain."

You're lying.

There were many factions in Dûhr that would pay handsomely for detailed knowledge of House Blackhand, and Tehru would certainly profit by selling them not only what he reported tonight but any other tidbits he chose not to share. While that prospect irked Welbley, it was of little consequence in the greater scheme of things. What bothered him was that Tehru was a sloppy man and therefore dangerous without intent. The possibility that he might unwittingly interfere with Church designs was too great to ignore, and Welbley could not afford additional complications. Not now.

Welbley could not allow the man to leave.

The priest rose to his feet and addressed the spy.

"It would appear, then, that our discourse is at an end, Tehru."

Tehru followed the priest's lead. He stood and wiped bits of clover from his clothes with short, sharp strokes. After a cursory inspection, he turned back to the priest and smiled unctuously.

"If m'lord wishes, I can look deeper."

"Under similar terms, no doubt?"

Tehru smiled, offered an almost respectful nod. "No doubt."

Welbley was unsure whether he was more amused or angered by the man's inadequacy as a liar.

"No doubt," Welbley said softly, almost to himself, as he turned to leave. "No doubt."

Welbley's eyes slowly narrowed. He allowed his anger and distaste to rise until it sparked rage. When he spoke again, his voice was no longer cool, no longer controlled. It was fearsome.

"No doubt," the priest hissed, turning back to face Tehru. His left hand was clutched at his breast. His right hand pointed his staff menacingly at the spy.

"You, Tehru Shaddoht, are an idiot! You dare to withhold information from me and then try to make me pay further for what I've already purchased? You must think me a fool to fall for such an artless scheme. Similar terms, indeed! By Sathiis's Bloody Coils, I should strike you dead!"

Tehru leaped back and threw aside his cloak. He instinctively snatched a poisoned knife from his belt and dropped into a combat stance. He started to speak—

Oh yes! That is a wonderful pose!

—but Welbley's body began to convulse before Tehru's words found breath. Spittle began to fly from the priest's lips as he gagged out words in the Old Tongue and traced a green smoking arc in the air with his staff.

Tehru lunged to attack—

—doubled over as sudden pain racked his body.

The spy screamed.

The priest laughed.

Such lovely anguish!

Tehru ground his teeth and frothed curses at Blaythe. He forced himself to straighten, face the priest, bring up his blade to strike—

The pain immobilized him. His flesh hardened and blackened. His mind failed. His senses faded…

… vanished…

… and he became a thing of iron.

Welbley chuckled. Pleasure poured through his body as he stepped forward to examine his handiwork. He thought it magnificent, exquisite. No sculptor could capture such torment. As he ran his fingertips lightly over the statue's face and neck, he could feel the last vestiges of heat fade from the metal. It aroused him.

And so shall you sleep, Tehru, until we speak again. And when we do, you will tell me everything.

Closing his eyes, Welbley forced himself to breathe slowly and evenly, suppressing the physical excitement brought by the weave. Such pleasure would have to wait. There remained work to be done before the night was over.

He called his attendants and waited patiently until two adepts approached. They bowed their shaved heads low to their master.

Welbley greeted them with courtesy and motioned to the statue.

"Please take this to my workshop," he said calmly. "I have a meeting to attend."

CHAPTER 6

WHEELS IN MOTION

T he four men looked down upon Ciridan without com-passion or concern. She lay crumpled where she'd fallen, her cup overturned, a pool of spilled wine bleeding into her clothes and staining her golden hair.

"She is strong, Rahain," Arwynn said, then turned to face his blademaster. "You did not misrepresent her, and I retract my earlier accusations to the contrary. I do believe that she will make a fine Sahadi. With the proper training, of course."

"Of course."

"When can you be ready to leave?"

"Leave?"

"For the Mindbender's."

"Four, five days. I need to assess Morghanti ranks and deployments in light of Ciridan's promotion."

Arwynn nodded.

"Take a week," he said, "then deliver Ciridan to the Mind-bender. Set out an hour before dawn. Minimal complement: yourself, Ciridan, and one or two Bloods. Have two other parties of varying sizes ride out after you leave. Two-hour intervals. That should sufficiently confuse the other Houses.

They haven't the sulari to shadow every group that leaves the city, so they won't follow you straight away. They can always track you, so they'll bide their time. Your departure will be the most suspicious, so they'll assume it to be a ruse and follow the second or third group."

"Doubleruns or siderides?"

"Don't waste the time. Without a silver eye, anyone tracking you will be stymied by the Mindbender's defenses. Deliver Ciridan and arrange for Mirithwin's payment, then return."

Morkainen nodded. "Understood."

"Good. Now, to other business." Arwynn tapped his fingers on the wooden table. "Loquay's recruiting and likely alliance with the Sathiians is a proximal threat but doesn't necessarily portend an attack against us. It's more likely that she has another target in mind. Savarat, perhaps. Or Tanjneen. Both of their Houses hold sections of the Underwet under the Gardens of Twilight bordering her own. Of course, that may be precisely what she wants us to think… Loquay is cunning—she might just attempt such a misdirection before an attack. It would be wise to investigate matters beneath the temple district. Not right away, though. Moving too quickly after receiving Blaythe's messenger will alert Loquay of our suspicions. Wait a week or two."

"I agree," Lindrowe said breathily. "I recommend a single small contingent."

"What do you have in mind?" Morkainen asked.

"Hmm. Two Morghanti, I should think. Preferably Bloods, if you've any to spare; otherwise good Blades will do. One Maranth, one Sadri."

Malaraphi looked up, displeased at the mention of his Sadri.

"I don't want my Sadri's talents wasted. There are dangers in frivolity."

Arwynn nodded. "Malaraphi's right. Until we know more, we'll limit ourselves to a small reconnaissance party: two Morghanti, two Vehem. Then"—he turned to meet Malaraphi's red eyes—"should the situation merit, I will commit a Sadri."

Malaraphi grumbled under his breath, but nodded consent.

To Lindrowe, Morkainen said, "Two of my Morghanti—Sieda and Maro—are well acquainted with the Underwet. I'll instruct them to follow your orders."

The fat man smiled. "Excellent. Most excellent, indeed. Perhaps we will be able to straighten out this little wrinkle before you get back, Rahain."

"Perhaps," Arwynn said, though he was not convinced. He eased himself into a more relaxed posture in his chair. "Urath, about these barges—"

"Blaythe's?"

"Yes, Blaythe's. I'd like to know what supplies his temple requires for 'clerical responsibilities.' I doubt we're talking about incense and ornaments."

Lindrowe chuckled. "Most unlikely. When do you want it?"

"Next month," Arwynn said. "Even if Blaythe anticipates betrayal, he knows that his first few shipments will face no threat from us. That kind of inelegant treachery would only sully the value of our covenants. The cargo on the next two barges to arrive will have left Wirith before we struck our covenant, so ignore them. The next one will be a test. Nothing of value to us. I don't expect any delicate cargo until the fourth or fifth barge. He won't deliver anything of real value until his temple in the Gardens is more secure and his people can maintain constant possession, so we'll have to time our actions appropriately."

"The mir would prove useful for this," Lindrowe said.

"Agreed," Arwynn said. "Deal with them."

"And if the Sathiians already have?"

"Strike a better bargain. The mir are fickle; they will have no problem shifting their loyalties if the price is right. I don't care what you promise them. If we can deliver, fine. If not, well… we'll deal with that later. We won't need them for some time, but set things up now."

Lindrowe nodded. "Beya."

Arwynn turned to his loremaster. The old wizard ceased his doodling and waited patiently for his assignment.

"I want you to travel north," Arwynn said. "As soon as you're able. Confer with the Clubfoot."

"The botanist?"

Arwynn nodded. "Blaythe's messenger bothers me. I want to know if there was any significance to that oppressive smell of flowers. If that thing was a liche, I want to know what we're dealing with before we move against Blaythe. Find out everything the Clubfoot knows about Blaythe, his organization, and his messenger. Take some Sadri with you. Sartahex could use some time away; her cruelty needs focus."

Malaraphi gave a curt nod.

"Oh, and one more thing."

The old elfi raised an eyebrow.

"Send back a dozen or so gobli, will you? Alive, please."

CHAPTER 7

SERVANTS OF STONE

Deep beneath Wirith's Temple of Wargrum, Lord Priest Aerkon Kharae (*Stone, Animus*) worked late into the night under the warm glow of sunstones. Aerkon's desk was a slab of polished basanite supported by two irregular blocks of basalt, older than the temple itself. Yellowed papers and parchments, battered books, and tattered maps cluttered the desktop and lay scattered on the floor around him.

The old priest straightened in his chair with a low groan and rubbed his tired eyes. Once broad and strong, his back was now bent and frail—like the rest of his body, robbed of its vitality by the thief of years. His hair was blanched and stringy, his teeth were yellowed. His eyes were sunken; his hands, gnarled and arthritic. But his mind remained sharp, and for that he thanked Wargrum.

He leaned back and rubbed his neck.

Without mats or pillows, the gray stone seat pressed hard against his old bones and chilled him through his cassock. He grimaced and half wished for the comforts of silk and stuffing, then snorted at the irony of those desires. Had it not been the asceticism demanded by Wargrum that had first attracted him to service? Where was his vaunted discipline now that his body argued with him so persistently? So painfully.

It was a battle he found himself fighting with increasing frequency as the years progressed: strength of faith versus frailty of flesh, with his spirit caught in the middle. In moments of weakness, Aerkon would find himself wishing for respite from the agonies of age. Then the moment would pass, and he would chastise himself for his failings. It was a small grace that his adherents never witnessed such moments, that his will remained ironclad when surrounded by the faithful. It was only when he was alone… only when he…

"Bah!"

Aerkon chided himself for his lack of focus as the echo of his outburst faded. He had no time for self-indulgence; important matters demanded attention. Arael would soon return from her meeting with Bortran Harnath. He must be ready, regardless of Bortran's decision.

The lord priest set back to work, ignoring the clumsiness of his hands as he organized papers and hid the ring among them.

There was a knock at the door. Two sharp raps.

Aerkon barked a word in a dead language.

With a soft rasp, an octagonal slab of rock in the far wall of the lord priest's sanctum slid away. Arael Laran (*Earth, Will*) stood in the corridor beyond. Aerkon's high priest paused before entering, careful to identify herself to the unseen stone sentries that guarded the entrance to his chamber.

Arael crossed the threshold and offered a formal bow. Her long hair was blue black, like the wings of a raven, and her brilliant blue eyes glittered in the low light. Her features were strong, angular. Her light skin looked dark against her crisp white raiment.

"My lord." Her voice was deep, almost masculine.

Aerkon beckoned his high priest forward. A rough chair rose from the stone floor in front of his desk as she crossed the chamber with easy, confident strides.

"Balistrahd's increased the watch numbers to half a myriad," she reported as she approached.

"Three hundred soldiers?"

Arael nodded. "And three full myriadi patrol the proximal croplands and ranches."

"Royal?"

"Yes."

Aerkon shook his head and grumbled, "He's starting to position his forces for his damned war."

"It was only a matter of time before he deployed the Myriadi Royal," Arael said matter of factly as she sat in the stone chair. "The House Royal's been ratcheting up their militant rhetoric for months. Balistrahd himself has—"

"Balistrahd's a puppet." Aerkon scoffed. "He's been doing Blaythe's bidding from the start of this nonsense. And he has no idea what he's gotten himself into. The hardships of war with the Gobli Horde will only weaken his House and strengthen Blaythe's chokehold on his Family. Beya, the man's an idiot."

"Unfortunately, Blaythe is not." Arael spoke solemnly. "We've confirmed that he's already secreted adepts among the Myriadi Royal and are investigating rumors that he's negotiated covenants with two Houses Assassin."

The lord priest rubbed his wrinkled brow with a twisted hand and sighed exasperatedly. "He's setting everything up just like he did in Isitar… We will need to prepare for an attack."

"How shall I assign the priests?"

"That depends on Bortran Harnath. What did he say when you delivered my letter?"

Arael reached into her robes and withdrew a folded paper that bore the seal of House Harnath. She leaned forward and placed it on Aerkon's desk.

"He said he was happy to finally be free of you."

Aerkon raised a quizzical eye.

"He said that?"

"He said that."

The lord priest chuckled. He picked up the letter, broke the wax seal and read the message, then tossed it on the desk and leaned back in his chair. There was a hint of a smile on his craggy lips.

"How familiar are you with the Underwet, Arael?"

"The sewers?" The priest shrugged. "The Houses Assassin use them as a private highway, but I don't know much beyond that. Why?" She glanced at the letter. "What did he say?"

"It so happens that Bortran has maps to a system of tunnels that undercut the sewers," Aerkon said. "Ancient and forgotten tunnels. So old, they predate Wirith itself. He uses them for smuggling. To clear his debt, he's giving us access to those tunnels and a guide."

"And why would we need those things?"

"I need something smuggled out of Wirith and into Dûhr."

Aerkon reached out to pat a leather-wrapped bundle, which he then slid to Arael.

"I need you to deliver this to Kargan Teahl in Dûhr. Swiftly. And discreetly."

"Hence, the tunnels," Arael said, accepting the bundle. "Does the prince know of Harnath's tunnels?"

"I doubt it. Even if he did, he doesn't have maps. The best he could do would be to flood the tunnels with soldiers, but without a guide, that would not end well. The Houses Assassin don't take kindly to intruders."

"Unless they have covenants with Balistrahd or Blaythe."

Aerkon shook his head. "They would never form a covenant that would jeopardize their control of the Underwet."

"Fair enough," Arael acceded. She thought a moment, asked: "And how did you know…?"

"About the tunnels? Bortran and I have a long history."

"Of course. The debt."

Aerkon smiled.

"And the guide?" Arael asked.

"Bortran's daughter, Gabrael."

"The half-dwarfi?"

Aerkon nodded. "She volunteered."

"Didn't she and Pendaro…?"

"They did. It ended poorly."

"Oh."

"It will be tricky to reach Bortran's tunnels," Aerkon said. "Avoiding the sulari of five Houses Assassin will be difficult. And it's possible that some of Blaythe's snakes may have slithered into the Underwet. You'll need to take several adepts with you."

"That will leave you vulnerable to a Sathiian attack."

"There's no other choice, Arael. This parcel *must* get to Kargan Teahl."

Arael started to protest. Aerkon raised his hand to silence her.

"Wirith has fallen," he said soberly. "The snake has the House Royal trapped tight in its coils. The same with Isitar and Rha. If we have any hope of defeating the Black Church, we'll need Kargan's support."

Arael sighed in resignation. "When do I leave?"

"Next week, after the Feast of Famik. The Sathiians will think us stronger if they count you and your adepts among our delegation. You can slip away after the festivities."

"I understand." Arael nodded.

She turned to leave.

"Oh, and Arael?"

"Yes, my lord."

"You should know that this is not about Balistrahd. Or the Gobli Horde. Or even Welbley Blaythe, for that matter."

"My lord?"

"It's Adderash," Aerkon said grimly. "It's been Adar Ashan all along."

CHAPTER 8

A SWIFT AND SPLINTERED MIND

The woman in the doorway scowled as she peered into the vacant chamber. Though the room was spacious and lavish even for the office of a lord priest, its grandeur neither impressed her nor stirred her mercenary spirit. She was interested only in the lord priest himself, and he was not here.

The woman's frosty blue eyes narrowed, and her pointy nose wrinkled.

"It would appear that your master is elsewhere," she said without looking at the acolyte that held open the door.

"I fear so, my lady," the man responded. "My apolo—"

"Find him," she said curtly, stepping into the chamber. "I will not be kept waiting."

The acolyte bowed his shaved head.

"Yes, my lady."

Selene shot him a venomous glare.

"Now!"

The acolyte took a half step back, considered a reply, then thought better of it and turned sharply on his heel to hurry down the hall.

Selene, princess of Dûhr, abandoned her indignant facade as the door closed behind her. She was not angered at Blaythe's absence; in fact, she was pleased to have the opportunity to be alone among his personal effects. Her show of outrage had been enough to send her minder dashing off after his master, but it would only be a matter of minutes before someone else arrived. Solitude would not last long.

Time enough.

Selene surveyed the room as she moved to its center. She allowed her eyes to linger briefly on every feature, article, and fixture: wood and eel skin furniture, cabalistic tapestries, heavy velvet curtains, crowded bookcases, low wyrm-bone table. Everything was scrupulously arranged and well guarded by mechanism and magick, or she would not have been left alone.

Reaching the middle of the room, Selene took a long, deep breath and stretched her neck. She turned in a slow circle and let the chamber's features and decorations draw her attention where they would. Then, she released her mind.

In a twinkling, she was caught up in four distinct whirl-winds of images, ideas, and insights.

Eight seconds later, she was done.

The ill-fated Mindbreaking that shattered Selene's mind as a child had reduced her consciousness to a collection of independent mental fragments held together by sheer will. Over the years, Selene learned to maintain these fragments in a stable pattern that preserved her awareness, intellect, and identity with minimal effort. But, should she desire, she could partition those fragments into distinct mosaics and allocate an independent portion of her consciousness to each. This enabled her to devote her complete concentration to different mental tasks simultaneously. Mosaics of disparate fragments facilitated creativity; mosaics of similar fragments fostered pure and perfect thought.

But it was not without cost. Maintaining multiple mosaics for any appreciable length of time carried a great physical toll, and the possibility of self-reference was a constant threat. A poorly constructed mosaic could loop back on itself, drawing in more and more fragments of Selene's mind with each iteration until it trapped her entire consciousness. Once trapped, there was no telling how long her imprisonment would last. To Selene, it would seem no more than an instant, but the world might just as easily pass through a year as a second.

Selene sighed and rubbed her eyes as the fragments of her mind fell back into a single pattern. She was drained from the effort of maintaining four distinct mosaics for eight seconds, but the insights she gained were worth the effort.

With small, deliberate steps, the princess made her way to one of the chairs before the lord priest's desk and eased herself into it. She closed her eyes and sighed again as she massaged the bridge of her nose with her thumb and forefinger. After a few moments, she could feel her strength returning.

Soon, the priest would arrive, and she would be ready for him.

In more ways than he suspected.

THE CHILDREN OF ELEM

The Elem taught that all humani were composed of four primal forces: the soul, the emote, the kih, and the eie. These forces were represented in nature by the four elements and personified by the four gods of the Elem.

Pheon, Lord of Fire, breathed the soul into the humani—the living fire of spirit.

Anwin, Lady of Water, granted the emote—the sea of passion that shaped the fire of the soul.

Wargrum, Lord of Earth, gave the kih—the will and strength to control the emote.

Sheeshee, Lady of Air, provided the eie—the ability to perceive and define the kih.

The Elem also taught that there existed dark and terrible forces beyond the reach of the four gods, in the Churn of Chaos. The manifestations of these forces were the Selfish Ones, the lords of the daemin.

Azalith, She of Flame.

C'thoq, He of Sea.

Zanyr, She of Stone.

Xoltith, He of Wind.

These forces existed to undermine the Elem and pervert their gifts.

The Elem did not speak of Sathiis, for Sathiis did not exist.

A rael thought about her conversation with Aerkon as she made her way to her private rooms, the bundle of papers he'd given her tucked neatly under one arm. She shuddered involuntarily. Just thinking about Adderash and his followers made her skin crawl.

The Church of Sathiis was not a church at all. It was a cult cloaked in ecclesiastical trappings, dedicated to serving the avarice of a single man. Where the Elem professed harmony with nature, the Sathiians advocated control. Where the Elem sought to raise the downtrodden, the Sathiians sought to destroy any that stood in their way. The Elem preached a time-honored philosophy that sought to bring together mind and body, life and spirit. The Sathiians adhered to little more than a hierarchy of objectives disguised as religious doctrine, with no care for the spirit and no concept of the soul.

Arael detested Adderash and despised his sycophants. She held nothing but contempt for Welbley Blaythe and the gutless politicians that allowed him to slink into Wirith.

And for what? A few elfin laef and a pittance of favor?

These were not leaders. These were creatures of corruption, beasts in humani skin concerned only with advancing their ends through false piety, phony ritual, and colored smoke.

And yet…

Arael stopped walking. She slumped her shoulders and sighed heavily.

They are but people, after all. Humani.

Children of Elem.

Arael's duty as a high priest was to minister to all Children of Elem, regardless of station or affiliation. Even the Sathiians. The soul of Pheon burned within them with no smaller flame than that which burned within herself. The Soul Lord granted his gift freely to all: priest and peasant, pious and pagan, virtuous and ignoble. For Arael to pick and choose in her works of salvation would be to ignore her eie and allow her emote to control her kih. That path was unacceptable.

That was the path of the Sathiians.

By the time Arael reached the vicinity of her private chambers, she was so engrossed in thought that she didn't notice a priest step into her path from an adjoining corridor.

—Whump!

Arael bounced off the man's large body, staggered back a half step, and fell to the floor.

"My lady!" Pendaro gasped, eyes wide.

He extended his hand.

"Oh, my lady! Please forgive my clumsiness!"

Pendaro (*Stone*) was a mountain of a man, well over six feet with a great barrel chest and shoulders like a bear. His huge limbs were heavily muscled and covered with coarse dark hair. Unkempt inky waves tumbled from the left side of his head; the follicles on the right had been destroyed by fire. The scarring was hideously bright against his dark skin from behind the ruined helix of his right ear to the middle of his right eye and down most of his cheek and chin.

Seeing him tower over her, Arael remembered how apprehensive she'd first been when assigned to instruct Pendaro in the Ways of Wargrum, how frightened she'd been by his size, strength, and physical ugliness. But high priests were supposed to be above bias, so she accepted him as her pupil and tried to see beyond his outward aspect.

She never regretted that decision.

Pendaro was a kind and gentle man despite his grotesque appearance, wholly at ease with himself and his disfigurement. He was fond of saying that Wargrum had given him a large and knobby nose to offset his delicate beauty, so his scarring was a blessing, for it drew people's attention away from his actual deformity. His eyes would sparkle as he said this, and his smile would grow childlike in almost painful sincerity.

In many ways, Pendaro already possessed the qualities Wargrum's disciples struggled to attain: strength guided by maturity, purpose softened by patience, knowledge tempered by wisdom, insight nourished by mercy. He saw the grace of Elem in everything and bore no malice for any humani—not even those responsible for his disfigurement or those who acted in darkness. They could be saved, he said, if only they could be made to understand the fundamental flaws in their philosophies. And that, he claimed, required patience, not force.

Arael was hard pressed to say who had learned more from whom. She had taught Pendaro the catechism of Wargrum's Church and the secrets of the Strand of Stone, but Pendaro's example constantly assured her that the inner peace she craved was attainable in life.

The high priest took Pendaro's hand. He lifted her to her feet and apologized again for his clumsiness.

Arael shook her head and waved away his words.

"The fault was clearly mine, Pendaro," she said. "I wasn't watching where I was walking."

"Yes," he agreed, "but had I the agility to step aside—"

"Pendaro."

"Had I the foresight to look where—"

"Pendaro!"

That silenced him.

Arael glowered at him in mock anger.

"Beya! Sometimes you can be so exasperating!"

Pendaro looked surprised.

"Sometimes? You mean there are times when I'm not?"

Arael tried to suppress her chuckle. She failed, and it turned into a snort.

Pendaro bent and retrieved Arael's leather-wrapped bundle. He handed it to her with a wink and a smile, then turned to go about his business.

"Pendaro?"

He turned back.

"Lady?"

Arael tapped her foot as she looked Pendaro up and down.

She held up her parcel and said, "Lord Aerkon has charged us to deliver this to Lord Kargan Teahl in Dûhr."

"Us, my lady?"

"Me, specifically. You, indirectly."

With a glimmer of interest and half a grin, Pendaro said, "The roads to Dûhr are closed, of course."

"Of course."

"And travel beyond the border is frowned upon by the prince."

"It is."

"Except for sanctioned traders," he added.

"Which we are not," she replied.

"So, we will proceed by another route?"

Arael pointed to the floor.

"Ah, the Underwet."

Arael nodded.

"We have a guide, then?" Pendaro asked.

"Gabrael Harnath."

Pendaro stiffened. The playful sparkle in his eyes vanished.

"Bortran's daughter?" he asked.

Arael nodded. She could feel his trepidation.

"She has a fine reputation as a scout," Arael said.

"So I've heard."

Pendaro rubbed his chin with a gigantic hand.

"When do we leave?" he asked.

"Next week," Arael said. "After the Feast of Famik. Inform Rahne, Wylen, and Misha that they're to accompany us. Illiashi and Baccaro, as well. Minimum gear. We'll use the Enchantment of Vitality, so food and water won't be necessary."

Pendaro hesitated.

"What about the Sathiians?" he asked.

"I've not invited them to join us."

"That's not what I meant."

Arael shrugged.

"Let's hope they haven't slithered into the sewers yet."

"That's not what I meant either."

Arael said nothing. She knew precisely what Pendaro meant. Aerkon had sent several high-ranking priests on clandestine missions of late, and none had yet returned. When she and her adepts departed for Dûhr, there would be few remaining to defend the temple against a Sathiian attack. Aerkon was a powerful and holy man, but he was very old. And the Sathiians were many.

She tried to conceal her worry.

Pendaro nodded and turned to leave.

CHAPTER 10

THE PRINCESS, THE WITCH, AND THE PRIEST

When Welbley returned to his office, he was accompanied by a striking woman.

The woman's hair fell from her head in a dark tangle, streaked with red where gray was expected. Her milky skin was almost luminous. Her black eyes were rimmed with red, iris and pupil alike. The woman's cloaks were supple swaths of cerise suede and crimson velvet joined together by spidery bands of black silk. They seemed to crawl over her like a living thing, the depth of their redness waxing and waning as they moved. A black earring dangled from her left ear, a companion piece to the black chain necklace that snaked through the eye sockets of a child's skull. She wore three rings: one of bone, one of iron, and a band of red crystal that encircled the thumb of her right hand.

"Ah, Lady Selene," Blaythe said brightly as they entered.

He closed the door behind them and locked it.

"I apologize for my tardiness," he said. "I trust your wait was not unpleasant?"

"Not at all," Selene replied with practiced courtesy. "I've been made quite comfortable."

"Excellent," Welbley crooned. "Marvelous."

Welbley eyed Selene as he ushered his guest into the room. The princess wore a satin semigown that hugged her slender frame, lustrous white trimmed with vibrant blue embroidery that matched her azure lips, nails, and eyes. Her indigo hair was tied away from her pointy face with braided white silk. Her jewelry consisted of three silver rings and a moonstone pendant.

"May I present the Lady Selene, princess of Dûhr and sister to Melkor Kythidûhr," Welbley said to the woman in red. Then, to Selene: "This is the Lady Kaleena of Dûhr, better known to you perhaps as the Crimson Witch."

Selene's brow rose slightly. She'd had many dealings with the Crimson Witch over the years, but they'd never met face to face. Seeing her now, she thought the witch both younger and more handsome than her notoriety implied.

"A pleasure, Kaleena," the princess said. "I've looked forward to meeting you for some time."

Kaleena acknowledged Selene with a tilt of her head and took the remaining seat before Welbley's desk as the priest moved behind it.

"You've not met before?" Welbley asked, pulling out his chair.

"Not in person," Selene said to Welbley. Then, to Kaleena: "I do find it curious that we should meet in this manner. I never understood you to be interested in any politics but your own."

"I'm not," Kaleena said in a controlled voice.

"Then why are you here?" Selene asked.

"Blaythe promised me a tool to destroy Arwynn Blackhand," Kaleena said. She looked at Welbley, obviously displeased. "My aid in his schemes is the price of that tool."

"Oh! You wound me, Kaleena!" Welbley said as he sat, an affected expression of hurt on his pudgy face. "Where is the call for such hostility? We are all friends here, are we not? Partners in this venture."

Selene looked curiously at the priest.

"Partners, Welbley," she said. "Not friends."

"Tut-tut." Blaythe waved Selene's words away with a flutter of his fingers. "We have far more important matters to discuss than word choice."

"Then let us discuss those matters, Welbley," Kaleena said dourly. "Speak clearly and spare no detail. Then I will tell you if your promise is worth your price."

Welbley looked from Kaleena to Selene and back. He smiled unctuously and offered his hand in mock surrender.

"As you wish."

He cleared the papers on his desk to reveal a large map of the northern Realms Humani.

"Wirith is failing," he said, tapping the map. "The recent spate of gobli attacks across the Aenin have devastated land trade with the eastern realms and forced Wirith to rely almost exclusively on sea trade. This increase in sea trade has been met with a comparable rise in piracy, compounding Wirith's plight. The Houses Mercantile have reduced their patronage of the Houses Mercenary in the face of dwindling trade volume and increasing security premiums. The Houses Mercenary have chartered more of their myriadi to support Balistrahd's campaign against the gobli. The Houses Assassin now find themselves at war over lucrative covenants offered by desperate Houses Mercantile seeking to eliminate competition. Add rising prices, declining employment, and fearmongering, and you have the makings of potentially violent uprisings against those believed responsible."

"The Family Royal," Selene said.

"Yes," Welbley said. "House Balistrahd. The natural scapegoat."

Welbley gathered a few documents from his desk and handed them to the witch and the princess.

"What are these?" Selene asked.

"Reports from my agents in Wirith. Read them, if you like. You'll see that I do not exaggerate. House Balistrahd's survival depends on restoring trade across the Aenin, and to do that the prince needs to rout the gobli."

Selene scanned the documents Welbley had handed her. The reports appeared genuine and supported the priest's assertions, so she assumed them false. Kaleena looked over the papers she'd been given, chuckled, and set them aside.

"Where do the people stand on the gobli?" Selene asked, returning the documents to Welbley's desk.

"With the prince," Welbley replied.

"And the Elem?" Kaleena asked. She casually dropped the papers she held to the floor by her chair. "Where do the Elem stand?"

"Opposed, naturally."

"And the Black Church?"

Welbley smiled. "Why, Kaleena, do you really think that Balistrahd could incite Wirith to start a war with the Gobli Horde without our… guidance?"

Selene scowled.

Something didn't feel right. She needed to think.

The princess closed her eyes and apportioned her mind into three homogenous mosaics: one to process the information Welbley provided; one to integrate what she had learned of Welbley from his office, his affect, and his behavior; one to deliberate the motives and means of the Black Church.

Three seconds later, she opened her eyes.

"You're going to turn on Balistrahd once the gobli are routed," Selene said flatly.

Welbley was obviously surprised, but quickly regained his composure. He looked at Selene intently, then chuckled and offered a small smirk.

"Yes."

"And Dûhr?"

Welbley smiled with pretention. "My dear princess, had we the same designs for Dûhr, I would never have invited you here."

Selene returned the smile. Welbley's was smug—hers was cruel.

"My dear priest," she said, softly and calmly. "I afforded your emissaries access to my brother and convinced my Family to grant your church a place in the Gardens of Twilight because it served my purposes. Tell me why I should not now have those emissaries killed and that temple razed."

Welbley was taken aback by Selene's bluntness. He glanced at Kaleena. The witch looked amused.

The priest softened his smile. He raised his hands in conciliation and settled back in his chair.

"Rest assured, Lady Selene," he said, "we have no designs on Dûhr."

"Your history disagrees."

"Consider things from our perspective," he said. "Dûhr's Houses Mercantile have access to significant markets; her Houses Mercenary are fiercely independent; her Houses Assassin are masterfully organized. It would require far too much effort simply to maintain control, let alone extract value. No, we seek a partner in Dûhr, not a puppet. Someone with the charisma and resources to manage the realm, and the intellect and guile to manage the Houses."

Welbley eyed Selene appreciatively.

"That partner is you, Lady Selene," he continued. "Your Family both respects and fears you. Your influence has already proven invaluable. Your continued suasions will ensure that Melkor withholds Dûhr's aid long enough for Balistrahd to become vulnerable. We will then use the consequences of Melkor's inaction to persuade the Dûhrani, and your Family, that they prefer their princess to their prince."

"Very persuasive," Selene said. "I will think about it."

"That is all I ask."

"Very persuasive indeed, Welbley," Kaleena said coolly. "You've made clear why you need the princess. Why do you need me?"

Welbley turned his attention to the witch. Her cloaks appeared darker, the red in her eyes brighter.

"Ah, Lady Kaleena," Blaythe said, "you are crucial. Once House Balistrahd has fallen, there will be a period of disorder until a new House Royal ascends—and the Elem will certainly use this time of unrest to move against us, despite their peaceful tenets. It will be essential that our temples in Isitar, Rha, and Dûhr are prepared to support our allies in Wirith, lest the Elem and those Houses still loyal to Balistrahd join forces and retake the city. Lend me your magicks to shore up our temple in Isitar and fortify our fledgling temple in Dûhr, and I will provide you with the tool you need to topple House Blackhand."

"That tool being?"

"A flower."

CHAPTER 11

LIQUID CHAINS

Prince Melkor Kythidûhr paced alone in a luxurious room, head low and hands twisting behind his back. His face was gaunt and pale. Dark rings circled his red-rimmed eyes. Chills were upon him, and beads of sweat dotted his brow. The night was late, but sleep would not come.

It never came anymore.

Melkor stopped pacing and turned his head. On the polished surface of the bone table in the center of the room was a long-stemmed glass filled with violet liquid. The warm firelight flirted with the liquid, sending violet tendrils twisting on the tabletop. He took a step forward, reached out—

No!

—jerked back his hand and clenched it. He bit his lower lip and shook his fist, then thrust his hands behind his back and resumed pacing.

I should send myriadi to Wirith. I should rally the Houses now, and...

And what? Send a glaring signal to the Gobli Horde that House Kythidûhr stood ready to oppose them? That would only draw their attention to Dûhr. But if he did nothing...

... Wirith would fall.

No!

The Horde would ignore Dûhr if he did nothing. His advisers had assured him of that. Let them have Wirith and they won't crave Dûhr, they'd told him. Let them take the Aenin, and they will forgo the east.

Let them have it.

Melkor shook his head and tried to clear the fog as a painful stab of need sliced through his belly. If only he could get some sleep, he could think clearly. Surely there was a solution that need not compromise Wirith.

The prince collapsed into a stuffed armchair and lolled his head to one side with an exasperated groan. He could feel his forebears silently judging him. Relics predating his House's ascension to royalty sneered at him from ornate cases and cabinets. Tapestries and trophies commemorating the accomplishments of his extended Family mocked him from cold walls and laden shelves. Nereen, his great-grandmother, had codified the Laws of Kyth and chartered Dûhr's first guild and College. Meloch, his father, had built the Gardens of Twilight and forged lasting peace with the mir clans and jhediri tribes.

And what have I done?

For the nearly eight years of his reign, Melkor had endeavored to build on his father's work. Though his reforms had met resistance from the city's dissolute populace in the early years, he'd managed to retain his crown and make progress toward his father's vision of the jewel the realm could become. By the sixth year of his rule, he had successfully quelled four insurrections, balanced Dûhr's trade deficit with Wirith and

Khâlir, rebuilt the ruined portions of the eastern city, and instituted bold food storage policies to ease the strains of Dûhr's harsh winters. But it wasn't enough. He still felt undeserving in the shadow of Meloch. By the end of his seventh year as sovereign, the resources required to maintain his programs exceeded what the realm could provide.

That's when the Sathiians came.

I should never have listened to you, sister.

It was Selene's idea to approach the Black Church. She extolled the wealth and industry they had brought to Wirith and insisted they would bring the same to Dûhr. Melkor resisted at first, not only because he distrusted the Sathiians but because he knew that Selene coveted his throne and that her advice was motivated more by her desire to improve her standing than to serve the realm. Eventually, he relented, and the Black Church came to Dûhr, with promises, platitudes, and presents.

Melkor looked at the table.

Painfully.

Wistfully.

The drug was there, a gift from the Sathiian delegation in appreciation of the Family Royal's official invitation to build a temple in the Gardens of Twilight. An elixir to drive away insomnia, they said, for when the stress of leadership grew too great.

It called to him from its glass prison.

Come, Melkor, it whispered. *I can bring you sleep.*

A slash of yearning forced Melkor from his chair. He stood, uncertain for a moment, then lurched toward the table, stumbled, and fell. He reached up and snatched the glass, pressed it to his sweaty lips.

Sweet aroma.

Exotic blossoms and faraway flowers hung in the air like a heavy perfume.

His hand trembled.

Great Pheon, what am I doing?

The gobli. Wirith. He should help them. He should—?

Oh, Calista. My love. My—

As he bent forward in tears, the glass slipped from his hand and shattered on the marble floor.

And Melkor found himself sprawled on the floor, licking up the spilled violet fluid, shards of glass biting deeply into his tongue.

CHAPTER 12

OF PRINCES AND PRIESTS

Arwynn sat quietly in his sanctum, alone with his ruminations and his tiles and his maps. It was a large room, furnished with a single armchair and a wide side table bestrewn with pouches of ceramic tiles. Despite its lack of appointments, the room was far from plain: the floor was painted with an enormous map of Dûhr and the surrounding countryside; the walls and doors and shutters depicted the known world; the ceiling, the byways of the Underwet. Sunstones hidden in the walls allowed selective illumination of any portion of the room.

Scores of colored tiles were carefully arranged over the map of Dûhr at Arwynn's feet. Black tiles marked the placement of his sulari. Other colored tiles marked the placement of his rivals' forces: Loquay the Yellow, Tanjneen the Green, Savarat the White, Ledico the Orange, Corsetti the Brown. All but silver and red designated a House Assassin. Silver was the most prevalent color on the map, denoting the forces of the Family Royal. Red tiles, representing agents of the Crimson Witch, were few.

Arwynn's position was strong relative to his rivals, both visible and not. All Houses Assassin kept at least one clandestine sulari for each one they allowed to be seen. Two sulari hidden for each one visible was risky; three was adequate. He assumed his rivals held four. Arwynn held five.

The buffer between Arwynn's dominion and the prince's was another matter. Including Hotath's territory, recently won, House Blackhand's holdings now abutted Family Kythidûhr's in several locations. Arwynn had planned to divest himself of those holdings shortly after their seizure, but economic instability precipitated by recent gobli raids had curtailed the interest of potential buyers. For the moment, he was trapped in a dangerous position.

And Melkor knows this. He will move against me soon, but not directly. More likely, he will contract a rival House Assassin. Loquay or Savarat, I should think. Probably Savarat—Loquay would be too obvious.

Arwynn leaned forward and placed a new color on the map. A single purple tile.

Or... this new church.

He leaned back in his chair and stared at the new tile in the Gardens of Twilight.

Arwynn found it strange that Melkor Kythidûhr would allow the ill-famed Church of Sathiis a foothold in Dûhr. Although he would certainly find the tax revenue enticing, the Dûhrani people held no love for the prince; the presence of another political force would only undermine his tenuous authority. But Arwynn had confirmed Family Kythidûhr's endorsement of the Black Church and that the prince himself had offered them a place in the Gardens.

Arwynn picked up another purple tile from his table and turned it slowly in his fingers.

If Melkor intended to use the Black Church as a tool to attack the Houses Assassin, he would have little trouble gaining his Family's support.

He scowled.

It wasn't hard to see the attractiveness of a Sathiian covenant from the Family Royal's perspective. The Sathiians and the Family Royal both stood to gain if they managed to topple only a few of the Lesser Houses Assassin: the House Royal would claim credit and regain control of their sequestered wealth; the Black Church would fill the power void and gain standing. The social and political realignment would disadvantage the remaining Houses Assassin. Tensions would rise, altercations would escalate, and more Houses would collapse.

Clever.

Arwynn held the purple tile to his lips.

Too clever for you, my prince. Could it be that one of your advisers was forced awake? Or perhaps the idea came from another, hmm? Selene, that scheming sister of yours? Calista, perhaps? I've always thought her more politically savvy than she appears...

He narrowed his eyes, tightened his lips.

Welbley Blaythe?

If the alliance had been proposed by the Sathiians, it was unlikely that the prince would remain in control for any length of time. If Arwynn knew Blaythe's intentions, he would be better positioned to influence events. Unfortunately, his information was sorely limited when it came to the mysterious priest.

More than anything, Arwynn hated not knowing.

Gossip flowed freely since Wirith's recent push toward isolationism, but facts were difficult to find. Arwynn's spies in House Balistrahd and the Churches of Elem were hard pressed to divine Blaythe's plans, let alone his whereabouts. Even now, after more than a week of pointed inquiry, Arwynn knew very little about the man or his coteries within the Black Church.

I wonder, he mused, *to what do you aspire that you employ liches as messengers and bed with princes?*

Arwynn sighed.

He needed more information.

He needed sleep.

Arwynn rubbed his eyes and stretched his neck, then rose from his chair and walked along the map's perimeter until he came to the western reaches of Dûhr. He glanced over the dozen or so colorful tiles scattered about the Aenin, then carefully placed the purple tile he held on the River Fwaer with a soft clack. Arwynn hoped that Lindrowe would be able to cajole the mir into capturing a Sathiian barge. If not, his sulari would seize one under cover of a gobli raid using the creatures he'd tasked Malaraphi to fetch.

Blaythe's messenger was correct. These are dangerous times.

INTERLUDE ONE

THE SERPENT AND THE FROG

The two men faced each other across a wide expanse of scorched land, purple robes and colored sashes flapping in the breeze.

The man in the green sash was young, beautiful. His skin was golden and taut over wiry muscles, as smooth and unscarred as virgin marble. His hair was soft and delicate and flowed black in the breeze. His eyes, too, were black. Haunting.

The man in the blue sash was old, ugly. His body was ravaged by time, cadaverous and gaunt. His hair was red straw that grew in irregular patches about his mottled head and spotty arms. His eyes were white and cloudy.

With a sudden lurch, the old man began to gibber and trace patterns in the air before his face. His robes clung to his body as he generated a static charge. Within seconds, jagged blue ribbons pranced about his fingertips and the air about him began to crackle with energy. The old man teased the energy he held, coaxed it, allowed it to build. Then he screamed and threw a ball of blue lightning at the man he faced.

The man in the green sash allowed the lightning to strike him squarely in the chest. It lifted him from his feet and threw him away like a broken toy. He landed limp, bounced once.

His robes were obliterated.

The flesh of his chest was blistered and crusted black.

PART TWO

MACHINATIONS

In which betrayals are prepared,
agents are dispatched,
and difficult questions are posed.

CHAPTER 13

THE UNDERWET

Arcturi Lacosia (*Transmutation, Rifts*), sage viper of the Black Church, and two Sathiian priests moved warily through the Dûhrani Underwet.

Lacosia wore black robes, embellished with green and gold regalia, gathered at his waist with a brocade sash. His features were obscured by his hood, except for the black patch with a painted green eye that covered his empty left socket. He wore a black glove on his left hand, matching his high leather boots. From shoulder to fingertips, his right arm was sheathed in black chitinous armor. His companions, Ilyara Alil (*Echoes*) and Myrissa Dorumo (*Darkness*), wore silver-embellished purple robes suited to their station.

Lacosia tolerated Ilyara. She was a believer, devoted and incorruptible. Myrissa, on the other hand, was a cynic like him. Neither Myrissa nor Lacosia cared about spiritual fulfillment; they wanted to be feared. They wanted to weave the blackest threads for the darkest purposes and be admired for their boldness. They were drawn to the Black Church because it offered them an expedient path to fulfill their desires. Adar Ashan didn't care that Lacosia was an opportunist or that Myrissa was a sadist. He cared only that their iniquities served the Church.

The three moved slowly through the Underwet, examining each area they passed for signs of tampering. The Black Church's covenant with the House Loquay obligated the assassin to ensure the temple's safety from below, but Lacosia was wary and insisted on inspecting the local underways every few nights himself. Tonight, all seemed in order.

So far.

Lacosia distrusted all assassins.

"How many?" Sieda asked softly in Dûhrani. Lindrowe had ordered Sieda's splinter to remain incognito as they investigated Loquay's doings under the Sathiian construction site, so they wore unidentifiable outfits, used stolen gear, and spoke in the local tongue instead of House Blackhand's secret one.

"Three," Maro answered. "Single file."

"Channel side?"

"North."

"House?"

"Not enough light."

Sieda grunted.

"We're skimming Loquay's turf," Sieda said, glancing around the sewer. "Probably one of her perimeter patrols."

"And if not?" asked the woman beside Sieda.

"Savarat and Tanjneen are the only other Houses Assassin with a stake in the Gardens," Sieda answered.

"Sathiians?" asked the woman to Sieda's other side.

Sieda shook her head.

"They're priests," she said. "They won't get their own hands dirty."

The sewer tunnel was wide and tall, though the broad canal left the walkways on either side scarcely wide enough for two people to walk abreast. Long, narrow ledges ran the length of both walls, three feet wide and ten feet above the ground. Clumps of lichen spilled over their edges here and there. She could smell snakes. And rats.

"We'll wait on the north ledge," Sieda said, pointing. "Maro, you're a few yards east—there. Then Jenya... Vesta... me. Ten feet apart."

To Jenya and Vesta, she said, "If they're Loquay's, let 'em pass. Anyone else, drop a cloud when they're between your positions and throw some Dream."

The two Maranth nodded.

Sieda turned to her Blade.

"We drop when the Dream pops. It's too cramped for spraydarts or tazagûhl. If they're Tanjneen's, they'll pull rakesi knives and go straight for the belly. If they're Savarat's, it'll be flingblades. They'll aim for our necks on the fling and try to gut us on the back-snap. Either way, we hit 'em fast and drop low. Tanglers. Let the Dream take 'em out."

Lacosia and his companions slunk through the underways with deliberate care. Two of Savarat's patrols had been recently sighted at the periphery of their holdings, and rumor put Tanjneen's sulari in the general area. Lacosia feared that a confrontation with either would spark a larger conflict and embroil his forces before they were ready. It was better to remain unnoticed. So, they moved as shadows in the darkness, using Ilyara's weave of SoundKilling to silence their passage and Myrissa's spell of BlackVision to enable them to see without a lantern giving away their position. The price of such stealth was limited communication and reliance on visible movement to alert them to danger, for the SoundKilling prohibited conversation and the BlackVision excised all color and shadow from their sight.

There were four sudden pops in rapid succession, followed by billows of blue mist.

Savarat's sulari responded immediately.

"Sko sko!" one shouted. "Ema!"

Savarat's sulari briskly locked into combat stances. The first and last in line drew crescent blades and turned their backs to the one in the middle. The middle one began to mutter and twirl her finger in the air.

Sieda's eyes widened.

They have a weaver!

There were four more sharp pops as the blue mists of Dream thickened into fog.

"Weaver!" Sieda yelled as she dropped from the ledge. "Darts!"

Maro held his breath and jumped from the ledge. He hit the ground twelve feet from his target, threw his tangler at the man's legs, and dropped to his belly. Maro could feel the draft of the assassin's flingblade as it sliced through the air above him. He heard the snap of its tether and tried to flatten himself even more as the flingblade returned to the thrower's hand.

On the ledge, Jenya and Vesta crouched forward and flipped their wrists back. The slim flights of long darts slid into their hands. As they prepared to throw, the ledge cracked beneath them.

Sieda threw her tangler as she hit the ground and rolled away from the Dream fog. The assassin threw his weapon toward the sound of her landing and twisted his stance to face that direction. His flingblade nicked Sieda's shoulder on the back-snap as her tangler took him down. He landed hard on his side, knocking the breath from him, but he was within the Dream and unconscious in seconds.

The weaver finished her spell. A shimmering red disk spun into being at her twirling fingertip, growing and building speed.

The ledge gave way as Jenya and Vesta threw their darts. They barely had time to hold their breath as they fell. Their darts missed their targets and clattered off the stone. Jenya tumbled to the ground between the weaver and the rear sulari just as Maro's tangler wrapped around his legs. Vesta skidded into the weaver and knocked her off balance. The weaver lost control of the whirling red disk as she and Vesta struggled to separate themselves.

The disk began to wobble and spin faster as it grew; then it shot from the weaver's hand. It sheared off the top of her head, sliced Vesta in half without sound or blood, flared brightly, and vanished.

The entangled sulari fell trying to free himself from Maro's tangler. He landed on half of Vesta's corpse, gasped in horror, and tried to push himself away. He lost consciousness before he could escape the fog.

When it was quiet again, Maro, Jenya, and Sieda clambered clear of the Dream cloud. They moved twenty feet away before they let out their breath and inhaled again. Sieda checked her shoulder. The leather was torn, but there was no blood.

They waited for the fog to dissipate before they inspected the area.

"No blood," Maro noted. He looked at the ledge. "And the break was natural."

"Good," Sieda said. "There'll be no trace of this encounter."

She looked at Jenya. "Was Vesta under a parts contract?"

Jenya checked for a tattoo behind her dead comrade's ear. "No."

"Then we can dispose of her body with the others."

Sieda held her chin as she looked over the scene of the battle. One dead Maranth. One dead weaver. Two sulari lost to Dream. They'd be unconscious for an hour. More than enough time.

Savarat has weavers.

"Jenya, take anything from Vesta that could lead to us."

Jenya nodded.

"Maro, search the weaver and her friends for anything of value and take their livery. We'll dump the corpses in the canal and bleed out the dreamers over them. Something should eat them within an hour."

Maro nodded and bent to his task. He paused as he knelt over one of the unconscious sulari.

"Why their livery?"

"To wear over our drabs. If we run into anyone else, I want them to think we're House Savarat."

Myrissa froze.

She held out a hand to halt Ilyara and Lacosia and stared down the passageway for several seconds, then ushered them back around the corner they'd just rounded.

Myrissa tapped her eye with a forefinger, then brought her palms together, fingers straight and pointing away from her sternum. She moved her hands away from her chest and turned them to the left, then extended her arms a few inches and pulled away her right hand. When she held out three fingers, Lacosia nodded.

Around the corner. Ahead. To the right. Three creatures.

Lacosia made a gesture. Myrissa nodded.

Humani, or similar.

Lacosia walked two fingers of his gloved hand along the armored palm of his right, first in one direction, then the other.

Myrissa shrugged. Lacosia frowned.

It may be Loquay's sulari on patrol. Then again...

He pressed a finger to his lips and brought the index and middle finger of his other hand sharply together like scissors. The adepts nodded and let their weaves unravel. Their vision faded to normal sight. The muffled sounds of the sewers sharpened and intensified.

Lacosia whispered softly to Myrissa, "BlackestNight. On me. Give me one second of color before you throw." Then, to Ilyara, "Echoes."

Ilyara nodded. She took a deep breath and let it out slowly, tracing a pattern in the air with her forefinger, a duplicate pattern within the first, and a third within the second. Then she closed her eyes and listened. She sifted through the Underwet's miscellany of tone and pitch and timbre, muffled its skitters and slithers and drips, muted its ripples and rebounds and resonance until she could hear the others. She tightened her weave and focused on the soft, deliberate footfalls around the bend. She could feel their gentle tread, see the subtle echoes of their steps.

Ilyara held up three fingers, then opened her left hand and walked two fingers of her right over her palm, toward her wrist. Then she held her hands shoulder width apart, palms inward, and began to bring them together slowly.

Myrissa and Lacosia began to whisper dead words.

Ilyara's hands were six inches apart...

The faintest glimmers of stray light shimmered on the water at the corner. A depthless blackness began to trickle down Myrissa's arm.

... four inches...

The faint glow of a muted sunstone began to spill around the corner. The blackness began to flow in rivulets down Myrissa's arm and snake around her open hand like a living thing.

... two inches...

The eye painted on Lacosia's patch began to pulse with violet light.

Sieda held up her hand to stop their advance. The white-banded leather on her wrist looked strange to her. She wondered how Maro and Jenya felt wearing another House's livery.

"Maro," she whispered, "did you hear—"

A figure stepped from around the corner before Sieda could finish her question. She had a brief glimpse of robes and color and patches of violet fire; then the figure was engulfed in a sphere of complete darkness.

"Weaver!" Sieda yelled.

She grabbed Maro and pulled him to the ground.

"Spray!"

Jenya threw aside her cloak and pulled her shoulders back. A dozen poisoned darts shot out of the harness on her chest toward the blackness—

Lacosia raised his glowing hand and ripped a hole in the air. Without a sound, the space between himself and the three humani split and peeled away.

—and vanished into a tear in space.

Where there had been a sewer and a black sphere, the sulari now saw a gleaming patch of stars against complete blackness.

For an instant, they felt a terrible cold. Then they were sucked into the starry void.

Lacosia sealed the Rift and lowered his hand. He allowed himself a moment to let his pleasure fade. He had channeled too much of late.

"They're gone," he said.

Myrissa retracted her darkness and banished it from the world.

"Were you able to see who they were?" Ilyara asked.

"Assassins," Lacosia said. "Savarat's."

CHAPTER 14

EVEREVE MARSH

Fedahi and Morgru followed Blaythe's messenger by barge for several days, never more than a few hours behind, stopping only when the messenger stopped or when they needed to change transport or obtain supplies. It was slow going; the Fwaer had been overburdened with traffic since the closure of the Aenin.

On the eve of the fifth day, the messenger left the river at the village of Norbruck, seven miles east of Evereve Marsh. As in other towns along the way, the messenger met with one or two people before continuing. Fedahi kept a written log of these meetings, complete with physical descriptions and the time and place of contact. He passed his logs to Ciridan through Blackhand's local agents.

From Norbruck, Blaythe's envoy followed the Fwaer westward. He traveled on foot, far enough away from the river's banks to avoid detection from the water, stopping for neither food nor rest. By the afternoon of the seventh day, Arwynn's sulari were hard pressed to maintain his pace. Worse, he did not turn from the Fwaer to follow the road to Amsted but continued along the river toward Evereve Marsh.

Morgru and Fedahi moved silently among the thick rushes that lined the Fwaer. The ground became increasingly soft and treacherous as they neared Evereve's outer reaches. The air began to stink of dead things left in heat as the plant growth thickened with the flattening and wetting of the terrain. Wisps of noisome mist wafted from the scattered sumps that pocked the outskirts of the deadly swamp. Insects began to attack their eyes and feast on their blood and sweat and skin.

"We should track'm," Fedahi said, swatting a bug.

"Why?" Morgru asked. "We can still keep up."

"Yeah? For how long?"

Morgru shrugged. "Few hours."

"Doesn't buy much." Fedahi snorted. "I don't know 'bout you, Morg, but this place gives me the knogglies. And this's just the outwet. You know what's next."

Morgru chewed his lower lip and surveyed their surroundings. Through the tangled vegetation, he could see Blaythe's envoy moving steadily and artlessly deeper into the poisonous fen. Soon, he would vanish beneath Evereve's dark canopy with only trampled undergrowth and jostled foliage to mark his passing. Keeping to his path would not be difficult, but it would be much slower than simply following him.

Morgru shook his head.

"Take too long."

"Beya," Fedahi protested. "Ciridan never knew we'd be goin' *inta* Evereve. There's no—"

"Doesn't matter!" Morgru cut him short with a sharp wave of his hand. "Ciridan made it clear: speed is greed. So, we give her speed."

"Speed?" Fedahi sneered. "Speed? Speed ain't gonna mean nothin' if we're dead! Who's gonna report back? Ghosts?"

Morgru scowled at Fedahi.

"Look," he said, "you're right. I know you're right. You know you're right. But orders are, beya? An' it's my neck in the noose. You're second man, Fed. I'm point. If we pull bones, I get th' blade. So, we bleed for speed. Beya?"

"You know what's in there," Fedahi said gravely. "The *things* that live in there. You've heard stories, same as me."

"Yeah," Morgru said. "I know th' stories. But it's bog or blade, an' we have better chances in the bog."

Fedahi grunted, then offered a defeated shrug.

Morgru turned and started after the messenger. "Wargrum protect us."

"Protect us?" Fedahi grumbled. "Even Wargrum won't go in there."

The sulari moved invisibly through the gloom, matching their quarry's path and pace. As they got deeper into the swamp, the wispy mists settled into a carpet of fog as the vegetation thickened and tangled. The canopy overhead grew more entwined, the shadows, more ominous. The sickly sweet tang of rot and decay deepened as the Fwaer stagnated.

Then the mire exploded.

Barbed vines and tendrils lashed out from all around them, whipping and flailing. Morgru spun about, caught a vine across his throat, and staggered, stunned. Fedahi dropped low, drew his shortblade, and pivoted as creepers clutched the air above him. Two large kalypshia vines snatched up Morgru as he faltered and pinned his arms to his sides, locking into his flesh with long curved thorns. Fedahi caught the briefest glimpse of his companion being dragged into the foggy underbrush; then his right leg was pulled from under him.

Morgru's screams were cut short as the breath was crushed from his body, replaced by the dull popping of his ribs and spine.

Fedahi severed the vine snaring his leg before it could bore into his flesh. He rose to dodge a second vine, cleave a third. He wheeled about—

—was jerked backward.

The kalypshia had lashed a thorny vine around Fedahi's left wrist. Tendrils were worming into his skin and starting to twine along his bones. He hacked with his shortblade, but the plant's fibrils had pierced his arteries and were using his blood to regenerate.

Fedahi screamed and cursed and thrashed against the plant. The kalypshia tightened its grip and pulled him closer. More vines rose from the fog and began to sway to and fro like serpents waiting for prey to come into striking range.

Maddened with pain and desperate, Fedahi began to chop at his forearm.

Again and again and again.

Until his hand was torn away.

CHAPTER 15

STONE HEART

Arael's company slipped quietly into the sewers beneath Wirith with the first breath of dawn. Gabrael Harnath's penchant for the Underwet enabled her to shepherd them deftly through its convoluted passageways. So perfectly did Gabrael's hematite hair, mottled gray cloaks, and schorl skin blend with the stonework and the shadows, she was often indiscernible in the gloom. Only the occasional glint of her copper-gold eyes gave her away.

They navigated the main sewers easily and soon entered the older, more convoluted passages beneath Wirith's southern districts. Two hours later, they entered the Underwet's lower levels, and from there a maze of antiquated tunnels that undercut the deepest foundations of Wirith. Gabrael guided the Wargrumites through the ancient passageways with confidence, knowing that her family alone possessed maps of the forgotten tunnels.

She was wrong.

They'd scarcely covered a furlong when a Sathiian caught them unawares and engulfed Misha and Baccaro with a silky black fire. They fell to the ground screaming as their long bones shattered and their flesh fused, blackened, and scaled. By the time Arael formed an Aethic shield, Misha and Baccaro had transformed into monstrous serpents and were attacking their former comrades.

Arael gave in to her rage. She hurled her shield at the Sathiian and enveloped him in a shimmering sphere, then collapsed the sphere upon itself until it and the man inside vanished. When she looked around, the serpents lay still, with Wylen and Illiashi alongside, dead by their venom.

When they encountered a second Sathiian twenty minutes later, Arael wasted no time. She stepped forward without shields and turned the Sathiian to stone, then spat on the ground at his feet and cut the air before her with a flat hand. The earth softened and bubbled where she'd spat and sucked the petrified man deep into its bosom. Arael clenched her fist, and the earth hardened. When it was solid, she released the Sathiian from his stone form and allowed him to suffocate in Wargrum's embrace.

When they'd sufficiently distanced themselves from Wirith's middle ring, Arael held a modest service for their fallen comrades. Gabrael stood guard while Arael, Rahne, and Pendaro entreated Wargrum to restore their stolen humanity and guide their lost brethren safely into the Afterworld. They also prayed for the Sathiians, that they might find in death the humanity that eluded them in life. When they were finished, Rahne and Pendaro took a few moments for private meditation. Arael watched and wished she could do the same.

Rahne and Pendaro had drawn strength from the brief service. Arael, however, felt only sorrow. And regret for the terrible weaves she'd used in anger to kill.

Is my anger so powerful that I am lost to it?

Arael's capacity for rage terrified her. It was her greatest weakness and the single reason she'd committed herself to the Lord of Stone: only Wargrum could grant the strength she needed to forge her kih and hold her emote in check. Yet having now killed two men, she wondered whether she would ever be strong enough to rein in her fury. It seemed that as her Aethic mastery grew, so too did the heat of her rage and the depth of her sorrow.

Six have died this day.

She looked at her hands and sighed sadly.

By hands that pretend to heal.

Which was the greater evil: to kill one's fellow humani over an unshared belief, or to strip them of their humanity and let them die an animal? Was she any better than the Sathiians who sought her death in the name of their faith? Were they not heroes in their own eyes?

She wiped her eyes and sniffled.

Though she told herself that her mission's urgency justified extreme actions, she didn't believe it. That reasoning was too indulgent and too easily twisted to legitimize willful evil. If urgency was the only predicate that mattered, what separated the Elem from the Sathiians? What distinguished her from Welbley Blaythe?

Arael felt unworthy of her station when the tears finally came.

Sometimes, Wargrum demanded a heart of stone.

CHAPTER 16

DISCOVERIES AND DETAILS

Welbley Blaythe sat behind his desk in his private office, toying distractedly with the green crystal ring on his right thumb. His messenger stood dutifully before him, silent and still.

It was a remarkable creature, as humani in appearance as it was unnatural in nature. More plant than liche, it was impervious to magicks directed against flesh and resistant to weaves tuned to the unliving. That Adar Ashan could conceive of such a creature, let alone devise the means to create it, was a marvel to Welbley. When he looked upon the thing before him, he did not see the mutated shell of his former high priest, Draka. He saw a testament to the power of the Church of Sathiis.

Welbley stood, approached the shell of what was once Draka, and ran a finger lightly over the creature's cheek.

You were warned not to answer X'theX'lo's questions, he thought.

Welbley smiled, remembering the night Draka declared he would summon the daemon. He chuckled as he imagined the stark terror on Draka's face when he realized he'd answered a question and his mind was stolen.

And here we are.

Welbley sighed. There would be time for pleasure later.

The lord priest traced a complex pattern before his creature's face, then closed his eyes and pressed a palm to its forehead, as he'd done several weeks ago before sending it to meet with Arwynn Blackhand. This time he did not program the creature with careful dialogue or imbue it with the intellect to deal with an assassin. This time, he furnished the creature with the cognizance necessary to recall details and answer simple questions.

"How many followed you?" Welbley asked, returning to his chair.

"Two," the creature replied dully.

"Humani?"

"Yes."

"Did they observe your meetings?"

"Yes."

Welbley had expected Blackhand to shadow his courier and arranged a trail of false agents along its return path. Resources Arwynn committed to investigating those agents would be wasted.

"Were you followed from Norbruck?"

"Yes."

"By how many?"

"Two."

"The same two?"

"Yes."

"How far?"

"The swamp."

"And then?"

"They died."

"How?"

"Vines."

Welbley leaned back in his chair and tapped his fingers lightly on the edge of his desk.

"Describe Blackhand," he said softly.

"Humani," the liche responded. "Average man. Dark eyes. Dark hair. Narrow face. Light skin. Dark beard."

Welbley glanced at the letters on his desk, reports from four agents over six months. No two described the assassin the same way, and his creature's description was different again.

Always in disguise? Is that possible?

"Did Blackhand have any distinguishing markings?" Welbley pressed.

"No," the messenger rasped.

"Scars?"

"No."

"Jewelry?"

"A ring."

"Metal?"

"No."

"Crystal?"

"Yes."

"Color?"

"Red."

Blaythe frowned. The ring could be anything—a symbol of status, a gift, simple ornamentation…

Or a crystal ring of power.

Welbley frowned again and looked at the green band on his right thumb. The Church of Sathiis favored emerald and promoted from the little finger of the left hand: Blaythe's ring on his right thumb marked him as a sixth-tier weaver. But Blackhand was an assassin—there was no reason to suspect his ring to be anything but adornment. Then again, until Tehru Shaddoht's report there had been no reason to suspect a wizard in his House either.

Perhaps therein lies the deception, Welbley thought. *Simply wearing a crystal ring does not make one a magickan, except in the mind of another.* And yet, to discount such a possibility was to be doubly disadvantaged should they, in fact, be a weaver. *For the moment, we will assume that Blackhand possesses at least a smattering of Aethic training.*

Welbley returned his attention to his messenger.

"Did the assassin use tehelu?"

"No."

"Did you expel the somphora?"

"Yes."

Good!

Without tehelu, Blackhand would be blind to his creature's true nature and oblivious to the somphora spores it expelled from its body during their meeting. Spores that now worked within him to nurture a horrible affliction.

The thought of Blackhand's pending torment brought a smile to Welbley's lips.

"Did you reach an accord?" Welbley asked.

"Yes."

"What are the terms?"

Draka's husk did not respond. The question was too general.

"Does Blackhand protect our shipments?"

"Yes."

"From Westgate to temple?"

"Yes."

"What is his price?"

"Ten black lotos leaves. Ten feet of achaelos vine. Ten arrowheads of saurin redsteel. Fifty silver coins."

"Per barge?"

"Yes."

"Are the terms negotiable?"

"No."

Welbley's smile fell. The assassin's demands were excessive, but not prohibitive. Though he hated to pay such a high premium, only House Blackhand could provide the level of security he required. He could not afford a shipment falling into the wrong hands at this stage.

"How do we signal acceptance?"

"Church standard on the bow accepts. Stern refuses."

Welbley steepled his fingers in front of his face.

At last, his preparations were complete. Soon, Selene would supplant Melkor and the Great Houses of Dûhr would bow before the Black Serpent of Heaven.

One by one.

And yours will lead them, Arwynn Blackhand.

CHAPTER 17

CLAN C'THQUI

The waters of the Zemi were home to three mir clans: the C'thqui, notorious for their poisons; the Qithq, renowned for their subtlety; the C'thoqa, feared for their weaving. Each clan adhered to an idiosyncratic social order dominated by a ruthless warlord and overseen by a coterie of magikkas, weaver-priests devoted to strange gods. The mir trusted few in their own clan and none outside it. They maintained an uneasy peace with the humani and sauri solely for the benefit of trade, though they rarely took payment in silver. They preferred weapons of steel, exotic materials and foodstuffs, poisons, drugs… and slaves.

Urath Lindrowe and four Alyl waited amid the trees that lined a bend in the Fwaer, two miles east of Dûhr. They were dressed in hooded black robes tied at the waist and upper arms with short lengths of gray cord. The Alyl's faces were painted black with a white alyl flower over the left eye. Lindrowe's face was half-black and half-white. They stood silent and unmoving, shadows among the trees, watching and waiting.

One of the Alyl held a glass globe of yellow surath powder on a short length of copper chain, prepared to throw at Lindrowe's command. The other three stood slightly ahead to obscure her and protect the poisonmaster, armed with spraydarts coated with surath resin. Lindrowe had two short daggers and retractable knee spikes, all coated with achaelos syrup. The mir suffered a grievous vulnerability to surath, but he suspected that achaelos would prove even more virulent. While Lindrowe hoped their negotiation would go smoothly, he was happy to test his theory should things get out of hand.

Time passed slowly.

Tensely.

Though it seemed not to pass at all.

It was past midnight when the first mir broke the water's surface. It rose soundlessly from the river with scarcely a ripple, its thin and chalky body pallid in the pale light of the moons. Out of water, its stringy hair glistened like flat glass against its neck and shoulders. It remained perfectly still as it scanned the trees; then it sank noiselessly back into the Fwaer.

A scout, Lindrowe thought. *It knows we're here. It's trying to draw us to the water.*

He found the mir fascinating and unnerving in their elegant strangeness. Their hair was threadlike tubules that grew full upon the crests of their heads in rich variations of green, blue, and white. Their large eyes matched the color of their tubules, though brighter and flecked with silver. From the waist up they appeared humani, albeit eerily emaciated, as though their milky skin had been stretched across too much bone. Below, they were water serpents, solidly muscled and heavily scaled. Their part-serpentine bodies allowed them to rocket through water and glide easily over land.

It had been their spectacular poisons that initially enticed Lindrowe, but he quickly realized the mir had far more to offer: access to rare plants, salvage services, and exceptional espionage along waterways.

Another tiny ripple spread across the water as a mir warrior silently broke the surface.

And another.

So, it begins.

Five figures emerged from the water, four warriors and an ancient magikka.

The warriors wore deceptively fragile-looking light armor of interlocking shells adorned with brightly colored scales. Each held a barbed spear, artistically graven, carved from a single bone.

Lindrowe noted the knives on their belts. *Poisoned or they would be unsheathed. A resin coating of some kind.*

The magikka wore a dark cloak of dyed humani skin, clasped at the left shoulder with a large golden brooch that bore the sigil of Clan C'thqui. It paused to examine the shoreline before moving forward, trailing its retinue like a wake, two on either side. The moonlight slid down its waxy bald head and neck, flowed like oil over its pale flesh.

Lindrowe stepped from the cover of the trees to meet the weaver-priest as it left the water. His Alyl struck a defensive posture at the tree line as the mir warriors slithered nearer the shore.

The magikka's voice was unused to air.

"Ithoq, Lindrowe," it rasped.

It splayed the fingers of one hand over its breast and recognized the assassin with the common greeting of its clan.

Ithoq: you are here.

"Ithiq qui, Mad'rhaq," Lindrowe said, mimicking the gesture.

Lindrowe offered the more formal greeting, *Ithiq qui*: you are before me. Formality and delicacy were warranted, as the mir were known to attack without provocation. A subservient posture would also play well to the mir's arrogance in negotiations.

The assassin and the magikka eyed each other with suspicion.

Mad'rhaq broke the silence.

"There is no trade this cycle, Lindrowe Black House," it rasped. "C'thqui asks for what purpose you summon us."

"Truth told," Lindrowe said. "There is no trade this cycle. Nor have I summoned you for trade."

Mad'rhaq narrowed its eyes and frowned. "I do not like leaving the waters of my home, Lindrowe Black House. I like riddles even less. We have traded much, you and I, and our clans have prospered. For this reason, I will listen. Speak. Plainly."

Lindrowe bowed politely.

"There are barges," he said, "that travel the Fwaer between Dûhr and Wirith. They are black and green and bear the standard of the Church of Sathiis."

"These vessels are known to us."

"There will come a time that I will want one of these vessels destroyed and its cargo seized."

The magikka considered Lindrowe's request for some time before responding.

"No, Lindrowe Black House," Mad'rhaq said at last. "That is not possible."

Lindrowe let his face drop in disappointment, though he was unfazed by Mad'rhaq's blunt refusal. The mir often claimed a task was impossible until the price was driven high enough to justify their risk.

"Not possible?"

"The barges are under the protection of Clan Qithq," Mad'rhaq said. "Attacking one would open war between Qithq and C'thqui. Qithq is strong. War is not wise."

Blaythe is using mir guards, Lindrowe thought. *What cargo would justify that expense?*

Lindrowe called the woman with the glass sphere. She stepped from the forest's edge, glass orb in one hand, copper chain in the other. She approached Lindrowe and slowly presented the orb to her master. Lindrowe lifted the glass ball by its chain and eyed the yellow powder trapped within.

One thousand gold pieces' worth of surath powder. Enough to poison a hundred humani.

"You know what this is?" Lindrowe asked Mad'rhaq.

"I know," Mad'rhaq said, glaring at the yellow powder. "It is the powder that brought down Clan Icthx."

"Yes," Lindrowe said. "Surath. Deadly poison. More so to your people than mine."

The magikka's eyes burned with hatred.

For the powder.

For the reminder of his people's weakness.

"With this powder, C'thqui is strong." Lindrowe smiled as he spoke. "With this powder, C'thqui can lay low Qithq. With this powder, war is not unwise."

Lindrowe allowed his hand to tremble slightly as he extended the poison to Mad'rhaq. The magikka drew back, as though the powder might seep through the glass, then very carefully moved forward and accepted the orb by the chain. For a moment it stared at the powder inside the orb. Then a smile crept across its withered lips.

"A barge you name will go down when you say," Mad'rhaq said.

Lindrowe grinned broadly. "Excellent."

CHAPTER 18

PASSAGE

Arael intended to use Harnath's secret tunnels to slip under Balistrahd's guarded perimeter, then return to the surface and travel to Dûhr across the lower Aenin. However, when her company reached the first of Harnath's tunnels, they found the entrance collapsed.

At Arael's behest, Rahne moved forward and crouched a few feet from the rubble. He traced a sign in the air above the ground and placed a hand flat upon the earth. The tunnel floor began to glow a faint gray, gaining blue as it brightened. Seconds later, luminescence flowed away from his hand toward the rubble, spreading out over the broken stone, seeping into its dark recesses, before fading away. When the last glimmer vanished, Rahne returned to the others.

"This was a deliberate collapse," he said. "Several weeks old. Sathiian signature."

"The Sathiians are thorough," Pendaro said. "If they sealed one tunnel, they will have sealed them all."

"The ones heading east, at the very least," Rahne added.

"Still, the barrier is stone," noted Gabrael. "You can remove it easily."

"Yes," Pendaro said. "But should we? The Church of Wargrum is the only one of the Elem to openly oppose the Black Church. Few but our associates would be likely to travel this byway, so deep within the earth. The Sathiians would not overlook that. Yet this barrier is made of stone, the very element we command. Doesn't that strike you as odd?"

Gabrael offered Pendaro a faint but familiar half smile, then looked at the collapsed passage.

"A trap, then?" she asked.

"It seems likely," Pendaro said. "Lady?"

"I've seen many devilish Sathiian traps," Arael said. "One was not unlike this, a barrier easily removed with a skeleo trapped behind it. I've seen others designed to weaken rather than kill. Trivial obstacles, easily overcome, but high in count. The more Aethic energy we wasted clearing them away, the more vulnerable we became to the creatures that prowled the caverns. We were lucky to survive."

Arael looked at the ruined passageway and sighed. "The Sathiians do nothing without malicious intent. We will not risk clearing any obstacles they put in our path."

"Then, what do you suggest?" Gabrael asked.

"We'll go southeast."

"Toward Evereve?"

Arael nodded. "It's the one path certain to be free of obstruction."

The darkness thickened as they moved through the long, wet tunnels and began to curtail the reach of their sunstones. The silence was broken only by the slow drip of trickling water and the soft sounds of their footsteps on the wet rock. The air was fetid and damp. Arael was thankful the Enchantment of Vitality averted their need of food and rest.

"We're getting close to Evereve now," Gabrael commented.

"How much longer?" Arael asked.

"Till we reach the swamp? A couple hours if we keep this pace and the tunnel ahead hasn't collapsed or flooded. These old passages run deep, but there are still risks."

"Until we surface."

"Ah."

Gabrael consulted her weathered map.

"There are two paths to the surface. The first is about an hour ahead. It comes out in the Bahli, about a mile from Evereve's fringe. The next is a couple miles beyond that and leads into the swamp. If I had to choose, I'd pick the second. The Myriadi Royal are dogged, but only to a point: they'll patrol the Bahli but won't enter the swamp."

Arael was silent, thoughtful. The creatures that prowled Evereve Marsh were among the most fearsome in all the Realms Humani and grew steadily more lethal as one approached the Dead Gate at the center of the morass. Given a choice between a trek through Evereve's outer fringe and a confrontation with Balistrahd's patrols, Arael was hard pressed not to choose the latter. But Blaythe's priests traveled with the prince's soldiers, which tilted the scales considerably.

"We cannot stay in these tunnels much longer," Pendaro said.

He ran a finger along the tunnel wall and wiped it on the cuff of his cassock. It left a grimy, dark stain.

"Already the Black Moss weakens the stone," he said. "The corruption will worsen as we draw nearer the Dead Gate. It may be better to face mortal dangers."

Arael rubbed her chin. Pendaro was right: as they moved deeper into Evereve, the power of Wargrum would dwindle against the combined might of the Daemin of Earth and Water. As Wargrum's power waned, so too would their magicks.

Again, the scales tilted.

"Perhaps," Arael murmured, "we have a third alternative."

"And that would be?" Gabrael asked.

"We stay underground and go east."

"There isn't a tunnel in that direction."

A flicker of silver light danced behind Arael's brilliant blue eyes.

"Not yet."

CHAPTER 19

TIGHTLY WOVEN THREADS

The Caba Gehnan taught that existence was underpinned by a fundamental force called the Aethios and that reality was an intricate and transient tapestry woven of Aethic threads. Each thread represented a unique shaping of some fraction of the Aethios. Threads of common character combined into strands. Strands interlaced to define the pattern of reality.

All magickal disciplines were based on Strands. Through the Strand of Flesh, a priest healed living bodies; through the Strand of Death, a necromancer bound the dead to service; through the Strand of Sensing, a wizard struck their enemy blind; through the Strand of Cognition, a seer glimpsed unwritten futures.

A skilled magickan, a clever and able weaver of Aethic threads, might master a strand over the course of a lifetime, perhaps two.

With mastery of a strand, the magickan gained the power to affect its threads and thereby alter reality at its most basic level. Such power, however, was not without price. Manipulating a thread required the weaver to channel a portion of the Aethios and shape its energy as it passed through their body, like a lens focusing a ray of light. The greater the degree of manipulation, the greater the Aethic flow. But Aethic energy was anathema to mortal flesh and disrupted the magickan's physical structure. The damage could be assuaged by carefully managing the frequency and degree of one's channeling; otherwise such disruption quickly progressed to dissolution.

The structural breakdown was marked by sensations of pleasure that intensified to ecstasy as the dissolution advanced.

The ecstasy was addictive. The disintegration was cumulative, and irreversible after a point.

This was what the Caba Gehnan called Rapture.

Arwynn's Sadri guided their mounts cautiously through the darkening forest as night settled over the Gobli Lands. At the head of their staggered column rode Yarkossa (*Force, Planes*), followed by Sartahex (*Metamorphy, Control*); last in line were Agraxix (*Necrosis*) and Savishi (*Dominion*). Malaraphi held the middle position.

They had reached the forests north of the Tameron Pass in four days' traveling through the Shadow Plane and would now proceed conventionally to the Cerine Sea. When they reached the coast, they would separate: Malaraphi, Yarkossa, and Sartahex would continue to the Red Jungle to confer with the Clubfoot; Agraxix and Savishi would return to Dûhr, collecting the gobli Arwynn requested on their way.

Though it annoyed Malaraphi to be limited by the speed of their horses, he was unwilling to risk Yarkossa's planar weaves disturbing the thing imprisoned in Xotl.

Yarkossa remained ready to defend the group from attack while his companions manipulated threads of their strands to descry hazards beyond the range of their natural senses:

Sartahex by way of tissue, Savishi by way of cognition, Agraxix by way of ichor.

Malaraphi spent his time contemplating how best to deal with the Clubfoot.

"Lord."

Malaraphi opened his eyes. "Yes?"

"Several gobli wait beyond the next hillock," Sartahex said.

"They are aware of our presence," Savishi added.

"How many?" Malaraphi asked.

"Eighteen," Sartahex replied. "All male. One is very strong."

"What is their intent?"

"To encircle us," Savishi answered, "kill us with projectiles, steal our goods, and eat our remains."

"How droll," the loremaster muttered. "Shamans?"

"I sense no Aethic marks," said Sartahex.

"Nor I in their intent," said Savishi.

"Good." Malaraphi thought a moment, then nodded.

"Keep moving. We will maintain our approach as though unaware of their presence and try to bluff our way past. This will almost certainly fail, but any chance to conserve our strength is worth taking, with Xotl so close."

He glanced up at the two moons. Ilia trailed Glae by a good measure.

"The night is still young; the gobli will be active for some time. If it comes to violence, we must be swift and efficient. We can't afford survivors or alarms or lingering Aethic echoes.

Yarkossa, prepare a barrier against their projectiles. Agraxix, form a killing fog. Savishi, when the fog coalesces, turn it upon their thickest portion. Sartahex, wasps. My signal to attack will be the death of their leader. Hold your weaves ready until then—especially you, Yarkossa."

The gobli broke into three groups of six as the Sadri neared. Two groups deployed to flank the Sadri; the third blocked their path.

The gobli were nightmarish anthropoid beings, four feet wide at the shoulder and twice as tall, despite the oppressive musculature that warped their spines and bent their bones. Their eyes were large and luminous; their noses, broad and squat; their mouths packed with jagged teeth. Tufts of wirelike hair burst from their gray hides in irregular patches, dark and disheveled and matted with mud.

Their armor was a patchwork of metal and bone strung together with strips of sinew and hair. One clutched a gigantic spiked club. Two brandished steel-headed spears. Three held jhediri crossbows cocked with steel-shod bolts.

Malaraphi scowled. *Where would a gobli get such a fine crossbow? Or steel, for that matter?*

The club-wielding gobli stepped forward. Its armor was of higher quality, fashioned mostly of bronze scales and iron rings. Mummified humani heads were slung around its waist. It pointed the club at the Sadri.

"Stop!" The guttural gobli language tumbled from its mouth like a wet cough.

Malaraphi halted his company. He slowly raised his head and allowed the gobli leader to view his aged and wrinkled face.

"Who stop red man?" Malaraphi growled, the gobli tongue grating his throat.

The gobli cocked its head to one side. It squinted at the old elfi, then glared at each of the Sadri.

"Grahak!" it bellowed. It pounded its chest with a fist. "Ehtman Bone Tribe!"

It motioned to the surrounding forest.

"Land Bone Tribe! Pay to pass!"

"Say pay."

"Men go," Grahak barked. Then it pointed at Savishi and Sartahex, and its scarred lips twisted into a gruesome smile.

"Notmen stay. Good pay."

The gobli behind Grahak grunted and stamped their feet.

Malaraphi hardened his gaze and leaned forward in his saddle. He was grateful his cloaks concealed the weakness of his limbs. To the gobli, his age commanded respect—it was testament to his survival and his power. But if they were to see the weakness of his body...

"Red man shaman!" Malaraphi barked back. "Red man no pay!"

"Red man pay," Grahak growled.

"No."

"Me say pay!" Grahak boomed, temper flaring.

It smashed its great club upon the ground and narrowed its eyes, gnashing its teeth with a loud grinding noise.

"Red man pay!"

And so it goes...

Malaraphi spat on the ground between himself and Grahak.

The enraged ehtman howled and hefted its massive club with both hands. Malaraphi rose in his saddle and thrust a spindly arm skyward as the gobli began its swing. Red flames exploded from Malaraphi's eyes and mouth, rushed up his outstretched arm, and ignited his raised hand. He threw the fire at Grahak. It struck the ehtman squarely in the center of its chest, vaporized its torso, and blasted away the head of the crossbowman behind it.

There was a stunned silence as Grahak's burning head and arms fell to the ground. Then one of the gobli roared and sent its spear hurtling at Malaraphi as others let loose a rain of crossbow bolts.

Yarkossa was faster. Having already woven his spell, he had only to release it.

In an instant, the air about the Sadri sparkled and solidified into a shimmering green barrier that neatly trapped and held the gobli projectiles. The gobli gawked at the barrier, unable to grasp the implications of Yarkossa's magick. Then they hefted their weapons and rushed forward to swarm the mounted weavers.

As the first gobli slammed into the barrier, Agraxix clutched the air before it and pushed sharply. The gobli flew back as though struck by a great force. It landed on its back and was trampled by the others. As the creature choked and wheezed its way to death, Agraxix's magick took hold and transformed the gobli's dying breath into a pale blue vapor.

Savishi started to chant and sway in her saddle as her will possessed the vapor and her words coaxed it to condense into a fog. Savishi's control strengthened as her incantation swelled into song, making the fog roil and churn with the rhythm of her words, moving with her will. She sent it among the thickest group of gobli, singing its praises as it dutifully engulfed them in turn and sucked away their life.

Sartahex waited until the melee reached its peak. Then she chose a victim not touched by the fog and loosed her spell.

The gobli screamed and staggered backward. Blood spewed from its mouth and nose in a great gush as its lungs collapsed. Its flesh sank and cracked and pulled away from its bones at the joints while the bones themselves snapped under the weight of rotting muscle. The creature collapsed into a heap of dead tissue. A heartbeat later, a wasp the size of a muskrat ate its way clear of the carrion and fanned dry its diaphanous wings.

The wasp launched itself at the nearest gobli and buried its stinger in the creature's shoulder, paralyzing it with venom. Immobile yet fully aware, the gobli watched the insect tear through its patchwork armor and burrow into its warm flesh.

Feeding. Breeding.

Unable to even scream, the paralyzed gobli suffered silently as it was devoured from within, dying as its belly ruptured to spawn another wasp. Each wasp that bored into a host bred a second; where one entered, two emerged. Savage and bloody and ravenous.

When the final gobli fell, Agraxix dispersed his killing fog while Savishi sang the wasps to sleep. As the last wasp fell still, Yarkossa lowered his barrier and Agraxix dismounted to check the bodies.

Malaraphi turned to Sartahex. "Keep one of the wasps and bring it with us. We may need it later."

Sartahex nodded, dismounted, and bound one of the fallen insects with a minor weave. She wrapped it tightly in a strip of cloak torn from a gobli and placed it gingerly in her saddlebag before remounting her horse.

"Lord?"

Malaraphi turned. Agraxix was a few feet away, crouched by Grahak's remains. He held something shiny in his hand.

"Eh? What is it, Agraxix?" Malaraphi asked.

Agraxix stood and walked to his master's side. "A gobli war party wielding steel is one thing, but this?"

He held out his hand. In his palm were two gold coins.

Malaraphi leaned over in his saddle and picked up one of the coins. He examined it carefully, turning it slowly to catch the moonlight. Though battered and burned, it was unmistakably an elfin laef.

"A most valuable and uncommon coin," the old wizard muttered. "Interesting."

He looked over the remains of the gobli. "How is it, I wonder, that these brutes came to possess such currency?"

He pursed his lips thoughtfully, then grunted and dropped the coin back into Agraxix's hand.

"Give them to Arwynn. Let him deal with it."

"Yes, Lord," Agraxix said.

"We're close enough to the coast to separate," Malaraphi said. "Sartahex, Yarkossa, and I will continue from here.

Agraxix, Savishi—circle back to Dûhr through the Tameron and deliver a full report of our findings to Arwynn along with a score of live gobli by the week's end. Warriors preferably, but a shaman wouldn't hurt."

"Yes, Lord."

"Yes, Lord."

The old elfi nodded and took a last look around. He counted eight wasps interspersed among the slaughtered gobli.

"And kill the rest of those little devils before you go," he said brusquely.

CHAPTER 20

GATEWAY

The earth exploded before Arael's party in a continuous maelstrom of stone and dust and gravel. Spinning chunks of rock hurtled at them from all angles, fragmenting and splitting as they came, only to lose all form and integrity in a haze of eerie silver bursts just before impact.

Once Arael's intention was clear, Pendaro and Rahne acted to accelerate their movement through the tunnel she was creating. They wove their spell together—neither had sufficient Aethic reserves to contract dimension alone. While they met with less success than they'd hoped, their spell did not fail; each step their party took now covered yards.

And they were running.

With Gabrael protected between them, the priests rocketed eastward through the earth, as neatly and effortlessly as eelsharks through still water. At such a rate of movement, it was no wonder that Arael's disintegration of the stone ahead seemed a staccato sequence of violent discharges rather than an elegant dissolution of matter.

Their passage, however, was not without cost. Arael had to forgo the Enchantment of Vitality to weave her Dissolution spell. With its annulment, the sharp fangs of repressed hunger bit savagely at their empty bellies and the dead weight of forestalled fatigue sucked the strength from their limbs. They were up to their necks in the thick fluid of exhaustion and sinking fast.

The silver bursts that marked their progress soon lost their purity and dimmed to gray.

As the gray dulled, Arael turned her failing spell in the direction that she hoped was up.

CHAPTER 21

EMPTINESS

Rahain Morkainen and his Blood pressed their mounts for more speed as they raced through the evening rain. The limp bodies of their fallen comrades—one dead, the other drugged—lay tied over the back of a third galloping horse. It had been hours since either of the two assassins had rested, yet neither complained. They simply rode on through the thickening darkness and tried to ignore the fatigue pressing down on them. When they reached the outskirts of Dûhr, they separated. Morkainen made his way into the city while his Blood slipped away to deliver the fallen to a healer north of the river.

It was after midnight when Morkainen, still cold and wet from his journey, found Arwynn and Lindrowe in the master's conference chamber, locked in debate over a worn map. The table between them was laden with a slew of papers and markers, looking much the same as it had when Morkainen left with Ciridan. Neither man acknowledged Morkainen's arrival with more than a casual glance.

Morkainen showed no sign of ache or weariness as he crossed the chamber. He stopped at the blazing fireplace in the center of the room only long enough to remove his sodden cloak and tunic and lay them on the hearth.

He loosened the fastenings of his wet leathers as he dropped heavily into a seat across from his cohorts. His silver eyes scanned the cluttered table for food. None immediately presented itself.

"You were expected yesterday morning," the master said evenly. "What happened?"

"Gobli," Morkainen grunted. "They hit us two days ago. Khael was killed. Kavna took a spear to the belly."

He shook his head and scratched some wet hair loose from his scalp, adding: "Lydia took them to Falcroft's place up north."

"A pity," Arwynn said. "Khael had potential."

Morkainen nodded. "He served under a parts contract. Falcroft will salvage what he can and take his cut, then forward half the remaining payment to us and the other half to Khael's family. Kavna will be fine. Falcroft's very good."

"He should be for his prices," Lindrowe grumbled.

Morkainen looked at the poisonmaster. "Better his fee than the time and money it would cost to train another Blood."

"True enough, true enough," Lindrowe acceded. "Speaking of Bloods, Lydia is Blood as well, is she not?"

Morkainen nodded. "Two years come winter."

"You are satisfied with her performance?"

"Very."

"You have plans for her advancement?"

Morkainen narrowed his eyes. "I do."

He glanced at Arwynn, back to Lindrowe. "Why?"

"Show him," Arwynn said to Lindrowe.

The poisonmaster picked up a worn paper from the table and passed it to the half-elfi.

"Morgru's last report," he explained. "Came in last week from Norbruck. They were shadowing Blaythe's messenger west along the Fwaer."

"To Amsted?" Morkainen asked, scanning the paper.

"One would suppose. As far as we can tell, they never arrived."

Morkainen looked up. "What happened?"

"We believe they entered Evereve," Arwynn said.

Morkainen tossed Morgru's report aside. "They're dead."

"Most likely," Arwynn said.

"Hence your concern over Lydia," Morkainen said.

"Without Morgru, we're short a splinterhead," Lindrowe said flatly.

"You see a need?"

"I don't discount it."

The blademaster pursed his lips and scratched his chin. "She's slated for Shadow. This just accelerates the timetable." He turned to Arwynn. "She'll return from Falcroft's in two days. Give me another week to make certain she survives promotion."

"Done," the master agreed.

Lindrowe eased back into his chair, satisfied.

"Now," Morkainen said, "is there anything to eat? I'm starving."

"Under those maps." Arwynn cocked his head toward two large charts to Morkainen's left.

The half-elfi pushed the maps aside, uncovering a plate containing a few slices of pink fruit, several chunks of cheese, and two large pieces of dark bread. He snatched up a piece of fruit, ate it, and reached for another.

Arwynn sat back in his chair and rested his chin in his palm. "How fares Ciridan?" he asked. "Well received, I trust."

Morkainen nodded and swallowed. "Very."

He wiped his mouth with the back of one hand. "Mirroreye was impressed."

Interest twinkled in Lindrowe's torpid eyes. "Impressed, you say? How so?"

"I believe she said, 'I expect a gem and you deliver a jewel,'" Morkainen said, reaching for the bread. "She thinks Ciridan will be easy to train."

"How long does she estimate?" Arwynn asked.

"Two months to the ring."

"Two months?" Lindrowe's eyes widened. He shook his head, amazed. "Beya! How the Mindbender can do in one year what takes the College five is beyond me. But two months?"

Morkainen took a large bite of bread and nodded as he chewed and swallowed. "That's for the first tier. The second will take another four."

"How far can she rise?" Lindrowe asked.

"Mirithwin wouldn't set a limit."

Lindrowe raised his heavy brows and glanced at Arwynn. "We may have a Sadri in the making."

"Perhaps," Arwynn said. "Let's see where things stand in six months."

Morkainen nodded and reached for the cheese, glancing at Lindrowe. "How'd things go with the fishfolk?"

"A bit more complicated than expected." The fat man chuckled. "It turns out Blaythe hired Clan Qithq to provide guards for his barges."

Morkainen raised an eyebrow, popped the cheese into his mouth. "Mir guards don't come cheap."

"No," Arwynn said. "They don't."

"How do things stand?"

"We've contracted Clan C'thqui to acquire the goods from one of Blaythe's barges for us," Lindrowe said. "We'll stage a raid using gobli that Malaraphi's Sadri will provide. The attack will draw the Qithq guards to the surface to engage the gobli. They will defeat the gobli but be sufficiently weakened for the C'thqui attack to follow."

"That fight will be underwater," Morkainen said. "How sure are you the C'thqui will win?"

"They have surath."

"Oh."

"But they will not win."

Morkainen gave the poisonmaster a quizzical look.

"Before the C'thqui use the surath," Lindrowe said, "we will slay them. We'll use a Sadri to force them to the surface, where our sulari will cut them down."

Morkainen started to speak, but Lindrowe stopped him with a raised hand.

"When all is done, only the Qithq will know of our involvement. The mir are proud to a fault. We will shame the Qithq into submission by saving them from the C'thqui. Ceding Blaythe's cargo and binding themselves to our service for a year will seem a bargain for the return of their honor. In the end, Blaythe will believe his barge lost to a gobli raid, and we will have both his cargo and mir spies in his employ."

Lindrowe smiled and lowered his hand.

"Clever," Morkainen granted. "But surely the C'thqui will want revenge."

"The C'thqui will not pose any threat," Lindrowe assured him. "Ungi."

"Ungi? White Plague?"

Lindrowe nodded.

"The whole clan?" Morkainen asked.

"The whole lake," Lindrowe answered.

Morkainen was neither a gentle nor a caring man, yet sometimes the callousness with which he and his associates conducted their affairs troubled him. That his House would turn against the C'thqui did not disturb him—they accepted the risk of betrayal when they struck their bargain with Lindrowe. But, to Morkainen's mind, treachery was a purposeful thing, to be carefully planned and targeted and effected with implements that transcendentally bound the betrayer and the betrayed. Garrotes and knives were licit enough, and poisons and potions permissible, but plague? That tool was too indiscriminate and too extensive.

The ungi will lay waste to every clan in the lake.

It was proper that the plotter should suffer the consequences of their plotting, but those uninvolved should be shielded by their innocence. For his House to loose a plague in the Zemi simply to thwart the C'thqui's legitimate revenge was—

It hit Morkainen then.

The Emptiness.

It came whenever he reached outside himself, tried to care, started to feel. Whenever his cold heart warmed with concern or kindness or mercy, it was there. An indefinable melancholy that slowly deepened into hollow, aching despair. Sometimes it was so overpowering that he could do nothing but weep. He would lie on his side, knees pulled tightly to his chest, and sob for hours.

It had been like that when his Sahadi Lyete… unraveled. For two days. Nor could he deny its icy presence the night Ciridan was tested, when he'd driven fingernails into his palms to push back its terrible grip. With Mirithwin, too, he felt it stir, though he could find no reason.

Did I care for these women?

"R… h… n?"

Do I love them?

"Rahain?"

Morkainen blinked, felt a sting that heralded tears. He set his jaw and rubbed his eyes with his palms to pass off his despair as fatigue.

"Unghh," he groaned. "Sorry. I'm tired."

He took a deep breath and focused his attention on the business at hand, again digging his fingernails into his palms. The Emptiness faded with the pain.

"When does the attack take place?" Morkainen asked.

"The time is not set," Arwynn said. "Malaraphi's Sadri have not yet provided the gobli."

"And the plague?" he asked.

Lindrowe shrugged. "A week before the attack. Maybe two."

Morkainen's hunger returned with his composure. As he reached for more food, he noticed the map that had been the subject of debate when he arrived. It depicted Dûhr's sewers, specifically those beneath the Gardens of Twilight.

Morkainen thrust his chin at the map. "What were you discussing when I came in?"

"Beya." Lindrowe glanced at the map, immediately looked disgusted. "Eight high-ranking sulari lost without a trace in the last weeks, in or around this area." He traced a fat finger around the underways servicing the Gardens of Twilight and the Sathiian construction site, then fell back in his chair with an exasperated grunt.

"The splinters sent to investigate Loquay's doings?" Morkainen asked.

"Yes," Arwynn answered. "One was a Sadri."

"A Sadri? I thought you'd decided not to send Sadri into the sewers."

"That was before the first group vanished."

"Two groups?"

Arwynn nodded grimly. "Three Blades, a Blood, a Whisper, a Vipira, and a Scorpia. And a Sadri."

"Beya," Morkainen whispered. "And without a trace, you say?"

"None."

Morkainen frowned. His Morghanti and Lindrowe's Vehem would not be taken easily by common assassins, but a Sadri? Malaraphi's Sadri were among the most powerful weavers in Dûhr. Even the College feared the Sadri.

Morkainen looked at the sewer map again, more critically this time.

"I know what you're thinking, Rahain," Lindrowe said. "Loquay owns those sewers. And she's been recruiting."

Morkainen met Lindrowe's lazy gaze.

The fat man smiled, leaning forward in his chair. "Loquay has a fine sense of the strategic—indeed, the dramatic—but she lacks the power to bring down a Sadri without leaving at least a few traces."

"Then someone else is responsible," Morkainen said firmly.

"Yes… but whom?"

Morkainen leaned on the table and rested his chin on his left fist, forgetting his hunger as he considered other candidates.

The Crimson Witch immediately came to mind—both the most and the least likely suspect. Kaleena possessed incredible power, but the lack of evidence was not her style. If she was responsible, she'd want everyone to know.

Who then?

The prince was unlikely. Kythidûhr was sly of late, Morkainen granted him that, but he tended to work through agents external to the House Royal, none of whom had the power to wipe out one of Blackhand's reconnaissance squads untraceably. The wizard royal? Doubtful; even Mordavo couldn't defeat a Sadri without leaving evidence. It wasn't the prince or his wizard.

Only one other option came readily to mind.

"The Black Church," Morkainen said.

"Ahh," Lindrowe breathed. "The ever-enigmatic Black Church of Sathiis."

His chair creaked in protest as he shifted his great bulk.

"We've already discounted the Sathiians, Rahain. They are too weak at present. Besides, our spies would have reported any redeployment of their forces."

"Their visible forces," Morkainen corrected. "You said it yourself, Urath, many times—the Black Church is a House Assassin bundled up in religious doctrine. Why, then, shouldn't they use our tactics against us? Are we the only ones who keep secret forces?"

Arwynn raised an eyebrow. Morkainen's point was well made; the Black Church may indeed maintain unseen forces. Blaythe could conceivably shelter a militia in some secret place—a catacomb, perhaps—and discreetly use it to carry out delicate missions.

Yet, to Arwynn, even this seemed too direct for the Black Church. The trail wasn't convoluted enough to fully cover their hand.

"I don't think Lacosia would be so direct," he said.

He scowled, tapping his lips with a finger.

"For the sake of argument, suppose that Lacosia does maintain covert forces. Where does he house them? In his unfinished, unsecured temple? Unlikely. Some secret den in or around the sewers? Perhaps, if he paid Loquay enough. But even then, how would he arm them? Or feed them, for that matter?"

Arwynn shook his head and sighed heavily.

Wearily.

"Given a strong Sathiian presence, these questions would be moot," he said. "But under present circumstances, after the arrival of but one of Blaythe's barges?"

Arwynn shook his head. "I don't see it."

Lindrowe and Morkainen said nothing.

"Lacosia is not a fool," he continued. "He knows that the discovery of covert forces would compromise his covenant with House Kythidûhr. Several members of the Family Royal opposed their covenant; they would annul it if they learned that Lacosia maintained a hidden militia. That would force Lacosia to rely more heavily on Loquay and Blaythe to rely more heavily on us, putting them in very unenviable positions."

Morkainen slumped back in his chair. He was tired after his long ride. He pinched the bridge of his nose and sighed.

"I have a bad feeling," he said, "that there is magick at play here."

"I have a bad feeling," Lindrowe grumbled, "that you are correct."

Arwynn stroked his chin thoughtfully. "It could be Kaleena. It feels wrong, but it's possible."

"It is possible," Lindrowe affirmed, "but unlikely."

"Highly unlikely," Morkainen added.

"Put Zehedros to work on it, nonetheless," the master ordered. "If there's a magickal element involved, he should be able to ferret it out and determine its source. Whatever he discovers, I want to be prepared. I want fresh poisons brewed by week's end and distributed to all our sulari. Insinuative and ingestive: maddram, achaelos, and that new one you've been working on… kakaehli."

Lindrowe nodded. "Consider it done."

"I do," Arwynn assured him.

"Now"—he turned to the half-elfi—"Rahain, I have a task for you. I want some people retired. Not right away, though—wait a week or two. I don't want to arouse suspicion by acting too soon after your return."

"Targets?"

"No one of consequence, just a few midlevel city officials in areas that may or may not affect the Black Church. These aren't contracted retirements, so I don't care whom you choose—I'm more concerned with the fallout from the deaths than the deaths themselves. Use your judgment. Retire a few of Loquay's and Savarat's sulari as well. Make it look like they killed each other. Let's get a little tension going between their Houses and see what happens."

Morkainen nodded. "Understood."

"Good," Blackhand said. Then he looked over his two lieutenants and nodded. "Very good."

CHAPTER 22

HOUSE OF THE HEALER

Fedahi coerced his eyes open and waited for the ensuing cascade of filmy, blurred images to congeal into something meaningful.

A cluttered hut settled into focus: a single room, scarcely a dozen paces in length and breadth, fashioned from unfinished lumber and uncut saplings. Broad wooden shelves covered every bit of available wall space and sagged under the weight of old books, alchemical paraphernalia, and bundles of plants, weeds, and spices. The bed beneath him was soft and yielding.

A faint smell came to him. Smoke and herbs.

Somewhere, water bubbled.

Thirsty.

"So, you are awake, eh?"

The voice was old. Peaceful.

Fedahi rolled his head toward the speaker. He tried to raise himself from the bed—

—a hot wash of pain flooded his face and chest, coursed down his left arm, and crashed against his wrist like a tide of acid. He slammed his eyes shut and bit down hard, twisting his neck as his back arched involuntarily.

"Easy, young one," the voice said. "Easy. You've had quite an ordeal."

Fedahi stilled and breathed. The pain faded. Slowly, he relaxed his clamped eyelids and unclenched his jaw. A blurred image shuffled closer, took on femininity. He tried to speak, failed.

Weak.

The speaker was an old woman. She sat on a squat stool next to his bed and placed cool, damp cloths on his forehead and neck. Her hands were soft and gentle, like flower petals lightly brushing his tender skin. Her azure eyes were almost too large for her slim, frail face. Her silvery hair was a tangled mop that took no mandate from gravity, flying away from her head in all directions. She wore little jewelry: a simple necklace of plain wooden beads about her wrinkled neck and smooth hoops of ivory through the loose lobes of her pointed ears.

Elfi.

She crushed dried leaves in a wooden bowl and stirred in steaming water. While the mixture cooled, she muttered softly to herself in the lyrical elfin tongue and traced a simple pattern in the air above the bowl. After a moment, she sampled the mixture, grimaced, then smiled.

Gently, she placed a hand behind his head and raised it slowly from the pillow, whispering soft words of comfort as she held the bowl to his lips. He was far too thirsty to be bothered by the fluid's foul odor and downed it in great gulps, gagging only once. Almost immediately came a sense of light euphoria.

The woman smiled and proceeded to grind fresh green sprigs into the fluid remaining in the bowl, until she had a thick greenish paste. With skilled hands, she smeared the paste over the numerous punctures and lacerations that covered Fedahi's face, upper chest, and left arm. He felt an instant of pain when she pressed the paste to his skin, followed by a pleasant cooling sensation.

When the woman finished, she asked, "You feel better now?"

Her voice was melodic, tranquil.

"Better… now…" Fedahi tried to smile.

He lolled his head as the medicines dulled his senses and relaxed his muscles.

"Who… where…" His speech was hoarse, slurred.

"I am Sadrahehn," she said. "A healer. This is my house."

"H-he—healer? How…"

"Shhhh. My sisters brought you here yesterday morning. Your wounds were severe, the infections powerful. Thank Nimwe, the worst is over."

She smiled warmly. "Rest. Sleep."

She closed his eyes with a gentle sweep of her hand and muttered softly.

He fell into a deep sleep.

Sadrahehn (*Flesh, Spirit*) gently rolled Fedahi's head to the side to treat the minor wounds at the base of his neck. She'd removed the thorns and creepers the day before, but their legacy remained and would scar horribly if not appropriately tended.

Kalypshia. No doubt.

As she daubed his wounds with her healing unguent, Sadrahehn marveled at the man's survival. Victims of the kalypshia vine seldom lived. Yet here was one who had cut off his hand to escape the plant. She shuddered as she pictured him alone, in pain, weak from blood loss, running blindly through the treacherous wastes of Evereve Marsh, tearing his flesh on its thorns and barbs in his flight.

Her sisters had found him the previous morning while gathering herbs at the edge of the swamp. He was sprawled by a tepid pool, barely alive, showing signs of sappha poisoning and boreworm infestation. They brought him to her home, and she tended his wounds throughout the day and night, twice pulling him from death.

And she prayed.

Nimwe, how she had prayed!

And her prayers had been answered.

You will be fine.

Sadrahehn finished spreading her unguent and set the bowl on a small table. She groaned softly as she rose and stepped away from his bed. Her back was stiff and her eyes were sore, but the task was done.

A breath of fresh air before I sleep.

Drawing her white shawl tightly about her shoulders, she shuffled to the cottage door and stepped out. The cool night breeze carried the smells of the Fwaer and the faint thunder of a distant storm. She leaned against the doorjamb for a time, enjoying the peace.

Sadrahehn and her sisters had kept vigil over Evereve's verge from the Glider to the Fwaer for as long as anyone could remember. It was a quiet, friendless life. She rarely had visitors, other than her sisters or Nimwe's watchers when they found themselves in need of healing or reconstruction. It was nice to have common company.

She shivered and pulled her shawl tighter.

It's colder than usual.

Sadrahehn shuffled back into her cottage, carefully added wood to the fire, and slumped into a soft chair by the hearth. As the fire's warmth and soft crackle lulled her to sleep, she thought about the man in her bed.

Who was he? How did he come to be in Evereve Marsh?

And why was he carrying poison?

CHAPTER 23

LOVE AND SORROW

The black mantilla of night settled gently over the face of Dûhr, like a veil woven of wind and rain. The sister moons, Ilia and Glae, hung fat in the velvet sky, full and milky. Alluring and alive.

Princess Calista Deluras of Ufwin stood in the arched window of a high tower, naked to the night. She was a striking woman, squarer of jaw and thicker of limb than the Dûhrani socialites of Kythidûhr's Court—yet no less compelling, for her poise was genuine and her beauty authentic.

The wind and the rain caressed her body and showered wet kisses upon her face and shoulders as she leaned out into the darkness. She loved the northern rains—so much more exhilarating than the warm showers of Ufwin. She closed her eyes and sighed as the cold raindrops pattered against her honey skin and trickled down her body.

Calista smiled and sighed again. She put her hands on her hips and stretched her neck, arching her back. Two joints popped in mild protest.

Azago, she thought, stretching again. *I must see Azago.*

She turned away from the window. The lamplight caught the flecks of gold in her dark eyes like sunrise on sand and accentuated her amber hair, meticulously cut to fall diagonally over her brow and drop straight to her shoulders in layered sheets, long in the front and rising sharply at the sides to skim the nape of her long neck.

Her smile faded.

The prince of Dûhr lay sprawled across her bed where he'd collapsed.

Oh, Melkor…

The prince found no peace in dreams these past months nor solace in Calista's embrace. Most nights, he didn't sleep at all. He would wander the castle until the cocks roused the Houses and courtly matters took him. Then, inexplicably, he would sleep peacefully for several nights until insomnia returned.

What has happened to you?

Calista closed her eyes and tried to remember Melkor as he was when they first met three years ago. She'd come to Dûhr reluctantly, duty bound to lead the Ufwinian delegation sent to witness Mordavo Morvaine's ascension to wizard royal. The prince's sincerity and integrity caught her off guard. She found herself captivated by Melkor's passion to continue his father's social and economic reforms, and Melkor became enraptured by her bold ideas and political acumen. When the delegation departed for Ufwin, she stayed behind to help Melkor shape policy and advance his agenda. They soon fell in love. On the second anniversary of their meeting, they pledged to wed.

Calista opened her eyes and looked at Melkor.

Where has that man gone?

The changes in Melkor had been subtle at first. He grew distracted, then distant. His character slipped from noble to guarded. As the weeks wore on, he grew increasingly cagey and restive and began to wander the castle at night. When Calista sought to console him, he pushed her away, each time more forcefully. Her concern deepened when he began entertaining Lacosia's adepts and receiving strange visitors at odd hours. She was astonished when he twice refused Wirith's pleas for aid against the Gobli Horde, and flabbergasted when he re-directed funding from his public housing initiative to secure the Sathiian construction site in the Gardens of Twilight. When she pressed him to explain himself, he cursed her and raised his hand to strike her. The physical blow never landed.

The next day, when Melkor bound half a Myriadi Royal to serve Loquay Yellowhand, she decided to leave.

She felt a tear in her eye…

I love you.

… a pain in her heart.

But I can't keep living like this… watching you…

Calista felt suddenly alone. Vulnerable. She moved from the window, snatched up her robe from the stool of her dressing table, and tugged it around her rain-wet body. Arms folded, she looked at him again.

Oh, Melkor…

The prince mumbled in his sleep.

I can't marry you. I have to leave.

Soft sounds cut through her thoughts. Melkor was sobbing. She ached to hold him and soothe him, but she knew it wouldn't help.

His words were unintelligible, save one.

Blaythe.

CHAPTER 24

SUSPICIONS

The system of Greater and Lesser Houses existed to maintain social cohesion under the sanction of the Houses Royal. The Houses Mercenary regulated warfare; the Houses Mercantile managed trade; the Houses Assassin controlled murder and vice. While the assassins' methods of maintaining control were necessarily merciless and severe, few among them reveled in brutality as much as Celwynn Blackhand of Dûhr, whose name became synonymous with gratuitous cruelty.

Some hours after the late-night meeting with his lieutenants, Arwynn Blackhand could not sleep. The mystery of his sulari's disappearance weighed heavily, but he did not understand why it should keep him awake. He'd never been unable to sleep before—even the night he retired his father.

The great Celwynn Blackhand.

Arwynn scoffed.

That odious thug.

Arwynn could not remember a time he hadn't hated his father. Yet, in the end, it was not Celwynn's brutishness or abuse of Arwynn and his sister that ended their relationship, it was a philosophical conflict: Celwynn idolized fear as the ultimate tool for acquiring and holding power; Arwynn believed that fear was a short-lived lever at best and that the ultimate key to sustainable power was the control and manipulation of information. Arwynn didn't hesitate when the opportunity arose to seize mastery of his House and prove his father wrong.

He remembered the night vividly. When the deed was done and Celwynn lay dead, when his dreams should have been plagued with guilt, he'd found peaceful repose.

Arwynn pushed away thoughts of the past. He shoved his covers aside and sat on the edge of his bed, rubbing tired eyes with pale hands. His sleeplessness was rooted in his sulari's vanishment, not old memories.

More than anything, Arwynn hated not knowing.

With one of Malaraphi's Sadri, the second band should have easily overcome any resistance. Perhaps Morkainen and Lindrowe were correct; perhaps there was formidable magick at play—but some trace would remain, even then. Blood. Scorching. Something…

Unless they gave up without a fight.

Surrender?

Or collusion?

Both possibilities had occurred to Arwynn after the meeting broke. Either would explain why his agents seemed to vanish without a trace. They were such simple explanations that he couldn't help wondering why neither Lindrowe nor Morkainen thought to mention them.

Or did they ignore them?

Arwynn scowled as he reframed the possibilities into a single word. A word that explained both the mysterious disappearances and his lieutenants' omissions.

Betrayal.

INTERLUDE TWO

THE SERPENT AND THE FROG

The two men faced each other across a wide expanse of scorched land, purple robes and colored sashes flapping in the breeze.

The man in the green sash was young, beautiful. His skin was golden and taut over wiry muscles, as smooth and unscarred as virgin marble. His hair was soft and delicate and flowed black in the breeze. His eyes, too, were black. Haunting.

The man in the blue sash was old, ugly. His body was ravaged by time, cadaverous and gaunt. His hair was red straw that grew in irregular patches about his mottled head and spotty arms. His eyes were white and cloudy.

With a sudden lurch, the old man began to gibber and trace patterns in the air before his face. His robes clung to his body as he generated a static charge. Within seconds, jagged blue ribbons pranced about his fingertips and the air about him began to crackle with energy. The old man teased the energy he held, coaxed it, allowed it to build. Then he screamed and threw a ball of blue lightning at the man he faced.

The man in the green sash allowed the lightning to strike him squarely in the chest. It lifted him from his feet and threw him away like a broken toy. He landed limp, bounced once.

His robes were blasted away.

The flesh of his chest was burned.

PART THREE

PREPARATIONS

In which agents on all sides lay the foundations
for the realization of their schemes
and past loyalties are called into question.

CHAPTER 25

SEVERED TIES

"And you've got Riban tomorrow. He'll want to discuss the initiate decline, of course. Now, you have to accept some blame there, but you can always—Mirithwin? Mirithwin, are you listening?"

"Hmm?"

"I asked if you were listening to me," the man repeated.

"Oh, yes. Of course. I was just… no, I'm sorry. What were you saying, Jamar?"

The skinny man snapped closed his appointment book with a grunt. He leaned forward in his chair and pinched the bridge of his sharp nose with a sigh.

"Madam, how will we ever get through this month if you refuse to take your responsibilities seriously?"

Mirithwin (*Phantasm, Mind, Emotion*) turned from the window to face Jamar. The afternoon sun caught her face, her silvery hair. It pranced about the topaz iris of her right eye and glinted off the silver mirror that filled the empty socket of her left.

"I admit, I'm a little preoccupied," she said.

"Preoccupied? You're completely distracted." Jamar paused a moment. "It's the woman, isn't it? The assassin."

Mirithwin nodded. "Ciridan."

"You should never have taken her on," he admonished. "Not now. You have too many important activities already scheduled. Far too many. You've no time to train a phantasmist. No time."

"I have time."

"Oh? Really? When?" Jamar reopened his book, flipping through its pages.

"Perhaps during Riban's visit, hmm? That would go over well. I'm sure he'd understand. Or... here we go, you have a day between his departure and Shila Hoth's arrival. Plenty of time to train a phantasmist! Plenty of time. Or... hmm... ah, Maelkith Grae is due to confer with you in two weeks. Well, we can just cancel that to free up some time. After all, who does he think he is to merit an audience with you? Hmm? Who, indeed!"

"Enough, Jamar," Mirithwin said. "You've made your point."

"Good. Then you'll send her back to Dûhr."

"No."

Jamar frowned. "Why not?"

"She intrigues me."

"Intrigues you? Please. It's not her that intrigues you—it's him."

"Him?"

"The half-elfi."

"Morkainen? Don't be ridiculous."

"Ah, ah, ah." Jamar wagged a bony finger at the Mindbender. "Don't try to deny it. I saw the way you looked at him."

Mirithwin scowled.

Jamar smiled smugly. "Ahh, I'm right. You do have feelings for the man."

"Yes," Mirithwin admitted.

"Deep feelings?"

"Very deep."

"Do you love him?"

"Yes."

"Does he know?"

"Not anymore."

There was a pause, a look, and Jamar closed his book and set it aside.

"He's one of the Severed, isn't he."

"Yes." Mirithwin nodded. "He is also my husband."

Jamar's eyes widened. "Your husband? But… how? How could you…"

"Sever my husband?" she asked. "Because I love him. Perfectly and terribly. And because if I didn't, the Kuluth Brame would have destroyed him."

"The Kuluth Brame?"

"Necrophaelis's assassins," Mirithwin replied. "Creatures of phantasm sensitive to lines of eie and emote. Necrophaelis set them upon me after I helped Nimwe imprison it in Xotl."

"Why?"

"By the terms of his imprisonment, neither Necrophaelis nor its agents may act upon me directly. The Kuluth Brame hunt those connected to me by cognitive and emotional ties in order to pervert them into their master's service. My friends, my family, my acquaintances… my husband. Necrophaelis believes that corrupting my friends and loved ones will undermine my resolve and weaken its bindings. I will not allow that to happen."

"So, you severed the lines of eie and emote that connected them to you," Jamar finished. "All of them."

"Every single one."

She remembered all too well the night she wove her spell. It was the last time she saw her love reflected in Morkainen's eyes.

Mirithwin had intricately interwoven the Strands of Mind and Phantasm to sunder all threads of eie and emote that bound her to others. It had cost one hundred years of her life and her left eye to braid and twine the Strands into that terrible spell. When she finally released its power after three days of weaving, she severed herself completely from all who had ever truly known her or cared for her or loved her. For them, it was as though they'd never met.

But not for Mirithwin. She remembered everything.

"And that saved them?" Jamar asked. "The Severing?"

"Yes. The Kuluth Brame could no longer connect them to me."

"What about your connections to them? Those still exist. Your feelings for Morkainen are clear enough."

"That is true. But, as I said, neither Necrophaelis nor its agents may act upon me directly. The lines of eie and emote that I radiate are invisible to the Kuluth Brame; they can only perceive those radiated by others. Even then, they would only recognize those who knew me by the same name and nature as Necrophaelis."

"Then… the Severed will never remember?"

Mirithwin shook her head sadly. "The Kuluth Brame are undying and relentless. They still search for links to me."

Jamar sighed. "All so Necrophaelis will remain imprisoned?"

"It is essential that it does. Forever. If it were to open the Dead Gate… it would be the end of everything."

"But the price?" Jamar said. "To live forgotten and alone, unable to know an honest relationship? Always afraid to let something slip, let someone know too much, bring the Kuluth Brame down upon them… Is that why the girl is so important to you? Because she's alive?"

Mirithwin took a deep breath, let it out slowly. "It's been so long since I've had living companionship. Someone to talk to… to listen to… to be with. You would not understand, Jamar."

She smiled weakly then and closed her eye. The mirror in her empty socket flashed yellow. Jamar vanished.

Mirithwin sighed. Why did she continue to play such games with herself? Rehashing the past, having conversations with illusory foils…

To keep things in perspective, she supposed. Or maybe just maintain her sanity.

Whatever the reason, it was better to talk to a phantasm than herself.

CHAPTER 26

WARGRUM'S WHISPERS

Aerkon Kharae was nervous. He shuffled back and forth across his chambers, head down and shoulders stooped, gnarled hands knotted behind his back. He'd spent most of his time grumbling and pacing since Arael's departure. And worrying. If Arael failed to deliver his parcel to Kargan Teahl, Dûhr too would fall before the Serpent.

And what hope will there be for Wirith then?

Aerkon feared for Arael's small company. Despite their magickal prowess, they were but eight against Balistrahd's mercenaries below ground, his myriadi above, and Blaythe's adepts secretly sprinkled throughout.

What chance do they really have? What chance do any of us have, for that matter?

Arael's departure left Aerkon with scarcely enough clergy to minister to the faithful. They couldn't fend off a Sathiian attack. And Blaythe knew it.

I have to save them—and I don't know how.

The old priest stopped in the center of the room, eyes downcast, one foot tapping nervously. He felt confused. Helpless. Old. It was as though his confidence had departed with Arael. Where he'd been cautious, he now felt disheartened; where he'd been anxious, desperate. No longer was he the rock of indomitable Wargrum. He was a pebble.

Damn.

He struggled to maintain what composure he had left.

The tears came unbidden.

I have to save them, and I don't know how.

Aerkon's detachment deepened as the night thickened. He was scarcely aware of the people he passed as he scuffled through the temple's stone passageways. Eventually, he found himself in the ebreth, the temple's inner presbytery.

It was a huge octagonal room of basanite and marble, one hundred and eighty-five feet across. The walls were seventy-six feet wide and rose straight to the domed and coffered ceiling. Great slabs of rock, as thick as a man's height, jutted from the north, south, and east walls, sixteen feet apart and ten feet above the polished marble floor. Each rock slab extended forty-two feet from its base wall toward the center of the room and hung unsupported like weightless things. From below, they looked like portions of octagons that floated on the air and strove to meet above the central altar but were held at bay by a hundred feet of open space.

A simple octagonal altar of bare stone stood in the center of the room, raised waist high on eight squat pillars. Fires burned in wide crystal bowls in the chamber's corners and cast dancing shadows throughout the room. The incense that burned in the bowls suffused the air with a heady aroma, earthy and woody. Overhead, on the enormous overhangs, heavy stone hauhantu kept guard.

Aerkon did not remember entering the presbytery. He did not recall closing the heavy doors behind him, nor setting the incense alight. Yet here he was, kneeling alone in front of a stone altar in a room that smelled of rich earth and rare wood.

I must have come here to pray.

Aerkon closed his eyes, folded his hands, and bowed his head.

No words came.

He groaned and let his head fall heavily against the altar. It thumped dully against the stone.

He opened his eyes and looked up at the ceiling. The lambent firelight from the braziers played about the patterns circumscribed in its coffered dome.

He let his head fall again. And again.

Over and over.

Harder and harder.

He had never felt so defeated, so terribly old and so completely helpless. It was as though the weight of all time had fallen upon him like a heavy rain, washing away his resolve and saturating him with despair. He felt hollow and hopeless, like a dead tree.

Worse, he felt shame.

Too many have placed their trust in me. I cannot fail them.

He set his jaw and clenched his fists.

I will not fail them.

Aerkon took a deep breath and steeled himself against the protests of his aching joints, the pain of his bleeding head. He straightened his back and closed his eyes, clasped his hands together tightly, and prayed.

This time, the words came. In the form of a child's prayer:

O great Wargrum, Lord of Stone,
bless me in my worldly home;
give me the strength to face my fears,
and the kih to persevere.
Like the pillars of your altar,
may my spirit never falter;
strong and mighty, wise and kind,
with iron heart and diamond mind.

Aerkon felt himself smile. How old had he been when he'd first learned that prayer? Six? Seven, maybe? It seemed so long ago, when the world was a happier—

Aerkon's eyes snapped wide.

"Of course!" he cried aloud. "Pillars! And statues! That's it! Pillars and statues!"

CHAPTER 27

AZAGO

Calista let out a long, purring sigh as Azago spread scented oils over her shoulders and upper back.

"Mmm," she hummed. "Mmmmmmm…"

"Feels good?" the masseur asked.

How could he ask such a silly question?

She responded with a low groan.

"Hnnnghmmm…"

As the princess lay contented, Azago prepared a paste of ladu root and psiga berries. When it was thick and yellow, he spread it over her back with a small towel, lightly at first, then more aggressively to work it deep into her skin. The princess would feel the cool paste grow warm as the psiga opened her pores, then hotter as the ladu seeped into her muscles.

"It smells different today, Azago," she murmured, eyes only half-open. "Sweet."

"I added honey."

That was a lie. He had not added honey. He had added kambra, a favored drug for closing eyes and loosening lips.

"Mmm… honey."

Azago lightened his touch as the paste absorbed into her skin; he did not knead her muscles free of tension so much as coax them into relaxation.

"You have been quite tense these past weeks, m'lady," he said as he worked the backs of her arms. "More than usual."

A pause.

"Yes," Calista agreed. "I suppose I have."

"The gobli?"

Calista gave a slight shrug. "No more than usual."

"Court, then?"

"Court's fine."

"The prince?"

She stiffened.

Ahh, Azago thought. *The prince…*

The masseur's mouth curled into a wry smile.

"The prince," he prodded gently. "I asked if you were having difficulty with the prince."

"No," she replied, a bit too curtly. "You overstep, Azago."

"Apologies, m'lady. Most stress tends to come from work or family," Azago replied matter of factly. "And your relationship with the prince is—"

"None of your concern!" she snapped, turning to face him.

Azago held up his hands in surrender and took a small step back from the table.

"Forgive me, m'lady," he said penitently. "My apologies. I mean no offence—I only want to help."

Calista silently cursed herself for her short temper.

The truth was that her relationship with the prince had deteriorated steadily since he accepted the first Sathiian delegation. And the castle halls were not free from rumor. Some already questioned Melkor's health, physical or otherwise. Then, two nights ago, Melkor muttered a single word in his tormented sleep that changed everything: *Blaythe.*

Though the name cut through her like a blade of ice, it raised the possibility that her betrothed might not be the willing perpetrator of his recent misdeeds. She'd summoned her most trusted retainers the following morning, clearly spelled out her fears, and enjoined them to investigate Sathiian activities within the Realms of Dûhr.

Answers were not long in coming.

Not only did Melkor suffer curious agitation and insomnia, so too did Mordavo and two public ministers. Further, several of Melkor's advisers met regularly with Sathiian priests to prepare legislation constraining the Churches of Elem.

There was no doubt in Calista's mind that a conspiracy was afoot, instigated by the Black Church, with Melkor its victim. Leaving was no longer an option.

Calista frowned. She should not have lashed out at Azago—such an emotional outburst would only lead him to assume the worst. She had to foil his curiosity.

"No. No, Azago. My apologies," she said. "I overreacted. I… I haven't been sleeping well lately. You understand…"

Azago understood. His sleep had been troubled of late, too, and was slow in coming. Some nights, he didn't sleep at all.

"Of course, m'lady," Azago said. "I know how distressing a touch of insomnia can be."

He smiled and stepped forward, resuming his massage.

"Perhaps you should see a healer, yes?"

"I have."

"And?"

"Nothing to worry about," Calista said. "Just bad dreams."

She took a deep breath and sighed. "Honey, you said?"

"M'lady?"

"The sweet smell."

"Ah, yes. Honey."

"Mmmm…"

Azago smiled. The kambra had done its work well. Calista was unaware of the few words the drug had drawn out of her.

Insomnia.

Melkor.

Blaythe.

Mordavo.

Conspiracy.

At last, he had something to go on: the prince and the Black Church were definitely involved in something.

Arwynn Blackhand's smile broadened as he bent back to his work. He always discovered the most wonderful information as Azago the masseur.

CHAPTER 28

EARTH, AIR, AND WATER

Alana Allelil, high priest of Sheeshee, and Raphael Pyryllax, high priest of Anwin, followed Aerkon Kharae to his sanctum beneath Wirith's Temple of Wargrum, through what seemed an endless thicket of statues. Every stairway, alcove, patio, and garden was replete with statues; every chamber, tabernacle, foyer, and hallway was a sea of fine sculpture. From the lowest acolyte to the lord priest himself, all were represented in perfect likeness, life size and in stunning detail. Even Aerkon's sanctum teemed with statuary.

Aerkon shuffled to his desk and slowly took his stone chair. He laced his crooked fingers before his face and looked at the high priests.

Alana (*Air*) was young, barely forty, with fair skin, dark hair, and the luminous pupilless white eyes that marked her as Sheeshee's high priest. Her gossamer vestments floated about her body like weightless things, sensual suggestions on a summer breeze—bright white and trimmed in a blue so pale it made them look whiter still. Her hands were smooth, like porcelain.

Raphael (*Water*) was also young, older than Alana but no less attractive for his added years. In the dim light of Aerkon's sanctum, Raphael's lucent eyes shone like emerald moons. His sea-green cloaks glistened like moving liquid and flowed about his body in thick waves. His hair was dark and unkempt, wild and wavy.

"I'll be blunt," Aerkon said. "My enmity with Adar Ashan and his nest of vipers is far more volatile than I care to admit, even to myself. He's as crafty as any daemon. And his lackey, Blaythe, poses no minor threat—the man's a psychopath with more power than a Blue Frog. Rumor has it that Arcturi Lacosia will soon assume stewardship of Blaythe's temple here in Wirith. If that proves the case, he will move against me soon after his arrival."

"That much we were told, Lord Aerkon," Alana said.

"Eh? By whom?"

"Our holy ladies," she answered. "They told us of the animosity between yourself and the Sathiians. They warned us of the danger in no uncertain terms."

"And of our duty to you, Lord Aerkon," Raphael added. "We were not given details, but our ladies explained that our Churches owe yours a great debt. We have come to service that debt. We pledge ourselves to you, regardless of the danger ahead."

Aerkon chewed his lip thoughtfully. "And you both agree to this freely? In full knowledge of the hazards that lie ahead?"

"Yes, my lord."

"Yes, my lord."

"Then I accept your service," Aerkon said. He scratched his head.

"Now, details. As you know, the Elem chose not to oppose the Sathiians or hamper their affairs in Wirith. There were many reasons for this, the main one being our doctrine to refrain from religious conflict. Adderash—as Ashan calls himself—doesn't believe that. To him, churches are just Houses Mercantile peddling salvation, competitors for wealth and power with the same motives and ambitions as he. For his world to make sense, he *needs* us to plot against him, precisely because *he* plots against *us*. So, we broke doctrine to give Adderash what he needed: a visible enemy plotting against him in every city of every realm."

"The Church of Wargrum," Alana said.

Aerkon nodded.

"Then the Wargrumites are not renegades?" Raphael asked.

Aerkon shrugged. "That depends on your perspective."

Then he chuckled and shook his head. "No. We are not renegades. Wargrum's Church acts as a dissident faction to serve three ends. First, we give the Elem a means to act against the Sathiians. Second, our 'dissension' enables the other Churches to distance themselves from us and thereby circumvent Adderash's scrutiny, affording them safety to covertly undermine the Sathiians in realms already under Adderash's control. Third, we give Adderash a powerful and aggressive enemy to hold his attention. Unfortunately, I played my part too well—which is why the Black Church needs to eliminate me."

"Then why seek our services?" Alana asked. "When Raphael and I join in defense of your temple, our presence will implicate the Churches of Anwin and Sheeshee."

"There will be no defense," Aerkon said.

"No defense?" Alana looked confused. "But you said yourself that Lacosia will soon attack."

Aerkon nodded. "He will."

Raphael knit his brow. "Without any defense, his forces will walk right through this temple. They will capture it effortlessly!"

"Precisely!" Aerkon clapped his hands and grinned. "Do you think I would've wasted my time making silly statues otherwise?"

"Then, I am confused," Alana said. "If you don't plan to defend your temple from Lacosia, what need have you for us?"

"It's quite simple, really," Aerkon replied. "Temples can be rebuilt; people cannot. I must save my people."

An impish grin spread across the lord priest's wrinkled face.

"What I need from you are explosives and poison gas."

CHAPTER 29

SECOND-GUESSING

Lindrowe had finally concluded his most pressing responsibilities to House Blackhand. Over the last seventeen hours, he had delivered his new poison formulae to his brewmaster, started a culture of ungi bacteria in his laboratory, and provided Savishi with the tactical information necessary for her to prepare their gobli captives to attack Blaythe's barge. Now, he could entertain personal matters.

He retired to his study and settled in an overstuffed desk chair with a glass of wine.

Lindrowe thought back to his last meeting with Blackhand and Morkainen. Many topics had gone around the table that night, but what preyed most upon his mind was the curious disappearance of eight sulari in the Underwet. Zehedros's investigation had proved fruitless. No sign of their passing remained: no remnants of boot or cloth, no hint of blood, no indication of battle. Nothing. It was as though they had just ceased to be.

As though they never existed...

Barring magick, the simplest explanation was betrayal—meaning both groups had been persuaded to break faith with House Blackhand before their departure or at some point during their mission. As to how and why, Lindrowe had no idea. Not yet, anyway. Those questions were not his immediate concern.

Betrayal was not a solitary beast. It traveled with conspiracy and suspicion.

Suspicion which must now fall upon Rahain and me.

Betrayal required association; the closer the affiliation with the betrayed, the better the prospects for the betrayer. Naturally, those closest to one suspicious of betrayal were usually the first suspected. Suggesting a betrayal did not remove the suspicion—more often than not, the person drawing attention to treachery was the mastermind behind the threat. It was because of this knowledge that Lindrowe had held his tongue when the possibility of the sulari's betrayal crossed his mind. It was surely also the reason Morkainen maintained his silence.

How could it not? Neither of us wanted to be the first to broach the topic.

Regardless, the damage was done. Arwynn would certainly consider the possibility of betrayal and wonder why his lieutenants failed to raise the concern. Given their silence, he would reach one of two conclusions: they had not considered it or were involved in it. Prudence favored the latter.

It was, therefore, in Lindrowe's best interest to give Arwynn the betrayal he was looking for. It was the only way to escape suspicion and satisfy his master. Provided, of course, that he could place the blame on someone else. Someone like Morkainen. Or Malaraphi.

Lindrowe took a sip of wine, rolled the fluid over and around his tongue. Hopefully, Rahain had not drawn the same conclusion.

Where is Tehru when I need him?

CHAPTER 30

AWAKENING

Tehru Shaddoht awoke in darkness to a vague impression of pain. His head throbbed dully. His muscles felt stiff and sore. His skin tingled with a distant numbness and felt strangely tight across his body.

He lay on his back, legs straight and arms at his sides. The cold surface beneath him was flat and smooth and hard, like metal or stone.

When he tried to sit up, he found he could not. He was held down by straps he could feel but not see, across his wrists and ankles, waist, chest… and head.

The darkness surrounding him was complete, as was the silence. He could not hear his breathing. Even the hammering of his heart was lost to his ears, drowned out by oppressive silence.

Around him, hints of fragrant vegetation wafted through the malodor of strange chemicals.

Tehru began to feel the chill of fear crawl across his belly.

It was crawling toward his throat, he was sure.

Welbley Blaythe sat in a chair in a corner of Tehru's cell. Though he sat no more than three paces from the stone table where the spy was bound, Tehru was oblivious to his presence. It was as Blaythe desired, and his weaves ensured it.

Though all forms of suffering thrilled Welbley, he found a creature's anguish particularly erotic when he could watch their experience firsthand. As he could now. By his magicks, Blaythe could see the spy quite clearly in the darkness. He could smell Tehru's fear. He could hear every quivering breath and whimper, while Tehru perceived nothing.

Marvelous.

Welbley's tunic had fallen open at the waist when he'd taken his seat, exposing his right leg. He made no move to cover himself; the chill of the darkness against his skin added to his pleasure. He sat still in his chair, toes curled against his sandals, grip tight on the staff that rose from his ankle to his shoulder. The smile on his lips was genuine. He enjoyed every minute of Tehru's anguish.

As the spy slowly lost himself to his terror, the priest began to touch himself in the darkness.

CHAPTER 31

DESPAIR

Fedahi healed rapidly as the days passed, and it became apparent that Sadrahehn mixed magick with her herbs and potions. By the third day of his convalescence, he could feed himself and move about the cottage. By the fourth, his scars had begun to fade. They looked like silken lace, not at all like the puckered mutilations he'd seen on other kalypshia survivors. Then there was the matter of his hand…

… or rather, his stump.

Over the years, several of Fedahi's friends and comrades had lost appendages in one way or another: assassins to traps, fishers to eelsharks, woodsmen and trappers to misadventure. They all spoke of inexplicably feeling their lost appendages, though that slowly faded over time—as though the loss of an extremity was a gradual process and not a sudden thing.

Fedahi's experience was different. Physically, his body reacted as though he'd had a lifetime to cope with his loss. He suspected that was Sadrahehn's doing.

Yet despite these positive turns, Fedahi was miserable and spent long hours brooding. With the loss of his hand, his career in House Blackhand had ended abruptly. Where, after all, was the need for a one-handed thief? A maimed assassin?

Nowhere, he sulked. *Nowhere at all.*

He was no good to Blackhand now. No good to anyone.

Hasraheed the has-been.

Better to have died in the swamp.

Fedahi's physical injuries responded well to Sadrahehn's ministrations. Mending his flesh was one matter, but his mind? His spirit? These were fragile things with which Sadrahehn was reluctant to tamper.

On the fifth day, she could bear his suffering no longer. While Fedahi slept, she opened his mind.

Just a crack.

Fedahi's hopelessness struck Sadrahehn like a physical thing. The stink of despair and bitterness of surrender filled her nose and mouth. Melancholia slithered over her skin as the echoes of Fedahi's silent whimpers hammered warmth from her heart. Writhing ribbons of oily blackness entangled Fedahi's spirit, affording her only sporadic glimpses of distorted images between its tightening strands—

—a bald man—

—a dying man—

—a severed hand—

—a woman—

All were memories rendered in gloomy stains of black and gray. Except the woman. His memory of her retained color: fair skin, yellowish hair, purple eyes. Where the other images resonated with fear and loss, hers radiated respect, admiration, and loyalty.

She will do.

Sadrahehn began to sing to the inky web that strangled Fedahi's emote. Softly at first, then with increasing voice as her melody evolved. Slowly and methodically, she plied her song to unwind the snare of hopelessness that bound the woman's memory to Fedahi's depression. The oily strands began to slacken and slide away until at last the woman's image shone like a beacon.

Focus on the woman. Let her be your guide.

Fedahi woke with the certainty that he'd been betrayed by Ciridan. He was never meant to survive his mission.

With Lyete gone, it was only a matter of time before Arwynn commissioned a new Sahadi. Yes, Ciridan, Tempek, Sandahl, and Praxis were Shades, but Fedahi was foremost among Shadows. Promotion from Shadow to Sahadi was not unprecedented. Ciridan no doubt sought to reduce her competition by assigning Fedahi to a mission destined to fail.

Why else would she have assigned Morgru a second?

Shadowing Blaythe's messenger was a one-man job. That was how it should have been. Morgru. Alone.

Wicked little bitch!

Fedahi's despondency faded as he came to appreciate the artfulness of Ciridan's treachery. His suffering was the result not of a cruel twist of fate but of a devilish plot in which he was the victim.

For that, my Shade, you will pay.

CHAPTER 32

THE SILVER DRAGON

Arwynn left the Palace Royal as Azago the masseur through the kitchens, with some playful banter with the cooks and staff. He reentered shortly after through the Merchant's Gate as Remi Orri, spice trader from Khâlir. Once inside, he slipped into Calista's tower and sought out her housekeeper, Magdalia Elani.

Though Family Kythidûhr saw Magdalia as only a servant, she was Calista's friend and confidante, as close to the princess as a sister. It was Magdalia with whom Calista shared her hopes and dreams and secrets. And fears. Arwynn hoped that Magdalia would be able to give flesh to the skeletal information he'd gleaned from Calista's drugged whispers.

Magdalia was overjoyed at the unexpected return of her lover and rushed headlong into his arms, covering his face with a barrage of kisses. After a long and passionate coupling, Arwynn artfully eased their conversation to the affairs of Calista and House Kythidûhr. Magdalia answered many of his questions and shed light on several others he'd only begun to entertain.

But it was mention of the prince and his wizard's mysterious sleeplessness that unsettled him the most…

The massive tapestry that bore the silver-and-black regalia of House Kythidûhr was the most imposing feature of the prince's throne room, stretching over the entire western wall. A silver winged dragon beneath three stars against a field of blackest night. Beneath the tapestry was the prince's throne, bounded by two heavy velvet curtains of deep indigo joined to marble columns by steel chains. The chamber floor was a tessellating mosaic of blue and black tiles lined with threads of platinum; the ceiling, a dome of cerulean crystal that illuminated the room with soft blue light.

Set into the east wall was an immense door of black iron, reinforced with polished steel. A palace guard, armored in steel plate and armed with a redsteel spear, stood to each side. A similar sentry stood at each of the other walls of the ten-sided chamber.

Except the north wall.

The sentry there was not what they appeared to be.

Arwynn looked over the crowd through the eye slits of his helm. Though the plate armor was heavy and the helm significantly restricted his vision and hearing, it was the perfect disguise. There was no better way to conceal one's features than to obscure them completely.

Arwynn scanned the room, taking note of those present and absent. Several members of the prince's Family, including a great-uncle and some distant cousins, were in place. He counted fewer representatives of the Elem than usual, and more officials than customary from Dûhr's more eminent Houses Mercantile and Mercenary.

The conspicuous absences spoke loudest: Calista, the prince's betrothed; Mordavo, his wizard royal; and the princess Selene.

Where could they be? he wondered. One such absence was curious—two, intriguing. But all three?

Arwynn found himself scowling behind his faceplate.

Just what have you uncovered, Calista?

The Sathiian delegation arrived as the last of the day's petitioners bowed to the prince's judgment. Two men in purple robes stepped imperiously into Melkor's throne room and glanced about the Court, then strode confidently toward the prince, retinue in tow.

Arwynn looked on with interest. The Sathiian barge was still two days from Westgate, as reported by his agents that very morning. Emissaries of Black Church were not expected before the next Court.

Most curious...

A retinue of five followed the Sathiian priests: Arcturi Lacosia, three blue-robed adepts, and a dark-haired woman cloaked in shifting shades of red.

Kaleena, the Crimson Witch.

Behind his visor, he frowned.

What in Xoltith's name is she *doing here?*

When the delegation reached the throne, the priests and adepts knelt and lowered their heads. Lacosia and the Crimson Witch remained standing. Lacosia offered a slight bow. Kaleena stared at the prince for a long second before smiling dryly and acknowledging his position with a slight tilt of her head. The prince chuckled and bade the Sathiians to stand.

"Prince Melkor Kythidûhr, Dragon of the Silver North," Lacosia said. "I bring greetings on behalf of the Lord Priest Welbley Blaythe. He sends his wishes for your health and good fortune and offers a gift of silver and steel. May I?"

Melkor nodded. "Please."

Lacosia smiled and clapped his hands twice. The sound of creaking metal filled the air as six servants wheeled a great silver-and-steel sculpture into the center of the room—a winged dragon, twenty feet long and six high, the image of the seal of House Kythidûhr. The dragon's scaled hide was fashioned from thousands upon thousands of overlapping silver coins, polished to a shimmering brilliance. Its teeth were daggers of saurin steel, as were the spines that lined its back and ridged its long tail. Saurin steel shortblades and scimitars served as fangs and claws. Beneath its smooth and polished silver belly lay an even greater treasure: a mound of steel weapons and armor.

The prince rose from his throne, his eyes fixed on the lavish gift, and strode to the magnificent sculpture. He ran his hand lightly over its neck in wonder, while the Sathiians watched and courtiers whispered excitedly among themselves.

Never had the prince seen such exquisite beauty.

All the strengths of House Kythidûhr were reflected in the wyrm's overwhelming presence: power, dignity, majesty, splendor. All the noblest ideals of his father were embodied in the sculpture, as were his own worst failings. For as much as the dragon was a testament to his father's greatness, so too was it a symbol of his weakness. As his fingers slid over its silver scales, Melkor wondered how things had gotten so far out of hand.

Two seasons ago, at the summer's end, Welbley Blaythe approached Melkor with a request to build a temple in Dûhr. The prince refused. It was difficult enough to overcome the obstacles constantly set before him by the Houses; the last thing he needed was another faction to undermine his authority. Blaythe had no choice but to yield to Melkor's will, but never relented in his desire. He sent countless envoys to Melkor's Court and innumerable couriers to his palace, each time with the same request: a temple in Dûhr. Each time, Melkor refused.

Until Selene convinced him otherwise.

Did you know?

"Lord Melkor?"

Melkor turned at the soft voice.

"The new law," Lacosia whispered. "It is prepared?"

You bastards.

"Yes," he whispered.

"You will announce it now?"

Melkor sighed, nodded.

Lacosia smiled. "We knew you would not fail."

Arwynn watched Melkor run his hand over the silver dragon while the courtiers marveled at the sculpture's extraordinary beauty and worth. While the value of the silver coin scales was staggering, it was the weaponry that fascinated him—the bluish sheen suggested dwarfin forging. If the steel was dwarfin, the value of the swords and daggers far outweighed the silver.

As he entertained the idea of purloining a sword or two, Arwynn noticed Lacosia approaching the prince. They appeared to exchange words.

Melkor slowly moved back to the dais and stood before his throne. He cleared his throat and raised his arms. When the excited buzz faded from the Court, the prince lowered his arms and spoke.

"My lords and ladies," he began, "ambassadors, emissaries, and loyal subjects, all. In the name of Family Kythidûhr and the city of Dûhr, I accept this gracious gift of silver and steel from our friend, the Lord Priest Welbley Blaythe of Wirith. Though I wish it were possible to keep it always in the magnificent form in which it is given, Dûhr's needs will be better served by its pieces."

Puzzled whispers purled through the crowd. The prince raised his arms. The whispers died.

Melkor turned his palms upward and lowered his hands to chest height.

"The Realm of Wirith now walks a precarious path, one that narrows with each step. To one side"—he looked to his left hand—"economic ruin. To the other"—he turned to his right—"war with the Gobli Horde. Soon Wirith will fall to one of these."

He curled his hands into fists and looked first to one, then the other, before finally turning to the congregation before him.

"Which will it be? Ruin or war?"

Courtiers looked around in bewilderment as the prince fell silent, unsure whether they were expected to respond. The flatterers and sycophants were doubly distressed—they were unsure whether to respond and saw no indication of what response the prince desired. A few of the older and more seasoned delegates nodded knowingly to themselves while those younger and less experienced blurted out replies to no one in particular.

War.

Ruin.

War.

War.

"War."

Arwynn stiffened, distressed. It wasn't the first time he'd caught himself unintentionally speaking his thoughts aloud. Sleeplessness was affecting him more than he thought.

He glanced about—no one had noticed his outburst. They were too engrossed in the prince's speech.

Then, out of the corner of his eye and across the room, he caught a glimpse of the Crimson Witch.

She was looking directly at him.

"—out of the question," the prince continued. "The only answer is war. And therein lies our dilemma. If we lend our strength to Wirith, we draw the attention of the gobli. If we withhold our aid, Wirith stands alone against the Horde. We thought the choice an easy one: sacrifice Wirith to save Dûhr. We refused their calls for aid. We chose to let Wirith stand alone. But now we know it was a fool's choice. Regardless of Wirith's victory or defeat, Dûhr *must* face the Horde."

Eyes widened, mouths fell agape.

"Perhaps Wirith prevails," the prince continued. "Perhaps Wirith's myriadi drive the gobli back into the Borowood. What then? With its economy devastated, Wirith hasn't the resources to pursue the gobli into the High Wild and secure a decisive victory. The gobli would remain free to regroup and attack the next logical humani target."

Agitated undertones skittered through the crowd.

Someone shouted, "Dûhr!"

"Yes!" Melkor called back. "Yes! Who else could it be? Not Wirith, not right away—their defensive position would be too strong. Isitar? Rha? Those realms are too far away and shielded by Evereve. No, it must be…"

"Dûhr!" someone shouted.

"Dûhr!" cried another.

"Dûhr!"

"Dûhr! Dûhr!"

The prince patted down their cries.

"Yes," he said. "If Wirith emerges victorious, they drive the gobli to Dûhr. But if Wirith falls to the Horde? What then? Will the gobli be sated? No. They will be emboldened. Invigorated by battle, fortified with arms and armor looted from Wirith's dead, unchallenged in the Borowood and Aenin, they will turn their hunger to Dûhr, and from there, Khâlir, the Greyglade, and beyond!"

Melkor held the Court with his gaze.

"No matter the fate of Wirith," the prince said, "the Gobli Horde will come for Dûhr."

Melkor paused and looked over the sea of anxious faces. He hated himself for what he would do next, but Blaythe left him no recourse.

He took a deep breath and straightened to his most regal countenance.

"Dûhr's best hope for survival lies in a swift and determined buildup and deployment of its myriadi, Royal and House," he declared loudly and firmly. "To this end, I hereby declare a tax on all religious, mercantile, and occupational organizations, Churches, Houses, and guilds, in the amount of one-half of all tithes, dues, and duties collected. These funds will be distributed among the Houses Mercenary to allow for their immediate expansion and provide for the purchase of mounts, armor, and arms. Furthermore, I declare a curfew on all nonmilitary persons within the city of Dûhr and its inner realms from the fourth to the twelfth hour of darkness. This curfew will begin one week from today. Anyone caught in violation of the curfew will face fines or military duty, dependent on age and physical suitability. So speaks the Throne!"

CHAPTER 33

MORDAVO

The knock on the door came just as Mordavo raised the glass to his lips. He paused, debating whether to drink. The cravings were insistent, but not demanding.

Yet.

He set the violet fluid on a round marble table, where it would go unnoticed amid a forest of bottles and flasks. Then he ignited small fires under two large ceramic containers on a worktable and stepped to the center of the room.

Mordavo Morvaine (*Dimension, Binding*) was an imposing man, portly and broad, with a tangled shock of curly blue-black hair, thin over the crest of his head and to his shoulders everywhere else. His mustache and beard were thick and full; his features, broad and pronounced. He wore an earring made of smooth polished wood in his left ear. His amber cloaks were linen and leather, open at his chest and upper arms. A ring of orange crystal encircled the middle finger of his right hand.

The wizard grumbled to himself as he hastily combed his hair and beard with stiffly curled fingers. A featureless iron hauhantu creaked to life and slowly pulled open the chamber door.

Mordavo struck his most irritated pose.

He hoped it wasn't the prince.

Calista spun to look, but the corridor behind her was empty. She listened carefully, but the footsteps did not return… if ever there at all.

She turned back to the wizard's door and raised her hand to knock again, but the door was slowly drawn open. She could see Mordavo standing in the center of the room, a scowl on his face, fists on hips. When he saw Calista, his expression brightened. He beckoned her forward and waved away the hauhantu, which returned to its position behind the door.

The wizard's chamber was dimly lit and cluttered with books and bookcases, scrolls and scroll racks, half-finished experiments, and curios from the world's ends. Behind him, a large window framed with rough-cut runes and blood-painted sigils overlooked the southern expanse of Dûhr. An enormous patterned rug of jhediri design covered most of the tiled floor.

Mordavo clapped his large, hairy hands.

"Well, well, child." He beamed. "It's been some time since you've come to see me! Some time, indeed! Tell me, to what do I owe this most welcome pleasure?"

"Come now," Calista returned with a smile. "It hasn't been that long."

"Beya," he sighed. "Time passes so differently for the young."

The princess laughed. "And not at all for the likes of wizards, eh, old man?"

Seeing the woman Calista Deluras had become warmed Mordavo's heart.

After the disappearance of her father in her infancy, her mother's request saw Mordavo take her under his care. As the years passed, his initial affection for the child deepened to a fatherly love, and Calista became his progeny in spirit, if not flesh.

—?

A stab of need struck the wizard's belly.

Beya!

Mordavo tensed his back and shoulders to hide his discomfort. After a moment, the pain faded. It would return.

"Alas, child," he said soberly, nodding to the table where his small fires burned, "I'm in the middle of a delicate experiment that cannot be interrupted. Perhaps we can visit another time?"

Calista's lips tightened. Mordavo was probably telling the truth, but she needed confirmation. She needed certainty.

Might it not be better to interrupt him now and ruin his work? Better for the House Royal?

For Dûhr?

For Mordavo?

"I know," she said bluntly.

Mordavo looked confused.

"I know," the princess repeated. "About you. About Melkor."

Mordavo's good humor fell away like an old mask. His features hardened; his eyes narrowed. He looked past the princess, out the open door, and into the hallway, then barked a strange word, and the heavy door slammed shut.

Calista's heart froze.

Oh, Sheeshee—it's true!

CHAPTER 34

WATCHFUL EYES

S elene stopped in her tracks and doubled back behind the corner. She held her breath and waited, her body pressed tightly against the stone, listening intently for the soft swish of cloth or the dull clatter of approaching footsteps. The silence remained unbroken. She chided herself and silently thanked the gods her presence had gone undetected.

Pressing her cheek to the wall, she leaned forward until she could peer around the corner to see who stood before the wizard's door.

Selene scowled.

Calista? What business could that sandcat possibly have with Mordavo? Now of all times?

The wizard's door opened, and the woman stepped inside.

Beya! Why isn't the old fool asleep?

Faint whispers of speech floated down the corridor to her ears. Though she could not discern their words, their tone was bright and cheery. She relaxed a bit—a social call would present no problems, provided it didn't last long. Calista would leave Mordavo's tower knowing no more than when she'd arrived. She would suspect nothing.

But the nagging question remained: Why wasn't Mordavo asleep?

Suddenly, the wizard's door slammed shut with such force that Selene let out a startled yelp. She clamped a hand to her mouth and slowly backed down the corridor.

CHAPTER 35

LOYALTIES

Mordavo crossed the room with surprising quickness and silently ushered Calista into a hidden alcove through an illusory wall. He sat her on a cushioned divan and dropped into an accompanying chair. He threw a sharp glance about the alcove, then turned his gaze upon the princess.

Up close, Calista noticed that the wizard's eyes were red rimmed and underscored with dark rings. His hair and beard looked split and frayed. Unwashed. His naturally ruddy cheeks appeared more rouged than rosy, and the flesh about his eyes and mouth looked waxy. His breath was stale.

"Perhaps," he whispered forcefully, "you should tell me precisely what it is you think you know."

There were four people in Dûhr the princess could have confronted with her suspicions, but Mordavo was the only one with whom she felt she had any chance of gain. The two lesser ministers her agents had identified were too removed from the Court to be any value, and the prince would evade direct questions, as he had till now. That left Mordavo.

Grampa.

Calista hoped that her relationship with the wizard would ease her task. Now, seeing him so stern, she questioned her reasoning. One thing was sure—she could not be the one to offer explanations, or Mordavo would quickly discover that she knew little of substance. Though she was certain treachery festered in the House Royal and she was certain of the players, she could prove nothing and implicate no one. She was the one that needed answers.

But Mordavo was no ordinary courtier to be plied with sweet talk and innuendo. He was a wizard—his mind sharper than shattered glass, quicker than lightning. Any verbal dance she might attempt would quickly fall to his lead.

How could she deflect the wizard's inquiries and initiate her own without revealing her ignorance?

There must be a way.

Calista's mind raced. Formal commands were out of the question. Mordavo was bound by his station to House Kythidûhr and, as she and Melkor were not yet wed, the prince's commands superseded hers. Extortion? She had no experience or capacity in that vein. And what could she possibly use as a wedge against the wizard? There was nothing in his actions, past or present, that would serve that end.

Or was there?

Mordavo was a loyal and noble man. A lesser man might fall to temptation and turn against his lord and land, but not Mordavo. Whatever she might discover, nothing could dissuade her from her conviction in his fundamental probity. Fealty was the key by which she would open him.

Not his fealty to House Kythidûhr; conferred by contract, that was not so powerful that it could turn him against the realm. An appeal to that loyalty would never do. She must call upon a deeper fealty, an imperishable allegiance born of honor, respect… and love. His fealty to her, to Family.

To her father.

If her worries proved unfounded, no harm would be done. But if her suspicions were correct and Mordavo was indeed an unwilling participant in some clandestine scheme, then she might rekindle the flame of fidelity in his heart and hope its light would burn away the darkness clouding his vision.

But can I do this?

The princess hesitated. Though she would rather die than break the man's heart, she had no choice. Her duty was to the realm.

Forgive me, Grampa.

Calista swallowed hard, forcing down the queasiness in her stomach, and assumed her most regal bearing. When she spoke, her voice was level and strong, confident and powerful, as Mordavo had taught her.

"Perhaps," she said, "you would do well to remember to whom you are speaking!"

Her tone caught Mordavo off guard. He involuntarily drew back, a curious expression on his face.

Calista feigned outrage and slapped the wrinkles from her clothes.

"Am I some petty waif to be bullied about? Am I some menial subordinate to be questioned—interrogated—at your whim? I think not!"

"No—of course not!" Mordavo defended. "It's just that—"

"That, what?" Calista spat. "Speak, Mordavo! Make something up quickly, for surely there is no excuse for your appalling hubris!"

Mordavo closed his eyes, lips thin, and breathed heavily through his nose as though struggling to ward off a rage of his own. At last, he spoke, softly but forcefully.

"Calista, will you please—"

"You will address me as *Princess*!"

Mordavo was stunned. His eyes opened wide and his jaw dropped as Calista's words slashed brutally across his heart.

She hated to see him so wounded and wished she could take back her words and tell him how much she cared for him—loved him. But it was too late now.

To save Dûhr, she had thrust a dagger deep into his heart. Now she must twist it.

"Perhaps you think you can treat me so disdainfully," she sneered, "because my name is not Kythidûhr? Is that it? Are you so blind that you cannot see a true princess when she stands before you?"

Calista rose to her feet.

"Well, here I stand!" she cried. "Royal born and heir to the Seal of House Deluras!"

She bent at the waist and stared into his eyes. "You do remember House Deluras, don't you, Mordavo? Or have you forgotten your fealty to my father's House? Have you forgotten the pledge you swore to my mother?"

She paused, then landed her final blow. "Or are your promises empty and conveniently dismissed?"

The wizard royal reeled under her verbal assault. Never had he seen Calista so enraged! Her accusations tore through his heart like a rusty blade, dull and jagged and brutal. And through it all, the painful need cutting his belly grew stronger…

She knows.

… intensified.

She knows!

… sharpened.

Mordavo could think of no way to assuage her fury without sealing the prince's doom, so he suffered in silence while the woman he had raised since childhood spat hateful aspersions on his loyalties, past and present. It was almost impossible to bear. He wanted to tell her how wrong she was, how she misjudged him and his devotion to her father's House, but he could not. He dared not.

She knows about the prince. She knows about… me.

Stabs twisted.

He winced, gnawing the insides of his cheeks until they bled and tightening his fists against the growing pain in his belly.

Need screamed.

He sank into his chair.

She knows about the drug.

He wondered if Calista understood the ramifications of the prince's addiction, let alone his own.

He was trapped.

Do you realize, Princess, if I tell you… I kill you?

If he confided in Calista, she would move against Selene and expose the Sathiian infiltration of the House Royal. Had she powerful allies, she might succeed. But she would fail, and her meddling would bring her death. Or worse, her own addiction and Blaythe's entry into Ufwin.

Yet if he revealed nothing, he betrayed both his princess and his pledge to her father's House. That loss of honor would be a terrible burden—but one he would bear happily if it would shield her from the sickness that now consumed House Kythidûhr. But it would not. She would be consumed as surely as the prince.

She is doomed as long as she remains in Dûhr.

Then it hit him.

Pain. Need. Want.

And an idea.

Mordavo forced back his craving. He narrowed his eyes and locked them on the princess.

"Very well," he said slowly, softly. "But I warn you, your life will be in great peril once you hear what I have to say."

"It is a risk I will take," she said boldly.

The wizard smiled weakly. He felt an undeniable pride in seeing her take such a stand—so strong, so proud, so regal! He'd sworn to raise her to be a true princess, an inspiration to her people. Now, he realized he'd succeeded. Perhaps her bravado did outstrip her abilities, and maybe her vision for the world did blind her to its ugly truths, but such was the way of youth. Such was the hope and passion that separated the great from the ordinary.

"There are many eyes upon my door these days, Princess," the wizard said. "Very few of them friendly. Before we continue, you must promise to allow me to send you back from whence you came when our discussion is ended so that this meeting might remain a secret."

Calista thought a moment, then nodded. "Agreed."

Good.

"In that case, Princess," Mordavo said, "we must talk about flowers."

CHAPTER 36

DILEMMA DEFEATED

Urath Lindrowe opened his eyes with a clear solution at last. A contrivance that would not only implicate Morkainen in a betrayal of House Blackhand but remove himself from suspicion.

Perfect! Wonderful!

The fat man smiled and took a sip of wine. As he rolled the rich liquid around his mouth, he noted that thin blades of daylight no longer sliced through the shutters of his study.

Evening now.

He smacked his thick lips and drained the remainder of his wine in one great swallow, placing the empty glass gently on his desk. He closed his eyes and basked in the moment. The wine's piquancy gradually faded from his palate, and its warmth slowly vanished from his throat. When the flavor passed into memory, the poisonmaster expelled a heavy breath and opened his eyes.

Much to do.

He lifted his corpulent body from the chair, cracking his fat neck as he stood. He bent as far backward as his bulk allowed, stretching his heavy arms high overhead and cracking the knuckles of his pudgy fingers. Then he slid the chair back beneath the desk and opened the shutters. The stars were just beginning to spy on the world.

Lindrowe looked from his window to the training field below. Several fresh recruits were still practicing at the far end of the field, while Morkainen worked with some of his Blades closer to the inner walls.

He smiled and ran a fat finger slowly over the windowsill. *Oh, Rahain, Rahain...*

Watching the sparring pulled the last threads of his scheme into a delicate weave. Then a loose end broke free—Tehru Shaddoht had not yet reported back from his meetings with Blaythe and Loquay.

The poisonmaster growled. The man's skills at espionage were modest, but he had extraordinarily loose lips. The man's inability to keep a secret and his weakness for silver ensured the spread of any misinformation Lindrowe chose to feed him. Of all his spies, Tehru Shaddoht was a precious commodity. Now the man was missing, just when Lindrowe would have found him particularly useful.

Perhaps he has been discovered? Or turned against me?

Lindrowe scowled and drummed his fingers.

Beya! That would be just like him, to throw a kink into my plans without intent! Ah well, it is of no immediate concern. I'll clean up his mess after Morkainen's retirement.

Without Tehru's tongue, it would be more difficult for Lindrowe to implement his treachery against Morkainen—but not impossible. He would simply have to leverage other assets.

Perhaps one or two of the blademaster's pupils...

Lindrowe was surprised at how many names came to mind after just a few moments of thought.

Smiling again, he raised a fleshy hand to his lips and blew Morkainen a kiss. As his kiss dripped like slow poison to the earth, he laughed and turned to leave.

He needed to consult with his brewmaster about the plague.

CHAPTER 37

STRANGERS

Sadrahehn and Fedahi were midway into their evening meal when the cottage door opened unexpectedly—two heavy knocks shook loose the latch; a third blew it open. Cool night air rushed in, fanning the fire and rattling the bunches of dried herbs hanging from the crossbeams. As they looked up at the sudden noise and chill, four figures appeared in the doorway.

One of the women was tall and solid, fair skinned and dark haired. The other was night given flesh, with jet-black hair and thick limbs. The men were of similar contrast—one was small and sharp featured, while the other towered over his fellows like a bear, with a face long ago ruined by fire or acid. Their vestments were torn and ragged, though the triangular mark of Wargrum was visible beneath smears of dirt and mud. Their flesh was bruised and coated with grime and dust. Clods of earth and small rocks clung to disheveled hair.

Sadrahehn sensed no physical or spiritual wounds, but she could feel exhaustion and hunger. She stood from the table.

"Please," the tall woman said, her voice deep and weary, "forgive the intrusion, sir and siri. We… we mean no harm. We… we saw your light… hoped we may…"

The woman staggered. The man with the ruined face caught her.

"We are lost in these wilds," the bear said. "We have pushed hard for several days and skirted the verge since crossing the Glider two days ago."

"And yet you smell of the swamp," Sadrahehn said.

"We traveled beneath it," the man said. His voice was stronger than she expected.

"The old tunnels?"

"Mostly."

"Please," the tall woman said. "We are tired and hungry. May we offer you silver for your aid?"

Sadrahehn held out her wrinkled hands, empty and open.

"Please make this small house your own," she said. "I will fetch food and drink while you warm yourselves by the fire."

Grateful mumbles tumbled from the strangers' lips as they shambled into the cottage, closing the door behind them. The scar-faced man smiled and bowed his head respectfully, then moved to help his less able companions make their way to the fire. When they were settled, he opened the lining of his soiled robes and withdrew five silver coins as payment.

Sadrahehn refused.

"Is there a problem?" he asked.

"That symbol on your robes…" Sadrahehn nodded to the gray triangle. "It's the symbol of Wargrum."

"It is."

"Do you follow the Lord of Earth?"

The bearlike man nodded. "Yes."

"In what capacity?"

"I am a priest of Wargrum," he said. "My name is Pendaro Parthas." He tilted his head toward the tall woman already half-asleep by the fire. "She is my master, Arael Laran, high priest of Wargrum. The others are our associates, Rahne and Gabrael."

"My name is Sadrahehn Nimwahehn. You are all welcome."

"You are one of Nimwe's?"

"I am."

Pendaro sighed in relief. "Then we are blessed. Nimwe is a friend."

He smiled and placed the silver coins on a small side table.

"We will not impose upon you for long."

"No, you won't," Sadrahehn said. "There is great urgency in all of you."

Pendaro nodded. "We travel to Dûhr. We would be grateful for any assistance you might offer. I have more silver."

The old elfi's eyes softened.

"Put your money away," she said. "My service to the daughter extends to the father, and to all who serve them. I will help you."

"As will I," called a voice from behind the healer.

Fedahi stepped forward, eyes bright.

He was smiling.

CHAPTER 38

THE MINDBREAKING

Ciridan's mind reeled under the force of Mirithwin's psychic attacks. The whitened flesh of her knuckles threatened to split as she further tightened her grip on the narrow wooden table between them.

Mirithwin's mental blasts seared her brain like skewers of fire, each longer and hotter than the last—but she refused to cry out. She would pass this test as she had passed the others: with the strength and dignity of a House Blackhand Sahadi.

Another attack.

Ciridan flinched, set her jaw against the pain.

I will not succumb. I will not fail.

Another blast.

I will not fail!

Then another.

Ciridan ground her teeth and held off the assault. She blew out her breath in a wet spray, sucked in another before the next. She would not be able to maintain her defenses much longer—each moment of recovery Mirithwin afforded returned less strength than the previous one. Despite her best efforts, she could feel herself slipping.

Weakening.

Her breath came in sucking, ragged gasps. Her muscles burned from exertion and tensed involuntarily against each blow, as though Mirithwin's attacks were physical and not mental.

It was by sheer will alone that she'd remained conscious this long, but giving up was worse than failing.

Ciridan could see her reflection in the mirror of Mirithwin's left eye. Her face was pale, her short blonde hair matted and plastered to her forehead and cheeks by the sweat that stained her clothes. Her gums and eyes were lined with blood.

Mirithwin's mirror eye sparkled as she launched another attack.

I… will not… fail…

Then another.

I… will… not… fail…

Then another.

Then another.

Then another.

CHAPTER 39

CLARITY

Fedahi's mind whirled with alacrity he'd never known, thoughts falling neatly into place as fast as they formed.

"I'll help you reach Dûhr, if you'll have me."

"And who might you be, friend?" Pendaro asked.

"My name is Fedahi," he replied. "Fedahi Hasraheed. The lands 'tween here and Dûhr aren't t'be traveled lightly. The gobli are everywhere. And the highwaymen… well, they've been busy. I know the terrain and dangers, all the safe paths 'n' shortcuts. And I know Dûhr, aboveground and below. I'll get ya there speedy safe."

Pendaro looked at the one-handed man skeptically, then glanced at his companions. Asleep. Their first true sleep in five days. Weaves only went so far to forestall the Enchantment of Vitality's inescapable debt.

He turned back to Fedahi.

"An interesting offer, Fedahi Hasraheed," he said. "And a tempting one. However, I'm bound to ask—if the road to Dûhr is filled with such danger, why would you guide us? You owe us nothing. Nor even know us."

"For Sadrahehn," Fedahi said.

Fedahi turned to the healer, said: "I was nothing to you, but you brought me into your house and cared for me. You gave me your bed, your food. I owe you more th'n I can say. If you'd help these people, so would I."

He paused a moment, then added, "It's a chance to repay your kindness. And to prove I still have value… even without a hand."

There, Fedahi thought, *that should satisfy them.*

Sadrahehn was surprised by the sudden change in Fedahi's mood. Although his despair had faded over the last few days, he'd remained withdrawn and pensive. His sudden enthusiasm unnerved her.

Something's not right.

"You are only just recovered," she said.

"Thanks to you."

She smelled blood on his breath.

"Are you strong enough for such travel?"

"Strong enough."

Sadrahehn looked into Fedahi's eyes and felt her own grow cold and strangely numb. A powerful sense of purpose began to fill her. The blackness was still in him. But now instead of misery, it brought him elation.

For an instant, she smelled a woman…

The woman in his mind?

… then, death.

Oh Nimwe! He means to kill her!

Fedahi's eyes brightened, and his smile broadened. He cared not about Sadrahehn or the Wargrumites, but the Aenin was dangerous; Pendaro's company would bolster his own odds of reaching Dûhr safely. He just needed the priest to see him as he wanted to be seen, a man lost to despondency suddenly afforded the opportunity to repay his savior and rediscover his worth.

Pendaro looked at Sadrahehn, raised an eyebrow. Sadrahehn stood silent and still.

Pendaro turned back to Fedahi.

"Very well, Fedahi. I will accept your offer if Sadrahehn feels that you're up for the journey."

Sadrahehn's first impulse was to declare Fedahi unfit for travel, but that was not entirely true. He was physically strong enough. It was his emotional state that concerned her.

Somehow, his debilitating despair had transformed into a murderous fixation, and the image she'd meant as a beacon of hope had instead become a focus of obsession.

At that moment, Sadrahehn was certain of two things— that the blonde woman of his memories was in Dûhr; that Fedahi would, immediately upon his arrival, seek her out and kill her.

I am the one that opened his mind. Her blood will be on my hands.

Sadrahehn had no choice but to let Fedahi leave with Pendaro's band. If she did not consent, she would certainly find him missing with the dawn.

At least she could warn the priests. Perhaps one of them could dissuade Fedahi from his obsession or find some way to prevent his attack.

CHAPTER 40

LICHOSIS

Tehru had no concept of time since he'd first awakened to darkness. All he knew was that he was bound and the full measure of his memory had not yet returned. He was aware of his identity and position, even his past to some degree, but everything since he left Dûhr was a jumble of blurred images and half-formed sensations.

"So, you are awake, eh?"

The voice sliced through the silence like a sharp knife through overripe fruit.

Tehru snapped his eyes in the direction of the voice—

—slammed them shut as a sudden flare of silver light, bright as the sun and cold as frost, shattered the darkness.

He caught glimpses of his surroundings through twitching eyelids.

Cables. Bottles. Shelves. Glass.

A man.

Not a man… a priest.

"I trust you slept well, Tehru," the priest said. "No nightmares? No bad dreams?"

A pause.

"Slept like a statue, didn't you? Heh heh."

Tehru blinked, trying to banish filmy tears and see clearly. He could hear the priest moving about amid metal and glass clanking and clinking.

A splash here. A scrape there.

A crackle of fire.

A smell of… compost?

Thick liquid bubbling.

"W-where am I?"

The sounds of movement stopped.

"Who's there? W-who are you?"

The priest chuckled softly and moved closer but remained just beyond visual range.

"You don't remember? Why, Tehru, I'm hurt. Really, I am. After all we've meant to each other."

Tehru tried to turn his head, but the strap was too tight. He could see only a dark blur from the corner of his eye.

Black. No… purple.

The words puzzled him. Tehru felt that he should know his tormentor, at least recognize the voice, but he did not. Recent events were nebulous, as though random pieces of his memory had been erased. He distinctly remembered traveling to Wirith, through a thick ring of soldiers, to deliver a report to… to…

What was his name?

It was a priest, he was sure of that much. A priest of…?

What's the matter with me? Why can't I remember?

The priest moved up the length of the spy's body, checking the bonds. He slightly tightened each, though they were not loose.

Tehru counted nine restraints in addition to the one across his forehead: each ankle and thigh, his waist, each wrist and bicep. The priest came into view as he bent to test the band that held Tehru's head.

Short dark hair, pudgy face, full lips, and little green eyes… *Welbley Blaythe.*

The sight of the lord priest jolted Tehru's memory. Everything came back in a sudden, chaotic rush—their nighttime meeting, his report on House Blackhand, the priest's strange detachment and sudden anger.

And their confrontation.

"Ahh," said Welbley happily. "So, you do remember me, hmm? Good. Very good. Perhaps you also remember certain bits of information you neglected to mention during our previous discourse, yes?"

He paused, leaned closer to Tehru's face.

"Certain things about House Blackhand, as I recall. Mmm? Yes?"

"I—I don't know what you're talking about," Tehru said.

"Tehru, Tehru, Tehru."

"No—really. I don't remember. I—I can't remember anything!"

"Really?" Welbley looked amused.

He leaned closer, his lips brushing Tehru's cheek.

"Do you know what I think, Tehru? Hmm? I think you do remember. I think you remember everything. And do you know what else I think?"

Tehru tried to turn away from the touch, but the strap held him fast.

Welbley smiled and ran his hand over the top of Tehru's head. Pleasure stirred within him as he felt the spy try to recoil.

"I think that you'd better take a good, long look around, Tehru," he said. "Before you further... inconvenience... yourself with lies."

Welbley unbuckled the band that held Tehru's head in place and stepped away from the table.

It was an expansive alchemical laboratory.

The chamber's walls were dark rock, graven with cryptic glyphs and overgrown with dark patches of lichen. Shelves and compartments had been carved into the walls at shoulder height, filled with ceramic flasks, clay pots, books, scrolls, and all kinds of miscellany.

Tehru could see two long stone tables to his left; one cluttered with mysterious equipment and paraphernalia, the other with glass bottles and flasks of colored liquids suspended over low flames. The vapors that boiled off the fluids were collected by bladders hanging from iron racks. The faint wisps that escaped tainted the air with the sickly sweet smell of rotting plants. There was a single heavy door in the middle of the far wall. It looked miles away.

Then Tehru stretched his neck to look at the ceiling behind his head.

And saw ominous glass globes.

Dangling behind his head like bloated testicles, suspended by an elaborate array of ropes and cables—four large glass orbs filled with a blue-black fluid, each connected to a translucent tube. There was a valve in each tube, some three feet above the table on which he lay. Above the valve, each tube was filled with the same dark fluid; below it, what appeared to be water. The tubes descended from the orbs—

—*Oh, gods!*

Following the tubes, Tehru got his first look at his body. And screamed.

Long incisions marred his flesh. Down the length of his arms and legs, along the lines that defined his muscles, and smaller ones through the flesh between his fingers and toes. His torso was partitioned by similar slices, curving along his pectorals and between ribs, separating his abdominals and outlining his obliques. He could only imagine what they'd done to his face.

Viscous, milky fluid oozed from his traumatized tissue, thinner than pus but no less revolting. A fuzzy white substance, like the downy head of a dandelion, grew in the furrow of each lesion. These fibers stretched across each gash like a spiderweb, thickest where the pale seeping fluid mixed with his blood.

The tubes descending from the orbs punctured Tehru's body at his inner thighs and elbows. The points of entry were swollen and discolored; dense masses of the white fibers seemed to be holding them in place. Where each tube invaded his body, a second was similarly affixed. These other tubes disappeared over the edge of the stone table on which he lay.

Oh gods oh gods oh gods oh g—

"Buckets."

Eyes wide, Tehru turned to the lord priest.

"Buckets," Welbley repeated casually. "They empty into buckets. To catch your blood."

Welbley did not normally speak to victims during lichosis. He'd carry on his work quietly, knowing his captives' ignorance fueled their fear more than anything he might say.

Tehru was different, his imagination more active. With the proper verbal stimulation, Tehru would amplify his fear to the highest levels of terror—bringing Welbley to the edge of ecstasy and perhaps… beyond.

Loins tingling with anticipation, Welbley inspected the penetration sites across Tehru's traumatized body. The flesh was distended and discolored, hard to the touch, and overgrown with lusetti fibers.

Excellent.

Welbley gently ran his hand along the dangling tubes that joined Tehru to the hanging spheres. He spoke as he checked a valve.

"The fluid you see above you is the Ichor of Unlife. It is the fluid that animates unliving things. Did you know that, Tehru?"

The spy's face was blank.

Welbley shrugged and checked the remaining valves. Satisfied they were adjusted correctly, he turned back to his captive.

"Once the valves are opened," he explained, "the Ichor enters your veins at these junctures."

He gestured expansively to the fiber-coated penetration sites at Tehru's thighs and elbows.

"From there, your heart will pump it to all parts of your body, where it will corrupt your flesh as it sucks away your life. Your blood, fresh and tainted, will be drawn out by the second set of tubes and collected in the buckets that lie beneath the table. Eventually, only the Ichor will remain. Do you understand, Tehru? Am I going too fast?"

Tehru stared at the priest, lips trembling.

"Under normal circumstances, the Ichor would kill you outright," Welbley said casually. "Of course, these are not normal circumstances."

He ran a finger down the long lesion that outlined Tehru's left pectoral. Then he grinned, little eyes agleam.

"You see, liches are created from the dead, not the living, as the Ichor has an unfortunate way of dissolving living tissue. There are no known methods of transmuting a living creature into an unliving one that does not require the creature's death as an intermediate step. Well, until now."

Tehru's eyes were wide, wild. Color had fled from his lips. His body trembled.

Lovely.

Welbley reveled in Tehru's anguish for several long seconds before continuing.

"Plant matter was the key—a bridge between Life and Unlife. It's more cohesive than animal flesh, so the Ichor can't undo it quite as easily. By transmuting a living creature's flesh and organs to a more vegetal material, we not only accelerate the lichosis but cross from Life to Unlife without passing through death. Do you have any inkling of what that means, Tehru? Hmm? Do you understand what a wondrous achievement that is?"

Welbley pulled a small tuft of white fibers from Tehru's body.

"Ah well, no matter," he said, examining the fibers. "You will understand soon enough. You are already entering the Green."

Welbley held the tuft before the spy's face, savoring Tehru's inability to look away.

Such delicious fear.

"This is lusetti fungus," Welbley said calmly. "It grows in your wounds and feeds on your blood. Even as we speak, it's hard at work breaking down the animal matter that comprises your flesh. As the infestation moves inward, its growth rate will increase. As it spreads and its growth requirements consume more and more of your animal matter, your body will be transmuted into a semivegetal material. Not quite plant, but definitely not animal."

The priest tapped the hard areas of Tehru's inner thighs where the cables pierced his veins. They thumped dully. "You see? It's happening already. Soon the process will be irreversible."

Tehru screamed, long and loud.

Oh, yes…

Welbley closed his eyes and smiled like a man lost to beautiful music. Tehru's cries washed over him like a lover's tongue, licking and flicking, tickling and titillating. It was a fleeting ecstasy, for the spy ran out of breath and fell to quiet sobbing. While his sobs were sweet, they were not nearly as satisfying as screams.

"Why?" Tehru choked at last. "Why?"

"To punish you, of course."

"Punish me?"

"You lied to me, Tehru."

"I—"

The priest cut him off with a raised hand. "Now, now—don't try to deny it. You knew far more about House Blackhand than you told me. I found that offensive, Tehru. Very much so. In fact, I still do. One way or the other, I will have that information. Now you can save me a great deal of time and expense by telling me what I wish to know, or…"

He glanced at the globes above.

"No! I-I'll tell you," the spy sputtered through his tears. "I-I'll… I'll tell you everything. Everything! Only p-please—please!—don't do this…"

His voice faded into sobs. "Not this… not this…"

Tehru's misery was everything Welbley had hoped. He moved to the head of the table and stepped behind the spy, gently running his fingers over his forehead. Tehru was too weak to resist.

"Please…" he whined.

"Now, now, Tehru," Welbley chided. "We mustn't whimper."

"You… you're…"

"Yes, Tehru? I'm…?"

"Insane!"

Welbley smirked. He licked his lips, smile unbroken. "Impertinent to the end, eh, Tehru? How pathetic." He paused in consideration. "But perhaps you're right. Perhaps I am insane."

Without warning, Welbley slammed the spy's head back down onto the stone table and roughly reaffixed its restraint.

"Then again," he chuckled. "So what?"

CHAPTER 41

STRENGTH

Ciridan lay where she'd collapsed over the table, beaten senseless by Mirithwin's brutal mental assault. Blood seeped from her ears, trickled from her mouth and nose, and darkly lined her open eyes.

She was so still, she looked dead.

Mirithwin sighed wearily and massaged the bridge of her nose as she sank back into her chair. She was exhausted. The level of Aethic channeling required for Ciridan's Mindbreaking had been far greater than she'd expected. She felt as though she'd just felled a practicing mage, not a fledgling phantasmist.

It had been a long time since she'd broken such a strong will.

Not since Selene…

The name conjured up memories long buried. How long had it been since Mirithwin had thought about her? How many years had passed since Selene had collapsed on Mirithwin's table, her mind shattered.

Ten years?

Twelve?

It seemed like only yesterday, so clear were the details. When Mirithwin closed her eye, she could still see the girl—barely fifteen years old—reeling under the mindblows, gripping the table so tightly that her fingernails broke off in the wood. She wore a mask of indomitable determination; the blood that streamed from her eyes stained her face like war paint.

Gods, she was valiant! Right up to the point where her mind imploded.

She never recovered.

And now there was Ciridan.

With her mind broken, Mirithwin could now begin the task of reassembling its pieces. Not as they were, but as they would be had Ciridan spent years training as a magickan. With the architecture of her mind reconstructed so, she would be prepared to channel the Aethios in a matter of days and weave illusory patterns in a few short weeks. By the time Ciridan returned to House Blackhand, she would hold the third tier in the Strand of Phantasm. Perhaps the fourth.

Mirithwin sighed wearily and rubbed her neck. Ciridan's strength and will had made for an unexpectedly taxing Mindbreaking. There was no doubt the young sulari had the makings of a fine weaver. Rahain had been right to bring her.

Does he love you?

The thought came unbidden—cruel and sudden.

Mirithwin hugged herself and closed her eye tight. She squeezed her arms and chewed on her lower lip as the painful question replayed in her mind.

It would be easy to find out. Now that Ciridan's mind had been broken into fragments, it would be easy to sift through the shards of her psyche and pluck out the answer. It would be easy to resolve the agonizing uncertainty.

Does he love you?

So easy.

Do you love him?

So very easy.

With a tired groan, Mirithwin stood and dragged her chair the length of the table to sit beside her senseless student. Ciridan's short hair was matted with sweat. Her eyes were vacant but undamaged; the blood that rimmed them flowed from broken capillaries in the lids. So too her nose and ears. A thin thread of saliva joined her lower lip to the table, darkened by the blood that lined her gums.

Then Mirithwin noticed that her irises were still violet.

Strange.

She closed Ciridan's eyes with a sweep of her hand, then gently touched the woman's cheek. The flesh was soft, yielding.

Odd.

She licked her palm and placed it before Ciridan's face. Ciridan's breathing was slow and even.

This is… not possible!

Mirithwin took Ciridan's face in her hands and closed her eye. She annulled the magickal vision in her mirror and redirected its energy to a spell of MindMapping. A yellow radiance glittered into being inside the mirror, then slowly moved out to dance on its surface. The radiance intensified, then burst from the mirror and bathed Ciridan's face in a bright effulgence.

Mirithwin kept her eye closed as her weave tightened.

At first, she saw only darkness. Then yellow motes of light began to twinkle. As the seconds passed, the yellow motes grew brighter and more numerous until an image began to form. It was Ciridan's face, perfectly rendered in yellow light, bright and strong.

Complete!

Mirithwin's weave unraveled as her eye popped open.

"Great Sheeshee, Mother of Air!" she whispered aloud. "Her mind is still whole!"

CHAPTER 42

TRICKERY

Passage through an interdimensional vortex, even one as tightly constrained as a short-range teleportive field, wreaked havoc on one's equilibrium. Although Calista was less susceptible to the disorienting effects than others, having been schooled by a wizard fond of such means of transport, she was stunned when she emerged from Mordavo's portal. So great was her stupefaction, she was only vaguely aware of falling to the floor.

For a long time, the princess remained where she'd fallen, unable to move or think, eyes closed. Slowly, her heartbeat ceased its rapid hammering and her breathing returned to its regular cadence.

When she felt strong enough, Calista carefully lifted herself. Her muscles complained but complied, and she tentatively regained her feet. Her eyes were still closed, but the warm breeze against the side of her face told her the window was to the left. Slowly, she turned her back to the breeze and began to cross the room with small steps, outstretched hands feeling for her bed.

She stopped when her hands hit a wall.

—?

Calista had arranged her sleeping chamber so that her bed was directly across from her window and her door in easy reach. The window was directly behind her. Her bed should be where she now stood.

Calista frowned. She turned and cracked her eyes open. Pale swatches of light appeared as her vision gradually returned. She could make out vague outlines of furniture… reflections of dim light off mirrors and metals… two large windows…

Two windows?

She froze.

A warm breeze?

Vision clearing, Calista saw her bedchamber.

Mordavo tricked me!

She had been so intent on obtaining information from the wizard that she'd fallen into the simplest of traps. How often had he warned her to listen to a wizard with her mouth, not her ears—to repeat spoken words mentally and search for hidden intent.

First, you must promise to let me return you from whence you came…

Calista had agreed to Mordavo's condition without thinking, sure that he meant to return her safely to her tower so that she might escape the notice of any Sathiian henchmen slithering about the palace. She never suspected that he would be so exact with his words, that he would return her quite literally from whence she came.

To the tower of her youth.

In Ufwin.

INTERLUDE THREE

THE SERPENT AND THE FROG

The two men faced each other across a wide expanse of scorched land, purple robes and colored sashes flapping in the breeze.

The man in the green sash was young, beautiful. His skin was golden and taut over wiry muscles, as smooth and unscarred as virgin marble. His hair was soft and delicate and flowed black in the breeze. His eyes, too, were black. Haunting.

The man in the blue sash was old, ugly. His body was ravaged by time, cadaverous and gaunt. His hair was red straw that grew in irregular patches about his mottled head and spotty arms. His eyes were white and cloudy.

With a sudden lurch, the old man began to gibber and trace patterns in the air before his face. His robes clung to his body as he generated a static charge. Within seconds, jagged blue ribbons pranced about his fingertips and the air about him began to crackle with energy. The old man teased the energy he held, coaxed it, allowed it to build. Then he screamed and threw a ball of blue lightning at the man he faced.

The man in the green sash allowed the lightning to strike him squarely in the chest. It lifted him from his feet and threw him away like a broken toy. He landed limp, bounced once.

His robes were singed.

The flesh of his chest was warm and red.

PART FOUR

TREPIDATIONS

*In which agents on all sides are confounded,
suspicions of betrayal are aroused,
and hidden relationships are made clear.*

CHAPTER 43

MISGIVINGS

Sadrahehn had warned Arael of Fedahi's intent before they left for Dûhr and begged her to intercede. As one of Wargrum's, Arael could not refuse a plea from one of Nimwe's daughters. She informed Pendaro and Rahne of Sadrahehn's warning, charging them to be wary and, if possible, dissuade Fedahi from acting on his mania when they reached the city.

Arael stood at the eastern rim of a small patch of wood and stared out over the starlit landscape, legs braced and arms crossed. Gabrael leaned against a bent tree behind her, absentmindedly picking away small pieces of bark with her nails.

"You're certain?" Arael asked.

"That the copses we've been camping in aren't natural? Or that Fedahi's an assassin?"

"Both."

"Yes," Gabrael replied matter of factly. "I'm certain. The growth is too precise, too cultivated. Too *clean*; no pesky roots or scrub to trip over; the usual irritant ivies have been removed.

Oh sure, there are tiny sprigs scattered about here and there, but no mature plants. Even the spray is wrong. Look—"

She nodded to the lacy network of interwoven tree branches that surrounded them.

"The canopy looks good, but it's not natural. It's been sculpted to provide maximum coverage with minimum bulk. Easy to see out, tough to see in."

Arael took a moment to look around, then nodded.

"My compliments on your perceptive abilities."

Gabrael gave her a half smile and shrugged.

"House Tedico trained me. I know an assassin's baglor when I see one. Even one as cleverly constructed as those we've slept in these past two nights. This copse of trees is just like the last two: an observation post and ambush point."

"Could it be a coincidence?" the priest asked. "Could it be chance that Fedahi led us to these places?"

Gabrael shook her head, frowning.

"Not three in three nights. The path he's cut since the first baglor has been almost a direct line to Dûhr. It's no coincidence that these wonderful camping areas pop up just as evening descends. He knows these places, and their purpose."

"That only testifies to his knowledge. It does not imply that he's an assassin."

"No," Gabrael agreed, "it doesn't. Not in and of itself. But consider also, he plans to take us into Dûhr by way of its Underwet."

"Blaythe must understand our destination to be Dûhr," Arael said. "His agents will already be in place and awaiting our arrival. Given the lethal reputation of the sewers, they will not expect us to enter the city by that route."

"Even though that's how we left Wirith?"

Arael frowned. "Beya… you have a point. Still, we stand a better chance of evading Sathiian minions traveling under the city than through it."

"That's true," Gabrael agreed. "But the sewers of Dûhr are no different from the sewers of Wirith. Sure as stars, the Houses Assassin divided them up long ago and keep tight rein over all traffic that passes through the upper levels. As for the lower levels… I have no map, and the ruins under Dûhr are even older than those under Wirith. Who knows what lives there?"

"Perhaps Fedahi knows a safe path."

"The Houses Assassin tightly control that information," Gabrael said. "Only their sulari know the safe routes."

She thought a moment, then added, "If Fedahi's an assassin, we may find ourselves in trouble in the Underwet."

"And if he's not?"

"It's been a long time, Pendy."

Pendaro turned and saw Gabrael leaning against a tree a few yards away. There was no campfire to betray their presence in the copse, but the moonlight was bright enough for him to see the half-dwarfi in the shadows. Though he had dreaded this moment since they left Wirith, he tossed back his cloak and patted the log next to him. She walked over and sat down.

"You've barely said a word to me since we started this journey," she said.

Pendaro sighed.

"I know," he said. "I'm sorry."

"Me too."

Pendaro looked at his feet and fidgeted with his ring.

"I wanted to, Gab. But I…"

He looked up at Gabrael. Her eyes reflected the moonlight in copper and gold.

"I never meant to hurt you," he said softly.

"But you did hurt me, Pendaro. Badly. It took me a long time to get over you."

Pendaro offered no reply. He turned his eyes back to his feet, and they sat in silence for a time.

"You never even told me why," Gabrael said at last.

"I couldn't."

"Oh, Pendy," she scoffed. "That's a lame excuse for lesser men."

"No, Gab," he said earnestly. "I *couldn't.*"

Gabrael reached down and picked up a twig. She looked it over in the soft light, then sniffed it and rolled it idly between her fingers.

"Can you now?" she asked without looking at him.

Pendaro sighed heavily and nodded.

"It was the fire," he said.

Gabrael glared at Pendaro. "The fire?" She tossed the twig aside and scowled. "Fo skok, Pendy! I told you that I had no issue with your—"

Pendaro shook his head. "Not the scars, Gab. The fire."

He took a deep breath, blew it out heavily.

"I thought I'd gotten past it. And I truly believed that you saw my soul and fully loved me for the man I was, not the body I wore. But… oh, Wargrum, this is difficult…"

Pendaro took a moment to compose himself.

"It was a few days after our last night together," he said softly. "I stumbled on a family heirloom in one of the south markets. It was a ring. My father's. It… it triggered something in me."

He turned to face Gabrael. The moonlight lent his scars a ghostly pallor.

"I lost my entire family in that fire, Gab. My parents, both my brothers, my sister… seeing that ring broke my kih. I…"

He closed his eyes and shook his head.

"I interrogated that poor vendor far too vigorously. I don't know what came over me. In the end, he begged me to take the ring and leave, swearing he knew nothing of its origin, only that he'd acquired it from a passing caravan weeks before…"

Pendaro slumped and looked back at his feet.

"I couldn't let it go, Gab. I just couldn't. I hired two of Tedico's fortari to trace the ring. The trail led back to Myrissa Dorumo."

Gabrael stiffened.

"Dorumo? Then Lacosia was behind it?"

Pendaro nodded. "The fire was payback. My father was a friend to Aerkon."

Gabrael's anger turned to dread.

"Was she…?"

"She hired sulari to set the fire. I don't know which House. But she was there."

"Tell me you didn't go after her."

Pendaro nodded weakly.

"I killed three of her attendants before she bound me with those black tentacles…"

Gabrael closed her eyes and shook her head despairingly.

"I'll never forget the look on her face," Pendaro said. "She reveled in my anguish. She grinned when those tentacles pinned me and… penetrated me… in ways I can't… I can't…"

Gabrael placed her hand on Pendaro's, squeezed gently.

"The last thing I remember was her licking my ear and whispering… 'Embrace and love, Wargrumite, and pass on my darkness.'"

Pendaro looked at Gabrael, eyes wet with tears.

"Oh, Gab… I'm so sorry. I was so afraid. I couldn't… I couldn't bear the thought of…"

Gabrael hugged him and buried her face in his shoulder.

"She lied," she whispered. "She lied…"

Pendaro began to weep.

"I love you, Gab," he choked. "I always have… I always will."

"I love you, Pendy," she whispered back. "I always have and I always will."

CHAPTER 44

THE CLUBFOOT

All the lands around Xotl were blasted and damned. Nothing lived there.

The sheer mountains that rose against its eastern edge were stripped bare of all markings and features, dressed only in a thin layer of fine white ash. The plains to the west were barren in a wide arc about the ruins, long ago seared into a glassy stretch of polished ground. Some days, when the clouds diffused the sunlight just right, a traveler could walk the wastes and see the scorched remains of creatures and constructs trapped beneath its burnished surface. Other times, when the sun blazed down hard and bright, the glare was brilliant enough to burn the sight from mortal eyes. But blindness was not the Glassy Wastes' only hazard. Its stillness belied its greater dangers—for it was not wholly solid, and it was always hungry.

Fearful that echoes of their channeling might disturb the thing sleeping in Xotl, Malaraphi and his Sadri made their way westward and skirted the Glassy Wastes using only the simplest and smallest of weaves to conceal their passage and calm their horses.

When they reached the Cerine Sea, Yarkossa twisted the planes and reduced the distance to the Red Jungle to fewer than a dozen steps. When they stood at the jungle's edge, their deception began. While Malaraphi and Sartahex bolstered their Aethic stores, Yarkossa minimized his own, tossed aside his crystal ring, and assumed the role of a servant. By the time they reached the overland tunnel to the Clubfoot's compound, all residual traces of Yarkossa's weaves had faded, and the minor Aethic store he retained was obscured by Malaraphi's and Sartahex's enormous reserves.

Malaraphi sat opposite Zaaldirn at the end of a long, scarred table. The meal was over, and the other diners had left, allowing the Clubfoot and the loremaster to discuss their business in private.

Zaaldirn (*Chaos, Plant, Shapes, Water*) was a hideously ugly man. His humped back and club foot conspired with his uneven features to so vilify his aspect that few could look upon him without revulsion. Yet trapped within his twisted frame was a brilliant mind.

Zaaldirn preferred to conduct his business through agents and attributed his talents in mathematics, magick, philosophy, and alchemy to different aliases. Only in botany did he maintain the name Zaaldirn—for his botanical prowess was his greatest genius and the reason that Malaraphi sought his counsel. If any man could shed light on the strange scent of flowers that enshrouded Blaythe's messenger, it was Zaaldirn the Clubfoot.

"Well, well, well, Vanir," Zaaldirn croaked, "it's been a time since last we spoke, hasn't it? Years t'be sure."

He narrowed his left eye, and a crooked grin spread across his scrubby face. He pointed at the wizard with his wine goblet.

"All pleasantries aside, Vanir, you're only here because you want something. Badly, too, or you wouldn't've risked Xotl to get here. Necro's still got it in for you."

"You are correct," Malaraphi admitted.

Ashen hair sliding over his narrow shoulders, Malaraphi leaned forward to place his elbows on the table. He clasped his withered hands before his face and looked at the Clubfoot over his knuckles.

"I need information on a matter most perplexing. One that requires your expertise."

"Really? And which might that be? I've so many talents."

"Plantlore."

"Botanica?" Zaaldirn smiled and clapped his hands together. "Truly the most noble of all scientia! Yes. Yes, indeed. Well, Vanir… I must admit I'm interested. Intrigued, even. Tell me what concerns you."

"You are familiar with House Blackhand of Dûhr," Malaraphi said. "The House I serve."

"Of course."

"And the Church of Sathiis, commonly called the Black Church?"

For a twinkling, Malaraphi thought he saw the Clubfoot's lips twitch at their corners—but when he turned his magickal perceptions upon Zaaldirn, he discerned nothing.

"I know it," the Clubfoot said.

Malaraphi pursed his lips. He again tried to probe the Clubfoot with his magicks. He was again stymied.

A deflection weave? Clever.

With practiced subtlety, Malaraphi reconfigured his weave into a spell of sensory enhancement and observed Zaaldirn more closely. He detected nothing beyond expectant curiosity and excitement.

"Arwynn Blackhand was visited by a messenger from the Black Church of Wirith," Malaraphi said at last. "The messenger was sent by Welbley Blaythe. You know the name?"

"Maybe."

You do.

"He is elusive, Blaythe. And mysterious."

"All priests are."

"I didn't say he was a priest."

"Who else would send a messenger on behalf of a church?"

Malaraphi smiled and offered a slight tilt of his head.

"As it happens," the elfi continued, "Blaythe's messenger had no wetness to its eyes or tongue and drew no breath. Yet it spoke. Quite clearly, I'm told. And quite eloquently."

Zaaldirn shrugged his misshapen shoulders and grunted. "Sounds like a liche to me."

"Yes," Malaraphi acceded. "It does. And it doesn't. You see, this envoy triggered none of our glyphs tuned to Unlife. Strange, eh? Quite strange. And that's not the whole of it. Using tehelu, Arwynn detected a strong smell of flowers emanating from the creature. Sweet and pungent, he described, and said the smell seemed to bore into him. I thought the odor's purpose was to mask the deadscent of a liche, but that leaves the lack of glyph activation unexplained. So, I come to you."

Zaaldirn was silent for several long seconds. He mumbled to himself and scowled and scratched his head, but Malaraphi suspected the Clubfoot was debating his reply rather than considering the information presented.

When Zaaldirn finally spoke, he asked, "How do you screen for liches?"

Two heavily armed guards escorted Malaraphi and his Sadri through an overland tunnel to the Clubfoot's compound. In some places, the interwoven tree limbs looked ominously skeletal against the sky; in others, stretching for some two miles, the interlacing was so tight and the darkness so thick that they were forced to use sunstones to light their way. Malaraphi knew these dark places were where the tunnel cut through the fields of achaelos and kalypshia that separated Zaaldirn's peninsula from the rest of the Red Jungle.

They exited the tunnel into an enormous circle of interlocking trees. Within this Woodwall, the open spaces were exquisitely landscaped and the structures meticulously maintained. It was as fair and fragrant as any dream garden; flowering plants of every imaginable color highlighted astounding greenery; blossoming vines and floret-speckled ivies wound around and over posts and pergolas and buildings; trees of all kinds reached for the heavens, tall and straight, well rooted in—

Rot.

—rich, black soil overlaid with sprinklings of caco shells and wood chips, where the dirt was not freshly tilled. Dozens of slaves in white tunics with colorful sashes wordlessly tended to the needs of the dazzlingly diverse vegetation.

Other overland tunnels opened in the Woodwall. Having been Zaaldirn's guest in the past, Malaraphi knew where these tunnels led:

to the marshlands and guest cabins, to the greenhouses and estates, to the docks, and to—

Rot.

—the slave pens. In the center of the compound, formed from twined boughs and bodies of innumerable trees and bushes and vines, was an enormous and glorious domed structure.

The Clubfoot's Great Lodge.

"Rot," Malaraphi said.

He scratched his chin, then took a breath to clear his head of the memory of their arrival and focused on Zaaldirn. The Clubfoot was waiting patiently.

Patiently? Zaaldirn has no patience.

"We detect liches by rot," the old elfi continued. "Internal and external. Also, by the unnatural degradation of the host meat by the Ichor. Bone denigration as well. And Spark."

He paused, then nodded. "Absence of Spark is the final trigger."

"And what links these together?"

"I don't follow."

"Meat," Zaaldirn said. "Bone. Rot. Spark. These're all unique to animalia. Anything not animalia would slip by your wards and wouldn't trigger glyphs. Of course, Ichor doesn't infuse mineralia... so, that leaves only—"

Plant.

"—vegetalia," Zaaldirn concluded. "The thing must've been vegetalia."

Malaraphi shook his head. "Impossible. Ichor can vitiate living meat, but it cannot corrupt vegetalia."

"Yes and no, Vanir," Zaaldirn replied. "Experiments only proved that Ichor couldn't directly corrupt vegetal matter."

He tapped his thick fingers on the armrests of his chair.

"But… what if it was possible to transmute a living creature from animal to an animal-vegetable amalgam?"

"You could…"

"Hmm…?"

"You could corrupt living tissue without rot," Malaraphi answered.

Zaaldirn nodded. "Not in the meat sense, at least."

"No… no. What you suggest… is transition from living to unliving without death as a conduit. Such a creature…"

The old wizard shook his head incredulously—then incredulity hardened into pragmatism.

"… would be undetectable. Glyphs and wards tuned to Unlife would be useless. Even the Houses Royal would be vulnerable!"

Then it hit him. Malaraphi narrowed his red eyes.

"You know how to do it."

"Yes." Zaaldirn grinned. "Yes, I do."

CHAPTER 45

RETIREMENTS

Morkainen examined the two dead men. There was no way to link his House to their untimely retirement. The bodies were clean.

He glanced skyward. Ilia still trailed Glae by a good two hours. He had plenty of time, but none to waste. The tumult following Melkor's declaration of the Gobli War Tax and curfew had already forced him to delay his mission longer than the two weeks planned; he did not want things to spill over into a second night.

Morkainen took a vial from his kit and collected some blood from one of the corpses. After he capped the vial with a white cork and returned it to its place, he removed a tazagûhl from one of the dead men and slid it into an outer pocket on his thigh.

Then he dashed across the roof and leaped into the night.

The woman's raka knife struck Morkainen's crossed daggers with a loud clang as one of her two companions died and the other sprang forward from the far side of the roof. Morkainen allowed her to force his guard down an inch, despite her poor stance.

How do you expect to overcome my strength with so much weight on your back leg?

He shot a glance at her charging companion.

Too much momentum.

Morkainen gave the running sulari another half second to get closer, then shifted his weight forward and threw his arms apart with a flourish. The curved knife flew from the woman's hands.

Morkainen pivoted sharply toward the charging sulari and thrust his right foot into the woman's gut. The force of the blow pushed her back but did not debilitate her. He needed her engaged. He left his leg extended for just a moment too long, hoping the woman would grab it.

She did.

As she trapped his foot and twisted it to break his ankle, Morkainen fell into a logroll that freed him from her grasp and threw him at the feet of her onrushing companion. The sulari leaped over him as he tumbled by. They were both in front of him now. A man and a woman. He just needed them closer together.

He'll cover her when she moves for her weapon.

Morkainen drew one of his black daggers as he broke out of his roll and spun to his feet. He dropped into horseman's stance and presented his left side to his enemies, arm extended and dagger weaving. With his right hand, he took hold of his stolen tazagûhl and cracked open the weighted cylinder's outer shell. From his opponents' vantage, he appeared combat ready—one dagger extended as a guard, the other eclipsed from view.

The woman made a quick hand motion to the man. He lunged forward to cover her as she dove for her weapon. She snatched up her fallen knife and wheeled about.

Now!

Morkainen threw the tazagûhl, snapping his wrist sharply as he released it. Ribbons of barbed razor wire spilled from the casing as it tumbled through the air. The deadly streamers snagged the man and the woman as they started to dodge and pulled tight, splitting the tazagûhl's inner casing. Six metal balls spilled free, sprung back on their razor wire tethers and entangled the man and the woman in a fatal whirlwind.

They were cut to pieces in under three seconds.

Morkainen collected his dagger and crouched beside the first of the sulari he'd retired. He relieved the corpse of a raka knife and a small stick of red resin.

After adding these to his kit, he removed the white-corked vial of blood he'd collected from Savarat's sulari he'd killed earlier. He opened it carefully, holding it away from his body, and walked to the southern edge of the roof, marking each footfall with a small droplet of blood. When he reached the edge, he recapped the vial and put it back in his tackle.

For a moment Morkainen looked out at the city below. Then he leaped into space.

CHAPTER 46

THE LOTOS ALLIANCE

The success of their trickery was apparent when they arrived at Zaaldirn's Great Lodge—Malaraphi and Sartahex were called to dine; Yarkossa was led away to the stables to tend to their horses.

There were no doors in Zaaldirn's Great Lodge. As Malaraphi and Sartahex stood before the massive structure of trees and brush, their guide muttered a few words and traced a pattern before his belly. A dull creaking followed as a living wall opened and allowed them to enter.

Once inside, Malaraphi found Zaaldirn's lair much as he remembered—a circular room two hundred feet across with a floor of packed clay, golden brown in the center fading to red at the periphery. The greatest and thickest trees formed the walls and created a domed roof high overhead, unadorned but for the natural ivies and florets of the surrounding wilds. Sunlight poured in during daylight hours through numerous open patches in the domed ceiling. With the darkening night, the moonlight was silver and fluid.

You...

Chairs and desks were scattered around the room's outer rim, along with a few pedestal tables laden with papers and sculptures and bowls of fruit. In the center of the lodge was a long wooden table, set for six. Three humani and an elfi were already seated when Malaraphi and Sartahex entered. They nodded their greetings as the Sadri approached, and the elfi called for dinner to be served as they took their chairs.

At the head of the table sat Zaaldirn the Clubfoot.

You…

He was smiling.

"You… can make such a thing?" Malaraphi said, amazed and aghast. "And Blaythe? How could Blaythe—"

Malaraphi's face tightened into an accusing scowl. He placed his hands flat upon the table and started to rise—

—found himself suddenly too weak—

What is the matter with me?

—and fell back into his chair.

"Yeah, that's right, Vanir," the Clubfoot said. He nestled back into his chair and clasped his hands loosely before his face. "I sold it to him. Well, not him. His boss."

"Adderash?"

"Yeah," Zaaldirn said. "Adar Ashan. Blaythe's master. My partner."

The Clubfoot belched loudly as he shifted his weight in his oversized chair at the head of the long scarred table cluttered with the remnants of their meal and an ornate centerpiece of yellow water flowers. Directly opposite him sat Vanir Malaraphi. Four others sat along the table's length, two on each side. The guests included Zaaldirn's groundskeeper, slavemaster, and liaison. The conversation was courteous and guarded.

Now that the meal was over and the wine was—

The wine?

—consumed, the conversation wound its way to the purpose of Malaraphi's visit. As it happened, both Malaraphi and Zaaldirn preferred to speak of their business in private. The groundskeeper and liaison offered their respects and withdrew. Sartahex took one last drink of wine—

The wine!

—and exited the Great Lodge with the slavemaster.

"The wine…" Malaraphi said. He looked at his goblet, then let his red eyes drift up to the Clubfoot. "You drugged me."

"Yeah," Zaaldirn said plainly. "Sartahex and your boy too. Just to be safe."

"Why?"

"Strictly business, nothing personal. You understand."

The wizard shook his head and cursed under his breath.

"No, Zaaldirn, I do not understand," he growled. "Never before have you—"

"Ptah!" The Clubfoot cut him off. "This isn't before. It's a new game. A new game with new players… and we're playing against each other this time."

He eyed the old elfi sharply for a moment and frowned.

"You really didn't know about the liche, did you? I thought you were lying, but you really don't know what's going on."

"Clearly, the Black Church is—"

"The Black Church," Zaaldirn interrupted, "is nothing. It's a vehicle."

"For what?"

"Lotos."

"The flower?"

Zaaldirn picked up his goblet and raised it in a mock toast. Malaraphi started to speak, stopped, looked confused, then eyed the Clubfoot apprehensively.

"It's nemsoma," Zaaldirn said.

Malaraphi raised a brow.

"The drug." Zaaldirn nodded at his goblet. "In the wine. Won't afford much concentration. And I wouldn't try any Aethic channeling. You haven't enough focus to shape the flow."

Zaaldirn took a slurp of wine and put down his goblet. He wiped his mouth with the back of his hand.

"A wonderful drug, nemsoma," he said. "It's not a poison or debilitator, so it doesn't trigger protection wards."

He leaned closer, as if sharing a secret.

"It's a memory enhancer. Small doses improve recall. Large doses… well, they tend to dredge up a lot of memory and ruin concentration. Pretty effective for unraveling weaves and preventing channeling. I mean, losing control over an existing spell's one thing, but opening a channel to the Aethios without being able to shape the flow? That'll get you killed."

Malaraphi eased himself back in his chair, hoping to remain upright as his spells of strength continued to fail. Zaaldirn watched him struggle with visible amusement.

"Feeling a little weak?" the Clubfoot gloated, reaching again for his wine. "Your resident weaves are failing. Same with your minions."

Sartahex!

Malaraphi took a deep breath and let it out slowly. He forced himself to remain calm. When his own weaves unraveled, he would be trapped in his aged body and limited to his natural senses. But—

—when Sartahex's spells fail…

Yarkossa reclined comfortably on a bed of fodder in Zaaldirn's main stable. He chewed absentmindedly on a piece of straw and watched the Clubfoot's servants go about their chores. The tray of food and wine beside him was untouched, though several fresh apple cores lay near it. Malaraphi had been clear on two points before they separated—eat and drink nothing provided to you, and keep the horses readied and well watched.

While the Clubfoot's servants brushed down horses, polished tack and harness, and prepared feed, Yarkossa played out his role as a lazy servant beyond his master's reach.

… zzzzz…

Yarkossa clicked his tongue and swept his hand over his ear to turn away the insect that disturbed him. It returned a few seconds later, stronger and louder.

… zzzzzzz…

When the noise didn't recede with the second sweep of his hand, Yarkossa paused to listen more carefully. The sound was not near his ear, but some distance away. He opened his eyes and looked in the direction of the buzzing.

The saddlebag on Sartahex's horse began to wiggle.

Yarkossa threw the straw from his mouth and began to gather the little power he retained, praying that it would be enough.

… zzzzzzzzzzzz…

Malaraphi felt himself slipping away from the present as his lapses into memory intensified. Images disturbed, sounds and smells distracted, tastes and touches teased, contexts confused. He fought to hold his focus—but to little avail. He was falling to the drug. He needed an anchor to the present.

Zaaldirn.

Malaraphi focused on the Clubfoot.

Zaaldirn is my anchor.

Zaaldirn was admiring a flower he'd pulled from the table's centerpiece.

"Tell me, Vanir," Zaaldirn said. "What do you know of asae lotosaio?"

Malaraphi managed a feeble shrug. "Yellow water flower. Poison."

"True enough, for the yellow." Zaaldirn placed the flower lightly on the table. "But did you know there are two other species?"

"No."

Zaaldirn seemed disappointed, then resigned.

"No, I don't suppose you would… but no matter. I'll tell you now, so you don't die ignorant. There're also red and blue varieties. People say purple, but it's blue. The red's quite rare… grows in only three places: the swamps on the west side of

Sador, a marsh deep in the Saurin Empire, and my fields. Its petals produce a curious acid—weak against mineralia and vegetalia, but aggressively corrosive to animalia."

Malaraphi clenched the armrests of his chair and stared at Zaaldirn.

"The blue petals yield a narcotic. The most potent and addictive I've ever seen. It's the cornerstone of Adar's church."

"Addiction?" Malaraphi sputtered. "For control?"

Zaaldirn laughed.

"Nothing so droll! You need passion to drive a priest and dedication to maintain a bureaucracy. Simple addiction can't give that. No, Adar's clergy fully believe his twaddle. Only a few know the 'Black Snake of Heaven' is just an artifice—a convenient lie that allows them to operate as a legitimate church, with all the social and political benefits that affords. Clever, eh?"

"Devious," Malaraphi agreed. "Such…"

The darkness that filtered through the domed ceiling seemed to thicken. Vines and creepers and tree limbs twisted together to blot out the sky. Sartahex and—

"… practical…"

—Yarkossa rode by his side through the overland tunnel to the Clubfoot's stronghold. The smells and sounds of the jungle beyond filled his mind—

"… diablerie."

—with phantom images of strange flora and fauna, filled his nose with exotic aromas, filled his ears with strangled noises that fascinated and disturbed. The darkness thickened as the tunnel walls grew more densely twined. Darker and darker.

And darker.

And darker…

"Such glorious potential!" The Clubfoot beamed.

Malaraphi's eyes snapped open, memory shattered by the man's voice.

Zaaldirn's exuberance fell away. He sighed.

"It's beyond you, Vanir," he said, clearly disappointed. "You and your Sadri. And those puny Houses. None of you have the wits to grasp the subtleties or the scope of Adar's scheme."

What is he talking about? What was I…?

Malaraphi struggled to rein in his wandering thoughts. Some memories were so strong… others, so weak…

The lotos. I must concentrate on the lotos.

"The lotos," Malaraphi whispered. "For outsiders." What began as a question ended as a statement.

Zaaldirn perked up. He eyed the old elfi suspiciously for a long moment.

"I'm impressed. Even under nemsoma? Go on."

"Sathiians addict outsiders," Malaraphi replied. "Addiction yields compliance."

Zaaldirn smirked and snorted. "Very good, Vanir. And close. But not quite. Even the lotos drug isn't powerful enough to guarantee submission. Withdrawal's excruciating, but possible. That's where somphora comes in."

Malaraphi raised an eyebrow.

Somphora?

The wizard tried to focus on the word, but his recent memories were too strong. Those memories reached out…

"Don't waste your time, Vanir. You never heard of it."

… embraced him…

"What is…?" Malaraphi asked.

"A fungus," Zaaldirn answered.

… pulled him…

Focus, damn you! Focus!

Malaraphi shook his head and swallowed hard. He took a deep breath and blew it out loudly to exaggerate his distress, hoping the Clubfoot would overestimate the effects of the nemsoma and think the end of their dialogue near at hand.

Neither spoke for a long moment. Then Zaaldirn said flatly, "You know, I'm gonna kill you when we're done here."

Malaraphi nodded. "Yes."

Zaaldirn grunted. "So, why do you care?"

Malaraphi smiled inside. He'd known Zaaldirn a long time and knew what he wanted to hear.

"I was bested," Malaraphi said. "You bested me."

There, toad. Now… brag.

Zaaldirn eyed the wizard askance and drummed his fingers on the arms of his chair, then picked up his goblet and took a long swallow. Malaraphi used the moment to bite the inside of his lip, hoping the pain would clear the fog and bring at least a few more moments of clarity.

It did.

"Somphora's a fungus," Zaaldirn said.

I knew you couldn't resist!

"Spores enter a host through the lungs," the Clubfoot explained. "It secretes a toxin into the blood that binds to the lower part of the brain. Builds up a matrix. Causes paranoia and insomnia as it thickens. The host can't sleep, eventually can't function. Eventually dies."

"The flower smell?"

Zaaldirn looked pleased. "Somphora spores. Blaythe's messenger was a liche. Carried the spores in its lungs. When it expelled them, your master breathed them in."

"Why?"

"Couldn't have him interfering. And he'd make a useful puppet."

Malaraphi felt anger bubble in his throat. He swallowed it and forced himself to remain calm—he couldn't afford to squander his few remaining wits. He needed to discover as much about Arwynn's plight as he could. Perhaps he could be saved.

Assuming I survive the night.

"The lotos narcotic?" Malaraphi asked.

"Yeah?" the Clubfoot invited.

"Lets them sleep."

"Yeah."

"Lets them function."

"Yeah."

"Lets them live."

"Yeah."

Malaraphi shrugged. "Any narcotic would."

"For a time," Zaaldirn said. "Eventually, a narcotic would fail. The matrix would grow too thick. The lotos drug is more than a simple narcotic. It erodes the matrix, allowing for—"

"Equilibrium."

Zaaldirn smiled. "Yeah. It's the only long-term solution."

"That's your game!"

"Yeah." Zaaldirn nodded. His smile broadened. "The blue lotos only grows in two places: Sador and my marshes."

"Adderash owns Sador."

"Yeah." The Clubfoot watched the wizard's head loll and smiled. "He does."

Yarkossa locked his weave as Sartahex's horse reared and shrieked. Eyes wild, foam flying from its mouth, the beast threw itself against its stall to dislodge the pain in its belly. It reared and landed heavily against the stall wall, breaking a leg as it crashed through into the next stall and Malaraphi's steed. Blood sprayed from its nose and mouth as its internal organs exploded and four gigantic wasps burst out of its side. After a few seconds drying their pellucid wings, the insects darted off in all directions, boring into horses and humani alike, splattering the stables with gore as they fed and multiplied.

Several of the Clubfoot's attendants were thrown to the ground by the wasps' paralytic stings as they sounded the alarm; others tripped over the fallen or slipped on blood and gore. The horses went berserk. The slaves, held fast by their chains, watched in terror as the wasps bore down on them.

Yarkossa stood witness to the carnage as he carefully siphoned power from the Aethios directly into his shield, all the while wondering what happened to Sartahex.

And Malaraphi.

The Clubfoot tossed aside his goblet and leaned forward in his chair as the cup clattered on the hard clay. Left eye squinted, he studied Malaraphi for a time while an ugly smile played across his ugly lips.

"The Sadori fields alone can't meet the Sathiians' needs if they want to overrun all the Realms Humani," he said at last. "And I own the only other source of blue lotos."

Zaaldirn slid off his seat and tottered down the length of the table toward Malaraphi.

"Can you imagine the power that gives me?" he asked as he approached.

A faint smile played on the old elfi's lips.

When Zaaldirn reached Malaraphi, he placed his hands on the arms of the wizard's chair and leaned into the elfi's face. Malaraphi was softly chuckling.

"Something funny, elfi?" the Clubfoot demanded, confused.

The wizard managed a nod.

"Your naivete," Malaraphi said weakly. "You think… Adderash will allow… your partnership… to continue… once he… no longer needs… your support? Once… he holds Dûhr… he will use… his influence… to join… with Khâlir… and Wirith… against the gobli… and… and…"

Memories battered Malaraphi. It was difficult to hold focus. The words tumbling from his lips sounded strangely distant, as though uttered by another. Images clouded his vision, like uncertain dreams at the moment of waking. He tried…

The foul creature stood before him—

… to center his thoughts, but the nemsoma was too powerful, too persistent. And he was too old, especially without his magicks to offset his curse. His memories were…

—huge and misshapen and hideous. Its torso—

… too powerful to quell.

—exploded from the firebolt. Melee broke out on all sides. Agraxix and Savishi—

"… and…" He struggled. "… turn on you…"

—turned their cloud on the beasts while he and Sartahex watched from behind Yarkossa's barrier. Then Sartahex—

"… undo you."

—made her wasp.

Zaaldirn growled. He pulled Malaraphi's chair from the table and spun it about, snapping the wizard's head against the backrest. The flash of pain released Malaraphi from the grip of his memories.

For the moment.

"Stupid old man!" Zaaldirn spat. "Do you think I'd let that happen? I've already poisoned my fields. Without the reagents I add to the water, my fields'll fail in a matter of weeks. By the time Adar's botanists figure out my sabotage, the land'll be dead. An' the snakes know it! If Adar turns against me, he slits his own throat. Ptah!"

Zaaldirn spat on the floor. He wiped his mouth on his sleeve and glared at Malaraphi. Gradually, his cheerless smile returned, and his tone turned condescending.

"As for the gobli," he said. "They work for us. How do you think I transport my goods to the Realms Humani, hmm? And get my money? And why do you think Blaythe refu—"

"Lord Zaaldirn!"

"What?"

The Clubfoot looked up at the slim green-cloaked elfi that hurried into his Great Lodge. The elfi's face was ashen; his eyes, wide and wild. He seemed unaware of the enormous wasp that loomed behind him in the opening in the wall.

"Lord Zaaldirn!" the elfi screamed again. "We must flee at once! We are—"

The elfi pitched forward as the wasp slammed into his back. He landed face down, flailing and screaming as the insect burrowed into his body. Zaaldirn half spun Malaraphi's chair around as he backed away.

"What in the underhells is that thing!" the Clubfoot shrieked. "What the—what in—"

Zaaldirn's words fell to unintelligible grunts as the elfi's screams faded to gurgles. Two wasps ripped through his chest and belly, gorged and bloody and ravenous. A third wasp hovered in the aperture the elfi had opened. The Clubfoot looked frantically for an escape. High above, two more crawled into the lodge through the open patches in the ceiling.

Malaraphi was too weak to move. He watched as the wasps tore free of the corpse and cocked their heads in his direction. They were thinner than those spawned by the gobli, more delicate, though no less vicious. As he prepared himself for death, the old wizard caught sight of two curious events at the periphery of his vision: to his left, the Clubfoot mumbling and fumbling with one of his rings; a familiar green glow to his right.

Then the wasps rushed to attack.

CHAPTER 47

RENDEZVOUS

With the arrival of inconvenient rain, Morkainen abandoned his killing spree on Dûhr's rooftops and turned to the more mundane murders on his night's agenda: Lylali Carathesis, the minister of river trade, and Portas Porteuos, the minister of common law. Neither was of much importance. At best, they were overworked public servants. Their deaths would raise questions because of their inconsequentiality, and Arwynn hoped that some of those questions might snag a few Sathiian scales or ruffle some royal feathers. And if the deaths of two ministers on a night filled with so many killings should cause Houses Savarat and Loquay to come to suspect each other's involvement, then all the better.

After cleanly dispatching the minister of common law, Morkainen traveled the rooftops to the home of Lylali Carathesis. He swiftly defeated the locks and alarms on its roof and slipped inside, making his way quickly and noiselessly through the unlit house. The nightsight he'd inherited from his elfin mother rendered the darkness little more than a shadowy gloom.

The upper rooms were disused storage areas, fallen into disarray. Morkainen searched them but found only scattered piles of debris and a few rats. The hallway ended in a bolted door that he opened easily.

Beyond the door was a small landing with steps down to another landing and another door. Morkainen moved silently down to find the door locked. He reached for his picks.

Click.

Morkainen replaced his picks, took firm hold of the door handle, and lifted the door against its hinges as he eased it open. The corridor beyond was empty. He could hear faint snoring and smell humani. He slipped into the hall and slowly closed the door behind him, releasing his upward pressure against the hinges only after its latch had caught.

There were five rooms on the second floor: a large closet and four modestly decorated sleeping chambers. After he satisfied himself that the household servants were asleep in their beds, Morkainen moved to the stairs that led down to the main floor.

There was a faint creak.

Morkainen froze.

For a tense moment, he feared that he had caused the sound, for it had started with his step and ceased when he shifted his weight to his back leg. Then it came again, this time without his movement.

A floorboard below.

Morkainen retreated to the landing as a warm light dissolved the darkness at the base of the stairs. He flattened himself against a wall and depressed the sheathlock on his left leg…

Lylali. And she's not alone.

… the slim black dagger slid from its housing with a faint rasp. Its blade was coated with kajhora, the favored poison of House Savarat.

Lylali Carathesis and her companion made their way to Lylali's office by the light of a small sunstone. Lylali cast a wistful glance upward as they passed the stairs. She hated being roused from her sleep and yearned for the warmth of her bed.

Lylali was an older woman, bent in body and face and soul. Even her nose was bent, though far less than her ethics. Her lips were taut across a mouth stretched wide by the passage of innumerable and enormous lies over the years. Her eyes were dull brown with a hint of red and set just close enough together to be unsettling. Her family had served as the Family Royal's ministers of river trade for three generations. But none had been as shrewd as Lylali—not a shipment arrived nor a vessel departed without passing through her convoluted web of paperwork and corruption.

And everyone knew it.

"I don't understand why we couldn't have done this earlier in the day," Lylali groused.

She shook her head wearily and withdrew a ring of keys from the pocket of her robe.

"It really would have been better to do this earlier."

"I wasn't in a hurry earlier," her visitor replied.

"Beya!" Lylali snorted. "You're always in a hurry, Miriam."

"Oh, stop complaining. We both know you prefer cold silver to a warm bed. Let's just get this over with so I can be on my way."

In her guise as the merchant Miriam of Khâlir, Princess Selene watched Lylali fiddle with her keys. She was already sick of the woman's complaining. It was bad enough that circumstances had forced this journey on her, but it would be worse if the prince were to discover her ultimate destination. There was little to the northeast save the jhediri tribes and mir clans, so word of her travel in that direction would spark interest from Melkor and his cronies. Detest it though she might, the only way to effectively misrepresent her journey was to deal with Lylali and pay her price for secrecy.

Time to play.

Miriam smiled almost warmly.

"My dear Lylali," she said, "I thought I made my position clear. I have pressing business that demands that I leave Dûhr immediately. I cannot afford to delay. All I ask is the discreet use of one of your vessels. Nothing fancy. A sail, perhaps. Or a reime."

Lylali cast a sidelong glance at the merchant as she found the right key.

"You already have a pilot, Miriam?"

"Of course."

"A good one this time?"

"A guild navigator."

"I don't want to lose another vessel."

"You were well paid for the last one."

"It's not the boat, it's the questions."

"Ahh."

Lylali grumbled and unlocked the door, pushed it open, and walked into the room, motioning Miriam to follow. Miriam glanced behind, stepped lightly into Lylali's office, and closed the door behind her.

"You say your business is urgent?" Lylali asked.

"Yes."

"And secret as well, no doubt."

Miriam smiled. "Very secret. And very profitable for you."

Morkainen watched from the stairway and listened carefully to the exchange. There was something familiar about the stranger's voice and bearing. When she glanced back before following Carathesis into her office, he recognized her immediately. Though she had dyed her hair yellow and wore commonplace clothing beneath her traveling cloaks, her large eyes and pointy chin were unmistakable. It was Selene Kythidûhr.

Now why would you need a watercraft, princess?

Morkainen glided to the door and pressed his ear against the keyhole.

And which gate will you use to leave the city, I wonder?

There was a great deal of circumstantial evidence suggesting that the princess was working with the Sathiians to overthrow her brother. Her departure by Westgate would add to that evidence, as that way led to Wirith. And Blaythe. However, if she departed by Eastgate… that path led to the wildlands and Lake Zemi. There seemed little there to interest the princess. The jhediri tribes would not align themselves with anyone but Melkor, and the mir…

The mir!

Morkainen frowned. Lindrowe had arranged for the C'thqui to secure one of Blaythe's barges for House Black-hand. If the C'thqui had dealings with Selene, and Selene had dealings with Blaythe…

Morkainen eased away from the door and retreated to the shadows at the far end of the hall. The princess would be on her way soon enough. Then he would talk with Lylali Carathesis.

CHAPTER 48

RETRIBUTION

The wasps had reduced Zaaldirn's gardens to a bloody wasteland by the time Yarkossa reached Clubfoot's Great Lodge. While most of the insects still flitted about in search of living flesh in which to breed, a few had begun to investigate the overland tunnels that connected the gardens to the rest of the compound. Yarkossa estimated that their numbers had already quadrupled since they escaped the stables. There was no telling how many now ran amok.

Protected by his shields, he ignored the wasps and circled the lodge to find a way in. As he rounded its northern expanse, Yarkossa caught sight of a gangly man in green entering through a hole in its side. The man seemed unaware of the wasp bearing down on him.

Yarkossa sprinted to follow before the aperture closed, but the wasp was faster. It dove through the hole before Yarkossa had covered half the distance.

He pushed himself harder, pulled his shields tight around his body, and threw himself into the opening. He hit the ground hard, bounced off his left shoulder, and slid three yards over the hard clay. His shields softened his landing, but it took several seconds to regain his bearings.

Through his shimmering barrier, he could see the Clubfoot backing away from a large chair in which Malaraphi lay sprawled. His master looked dead; his head bent awkwardly on his shoulders, and his arms hung heavy and still. To Yarkossa's right, scarcely two arm's lengths away, two wasps ate their way clear of the green-robed carcass of the elfi.

Yarkossa scrambled to his feet and sped toward Malaraphi as the wasps sprang from the carrion, gathering his shields and throwing them forward to envelop his master. For five terrible seconds, the wasps nearly pierced Yarkossa's shields, so thinly were they stretched. As he moved closer, his shields thickened and darkened. The wasps skittered about the green barrier for another few moments, then launched themselves at the Clubfoot.

Zaaldirn twisted the ring on his finger and invoked Nimwe's name as the wasps closed in. Instantly, his flesh darkened and split and grew craggy. His body stretched and twisted. His clothing ripped apart as his torso lengthened and thickened and his legs fused. Fleshy creepers burst through his boots, hardening into massive roots as his arms and fingers protracted and took to bud. By the time the wasps reached him, the Clubfoot had transformed into a gnarled tree firmly rooted near the center of the chamber.

Yarkossa drew his shields securely around himself and his master and glanced about the lodge. They appeared to be safe for the moment. The wasps couldn't penetrate his shields.

Zaaldirn was immune to the wasps in his tree form, but also immobile. He posed no threat while transformed.

"My lord," Yarkossa said softly, "can you speak?"

"Drugged…" came the weak reply.

Yarkossa took a deep breath and closed his eyes, then spread wide his arms and opened a channel to the Aethios. Green sparks began to dance around his arms and gather around his hands as he shaped the energy that flowed into him. The sparks coalesced into crackling bands that arced across his fingers and formed bright streamers of lightning surging from his hands to his shields. The shields thickened in substance and deepened in color as Yarkossa slowly widened his channel and intensified the Aethic flow. When he was sure that his shields would continue to burn unattended for several minutes, Yarkossa gradually constricted and reshaped the energy stream into a new weave.

The lightning stopped. The sparks faded.

Now came the danger—if his timing was not perfect, he would be lost to Rapture. It was one thing to draw power from the Aethios and feed it into an existing weave, but quite another to simultaneously channel and shape an Aethic current. Unshaped energy would unravel the threads that defined him until he was lost to the inescapable bliss of his undoing.

Pleasure blossomed in Yarkossa's belly and loins as he opened himself to the raw energy of the Aethios. It spread through his body and escalated into erotic giddiness as he began to shape the pattern of his weave, thickened into ecstasy as he pulled tight the final threads…

… eroded into mournful joy as he closed his channel…

… faded into wistful sorrow as he fell to his knees, sobbing, beside his master.

Yarkossa wiped his eyes and carefully cradled Malaraphi's head in his lap. He turned the old wizard's face so that it was directly beneath his own, gently opened Malaraphi's mouth, and spilled milky green saliva into his master.

Malaraphi gagged as Yarkossa's saliva slid down his throat but managed to swallow. A little at first, then more. After a dozen heartbeats, Malaraphi's lucidity began to sharpen.

By the time Malaraphi had locked away his memories and restored his spells of strength, Yarkossa had replenished one-third of his Aethic reserves.

"A most timely arrival, Yarkossa," the old wizard said. He stood and brushed the dirt from his robes. "Most timely, indeed."

Yarkossa rose with his master. "I was fortunate to reach you before the wasps."

"Did they try to restrain you?"

"No."

"Drug you?"

Yarkossa thought a moment and shrugged. "They sent food and water, but I didn't eat or drink any of it, as you instructed."

"Good. That likely saved us both." Malaraphi scratched his jaw and looked around the lodge. "So, let's see where we stand, eh?"

Other than the elfi's remains and the deformed tree that now stood near the room's center, all was as it had been before the wasps' arrival. The desks, chairs, pedestals, and tables were undisturbed. The ivied walls were solid; the entrance Yarkossa used had healed. Above, moonlight filtered through the organic lacework of the lodge's roof. Several wasps crawled over the interwoven boughs while more crept in through the openings between, attracted by the light of Yarkossa's shields. Accentuated by the green radiance, they looked strangely elegant.

The tree that stood in Zaaldirn's place was a distorted and scabrous thing. The cluster of roots formed by his misshapen foot was disproportionately large and protuberant, and broke through the surface of the chamber's floor in several places before vanishing beneath the russet clay. There was bulbous growth on the trunk where his hump had been, and the limbs were contorted. In the end, deformities of Zaaldirn's body remained with his transformation.

Malaraphi stared at the tree that had been Zaaldirn for a long time, quietly mumbling beneath his breath.

Then, he chuckled and whispered: "So, Zaaldirn, the rumors were true. You stole Nimwe's Ring of Wood. Heh heh. And to think, all this time I thought it was Maelkith."

He shook his head and snorted, amused, then fell back to staring and muttering. He seemed not to notice the wasps that occasionally bounced off Yarkossa's barrier.

After a time, Yarkossa touched Malaraphi lightly on the arm.

"My lord?" His voice was just strong enough to gain the elfi's attention. "Sartahex?"

"Eh? What of her?"

"Should we not begin our search for her?"

The old wizard thought a moment, then frowned and shook his head.

"No," he answered. "There is no time. If she survived, she will find her way back to Dûhr soon enough. We must return immediately. We may already be too late."

Yarkossa nodded.

"Can you form a path back?"

Yarkossa nodded again.

"Good. I need to get back and warn—"

The faintest of woody scrapings caught Malaraphi's ear. Slowly, he turned back to the tree.

Can it be?

"Lord?"

Malaraphi took hold of Yarkossa's arm and dragged him two steps toward the tree. The tiniest branches stiffened. He moved them two steps closer. The smallest boughs quivered. Malaraphi pointed at the tiny trembling things.

"Look, Yarkossa," Malaraphi whispered. "See how the tiny branches tremble? The Clubfoot is aware of us. He shudders as we approach. Even as a thing of wood, transformed by the power of Nimwe's ring, he is aware. Conscious. His emote betrays him."

"This disturbs you?"

"Yes," Malaraphi said. "If he is conscious, he can channel. If he can channel, he can return to his natural state. Once these wasps no longer pose a threat, he will assume his humani form and leave this place, no doubt to continue his work against our House."

"Then he must not be allowed to do so," Yarkossa said matter of factly. "Shall I destroy him?"

The little branches stiffened.

"No, Yarkossa, that would be too kind for one such as he. Too quick. I want something more agonizing."

He tugged at his lower lip, mused aloud: "If we could induce the wasps to remain in this area, Zaaldirn would be trapped in his present state, conscious always yet unable to regain his true form. It would require leaving the ring, but would be a fitting punishment for the beast."

"True," Yarkossa agreed. "But how can we induce the wasps to remain? Only Sartahex can control them."

"That's the tricky part…"

Malaraphi rested his right elbow in the palm of his left hand and tapped a finger against his nose. After a few moments, he looked at Yarkossa and asked, "What is the composition of your field?"

"Physical. My primary concern was repelling wasps."

"Any Aethic damping?"

"No."

"Good. Extend your shields."

Yarkossa complied. Slowly, the glimmering field moved away from the wizards.

"That's far enough."

"What do you have in mind?" Yarkossa asked.

Malaraphi only smiled and held his right hand away from his body, wiggling his fingers as he mumbled under his breath.

A faint grinding sound was followed by a series of dull pops as thirteen fist-sized chunks of clay sprang up from the earthen floor. Taking hold of Yarkossa's arm, he backed away until the thirteen earthen lumps lay outside the protection of Yarkossa's shields. Then he knelt and began to pound weakly on the ground with a closed fist.

After four seconds, his eyes rolled back in his head and his breath grew ragged.

After nine seconds, sweat beaded on his brow and his neck muscles began to quiver.

After thirteen seconds, Malaraphi could bear the stress no longer and released the power he'd amassed. Red pulses of energy streaked along the ground from his fist into each of the thirteen clay fragments. The energy carried with it a portion of the spell's power and one of thirteen specific instructions: gather, shape, twine, join, gather, paste, mold, lace, quilt, gather, wrap, twist, bind.

As each clay block received its impetus and command, it sprouted appendages and bent to its assigned task. In moments, the tree that had been Zaaldirn was swarming with tiny homunculi that gathered leaves and twigs from the walls of the Great Lodge and used them to construct a skeletal framework in the tree's branches. To Malaraphi's satisfaction, the smallest of the tree's branches quivered and trembled until the animated clay creatures eventually took hold of them and lashed them securely to the growing structure.

"What are you doing?" Yarkossa asked.

"Isn't it obvious?" Malaraphi chuckled. "I'm building a hive."

CHAPTER 49

DUPLICITY

Lindrowe stared at the murky liquid in the fragile glass prison between his thumb and index finger.

Soon now, he thought.

Carefully, he slid the vial back into its slot in the cushioned box, next to five others. Within the hour, a Whisper would arrive to take possession of the box and transport it to the western shores of Lake Zemi, where they would sling the vials into the lake.

Four days there, four days back, Lindrowe estimated. He leaned back in his chair and steepled his fingers against his chin.

By the time Rahain's Whisper returns, the stoppers will have dissolved and released the ungi into the deep water. The infection will have already begun to spread.

He smiled.

Soon.

Lindrowe had planned to decimate Clan C'thqui with an ungi plague. Once it was released in the deep water, mir scouts would carry the bacteria to their barracks and garrisons and marketplaces and homes. The infection would spread like an invisible dye throughout the entire fabric of the clan, wiping out half their number in a few weeks and most of the initial survivors over the next few months. The threat of C'thqui retaliation for Blackhand's betrayal would be removed.

This had been Lindrowe's plan—before he changed it. The unexpected need to provide Arwynn with a conspiracy forced Lindrowe to rethink his scheme. Ironically, Morkainen himself had provided Lindrowe with an unexpected and felicitous opportunity.

When the poisonmaster outlined his plan to eradicate the C'thqui, Morkainen had appeared strangely troubled. He'd tried to pass off his distress as fatigue, but Lindrowe noted tension in his shoulders, tightness in his jaw, and a curious despondency behind his eyes. Surely Arwynn had noticed as well. All Lindrowe needed to implicate his drossi colleague was a logical reason for that behavior consistent with the disappearance of their agents under the city.

It took him less than an hour.

He would convince Arwynn that their sulari had not vanished in the sewers but defected. To Morkainen. And the drossi now had them secreted away with the mir. If Morkainen had a secret pact with the C'thqui, he could easily launch a sneak attack against House Blackhand from below the sewers and cut deep into Arwynn's underbelly with one critical strike!

The circumstantial evidence was damning: Morkainen had been conveniently absent during the disappearances, the disappearances happened between the sewers and the Fwaer, and the Fwaer linked Dûhr to Lake Zemi.

The pieces fit together so well, it simply must be true!

Lindrowe smiled at his brilliance.

Properly framed, the tension Morkainen showed at the mention of the C'thqui genocide heralded not distress at the destruction of the clan but worry for the undoing of his traitorous labors—anxiety at coming so close to House Ascendance only to lose his footing as the endgame neared.

The ungi plague was the perfect vehicle to expose the blademaster's treachery. One of Morkainen's Whispers was to introduce the ungi to the lake: Who better to inform the C'thqui of their orders and intent? The clan would have the opportunity to address the plague and limit their losses immediately, but quietly. Discreetly. It would appear that the ungi had claimed them all… until they attacked with Morkainen's secret army of vanished sulari.

Oh, Rahain, how very clever. Such machination brings tears of jealousy to my eyes!

With the motivation, mechanisms, and ramifications of Morkainen's betrayal so clearly defined, Lindrowe's only remaining problem was to eliminate the C'thqui's capacity for retaliation while ensuring enough remained alive to appear as though they'd had advance warning of the plague. That was easily solved. The vials contained a weaker strain of the plague, fast acting but less lethal. Enough of the clan would survive to witness the treachery, but enough would die to forestall a retaliatory strike against House Blackhand until Lindrowe could redirect their vengeance.

Simply perfect.

CHAPTER 50

THE CRIMSON WITCH

A beating on the door woke her.

Kaleena (*Daemonism, Adaptation*) propped herself on an elbow and mumbled in the darkness as she wiped sleep from her eyes. A dozen candles sputtered to life.

Who's pounding this late at night? It's too late for business…

The banging came again. Stronger. Insistent.

Kaleena grumbled and sat up in her bed. Cool air swept over her skin as she tossed aside her furs with a sweep of her arm.

Bang! Bang! Bang! Bang!

"Black briars and bloody bulbs," she snapped. "I'm coming!"

Kaleena rose, tossed back her tangle of red and black hair, and snatched up her boots, muttering garbled curses at no one in particular as she forced her feet into the stiff leather. She felt better hearing herself complain.

She pulled the silk nightgown over her head as she stood, then wadded it up and tossed it over her shoulder. She put her hands on her hips and tapped one foot loudly against the floor, debating precautions to take before answering the door.

Her breasts and buttocks quivered with the clacking of her boot against the tile while her fingers drummed on the soft flesh of her hips. Her skin was pale and flawless but for long pink scars that cut across her lower back and buttocks.

Claw marks.

Settling on a spell of paralysis, Kaleena grabbed three rings from her night table and slipped them on her fingers: one of bone, one of iron, and one of red crystal. Whispering dead words, she crossed the room with her arms held wide. The shadows obediently congealed around her in thick strands of blackness laced with tatters of crimson. By the time her hand fell upon the iron door handle, her tenebrous cloaks had fully settled over her shoulders.

Bang! Bang! Bang! Bang!

Kaleena closed her eyes tightly and ground her teeth.

Just who in the four hells do they think they are to beat on my door at such an hour? By Xoltith's eyes, they'd better have a damned good reason!

Kaleena stormed out of her bedroom and slammed the door behind her, not stopping to check her appearance or straighten her hair as she tramped through her house.

She wanted to look as fearsome as possible when she confronted the lout at her threshold.

It was never wise to be seen around Kaleena's Hill; the Crimson Witch's perfidy was believed to be a communicable thing. Though the man that now pounded on her door had disguised himself before he came, the unexpected rain had ruined his masquerade. His carefully plaited hair hung flat against his head, and the paints and dyes that had completed his disguise ran from his face in runnels.

Without his disguise, he felt unnatural. Naked.

Vulnerable.

Damn it—it's me! Open up, Kaley!

The man clenched his teeth as the rain melted his cosmetics and pounded the warmth from his body like a hail of tiny hammers. Looking to the sky, he noted a faint red glimmer to the falling drops.

She's done something to the rain.

Suddenly furious with waiting, he renewed his beating upon the red door.

BANG

Open!

BANG

Up!

BANG

Kaley!

BANG

Again and again, he slammed his fist against the door until it was slowly drawn open from within.

The witch scowled at her visitor for less than a moment before she canceled her spell of paralysis. So much of his makeup had been washed away that his identity was clear; it was Arwynn Blackhand.

Her hated enemy.

Her beloved brother.

Kaleena waved him in and peered around him into the night, eyes narrow and brow furrowed. She focused her power. Her eyes began to shimmer, brighter and brighter, until twin beams of crimson light blasted from her pupils and sliced cleanly through the darkness. The world became gray and black where the beams struck, but living creatures caught in her gaze absorbed the crimson radiance and stood bright against the darkness. Their glow remained as her gaze moved on, slowly fading into the natural colors of the night.

When she was convinced they were alone, Kaleena closed her door and threw the bolt. Without a word, she ushered Arwynn deeper into her hill.

After a dozen steps, the corridor opened into a spacious room decorated in earthy tones and highlighted with an eerie red luminescence. Cryptic symbols were scrawled over every part of the chamber's walls, scarcely broken by the bunches of drying herbs and mummified hands and heads that hung from black pegs in the woodwork. In one corner of the room, a fire blazed in an enormous hearth and threw its living light out over the chamber's more prominent furnishings: tattered curtains of crimson velvet hiding nonexistent windows, brass and copper tools with no apparent function, and a long table framed by four chairs of tanned flesh stretched across frames of identifiably humani bone. The dirt floor was scantily covered by numerous rugs woven from the soft hair of infants.

Kaleena led Arwynn across the chamber. They walked to the stone hearth and stepped into the fire.

Kaleena and Arwynn had played the roles of mortal enemies for many years. Arwynn's true adversaries invited Kaleena to join their plots against him almost as often as Kaleena's rivals enlisted Arwynn's sulari to dispatch her. Kaleena provided Arwynn with the details of his enemies' schemes, and Arwynn saw that attempts on her life never quite succeeded. So masterfully did they play their parts, so carefully did they orchestrate their activities, that no one ever suspected anything but bitter hatred between them.

The rooms on the Dark Side of Kaleena's home were designed to reinforce her image as the villainous Crimson Witch and Eater of Children. Her actual residence was deeper in the hill, on the Light Side of her magickal partition. Here, the rooms were lavish and bright. The earthen floor of the Dark Side gave way to luxurious rugs and colorful ceramic tile as the walls became smooth and polished. Expertly rendered sculptures on cut marble pillars peeked from alcoves between tapered curtains; exquisite paintings of forests and seascapes hung proudly between clustered columns and tall amphorae filled with water, foodstuffs, oils, and wines. Soft pillows spilled onto the floor from a dozen chairs and couches, like fat grapes from an overripe vine.

Even the air was pure.

And sweet.

And safe.

Kaleena sat on the edge of a cushioned chair amid the warmth and pleasantries of a well-furnished den, eyeing her brother thoughtfully as she served tea with a delicate porcelain tea set. She stirred liberal helpings of honey into both cups with a slim silver spoon.

Arwynn stood nearby at a true fire, one foot on its hearth and one elbow on its crowded mantel, tugging on his lower lip as he stared into the flames. He looked more like a scholar wrestling with an esoteric dilemma than a master assassin pondering his next move in a changing game.

He had not taken the news of Blaythe's plans and intentions well. She decided to leave him to his musings until he was ready to continue their conversation.

It was not until the clouds of steam from the tea had softened into wispy curls that the master turned to face the witch. He was scowling.

"So," Arwynn said, "Blaythe is responsible for my insomnia."

"Yes," Kaleena replied.

"And when my sleeplessness becomes unbearable, he will offer me the lotos drug."

"No—I will."

"What?"

Kaleena took a sip of her tea and set her cup gently on the table.

"I will offer you the lotos drug. You were my reward for my service to the Black Church. And one that Blaythe was happy to consign, given our animosity."

"He believes that he will control me through you."

"Yes." Kaleena smiled, then looked off wistfully. "But that would make *me* his puppet, wouldn't it? And that just won't do."

Arwynn stepped away from the fire and took a seat opposite his sister. He toyed with the handle of his teacup for a moment before taking a sip. Frail wisps of steam rolled over his lips.

"It makes sense," he said. "After Blaythe has secured Wirith and begins to wrest control of Dûhr from Family Kythidûhr, he'll use my House to counter resistance from the Houses Assassin and Lesser Houses Mercantile."

"Rather clever, don't you think?"

"Yes," Arwynn agreed. "A bit linear, but viable."

"That was deliberate."

Arwynn cocked his head to one side. "How do you mean?"

"To make sure everything leads back to Blaythe," Kaleena replied. "Blaythe's just a lackey."

Arwynn thought a moment. "Adderash," he said softly. "He's behind everything, isn't he?"

Kaleena nodded. "From the start."

"Gods, I hate that man," Arwynn grumbled. "He thinks too much like I do."

He set his cup on the table and leaned back in his chair.

"His hand explains a great deal, Kaley, but one thing still bothers me."

"And that is?"

"How did Blaythe orchestrate my sleeplessness? I was exposed to no potions, no tinctures, no gases, no fumes… my food and drink were not contaminated. How did this priest ensnare me?"

Kaleena made a small, helpless gesture and shook her head.

"That I don't know. I only know that it will worsen."

"Can you undo it?"

"Not without knowing how it was done."

Arwynn frowned. "How long?"

"Until you need the narcotic to sleep? From the progression you described, I'd guess a week. Maybe two."

Arwynn's frown darkened into a glower.

"I'm sorry, Wynn," Kaleena said softly. "I can temper it for a time, but I can't restore you."

"The Enchantment of Vitality?"

She nodded.

"It will allow you to function without sustenance or sleep, but it will exact a heavy toll when it eventually fails."

Arwynn chuckled humorlessly. "Heavier than addiction?"

"That won't last," Kaleena said. "I'll pass the lotos drug over to you once I receive it when Blaythe arrives in a few weeks. Lindrowe should be able to replicate it, perhaps counter it."

Arwynn opened his mouth to speak, closed it, glared at his sister, and finally demanded, "Are you insane?"

"What? What are you—"

"Give the lotos drug to Lindrowe?" Arwynn rose, his voice growing louder and angrier with each question.

"Give Lindrowe the power to usurp control over every one of Blaythe's puppets? Give Lindrowe power over me? What are you thinking?"

"I didn't think—"

"No, you didn't!" Arwynn cut her off with a dismissive flick of his hand. "You didn't think at all. You should have contacted me immediately when you learned of Blaythe's schemes."

"Ptah!" Kaleena snorted. "You think I didn't try?"

Her cloaks darkened. Her fingernails sharpened.

"I tried to contact you as soon as I returned from Evereve! I sent familiars to your House to no avail—Blaythe's goons were constantly underfoot, coming and going and going and coming like weasels! I even went so far as to conjure a dream weave, but you didn't respond—of course, now that I know of your sleeplessness, I understand why that failed. The first opportunity I had to confront you without raising suspicion was at Kythidûhr's Court."

"By then, it was too late!" Arwynn spat. "I expected more from you, Kaley! Of all people…"

He glared at the witch.

"Or perhaps this was by design… perhaps you *want* me debilitated."

His eyes narrowed accusingly.

"Is that it, sister? Are you in league with Lindrowe?"

Kaleena stared at her brother in disbelief. She opened her mouth for a vicious retort but swallowed the words before they found a voice. Instead, she pushed herself back in her chair, arms crossed and lips sealed. Her shadowy cloaks grew darker still, and bloody. Her talons began to curl.

"Betrayal runs deep in our blood," she said. "If I wanted to destroy you, I would not need to sully myself with the likes of a priest."

Arwynn tensed. He was fast, well armed, and clever, but he was no match for the witch. She could turn him inside out with a snap of her fingers.

Arwynn stared at Kaleena. He knew she spoke the truth. Just as he knew that she'd done everything in her power to warn him of Blaythe's intentions. The bond they'd forged under their father's abuse was sacred and unbreakable. There was no one in all the world he cherished more than Kaleena and no one in all the world she loved as much as him. Neither could exist without the other.

He sat again, resting his elbows on his knees. He closed his eyes and massaged the bridge of his nose.

"I'm sorry, Kaley," he said.

His voice was soft. Penitent.

"I'm so sorry. I know you tried. It's… it's this damned insomnia… it's making me vicious and thoughtless."

He looked at his fingers and saw traces of makeup on them.

"And sloppy."

He sighed heavily.

"I should not have lashed out at you, Kaley. I'm sorry."

Kaleena's features softened. Her cloaks calmed; her talons receded. When she spoke, her voice was gentle.

"I can't know your suffering, brother," she said. "I only wish I could stop it."

She slid forward and placed her hand lightly on his, squeezing gently. Then she smiled and handed him his teacup.

"Drink some tea, Wynn. It will help you relax."

"You laced it, didn't you?"

"Only a little."

Arwynn chuckled and drank. The tension in his neck and shoulders eased as the tea passed from his mouth to his belly. He could feel his calm returning.

"You say Blaythe is coming to Dûhr?" he asked, returning his cup to the table.

"Yes. In a few weeks. He's coming in on one of his barges. I've already leaked the information; your fortari should report the news to you any day now."

"Why is he coming?"

"To take possession of the new Sathiian temple. Oh—that reminds me, I'll need two dozen of your sulari disguised as Sathiian acolytes when he gets here."

"Why?"

"Guards." Kaleena chuckled, picking up her teacup. "To prove that you are under my control."

"Ahh."

Kaleena took a sip of her tea.

"Deliciously ironic, don't you think, Wynn?"

"Indeed." Arwynn nodded. "And useful."

Kaleena gave him a wink and took another sip of her tea.

Arwynn sat back and steepled his fingers before his mouth. Blaythe's travel would adhere to a strict itinerary. Arwynn's sulari had reported that Blaythe's messenger made several stops along the Fwaer on his return. He could have been vetting waypoints for that itinerary and arranging meetings with collaborators.

"Kaley," he asked. "What do you know of Blaythe's messengers?"

"Guild contracts, as far as I know," Kaleena said, returning her cup to the table. "Why do you ask?"

Arwynn told Kaleena of his meeting with Blaythe's messenger and what he'd gleaned under the influence of tehelu. Kaleena listened carefully as Arwynn detailed the creature's oddities: its lack of breath, the lack of moisture about its eyes and tongue, and the sticky smell of flowers. He also shared his suspicions about a traitor among his lieutenants.

When he finished, Kaleena was silent for a very long time. When she finally spoke, her voice was thick with forced calm.

"Brother," she said. "To answer your questions, we would have to call upon X'theX'lo. Are you willing to pay that price for certainty?"

Arwynn thought a moment.

"I am," he said, looking into her eyes. "Are you?"

CHAPTER 51

INSECURITY

Morkainen returned to Arwynn's keep shortly before dawn, exhausted from the night's many kills and distressed by his discussion with Lylali Carathesis. The minister of river trade had provided him with as many questions as answers before she finally succumbed to his inquiries. He hoped that Arwynn (if he was available) or Malaraphi (if he'd returned from the Red Jungle) would be able to provide the missing pieces to the very dangerous puzzle he now faced.

The puzzle of Selene Kythidûhr.

Ambiguous worries flitted through the blademaster's mind as he approached one of the many secret entrances to Arwynn's keep.

Why would Selene travel northeast along the Fwaer? What is there besides the mir?

It was not in Morkainen's nature to entertain conspirative vagaries, but he found himself growing more unsure of Lindrowe's loyalties with each footfall. The man was the most brilliant strategist Rahain had ever met… and the only member of House Blackhand to have personal dealings with the mir clans. Surely he would know if Selene had contacted Clan C'thqui.

The princess's sojourns into the mountains were questionable by their very nature. But by way of the Fwaer? Surely this would not have been overlooked by Lindrowe's spies. Morkainen could draw only one of two conclusions—either Lindrowe's spies were withholding information from him, or Selene had secret dealings with the fishfolk that served a purpose to the poisonmaster.

A purpose he has not seen fit to share.

As he entered the keep, Morkainen noticed a cloaked figure preparing to ride out. He crossed the courtyard to confront the rider. When they turned to face him, he saw that it was one of his own Whispers.

"Aleati?"

"Lord Morkainen."

"Where do you ride?"

"Lake Zemi. Lord Lindrowe ordered me to deliver the ungi into the lake."

"So soon?"

The woman nodded. "He gave me the vials not twenty minutes ago and bade me leave at once."

Morkainen frowned. He and Lindrowe had jointly selected Aleati for the Zemi assignment and had gone to great lengths to impress upon her the need for secrecy. They had instructed her to prepare a strategy for gaining the lake swiftly and invisibly, and told her that her final orders could come from either of them, likely without warning. In that light, Aleati's departure was not suspicious. Still, Morkainen had not anticipated it for several more days.

This is bad timing. If my misgivings about the mir and Selene are true, then Aleati's mission will certainly fail. The C'thqui will be on their guard more than ever with the princess of Dûhr in their midst. Aleati will not stand a chance if they employ even one magikka to sense for intruders.

Morkainen knew he would tip his hand to Lindrowe if he denied Aleati's departure, a dangerous position if the poisonmaster was acting against House Blackhand. Worse still was the ungi. Even if Selene was not involved in Lindrowe's schemes, Morkainen could not allow the mir to gain possession of the plague. Their poisoners would certainly alter the bacteria and hold it for later use against Dûhr.

I cannot keep her here. I cannot let her go. What can I do?

"I will walk you to the gate."

He took hold of the horse's harness and began to lead it. He patted the horse twice on the neck, sliding his hand over the animal's throat after the second pat. It was a simple signal, but one he shared only with his Whispers. There were some things that even Arwynn Blackhand was not privy to know.

"As you please, Lord," Aleati responded.

She acknowledged his signal by stroking the horse's shoulder.

Morkainen held his head motionless as they moved toward the gate but scoured the darkness of the yard and the nearby windows.

His lips barely twitched as he whispered, "Listen to me very carefully, Aleati. When you pass these gates and the watchers beyond, you will not journey to Lake Zemi. You will ride to the house of the Mindbender and deliver a message to Mirithwin."

CHAPTER 52

X'THEX'LO

Arwynn and Kaleena rested, then descended a hidden stairway to a secret chamber deep under the hill. As they stood on the edge of her sunken trigram, Kaleena handed four of the eight red haja petals she carried to her brother. As instructed, Arwynn chewed them into a pulpy paste and smeared their sweet macerate throughout his mouth with his tongue. When they had both coated their mouths with haja, they climbed down into the witch's trigram and took positions in two of its three corners.

The trigram was Kaleena's power base, the physical manifestation of the open channel she maintained with the Aethios. Like the theurgic circles and pentagrams of other magickai, her trigram was imbued with the capacity to bleed power from the Aethios and store it in the glyphs that lined its border. Unlike traditional protective inscriptions, Kaleena's were not carved into the floor but rather etched into the inner perimeter of a triangular pit four feet deep and fifteen feet along each wall. The walls were angled inward, so the area of the trigram's opening was smaller than that of its base. This unconventional construction assured Kaleena's physical safety during summonings—the inward projection of the walls made it impossible to accidentally move outside the trigram's protective boundary.

Kaleena sat in her corner, legs crossed, shoulders against two walls, and back straight. She cleared her mind with three great breaths, then closed her eyes and began to softly chant. A few heartbeats later, she was half humming and half whispering the Song of Vision, preamble to the Song of Summoning.

While his sister prepared to summon the daemon, Arwynn knelt quietly in his corner and waited for the haja to bring its hallucinations, through which X'theX'lo would manifest itself.

It didn't take long.

The periphery of Arwynn's vision began to cloud, and a gentle tingling sensation crept over his body. The soft sounds of Kaleena's voice began to echo in his head, and the syllables she uttered seemed to slow and stretch as they fell upon his ears. A fresh gust of stale stone touched his nose on a breeze that could not exist. The taste of uncooked iron filled his mouth.

Then his sister began the Song of Summoning.

"What is the purpose of the haja, Kaley?"

"Protection."

"A drug?" Arwynn laughed. "As protection from a daemon?"

Kaleena sobered her brother with a solemn and steady gaze.

"To view a daemon is like nothing you could imagine, brother. It is opening one's mind to unbridled corruption… an invitation to madness and the death of thought. It is only by the haja that we can survive the

ordeal. The drug protects our minds by befuddling our senses. It allows us to view distorted images and dreamlike interpretations of the daemon rather than its true form. It is because of this misinterpretation alone that our sanity is able to survive the contact."

She paused, then added: "Unlike your tehelu, brother, which makes clear that which we cannot sense, the haja conceals that which we must not perceive."

Arwynn had never experienced anything akin to the effects of haja. Even under its full influence, he was fully conscious and fully aware. Though the drug distorted his perceptions, it had no effect on his wits. That realization brought him little comfort, however. Despite the apparent soundness of his reason, his vision and hearing lied to him, and his other senses played games without rules.

Soon, Arwynn could not tell whether his eyes were open or closed, whether he still knelt on the stone floor or floated above it. Strange sounds tickled his skin, and colors crawled over his tongue like serpents, wiggling and melting as they slithered down his throat. His eyes felt things that were not there, and his ears brought him impossible smells of roasting metals from faraway kitchens. It was as though he was a coherent mind in another's dream.

When the air in the empty corner of the trigram began to shimmer and thicken, Arwynn was uncertain whether it was a shadow of reality or his imagination.

He was still unsure when, at last, he faced himself.

"Since you are the petitioner, the daemon will assume your form when it appears," Kaleena explained. "As your dialogue unfolds, the daemon will gradually shed this guise and assume its true form. The haja will not allow you to see this. Instead, you will see a perversion of your image. The more corrupt your image becomes, the more likely the daemon will lie."

"What will be the form of this corruption?"

Kaleena shrugged. "It differs from person to person. Some have seen themselves age unto death and the rot that lies beyond. Others have witnessed their appendages being eaten away by all manner of parasite. You may see your image slowly transform into a daemonic visage, or watch it fall to performing perverse sexual acts with unnatural creatures. The precise form of defilement will be for you alone."

"And as corruption progresses, the daemon gains freedom to lie?"
"Yes."
"How will I know when the lying begins?"
"You won't."

Arwynn faced the image of himself that had congealed in the far corner of the trigram. Though his senses were lost to the haja, the image that stared back at him did not waver, nor did its voice suffer distortion as it spoke.

"Greetings to you, Arwynn Blackhand," the daemon said politely, almost cheerfully, a saccharine smile playing across its lips. "You have no idea how long I have waited to speak with you."

"Somehow, that knowledge brings me no pleasure."

X'theX'lo smiled but said nothing.

It simply waited.

"*The Song of Summoning will bind the daemon against all forms of physical and mental contact other than speech,*" Kaleena said. "*Spiritual shielding, however, is not provided by the summoning magicks. You must avoid asking questions that invite lengthy responses, as they will increase the duration of your exposure to the daemon and further compromise your soul. Unless absolutely necessary, refrain from asking probing questions to clarify the daemon's answers. These will also increase the duration of your exposure.*"

"*What do you suggest?*"

"*It's hard to say without knowing how much your insomnia has affected your faculties, and your lack of experience dealing with extraplanar entities is cause for some concern… we don't know the extent of your resistance to the daemon's corruptive influence. I recommend you ask only simple, clear, precise questions that call for simple, clear, and precise answers.*"

"*And what of other dialogue?*"

"*Such as?*"

"*Misleading questions to unbalance the daemon.*"

Kaleena shook her head. "X'theX'lo will manifest itself as a reflection of you in more than a physical sense. It will employ similar tactics against you if you initiate them."

Arwynn thought about this for a moment, then asked: "Have such tactics ever proven successful in the past?"

"*Yes,*" *Kaleena said. "Twice.*"

Arwynn scowled at the thing before him. It stood as quiet and unmoving as the reflection of a dead man. Though the walls of the trigram rippled behind it and curious scents and sounds bubbled up from places he couldn't determine, X'theX'lo's image did not waver. Arwynn thought it strange that the haja should so distort his environment while leaving the visage of the daemon unscathed.

"I have questions for you, X'theX'lo," Arwynn said flatly.

"And I have answers for you, Arwynn Blackhand." X'theX'lo smirked. "Perhaps they will coincide."

"Indeed," the assassin replied.

Arwynn forced himself to pause. It was imperative he ask the right questions in the correct sequence, or he would have no way of knowing when the daemon veered from the truth. As he prepared, Arwynn wondered what form of perversion X'theX'lo would wreak upon his image. As if in response, the daemon's smirk stretched and widened until its lips parted over perfectly formed white teeth.

Arwynn steeled himself and asked his first question.

"Are Welbley Blaythe's plans for my House as Kaleena described?"

"Yes," the daemon answered plainly, smile widening.

Arwynn frowned and let his shoulder slip ever so slightly. He hoped to appear disheartened, when in fact he was pleased. What had been speculation collapsed into certainty.

The question had served a dual purpose: it confirmed that Blaythe indeed sought to use the lotos drug to subjugate his House and fixed several points that he could use to gauge the truthfulness of the daemon's subsequent statements. Should the daemon's later responses conflict with those details, he would know the creature to be lying.

"Has Blaythe inflicted me with sleeplessness as prelude to addiction?"

The daemon's smile stretched wider still. "Yes."

Arwynn's heart sank. He'd thought himself prepared for the daemon's answer, but it still struck hard.

X'theX'lo's grin widened still further at the assassin's distress, so impossibly wide that its sharp corners sliced through its cheeks. A bloody pus oozed down the daemon's face from the wounds. Without the support of its cheeks, X'theX'lo's lower lip began to sag and pull away from its face, revealing fully the white teeth and pink gums of its jaw.

"You are a clever one, humani," X'theX'lo said, still in a voice that mimicked Arwynn's own, "to seek to bind me to honesty by asking me questions whose answers you already know. Why would you do that, I wonder? Perhaps you fear the knowledge that I possess? Is that it, manling? Are you afraid?"

"If the daemon senses any weakness, confusion, or loss of concentration on your part, it will try to usurp control of your dialogue. It will do this by asking a question of you. You must not allow this to happen. Once you start answering its questions instead of posing your own, you will never be able to stop."

"Never?"

"Never. The daemon will pull your mind out of time and absorb it into its own reality. You will answer its questions for all eternity. The

principal source of a daemon's knowledge is the combined intellect and experience of all those trapped in such a manner."

"And you, sister? As the summoner, what would happen to you in that event?"

Kaleena shuddered. "Please, Wynn... do not make me speak of such things."

Arwynn dared not answer the daemon. He needed to regain control of the dialogue—and quickly—before the daemon took his silence to be an answer. But to do that, he needed to pose a question backed by determination and strength of will. And uncompromisable specificity.

Ironically, X'theX'lo had provided Arwynn with just such a question.

Arwynn met the daemon's gaze and said: "Speak plainly, daemon: How precisely did Blaythe ruin my sleep?"

X'theX'lo accepted the assassin's question. Its cutting smile slashed fully around its head, and its lower lip fell away, along with the skin of its jaw and several of its teeth. The flesh about its eyes went white and split open at the corners. Bloody pus seeped out of the new wounds.

"An interesting question, Arwynn Black House," it said slowly, its words falling through teeth that cracked and rotted as it spoke. "It was Blaythe's messenger that did this to you, little man of many faces. By means of a poison it carried in its smell."

"The flowers I smelled that day?"

"Yes."

"Then they were the messenger's means of poison, not a disguise?"

"Yes."

X'theX'lo chuckled, then laughed.

Arwynn closed his eyes and choked back a sudden rush of bile as the laugh echoed through the chamber. Each reverberation struck like a physical blow, slapped his flesh and clung to his clothes. He felt sick and dizzy. His ego, his will, his whole sense of well-being, already weakened by his lack of sleep, seemed ready to buckle before the onslaught of the daemonic presence. He felt like he was being slowly crushed by the weight of a thousand sins, given the substance of rotten fish and the stickiness of tar.

The daemon ceased its laughter and caught the assassin's gaze once again. More of its teeth had rotted away, and its eyes had burst, leaving splatters of bloody jelly around empty sockets. Deep cracks lined the flesh of its face and hands. In the gore beneath the daemon's nose, Arwynn saw a second mouth waiting to replace the first.

It, too, was smiling.

Arwynn knew that he had little time before his will broke and his soul lay forfeit to the daemon, yet he refused to yield. The mystery of his vanished agents was too great to ignore.

"Is there a traitor among my lieutenants?"

More of X'theX'lo's face fell away in chunks of bloody pus as a new set of eyes rolled into place.

"There are many kinds of traitor, poison-handed manling. There are betrayers of the heart, traitors of the mind, and plotters of action. Are you asking me which types exist within your House? Or would you like to know their names?"

Don't answer. Don't answer.

Arwynn rallied the last of his strength into a final question.

"Does a lieutenant of my House seek my downfall?" he demanded.

The last putrid remnants of the daemon's face fell away and a new one, smiling and wet and slick with blood and white ooze, settled into place. The new face was also Arwynn's, more horrifying and distorted than the first.

X'theX'lo beamed.

"Even as we speak, Lindrowe plots against you."

CHAPTER 53

UNDER THE CITY

With Fedahi's guidance, Arael's band reached Dûhr swiftly and without incident. After a brief respite, they slipped into the city's sewers under cover of darkness and continued their journey underground.

Fedahi ushered them through the gloomy Underwet with tempered ease, pausing now and again to study the path ahead, turn a concealed lever, or disarm a trap. Occasionally he would stop and whisper, something like "avoid the raised stones" or "keep a hand on the wall." His actions and edicts must have seemed odd to the priests, but he didn't care. He cared even less whether they realized he was an assassin. He had but one concern.

Ciridan.

As they moved deeper into the Underwet, Fedahi's thoughts fixated on the woman that betrayed him. Far from Dûhr, he'd had little time to dwell on her. Truth be told, he'd been so busy avoiding the meddlesome priests and their unctuous moralizing that he'd had scant opportunity to focus on his mission. Their sanctimonious appeals to his sense of worth had both distracted and disgusted him. But now... now he could see her in his mind. Hear her. Smell her. Almost touch her. Each new passageway heightened his anticipation. Each new footfall brought her closer.

The narrow walkways along the sewer channels began to show signs of recent passage. Fedahi moved them off the main channels and into secondary canals through a series of twisting crawlways, barely wide enough to afford passage. The way was slow and laborious, but much safer than the main route. Still, the next several hours saw little progress. The priests spent much of their time huddled in darkness while Fedahi and Gabrael scouted the paths ahead.

It became a maddening pattern: huddle, move, stop, huddle together, wait, move, stop again. Their progress would have been easier, perhaps even restful, had the danger not been so palpable and the tempo so uneven.

As they moved closer to the city's center, their pace slowed even more as the Underwet's perils began to include patrols of rogues and thieves, soldiers and sulari.

As they neared the Gardens of Twilight, those patrols began to include Sathiian adepts.

Arael, Pendaro, and Rahne crouched in a cramped alcove off a secondary sewer canal, silent and still. They'd smeared themselves with mud and fecal matter to hide their color and scent from predators. Like Wirith, Dûhr had been built upon the ruins of an ancient civilization, and its sewers cut deep into its predecessor's remains. While the soldiers and sulari patrolling the Underwet navigated by sight and sound, the things that made their way up from the antediluvian ruins tracked the sweet smells of living things.

While they waited, the priests listened to the murmurs of the Underwet: the muffled scrabbling of rats; the skittering and buzzing of insects; the dull croaking of frogs; the dripping and gurgling of water. Gabrael had told them to pay attention to these sounds, for silence would herald danger. The glut of noise did not ease their tensions; it was a fragile veil to mask their presence.

Arael thought of her promise to Sadrahehn. The solution still eluded her. Despite Rahne's and Pendaro's efforts, she could see no way to save both Fedahi and his intended victim. She began to fear that the only way to save the woman would be to kill Fedahi.

Sshkhht.

Arael stiffened. Rahne and Pendaro tensed. Spells came to lips.

Sshkhht.

It came again. A soft scraping.

Then another.

A stone fell into the water.

Arael handed Pendaro the parcel she carried and gently tapped Rahne's arm twice with two fingers. *Paralyze*, the touch said. Then she rose to her feet and reached for the fragile curtain of foliage that covered the entrance to their alcove. Aiming to draw attention from her adepts, she took a deep breath, threw aside the creepers, and stepped fearlessly into the passageway.

Gabrael Harnath was prone upon the ground before her.

She looked dead.

CHAPTER 54

PAPER FOUNDATIONS

The woman approached a secluded table in a far corner of the tavern. She moved with an easy grace and sat opposite a balding man, placing her hands flat upon the table. She wore three rings: one of bone, one of iron, and one of red crystal.

The man wore a heavy traveling cloak, dark and nondescript, its cowl loose over his shoulders. He was short, stocky, and broad, with deep-walnut skin, blunt features, and hands that seemed strangely large for his body. He wore a ring of gray crystal on the small finger of his right hand. He was drinking from a pewter tankard.

"Drink?" He offered his tankard.

"No," she answered.

He grunted, shrugged. "Suit yourself. Me? I don't get out much. I rather enjoy sampling the local fare."

The woman pulled back her cowl. Her dark hair looked black in the low light, streaked with red that looked like blood.

"Do you have it?" she asked.

The man retrieved a slim bone cylinder from inside his cloak.

"Enchantment of Vitality," he said. "Single target, inkvane leech, ready to read. As promised."

The woman reached for the bone case. The man pulled it away.

"Ah, ah, ah," he chided.

He held out his other hand, palm up and fingers wiggling.

Kaleena smiled. She withdrew a small bundle of papers from a fold in her cloaks and handed them to the man.

"The plans, Kargan, as promised," she said, trading the papers for the scroll case. "Blaythe's temple in Dûhr, including all traps and automated defenses. I took the liberty of adding some dashed lines to show areas where the structure is weak. Not that he realizes it, of course…"

"Very nice," Kargan said, glancing over the papers. "What do these shapes signify?"

"Blocks are traps. Circles are glyphs."

"And the colors?"

"Red are active," Kaleena said. "Blue haven't been installed yet…"

She opened the bone case as she spoke, carefully removing a roll of parchment.

"… yellow are alarms and glyphs that Blaythe believes active."

"Believes active?"

"They're not."

"Your doing?"

Kaleena winked.

"Call it a bit of fun," she said, unrolling the parchment and scanning the symbols upon it. "Nice work, Kargan."

"Thank you. I do try."

"It shows."

"Really?"

"Uthic meter? Three-section rhyme?"

"So few people appreciate style these days."

Kaleena chuckled and carefully returned the scroll to its case, sealing it. Kargan folded the papers and stuffed them into his cloaks. Then he downed the remainder of his ale and wiped his mouth with the back of his hand.

Kaleena gave him a disgusted look.

"Don't you priests have any manners?"

Kargan smiled. "As I said, I don't get out much."

CHAPTER 55

THE MIRROR AND THE EIE

Mirithwin entered her study and turned to close the door. When the latch caught, she whispered words to blind the eie of would-be voyeurs. A faint glitter of yellow light played about the door and windows, slid over hearth and walls, and then faded into the floor and ceiling. When all traces of the unnatural light dissipated, she crossed the room to where her guest waited patiently in a chair by the fire.

"Well?" the elfi asked. "Who was it?"

"One of Arwynn's sulari," Mirithwin replied.

"And?"

"They want her back."

"What? Why?"

Mirithwin shrugged. She crossed the room and dropped into the chair opposite the elfi.

"I don't know."

"When?"

"Immediately."

The elfi frowned. His pupilless white eyes darkened against his pale skin.

"Ciridan's mental defenses alone make her a valuable asset to our cause," he said. "With Aethic training, she could turn the odds in our favor."

"I agree," Mirithwin said, "but restructuring her mental architecture is not an option. Her mind will not break. If I can't break it, I can't rebuild it."

"No," the elfi said softly. "I suppose not."

Mirithwin brushed back her long hair and stared at the ceiling. The elfi rested his chin in one hand and stared into the fire, drumming the long fingers of his other hand on his knee.

Neither spoke for some time.

"What about Sestigarthon?" the elfi asked at length.

Mirithwin stiffened and leveled a stern gaze at the elfi.

"Are you serious, Maelkith?"

"Quite."

"His methods are—"

"No more unorthodox than your own."

Mirithwin scoffed.

"Think about it, Mirithwin," Maelkith said calmly. "A skilled sulari with an unbreakable mind weaving the Strand of Sin?"

Mirithwin scowled. The thought at once enticed and scared her.

She shook her head. "It's a pointless discussion. They want her back. If I don't comply, we risk exposure."

"True," Maelkith acceded. "But consider, Ciridan's House knows her only by form and function."

"Your point?"

"Those can be replicated."

INTERLUDE FOUR

THE SERPENT AND THE FROG

The two men faced each other across a wide expanse of scorched land, purple robes and colored sashes flapping in the breeze.

The man in the green sash was young, beautiful. His skin was golden and taut over wiry muscles, as smooth and unscarred as virgin marble. His hair was soft and delicate and flowed black in the breeze. His eyes, too, were black. Haunting.

The man in the blue sash was old, ugly. His body was ravaged by time, cadaverous and gaunt. His hair was red straw that grew in irregular patches about his mottled head and spotty arms. His eyes were white and cloudy.

With a sudden lurch, the old man began to gibber and trace patterns in the air before his face. His robes clung to his body as he generated a static charge. Within seconds, jagged blue ribbons pranced about his fingertips and the air about him began to crackle with energy. The old man teased the energy he held, coaxed it, allowed it to build. Then he screamed and threw a ball of blue lightning at the man he faced.

The man in the green sash stood passively in the lightning's path. Before it could strike him, it lost both color and cohesion.

It sputtered and sparked inches from his body, like fire fed with wet wood, and dissipated into nothingness before it touched him.

The man in the green sash, known as Adderash the Snake, smiled. With this new weave of dissipation, his Black Church would be unstoppable.

"Now, Zithwathn," he called across the field to the man in the blue sash. "Now I am ready. Now it's time for me to visit Welbley Blaythe. But first, I need you to talk to Lacosia and Dorumo."

"About what?"

"Prospects and promotion," Adar said. He smiled slyly. "It's time to divest ourselves of a reckless opportunist and capitalize on a cruel darkness."

PART FIVE

CONFRONTATIONS

In which the Snake swallows Wirith,
a Great House is purged,
and new alliances are forged.

CHAPTER 56

A PARLEY OF SNAKES

Two hours ago, as the last of the sun's rays abandoned their efforts to pierce Evereve's somber canopy, Adar Ashan had appeared at Welbley's gate. Now, after a brief celebration to honor his arrival, the two men waited in Welbley's luxurious private study as servants prepared a fire and set out plates of sliced fruit and cups of infused water. When the servants departed, Welbley bolted the doors and activated an array of magickal wards.

Welbley was nervous. He'd had no time to prepare.

Why are you here? What do you want?

Welbley cast a sidelong glance at his master as he actuated the last of his wards, as though he might discern intent from his bearing or expression. The lord sovereign's mien offered no clues. Welbley watched the firelight play off his master's flawless skin, dance in his dark eyes, slide over his inky hair—

—and quickly looked away.

It was not so much Adar's exceptional beauty that disquieted Welbley but his mesmerizing presence. The man's overwhelming charisma engendered feelings of friendship, affection, and fidelity. Even the most hardened of hearts softened in his proximity. The infatuation deepened with prolonged contact and lingered for days. It was a weapon that Adar wielded with consummate skill in his quest to amass power as Adderash the Snake.

Welbley found these feelings unnerving. And frightening.

For the first time, he began to wonder by whose will he served Sathiis. His own, or...

Adar Ashan (*Dominion, Plant, Void*) settled back in his armchair, elbows on padded armrests and slender fingers laced before his chin.

"My arrival concerns you, Welbley," he said.

His voice slid over Welbley's ears like cool satin against freshly shaved skin.

"I have come unannounced, at a time when you cannot afford distractions."

Welbley smiled as best he could. He knew his discomfiture was obvious but tried to sound sincere.

"Your arrival is not a distraction, Master," he replied. "I am honored by your coming. It must be a matter of great importance to bring you so far from the Court of Coils."

A long second passed.

Stretched to two.

Three.

"You are correct, Welbley," Adar said at last. "For the most part."

He leaned to his right and took a slice of fruit from a nearby silver tray. Firelight glistened off the slim green wedge.

"Before I tell you what brought me to Evereve," he continued, "there are other matters we must discuss."

"Lord?"

"Our elfin laef, Welbley," Adar said. "Has it been discovered?"

"Six days ago, Lord," Welbley answered. "One of our agents in House Moramu arranged for their forward myriadi to discover the main camp of the Blood Tree Tribe. Both sides suffered heavy casualties, but the gobli were routed, and four small chests of elfin laef were found in the ehtman's lodge. As directed, Balistrahd used the discovery to mandate inspection of all shipments to and from the Elfin Republics, further impeding trade and adding to Wirith's economic woes."

"Can the laef be traced to us?"

"No."

Adderash took a small bite of the fruit he held, chewed it twice, and swallowed.

"Now is a most dangerous time, Welbley. All the pieces are on the table. The risk now is that someone might put the puzzle together before we have it locked in place. Our enemies are crafty. And they are cautious, as we must be. Cautious. And patient."

He paused, nodded to himself. "Delay our acquisition of Wirith by one month."

"Lord?" Welbley blurted. "Is that wise?"

"Do you question me?" Adar demanded softly.

"N-no, Lord," Welbley fumbled. "Of course not. It's just—it's just that—"

"What?"

Welbley chose his words carefully.

"Wirith is in upheaval, Lord," he explained. "Many affluent Families have dismantled their Houses and are preparing to abandon the realm. Evereve prohibits their migration southward, and the Gobli Horde blocks the Aenin. But these Families hold money for bribes, and the sea remains open. Until Balistrahd can form a blockade, they can escape."

"Are there enough to warrant concern?"

Welbley nodded. "If we delay a month, we should expect revenue loss between twelve and twenty percent. That's a total estimate, of course, considering the ancillary effects of House departure: lost employment, failed debts, inability to procure resources, what have you."

Adderash toyed with another piece of fruit.

"Of the Uli pirates under our sway, which Families are most feared?"

Blaythe cocked his head. "Hmm… Anjitsi… and Leymati. Houses Anjitsi and Leymati."

"Instruct those Houses to attack the two strongest seaports between Wirith and Tinagel Point. Completely obliterate them, as well as any nearby villages and hamlets. Spare no living creature. Butcher the elderly and infirm, rape and slaughter the women and children. As horribly as possible. Word will travel quickly to Wirith. That should dissuade the Houses Mercantile from emigrating and assuage the Uli pirates' thirst for plunder."

Blaythe bowed his head deferentially. "As you command, Lord."

Adderash ate the fruit and wiped juice from his fingertips with a white cloth. He took up his cup and looked at Welbley over its rim.

"Now, what is your projection?"

Blaythe muttered to himself under his breath, performed a few mental calculations.

"If they destroy Nibene and Black Bay…"

He licked his lips, reached for his drink, sipped it.

"Ten to fifteen percent," he announced.

Then he shrugged his shoulders apologetically, adding: "I know it's not much of a reduction, but I'm being conservative. Even if the Houses don't flee, most of them will have already dismantled their concerns before word reaches them of the raids. They'll still be in Wirith, but they won't contribute to the realm's wealth in the short term."

Adderash set his cup lightly on the table. He showed no outward sign of approval or displeasure.

"Would the realm remain viable with a fifteen percent loss?" he asked.

Welbley nodded. "It will be very weak, but it will not collapse. The more important and influential Houses Mercantile will remain intact; Balistrahd will support them with the funds we supply. With those Houses, Wirith should recover quickly enough once we reestablish trade."

"You did not mention House Harnath," Adar noted.

Welbley shook his head. "My apologies, Lord. House Harnath was strongly allied with the Church of Wargrum, and the threat of Elem agents operating within the House was too great. We were forced to implicate Harnath in a conspiracy against the House Royal. Balistrahd moved against Harnath two days ago. Harnath was crushed."

"That is unfortunate."

"Yes, Lord," Welbley agreed meekly. "Very. However, we were able to reroute the disbursements intended for Harnath to two Lesser Houses Mercantile: Kembari and Uthuk. When we reestablish trade, they will step in and take over Harnath's markets."

"Only two?"

"The price of maintaining our anonymity is very high. We have since managed to enslave key members of both Houses."

Adar nodded. It distressed him to lose Harnath, but Welbley had done well to secure Kembari and Uthuk. Kembari stood poised to make a play for Great House status once they secured a few more lines of trade. Claiming lines from House Harnath would accelerate their rise. Uthuk was weaker and less organized but could serve as a liaison between the Black Church and Wirith's Houses Assassin when they began to grow unruly.

That raised another question.

The Houses Assassin.

"Have Ularhi and Tedico given us any cause for worry?"

"Not as yet, Lord," Welbley replied. "Nor do I expect them to. They're parasites, feeding on the carrion of the Houses Mercantile. They plot and scheme and spy on each other… they kill off a few merchants here, a few agents there… a touch of graft, a bit of extortion… but in the end, nothing of real consequence. With Wirith's economy in shambles, there's not enough money available to take major risks. The Great

Houses Assassin will only become dangerous once they're certain that Wirith can support their ambitions."

"And the Lesser Houses?" Adar asked. "Surely now is the time for them to take risks."

"Negligible," Welbley said. "The Lesser Houses can't enter aggressions without dragging their allied Houses into the fray, and the last thing those Houses want right now is to throw their resources into an assassin's conflict. They'll wait until the winds settle before lighting any fires."

Adar leaned back in his chair and pouted. For the most part, he agreed with Welbley's assessment, and the points of contention were not worth discussing at the moment. He would address those later—personally.

CHAPTER 57

REFLECTIONS

Prince Melkor Kythidûhr leaned against the curved rail of his balcony and looked on his city with bloodshot eyes. Dûhr lay somber and silent below him. Like a graveyard. The only signs of vitality were intermittent flickers of light that now and again managed to pierce the darkness and remind the prince how few people could still afford to burn oil. Some Great Houses. A guildhall. Maybe a church. Dûhr's quality of life had deteriorated greatly since the levy of the tax and curfew.

If the stricture of trade across the Aenin was a wound to Melkor's sovereignty, the edict Blaythe had forced upon him was an infection that festered in it.

The legislation had been designed to weaken the Churches of Elem, but its repercussions had swiftly spread throughout the whole of the city. Taverns and inns suffocated under the curfew. Marketplaces, shops, and studios shut down before the daylight failed, fearful of the gangs and indigents that roamed the streets after dark. Day laborers quit early to avoid the highwaymen that prowled the forests and country roads. Each acted for their own welfare, and the combined effects of their actions worsened matters for everyone: reduced trade and shortened hours decreased production of goods; decreased availability drove up prices; higher prices stifled commerce; stifled commerce decreased orders for materials and labor; decreased orders reduced wages and eliminated jobs. In their attempt to avoid robbers, they made burglary more appealing.

The prince took a slow, deep breath.

He'd had such glorious dreams for his realm, even before Calista fanned the fires of his greater self. There were so many wide-ranging programs he'd still to launch, from moderniz-ing the city's irrigation and sanitation systems, to reforming Dûhrani labor and vice laws, to dismantling long-established mechanisms of institutionalized corruption.

"No more shall any in the Realms Humani speak of Dûhr in words of thievery, witchery, and corruption," he'd proclaimed when he ascended the throne. "We will breathe new life into the dreams of my father and aspire to the highest peaks of merit and propriety."

No one could deny Melkor's sincerity. Through the first three years of his rule, he never flagged from his vision and always pressed for truth, respect, and nobility in all things. Many of his reforms met resistance from the Houses—Mercenary, Mercantile, and Assassin. Even so, he managed to modestly advance his ambitious agenda during the early years of his incumbency, aided in no small measure by the shrewd insights of his wizard royal, Mordavo Morvaine.

Then he met Calista.

Melkor's whole world changed when he met Calista Delu-ras, and he found within himself new strength and renewed determination. As their love blossomed, he felt driven to further his reforms, push himself harder to accomplish the noblest of his father's goals. So great was his confidence, so strong were his convictions, that he began to empower others by his mere presence. Like a living magnet, he began to attract good, fair, and just people from all corners of his realm and draw out their greater selves.

Those times were gone.

The prince looked out over his city. It was a vast and beautiful hodgepodge of ancient buildings and modern structures enlivened by a diverse array of artists and crafters, builders and soldiers, servants and merchants. Dreamers and schemers. And ordinary hopeful people living out ordinary hopeful lives.

He let out a long sigh.

How did it come to this?

Over the last months, Melkor had lost everything—his sway over the Great Houses, his control over his dealings with the Black Church, his future with his beloved Calista, and, most painful of all, his self-respect. Instead of raising Dûhr as a pinnacle of wonder, he'd brought it to the brink of ruin. Now, he could only watch as Blaythe continued to tighten his hold over the realm.

Where did it all go wrong?

Melkor had asked himself that time and time again over the last months as he kept his nightly vigil over the city. In his sleepless hours between midnight and dawn, he replayed the events that had brought him to this point—and how a single decision had so radically altered the trajectory of his life and his city. He wondered how different things might be had he refused the Sathiian's request to erect a temple in the Gardens of Twilight.

"What's one more church in a sea of churches?" Selene argued. *"The others will certainly keep the Sathiians in line. And the Black Church's own taxes will help finance the very reforms that will eventually drive them from the realm."*

But the Sathiians were crafty, and in the end, it was Melkor who fell.

From prince to pawn in less than a year.

He'd been a fool to underestimate Blaythe, and the seeds of his destruction were sown the day he accepted the first Sathiian emissary. Noble Houses always fell when they bound themselves to the wicked. That was well known—and easily forgotten.

Melkor rubbed his eyes. Clenching his teeth to suppress a yawn, he tensed the muscles in his shoulders and neck to drive back his fatigue. It was a futile attempt; the fatigue was unnatural and would not be relieved by natural means. The attempt satisfied him nonetheless, as it reminded him how long he'd been free from Blaythe's potion.

What is it now? Two weeks? Three?

No, only two… this time.

It was getting harder to remain away from the potion and more difficult to maintain coherence as its effects ebbed. Yet each moment he held the purple sleep at bay was a victory in Melkor's eyes—a hollow victory, to be sure, but a victory all the same.

He tightened his grip on the rail.

Cali. Oh, Cali! If only you were here…

Long before she finally left, Calista had grown steadily colder to him. As the Sathiian drug claimed more of his soul, the heat of her passion dwindled and, finally, died. Through it all, Melkor knew that he could undo the slow decay of her love by confiding in her the cause of his ruin. She would try to save him and, in so doing, would bring upon herself the same addiction that consumed him. So he kept his silence.

In the end, it was because of his love for her that Melkor let Calista's love wither. The process was no less painful for that knowledge.

Oh, Cali… my love… if only I could have told you.

CHAPTER 58

A TIGHTENING OF COILS

Adar and Welbley discussed Wirith for a long time. They spoke of troop placements, agent deployments, and potential resistance they might encounter once Balistrahd's government collapsed. Eventually, their discussion turned to the Church of Wargrum.

"I've enjoined Arcturi Lacosia to deal with the Wargrumites," Adar said.

"Lacosia?" Welbley looked startled.

"This surprises you?"

Welbley squirmed uneasily.

"You may speak freely," Adar said.

"Lacosia has failed against Aerkon in the past," Welbley said hesitantly. "More than once. Why give him yet another opportunity to fail?"

Adar smiled coldly.

Because Lacosia has served his purpose.

"Because there is no downside. If Lacosia succeeds, then our enemy is eliminated. We gain our objective, and Lacosia's loyalty is strengthened because we tasked him with an important mission that afforded both the opportunity for vengeance and the chance to prove his worth. If he fails, Aerkon will still suffer heavy losses. As a lord priest of the Elem, Aerkon's first duty is to his congregation. After Lacosia's attack, Aerkon will lack the resources to both fulfill his responsibilities to his followers and block our move against Balistrahd. He will forgo the latter for the good of his flock. Either way, he will pose no threat to our plans."

"When will Lacosia move against Aerkon?" Welbley asked.

"Three days."

"He will not have an easy task."

"Perhaps," Adar said, unconcerned. "Still, it will be made easier by the adepts and scrolls I've given him."

"Scrolls, Lord?"

"Two Scrolls of Skeleo."

"*Two?*" Welbley looked astonished.

"Two."

Welbley blew out a deep breath and slowly shook his head. "Even so," he said, "Aerkon is crafty. He will have dark magicks and trickery ready. I doubt that Lacosia will find easy prey, despite the things he will command… and their shrieks."

Adar shrugged. "Either way, the Wargrumite threat will be eliminated in Wirith."

And Lacosia as well, with any luck.

"My lord?"

"Yes?"

"With Lacosia gone, who defends our temple in Dûhr?"

"Myrissa Dorumo. She is now high priest of Sathiis in Dûhr. She will oversee our temple's construction until your arrival."

Welbley raised an eyebrow, then bowed his head. "I understand."

Yes, I think you do.

Adar rose and walked to the fireplace, placed his hands on the mantel and smiled at himself in the mirror that hung there.

"Now is the time to bring the pieces together, Welbley," he said softly. "And for that, we need Dûhr."

Welbley shifted uncomfortably in his seat, elation flipping to dread.

"We… ahh… hit a snag, Lord," Welbley said cautiously, tapping his fingers nervously on the arm of his chair.

Adar's smile faded. "A *snag?*"

"Ahh… well…" Welbley sputtered. "It was the increase in lotos distillate. Selene has been able to smuggle in the small amount needed to gain and maintain control of the prince and our other initial targets, but not the larger volume needed to support our greater Dûhrani agenda. We needed another way to get additional quantities from Wirith to Dûhr."

Adar's eyes sharpened, but he said nothing.

Welbley took a deep breath to steady himself and wet his lips nervously before continuing.

"The land routes across the Aenin are not viable: the safe arrival of our shipments would be highly suspect, given gobli raids. The same with air transport; people would speculate on what cargo could justify the expense of a windrider. That kind of speculation would attract as many questions as thieves. Magickal transport was impractical. Deploying the required number of adepts would diminish our forces in Wirith, and a string of teleportive fields from here to Dûhr would not go unnoticed. Our best course was to ship our assets along the Fwaer and secure a covenant with a House Assassin to assure their safe delivery."

Adar frowned but nodded.

"I dislike involving assassins in our affairs. Still, you were right to use the Fwaer. Go on."

Welbley paused. He felt sweat begin to bead along his upper lip.

"Ten days before we were to meet with Kentu Hotath, Arwynn Blackhand launched a surprise attack against his House. Within four days, House Hotath fell, and House Blackhand seized control of their assets. Including Westgate."

"Unfortunate. How did you proceed?"

"When it was clear that Blackhand was unaware of our dealings with Hotath, and that his newfound authority over Westgate would stand unchallenged, I sent an emissary to meet with him. That alone took several weeks to set up—the assassins of Dûhr are very cautious, especially after a House war. But the delay was to our advantage. It allowed us to recruit several independent spies prior to meeting with Blackhand, one of whom had contacts within his House. He provided us with valuable information regarding Blackhand's operations, lieutenants, and the deployment of his sulari."

"He sounds like an exceptional spy."

"He was, Lord."

"Was?"

"He grew greedy. Unmanageable. It became necessary to dissolve our association."

"I see. What has become of him?"

"He is well into the Green."

"Ahh," Adar sighed. "It is always unfortunate to lose a meritorious spy, but worse to lose that spy to a competitor. Continue."

"We forged a covenant with House Blackhand," Welbley explained. "We agreed to provide them with poisons, weapons, and coin in exchange for secure transport of cargo from Westgate to the Gardens of Twilight. Once we are firmly established in Dûhr and able to assume control of House Blackhand, the payments rendered will become Church assets."

"Who negotiated the covenant?"

Welbley took a deep breath. "I used a liche."

The lord sovereign's expression quickly changed from pensive to piqued.

"A liche?"

Welbley swallowed, nodded his head.

A reproachful scowl spread over Adar's otherwise immobile features. He stepped away from the fireplace and slowly settled back into his chair, all the while keeping his eyes fixed on his lord priest.

"What were you thinking, Welbley?" Adar asked. "Surely you could not have forgotten the tehelu ceremony? The signature ritual of Dûhr's Houses Assassin? Even such liches as we employ stand naked before that infernal vision."

Welbley swallowed and replied: "That is true, Lord." His voice was subdued, deferential. "But I felt the risk acceptable."

"Explain."

"Blackhand was weak from the war with Hotath; he needed the wealth we offered and would not jeopardize a lucrative covenant. When the liche refused the tehelu, the assassin had no choice but to abandon the ritual. His suspicions were not aroused, and the liche delivered the somphora on its breath."

"That does not acquit you!" The lord sovereign glowered. "You were lucky, that is all. The assassin could have just as easily taken the drug. You were reckless."

"My apologies, Lord," Welbley said penitently. "I beg your forgiveness."

"Beya!" Adar spat. "My forgiveness is nothing. It is to your god Sathiis that you must make your petition. Your actions could have served His enemies more than Him!"

The lord sovereign said nothing more for several seconds. Slowly, the anger in his eyes dimmed and his enigmatic aplomb returned. He looked intently at Welbley.

"What is done is done," he said. "I will reflect and decide whether disciplinary action is warranted. For the moment, however, we will proceed. Tell me, Welbley, what you know of my plan from this point?"

Welbley took a moment to carefully compose his reply. He could not afford to upset his master a second time.

"My understanding," he began, "is that after the last of Wirith's Houses Mercantile are weakened, I am to provide Family Balistrahd with evidence that Dûhrani Houses Assassin were responsible for the gobli raids—that they sought to destabilize both realms, to strengthen their hold on Dûhr, expand their influence into Wirith, and that they used elfin laef and the gobli to cover their hand."

"That is correct," Adar said. "Houses Kythidûhr and Balistrahd will accept this evidence. Melkor will use it to move against the Dûhrani Houses Assassin, and Balistrahd will use it to relax restrictions and reopen trade. Our control over Family Balistrahd and select Wiri Houses Mercantile will grant us control over most of the reestablished trade. We will then pit Wirith against Dûhr... but there are preparations to be made. Tell me, other than this spy, have you any others in the final stages of lichosis?"

"Yes, Lord. Three others."

"Good. That should be sufficient."

"Sufficient, my lord?"

"For a different kind of liche."

Adar smiled and leaned closer to Welbley.

"Now, Welbley," he said softly. "I will tell you what brought me to Evereve. And you will listen very closely, for your next duties are more critical than any you've yet undertaken."

CHAPTER 59

THE ENCHANTMENT OF VITALITY

Arwynn's condition deteriorated rapidly in the days following his encounter with X'theX'lo. Without recourse, he returned to his sister's house. Kaleena was prepared. Within ten minutes of his arrival, they were in her trigram and she was reading the Wargrumite scroll.

The scroll deteriorated as Kaleena enounced its poetry. Ink slithered over her hands and up her arms as the parchment crumbled and she tethered herself to its magick.

Arwynn felt his strength, vibrancy, and alacrity return with each phrase Kaleena uttered. By the time the final stanza was spoken and its fragments fell from her fingers, he felt more energetic than he could ever remember.

It was almost intoxicating.

"Incredible." He beamed. "I feel my old self again—better, in fact!"

As he reveled in his restored vigor, out of the corner of his eye, Arwynn noticed his sister examining her hands.

"Is something wrong, Kaley?"

Kaleena looked up. "No."

"Your hands? Is that ink?"

She nodded. "From the scroll."

The witch held out her arms, revealing an intricate pattern of red-brown strokes from fingertip to elbow.

"Inkvanes," Kaleena said. "They bind me to the weave."

She looked at the remains of the Wargrumite scroll at her feet.

"The enchantment I released was a leech-weave," she explained. "The inkvanes are the conduit. It will sustain itself by drawing power from my Aethic reserves and persist until I rescind the weave or my reserves are depleted."

She looked admiringly at the back of her hand and ran a finger lightly along the russet patterns on her skin.

"They're rather beautiful, don't you think? It's a pity I can't channel, weave, or replenish my reserves without destroying them."

Kaleena looked at her brother and smiled sardonically.

"They're insidious, really," she said. "Leech-weaves, I mean. They limit you to your reserves while they drain them away."

Arwynn scowled. "So, you grow weaker the longer you maintain one."

"That's a bit naive," Kaleena said, gathering the remnants of the scroll. "Think of it as a resource management challenge."

Arwynn was pensive as he watched his sister delicately brush the parchment's ashes and remaining shriveled flakes into the scroll's case. She sealed the case and straightened.

"How long?" Arwynn asked.

"Until I deplete my reserves?"

Arwynn nodded.

"Normally, sixty days or so," Kaleena said. "But I have some unfinished business with Blaythe that could turn nasty, so plan on forty. Thirty, to be safe."

"That will suffice."

"Make sure it does," Kaleena said soberly. "You will face a crushing debt when the weave unravels."

CHAPTER 60

STATUARY

When Adderash and Zithwathn designed the organizational structure of the Church of Sathiis, they included two mechanisms to keep their foes off balance and minimize the likelihood of loose ends: the Cascade and the sage vipers. Under the assumption that their enemies might uncover one or more of their plots, they determined that several should be in process at any given time. That way, a few might succeed unnoticed among the many—or fragments of different schemes, gleaned individually, might be inaccurately assembled and lead their enemies astray while the true schemes progressed unperturbed.

To that end, the lord priests were encouraged to set new schemes in motion at irregular intervals, regardless of whether existing ones had reached fruition. They called the resultant effluence of overlapping machinations the Cascade.

It was the duty of the sage vipers to shepherd existing schemes to completion. They were the caretakers of plots in progress, moving from temple to temple as needed to maintain continuity, tie up loose ends, and provide closure. Through their efforts, the Black Church was able to maintain the Cascade.

The most notorious of the sage vipers was a humani named Arcturi Lacosia.

Of the few defeats Lacosia suffered during his career, two had been at the hands of Aerkon Kharae.

As senior adept to Zarthon Cabral, Lacosia had lost his left eye to the Wargrumite. Zarthon had deigned to replace the organ but had done so with the eye of a serpent, to serve as a constant reminder of his adept's failure. Lacosia hated that eye and kept it hidden by a black patch that he removed only on special occasions, such as the day he leaned casually against a taffrail and watched Zarthon drown.

Lacosia's second and last encounter with Aerkon came several years later, after they had both attained the rank of high priest. That engagement had cost the Sathiian his right arm, and its replacement had come from the Crimson Witch at a very high price.

Lacosia hated Aerkon almost as much as he'd hated Zarthon. That Aerkon was still alive was a stain on his prestige.

When the Blue Frog himself offered him the task of destroying Aerkon's temple, Lacosia enthusiastically accepted.

Lacosia cursed under his breath when he saw the statues. While he knew that destroying Aerkon's temple would not be an easy task, he'd hoped it would at least be a straightforward one. Aerkon appeared to have some kind of game in mind.

There were perhaps a dozen statues visible from Lacosia's vantage at the main gate, scattered haphazardly over the temple yard. Each appeared the same size and shape, though they were too distant yet to determine the exact form.

Aerkon is not given to extravagance. The statues have significance.

As they had not been present when Lacosia's adepts scouted the previous night, the old man must have ordered their creation that day or prepared them in advance and stored them in his temple. Neither situation was heartening. If manufactured that day, they must serve a purpose great enough to warrant the expenditure of Aethic power required for their creation. Retrieval from storage implied that Aerkon knew the time of their attack and would be well prepared.

Lacosia felt his lip curl into a snarl. Having been maimed in both their previous encounters, he had no choice but to investigate the mystery with care. He had learned not to underestimate Aerkon's cunning or resourcefulness.

Lacosia stepped back from the gate and returned to the nearby alley where his forces had been surreptitiously gathering for the past hour, arriving alone or in pairs at irregular intervals to avoid suspicion. He himself had arrived by way of the Underwet only a short time ago, accompanied by two cloaked and hooded companions. In all, they numbered fifteen. Six adepts were yet to arrive.

Time enough.

Lacosia signaled an adept to reconnoiter the area and scowled as he watched her slip through the unlocked gate and into the temple yard.

He hated Aerkon.

The adept returned ten long minutes later.

"There are thirteen statues on the lawn, Lord," she reported. "Each is of Aerkon crushing a snake with his heel."

"How smug," Lacosia said. "Describe them."

"They are made of white stone," the adept reported. "Masterfully crafted. All are identical except in jewelry. Each statue wears a different piece—a ring, a torque, an ear cuff. These are not sculpted but actual pieces of jewelry."

Lacosia frowned. "They could be enchanted. Wards, perhaps. Or Summoning Stones. I wouldn't put it past the old man."

He looked at the woman again.

"Did you sense any Aethic marks? Active or passive?"

The woman shook her head. "No, Lord. Your orders were—"

"I know what my orders were," he snapped.

The adept lowered her head. Lacosia turned away and looked at the statues in the distance.

What is your game, old man?

The jewelry might be enchanted. Then again, the pieces might be ordinary things meant to distract him. Aerkon was old. Aerkon was erratic. But Aerkon was clever.

Lacosia glowered as he ran his left hand lightly over the black armor of his right arm.

"Scan them," he said. "Scan them all."

CHAPTER 61

THE CABA GEHNAN

Mordavo proceeded immediately to his chambers upon his return to Castle Kythidûhr. He wore his longest, most exhausted face as he plodded the corridors to his private rooms, ignoring guards and passersby in his path. For the last three days, he'd been immersed in secret meetings with Dûhr's three greatest Houses Mercenary, seeking to strike an accord that could both protect the realm from the Gobli Threat and free it from Blaythe's political stranglehold.

Reaching his chambers, he sealed the windows and doors and whispered a few short commands to his hauhantu. The faceless iron statue creaked to life and stepped into one of the many small alcoves that lined the wizard's quarters. It passed through an illusory wall and into Mordavo's vault, a pocket of space without volume where only lifeless things could exist.

Mordavo flopped into a soft chair and closed his eyes. He took a deep breath and held it as he ran his fingers through his unkempt hair, then let out a low groan and cracked his neck. Now that he finally had a moment to relax, he began to appreciate how tired he was.

He felt drained.

Empty.

He knew much of his fatigue was attributable to his addiction, but dealing with three bickering warlords had taken a toll on his strength. Though he'd managed to secure their commitment, he worried that Melkor would be unwilling to pay the price.

Will he accept the responsibility? Will he accept the consequences?

Mordavo cracked the knuckles of his thick fingers and glowered in the low light. It had taken Princess Calista's passion to rouse him from his despondency and restore his sense of honor. He hoped that her sudden disappearance had similarly shaken Melkor, at least enough to rekindle his nobility. Without an unshakable commitment to duty, the prince would never agree to what Mordavo was now forced to propose.

The hauhantu returned from the alcove with a book in its rough hands. It was an old book, older than the memories of any magickan, sheathed in the ragged remains of a wyrm-hide cover and bound with strips of pitted metal. No title spoke to its contents. No symbol hinted at its origin.

Mordavo took the book and laid it delicately on his lap with unsteady hands. It was unnaturally heavy and cold to the touch.

How long has it been since any have turned to your power, Caba Gehnan? How many centuries since circumstances have been so dire that even a fool sought your counsel?

Mordavo steeled himself. He took a deep breath, set his jaw, and squared his shoulders.

A fool like me.

Gingerly, he opened the book.

CHAPTER 62

BONE AGAINST STONE

The jewelry Aerkon had placed on his statues proved nothing more than cheap trinkets, apparently intended to hinder Lacosia and slow the Sathiian advance. Still, the sage viper smiled when they finally reached the steps of Aerkon's temple.

The temple doors were twenty feet tall and half as wide, forged of solid iron and free of cracks, pits, and rust. Lacosia ran his hand over them. They felt as smooth as wet glass. His smile widened.

They might as well be made of paper.

He turned to his company and called, "Keleko skeleos!"

The two cloaked and hooded figures that had accompanied Lacosia to the rendezvous stepped forward. Their heads were bowed so their cowls covered their faces, and their arms were tucked into opposing sleeves, concealing their hands. Their long robes obscured their feet and dragged along the ground behind them as they slowly approached.

Lacosia pointed at the doors.

"Dokono Ke!" he commanded and stepped aside.

The figures stepped forward and straightened to their full height of eight feet as each placed a hand upon the doors. As their sleeves fell away, naught but clean bone emerged from their robes, white and perfect and shining. Faint glimmers of yellow and red light played about the bones of their hands and arms, like motes of twilight chasing each other. When their hands fell upon the temple doors, they pushed their fingers into the iron like knives into ripe fruit. Then, with no sound other than the groan of bending metal, they peeled the doors away.

A statue stood to greet them.

Aerkon.

The lord priest was sculpted smiling and wagging a crooked finger.

Lacosia snarled. He walked up to the statue and pushed it over. It shattered into pieces.

Hollow.

The snarl twisted into a tight smile, and he stepped into the temple followed by the two skeleos. With barely a shudder between them, the adepts fell into step behind their master and his angels.

Aerkon's temple was filled with statues. At first sparsely placed, they grew more numerous as Lacosia's force advanced deeper into the temple. All were likenesses of Aerkon, and like those in the garden, each wore a single piece of jewelry. Fearing traps, Lacosia ordered his adepts to take care not to upset the statues and to scan each piece of jewelry. He would be damned if he would let the old man take another body part from him. There would be time enough for the statues after they had destroyed Wargrum's altar.

By the time the Sathiian force reached the ebreth, the stone figures had grown into a thicket that filled every open space. Lacosia directed his adepts to carefully move aside statues that blocked the gilded metal doors, then commanded the skeleos to open them. As they had done at the temple's entrance, the creatures effortlessly peeled away the metal. Lacosia ordered the skeleos across the threshold so they might trigger any wards. When they stood safely beyond the portal's plane, Lacosia stepped into the chamber. The Sathiian adepts followed him in. Cautiously at first, then more boldly as the stillness and the silence remained unbroken.

The heart of Aerkon's temple was a huge octagonal room of basanite and marble, easily a hundred feet along the eight diagonals that spread from its center altar. The walls were over seventy feet wide and rose straight to a domed and coffered ceiling. Great slabs of rock, as thick as a man's height, jutted from the north, south, and east walls, supported ten feet above the polished marble floor by thick pillars of white stone. Each rock slab extended some forty feet from its base wall toward the altar at the center of the room, like portions of octagons striving to meet.

The center of the chamber held a simple octagonal altar of bare stone, raised waist high on eight squat pillars. Fires in simple metal bowls laced the air with incense and set shadows dancing.

Atop the rock overhangs, two massive stone hauhantu slowly became aware of the presence of living things.

The hauhantu attacked without warning.

They dropped from above like boulders, hitting the floor with a deafening, reverberating thud.

Each was twice the size of a man, a single massive chunk of basalt crudely cut into humani form. Their eyes glowed with red fire, and torrents of steam poured from their mouths and nostrils.

One landed squarely on the shoulder of an adept, tearing away their arm and upper rib cage before they realized they'd been struck. It reached out, took the stunned adept's face in one great hand, and effortlessly tore off their head.

The other hit the floor directly before Lacosia.

With blinding speed, a massive open hand shot toward Lacosia's face—

—and was caught by a hand of bone.

As preternaturally fast as the hauhantu were, Lacosia's skeleos were faster.

The skeleo took hold of the hauhantu's arm and forced it clear of its master's face. Though it could divert the blow, the skeleo could not negate the force behind the attack. An unearthly creak sounded through the chamber as a crack appeared on the skeleo's arm.

Then another.

Then another.

The eerie glimmers of yellow and red that flitted about the skeletal arm grew brighter, and an oily fluid began to ooze from the cracks.

Lacosia stumbled backward, overwhelmed by the speed of the hauhantu's attack, and lost control of his unliving servants as he scrambled away. He watched in horror as the stone monster struck at the skeleo's head with its free hand, which was also intercepted. The unnatural creaking grew louder, and cracks began to appear on that arm as well.

The second skeleo leaped upon the held hauhantu with a spine-chilling shriek. It began to tear out large pieces from the hauhantu's midsection, as though it were made of clay. Cracks began to spread across the hauhantu's torso, bright red against the black rock of its body.

Without his will to bind them, the skeleos attacked their nearest target, impossibly fast, and with every weapon at their disposal, including horrifying shrieks that shattered the resolve of living things.

Lacosia's adepts fell to panic. Some froze; others dropped to the ground trembling and babbling; some tried to flee. The unfettered hauhantu attacked randomly as it waded through the terrified adepts, caving in heads and tearing off limbs. Within the span of a dozen racing heartbeats, brains and skull fragments littered the area and arterial spray painted the smooth stone.

As the skeleos' summoner, Lacosia was not driven to panic. He moved away from the slaughter in disbelief, his ambitions crashing with the decimation of his forces.

It can't end like this!

He couldn't let it. He couldn't suffer another defeat at the hands of Aerkon Kharae—especially when the old man didn't even mete out his victory in person!

I would rather face the things in the Rift than—

Another horrifying shriek ripped through the chamber.

Priests howled with madness as their lives were blotted out.

—The Rift!

Skeletal arms shattered and spilled nightmarish jelly onto the cold floor.

Steam and magma blasted forth from the belly of a ruined hauhantu.

The things in the Rift could obliterate this temple!

Lacosia grinned. He could tear a hole deep enough if he used a channelweave. He began to mutter and draw shapes in the air. Violet fire ignited behind his eye patch and in his unarmored hand.

The adepts nearest the doors knocked over two of Aerkon's statues as they fled. The statues exploded. Shards of chiseled stone whizzed through the chamber like spinning knives, slicing through Sathiian flesh. Some were large enough to penetrate other statues, causing them to explode as well. A chain reaction started statues exploding in sequence, sending sharp fragments of stone through the air on gouts of green mist.

Aerkon had prepared well. He and his adepts were not secreted among the statues; it was clusters of sharp rock and compressed pockets of poison gas.

Erotic pleasure blossomed in Lacosia's belly and loins as he let the raw energy of the Aethios pour into him, then swelled into delight as he began to shape its threads into an elaborate pattern as they flowed through him. His delight intensified into unfiltered joy as he completed his pattern, and erupted into ecstasy when he started to rip reality—

A whirling chunk of rock struck Lacosia in the back as he spun the last of the pattern's threads. He cried out in pain and surprise, and lost control of his channel as the air before him split asunder to reveal a ghastly nightmare.

The vortex formed a split second later.

In the wrong direction.

CHAPTER 63

ONE TRUTHFUL LIE

Arwynn sat on the hearth in the center of his conference chamber, absently stroking a seam in the mortar as he thought about his encounter with X'theX'lo.

"Even as we speak, Lindrowe plots against you."

He'd initially refused to believe it. The daemon's aspect had grown so hideously corrupted when it implicated Lindrowe that it was most certainly lying.

But Kaleena was not so sure. She reminded him that the daemon knew that he knew it would lie, and that knowledge obviated its need to lie at all. X'theX'lo could sow discord as easily by lying as by speaking the truth and letting Arwynn believe it was lying.

Arwynn's pragmatism prevailed. The prudent choice was to retire Lindrowe.

If the daemon was lying, he would lose a poisonmaster and a strategist.

Unfortunate, but acceptable.

If the daemon was telling the truth, he would save his House.

Arwynn stood, clasped his hands behind his back, and began to pace, head low and shoulders loose.

An idea began to form.

CHAPTER 64

THE CRUCIX

Mordavo nodded to Melkor as he stepped onto the prince's balcony. He muttered under his breath as he lowered his barrel-chested body into an ornate wooden rocker. The wizard's words lingered in the air slightly longer than they tarried on his lips, like echoes that did not repeat, then slowly faded into the night air as his weave tightened. For the next several minutes, neither Mordavo's nor Melkor's voice would carry farther than the other's ear.

Melkor moved from the balcony rail to sit next to Mordavo. He knew the effects of the wizard's spell and didn't see the need to test it.

Melkor was more anxious than he'd been in many nights, from both lack of sleep and his anticipation of Mordavo's report. The three greatest Houses Mercenary in Dûhr stood to gain the most if his gambit succeeded. They also stood to lose the most if it failed.

"Well?" the prince asked. "What did they say?"

"All three agreed," the wizard replied.

Melkor fell back into his chair and closed his eyes with a sigh.

"There are, of course, conditions," Mordavo added.

Melkor opened his eyes. "Conditions?"

"Yes. First, no House will commit more myriadi than the House Royal commits."

The prince frowned but nodded assent. "Acceptable. The second?"

"You must personally lead the offensive."

"W-what?" Melkor sputtered. "Me? They can't be serious!"

Mordavo looked soberly at the prince. "Without your word that you will personally lead the army, the Great Houses will not commit their myriadi."

Melkor shook his head, patted his hands nervously on the arms of his chair.

"No. No, no, no," he murmured. "That… that's *not* acceptable. I-I'm in no condition to lead an army in a parade, let alone a battle! And against the Gobli Horde? No, no, no, no. There must be another way, Wizard. W-what about Dehrahk? She could lead them. Or K'jarmund—yes, yes—K'jarmund would be excellent!"

The wizard shook his head.

The prince moaned.

"There is no other way, Melkor," Mordavo said bluntly. "Your disbursement of money and weapons to the Houses Mercantile has enabled Dûhr to survive. Because the people believe that you drew on your personal treasury, they admire you and don't doubt your dedication to the Houses Mercantile. But the Houses Mercenary feel short shrift. The coins they receive from your new tax are swiftly spent to obtain the very weapons you freely gave to the Houses Mercantile."

"That was Blaythe's doing!" Melkor protested. "He was supposed to provide money, not weapons—certainly not dwarfin weapons! He knew I'd have to sell the lot to make up the shortfall, and that I'd have to turn to the Houses Mercantile to get the best price."

"That is immaterial," Mordavo said. "Things are as they are. As it stands, the three greatest Houses Mercenary see merit in your plan but will not bind myriadi without an unequivocal commitment. You are that commitment. You must ride at the head of the army that marches against the Horde."

Melkor slowly rose and drifted back to the balcony rail. He stared at the dark city below for a long time.

He knew that Mordavo spoke the truth and could see why the Great Houses would make such a demand. But… lead an army? He couldn't sleep without Blaythe's drug, and without sleep he could not function. Worse, what if he needed to take the potion on the march? The purple sleep lasted several days—what if the battle joined when he was asleep? It was ridiculous. He could not lead an army to war.

"I had such dreams," the prince said at last. His voice was low.

Hopeless.

"Such wonderful, beautiful dreams. For Dûhr. For my life. My Family. But no more. I now have only memories. Memories of dreams too painful to remember…"

He turned to face the wizard, smiled weakly like a man resigned to death.

"I'm sorry. I can't do it."

Mordavo knew that the prince could no more lead an army against the Gobli Horde than sleep of his own accord. They were both shadows of their former selves, slaves to the Sathiian narcotic.

The Crucix could give Melkor the power to turn the tables on the Black Church and free Dûhr from its coils, but the price was... so high.

Mordavo closed his eyes.

Do I have the right to even suggest it?

He thought of Wirith, already fallen. He thought of Dûhr, falling. He thought of Calista. Of Ufwin. Of Khâlir.

Do I have the right not *to?*

He opened his eyes. The prince was hunched over the balcony rail, sobbing. Mordavo could feel his despondency. It was no greater than his own.

If Melkor refused the Crucix, they would both bear witness to the fall of Dûhr with the knowledge that he willfully rejected an opportunity to save the realm. But if he accepted what Mordavo proposed... only Sheeshee knew the consequences of that choice.

Mordavo took a deep breath and let it out slowly.

"There is a way, my prince."

Melkor's back stiffened. He wiped his eyes and composed himself.

"To do what?"

"To lead the army."

Mordavo patted the chair beside him. "Please, sit."

Melkor watched the wizard intently as he returned to his seat.

"How?"

"The Crucix," Mordavo said.

A spark of hope flickered in Melkor's eyes. For a moment, Mordavo regretted speaking.

What must be done must be done.

"It is old magick, my prince," Mordavo whispered. "Older than you can imagine. And dark and wretched… and shunned."

"Tell me," Melkor said.

Mordavo closed his eyes and drew another deep breath, released it slowly.

"The Caba Gehnan describes a way to remove a soul," he said, "and place it in an enchanted jewel called a Crucix. While one's soul is held in the Crucix, their spirit and mind are freed from physical constraints. Their body becomes nothing more than an instrument, a tool…"

"… but?"

"It's irreversible."

Uneasiness crept over Melkor's face.

"If the subject is healthy and willing," the wizard continued soberly, "and the process is carefully executed, the body can be sustained indefinitely—until it is destroyed or it eventually enters a mummified state. Once a person's spirit and intellect are locked within a Crucix, their body becomes the puppet of whoever holds the jewel. Those who hold their own Crucix possess all their mental faculties, free will, and control over their physical bodies until they choose to destroy the gem and end their existence. Provided the flesh is maintained, of course. If the soul is torn away abruptly or the flesh is weak, the consequences can be... grisly."

Melkor's uneasy mien turned grim. "Are you proposing to place my spirit within such a device?"

"Yes."

"Why would I willingly submit to such a hideous end?"

"For Dûhr." Mordavo spoke plainly. "It would be the ultimate sacrifice for Family and realm.

"Without the limitations of your physical body, without the need for food or drink, sleep or drug, you would be free to lead the Myriadi Royal and the myriadi of the Great Houses Mercenary against the Gobli Horde. You would be able to reclaim the pride and honor stolen from your Family and your people.

"And you would have vengeance upon Welbley Blaythe."

CHAPTER 65

EXPULSION

Lindrowe felt that something was wrong the moment he stepped into the anteroom of his master's conference chamber, though he couldn't put his finger on what it was.

A smell, perhaps? Something odd with the light?

He paused a moment and—

Whack!

—staggered sideways from a blow to his right cheek. Purple blood spurted on the wall and the floor, though some splatter seemed to hang in the air.

Stunned, the poisonmaster reflexively heaved his great bulk in the direction of the attack and flexed his chest. Tiny darts streaked from hidden housings beneath his raiment and buried themselves in the stone wall and… something he could not see.

Whack!

A second blow struck him full in the face, flattening his nose in a purple spray. His legs quivered and gave way, and he fell to the ground.

Arwynn casually deactivated his invisible hauhantu. Floating spatter moved aside.

The master stepped to where Lindrowe lay unconscious, careful to avoid his poisonous blood. Behind him, in the conference room, a hidden door slid open. Malaraphi, Morkainen, and Ciridan entered the room, followed by Mad'rhaq and two mir.

"You saw?" the master asked without turning.

"Yes," the magikka said.

"I did not lie."

"You did not lie."

"Aru ke," Arwynn said, pointing to Lindrowe's limp form. He turned to lead the others into the room.

The invisible hauhantu swept up Lindrowe and carried him to a section of the chamber's north wall. The skeletal wall sconces dropped their torches and took hold of him. Dark blood dripped from his body, pooling on the floor.

Arwynn eyed Mad'rhaq as the mir joined them at his conference table. Mad'rhaq returned the master's stare, itself immobile and impassive. The mir could be unnervingly still when it suited them.

"Lindrowe has betrayed us both, Mad'rhaq," Arwynn said, gesturing for them to be seated.

"In my name, he secured your aid to capture a Sathiian barge. His words were lies. We neither sought nor sanctioned such action. His ruse was meant to avert your suspicion so that he might blight your clan with a plague for which he alone held the cure. I believe he sought to turn your people against mine. No doubt he hoped to sway one of my lieutenants—"

He nodded to Malaraphi and Morkainen.

"—to join his treachery and usurp my House."

"Your words are pretty, Arwynn Black House," Mad'rhaq said.

It coiled its body before the table, flanked by its two underlings.

"Why should I believe them? You gave me a vial of plague. For that, I have come as you requested. But what have I seen? You have beaten your creature. What have I heard? Words that sway, but do not convince."

Then it smiled.

"Am I so old that the words of an assassin are more valuable than the air upon which they ride?"

Arwynn was unperturbed. He knew the mir to be shrewd and skeptical creatures.

He extended his hand to the woman now seated at his left and said: "Ciridan. The vial."

Ciridan Lothloran drew a slim vial of cloudy blue fluid from her clothing and handed it to her master.

Arwynn looked at the liquid a moment, then smiled.

"This," he said, offering the vial to Mad'rhaq, "is the cure for the plague. With the two, you can eliminate your enemies and bring glory to C'thqui."

He handed the vial to the magikka. "A gift."

Mad'rhaq looked at the vial in its hand, then at Arwynn. There was no word for *gift* in the mir tongue, nor any notion of acquiring something without payment.

"Why do you do this?" Mad'rhaq asked. "Why give something so valuable?"

"A token of good faith," Arwynn replied. "With the plague and its cure, you can control Lake Zemi and the River Fwaer, perhaps even extend your influence over the River Coth. I will aid you in your expansion, in exchange for a pledge of cooperation and your aid against the Black Church."

"What are the terms of this pledge?"

"Your clan and my House will inform each other of dangers we discover that threaten us, and when possible, lend aid to counter those dangers. My loremaster will accept some of your magikkas to train in our magicks, and my blademaster will teach land combat to some of your warriors. Your people will train some of my sulari in water combat and poisoning and teach my Sadri your weaves of bodily regeneration. We will provide security for your land trade, and your people will protect our trade over your waters. The details can be settled later, but that is essentially what I propose."

The magikka scowled. Like all mir, it found the idea of forming close relationships with landfolk disagreeable. But the world was changing. The humani were strong and had much his people desired. And insight into humani weaving was more seductive than Mad'rhaq would admit.

Arwynn watched Mad'rhaq silently debate.

Lindrowe was correct; never deal with a mir without holding back an ace. How ironic that Lindrowe himself should now be that ace.

"It will be difficult to convince my warlord," Mad'rhaq said.

"Your warlord C'thqui already knows of the plague?" Arwynn asked.

"Yes."

"You will discuss with your warlord how to use the plague and its cure when you return."

"Yes."

"That discussion will lead to one of two outcomes: either Clan C'thqui will set out to conquer its enemies, or it will not. As a further show of good faith, I will give you something that will hold value regardless of the decision." The master paused momentarily. "I will give you Lindrowe."

"Lindrowe?" Mad'rhaq's eyes widened; its posture stiffened. "The Poison Lie? What value has he to us?"

"He is a traitor and of no use to me," Arwynn said bluntly. "To you, he is the personification of the plague. You could rally the mir for his public execution. The plague threatened all mir in Zemi—all the clans would owe a debt of gratitude to your warlord for preventing it and bringing him justice. Or you could unleash the plague on the lake. After sufficient suffering has accrued, you could stage Lindrowe's execution by your warlord's hand and distribute the antidote freely. Your warlord will be a hero to all the clans."

The magikka was silent for some time. Then it looked at Arwynn with narrowed eyes.

"There is merit in what you say, Arwynn Black House. I will take Lindrowe. I will convince my warlord to accept your offer."

"He is yours."

Mad'rhaq nodded and moved from the table. Arwynn stood and bade the others rise. The magikka gave a curt command to its companions. They bowed their heads and slithered to where Lindrowe hung on the wall. The skeletal hands released the poisonmaster at Arwynn's order, and he fell to the floor with a deep thud and a heavy bounce.

"Be warned," the master said, "his blood is poisonous."

Mad'rhaq nodded. "They are warded."

The mir stripped the former poisonmaster and cut away the mechanisms of spraydarts and springblades from his corpulent body. When he was naked, they took hold of his arms and pulled him upright. Lindrowe moaned as he was dragged toward Mad'rhaq.

"One last thing," Arwynn said to Mad'rhaq. Then, to the mir: "Hold him still and straight."

They looked to their master. The magikka eyed Arwynn for a moment, then nodded.

Arwynn approached Lindrowe, face stern and eyes hard. He reached into his tunic and removed a barbed black disk with cabalistic tracings inscribed on its sleek face. It was an Uth'q Q'wahi—a mir blood-disk. It protected its bearer from poison while it was wet with the bearer's blood.

Arwynn opened his tunic and pushed the Uth'q Q'wahi into his chest. He removed the bloodied disk and wrapped it gently in a damp cloth, which he slipped into a fold in his tunic. He extended his right hand to Morkainen. The blademaster handed him a slim curved blade scarcely the length of a man's hand and stepped back.

Arwynn sneered at Lindrowe.

Lindrowe stared back dumbly.

"You have betrayed us, Urath Lindrowe," Arwynn said. "You have damned us with your lies. Never again shall a falsehood fall from your lips."

Arwynn slapped him, hard. While Lindrowe reeled, Arwynn took firm hold of the former poisonmaster's lips and sliced them away. Blood spurted, thick and purple, spraying over Arwynn and spilling down Lindrowe's chin and neck and chest. Lindrowe screamed, sending spatters of deadly blood from his lipless mouth.

Arwynn stepped back and turned to Mad'rhaq.

"Now you may take him," he said coldly. He pointed to the chamber door with the bloody knife. "Do with him what you will."

CHAPTER 66

IN THE MOUNTAINS ICETOP

Baloth Kal Brathyr, lord of the Xûr and master of Tintaghûl Keep, stood before a tall, narrow window staring at the dark mountains beyond. He stood perfectly still, feet braced and hands clasped behind him, like a statue cut from rust-colored stone.

Baloth was a giant of a man—a humani warrior of heroic proportions with a body of chiseled brick and a soul of twisted metal. Heavy muscles coiled about his thick bones like iron serpents. His eyes were black, made blacker still by the red cast of his flesh. His hair, too, was black, with streaks of silvery gray. Long and crimped and wild, like a mane of battered wire, falling stiffly about his shoulders and upper back.

Behind Baloth, by a table in the center of the room set with food and wine, Selene Kythidûhr reclined on a cushioned divan and awaited his answer. She was dressed in a fitted gown of green chenille trimmed with gold brocade. She'd dyed her hair yellow blonde and painted her nails and lips golden orange. Her eyes were shadowed in shades of green and brown. Jewelry of emerald and sunstone completed her ensemble. The final effect was precisely as she desired: artfully seductive affability.

The princess watched Baloth calmly. What she asked of him was clearly reckless and certainly excessive, but no more so than what she offered him in return.

After a few moments staring into the darkness, Baloth spoke without turning. "What you ask is difficult, Selene."

His voice was deep. Controlled. "And dangerous."

Selene raised herself on the divan.

"It is," she replied. "But so, too, are the risks I face. I wouldn't have detoured up the Fwaer under a false identity and debased myself to that skok Rowayan if I wasn't prepared to take risks. It was disgusting—his price to open a portal to Tintaghûl."

She stretched an arm over the back of the divan and settled into its cushions, eyes fixed on Baloth.

"Still, the dangers you face are largely political," Baloth said, turning from the window to face the princess. "At worst, a few lives forfeit, a few careers ruined. A Wyrmsweep is another matter. A Wyrmsweep gone awry can destroy a realm. If the realm is destroyed, there is no value in what you offer."

Selene smiled wanly. "Surely you're being a touch melodramatic, Baloth. I doubt that a few wyrms could destroy the Realm of Dûhr. Even those such as you command. Besides, your wyrmsworn, your… your… what do you call them again?"

"Azûne."

"Yes, that's it. Your azûne are well trained and highly skilled, are they not?"

"They are."

"Then, what's the problem?"

Baloth moved to the table. He grabbed a piece of meat and tossed it into his mouth as he lowered himself into a heavy chair.

"Under normal circumstances, a few wyrms would be hard pressed to bring down the Realms of Dûhr. But circumstances are far from normal, and the timing is bad."

The curve of Selene's smile straightened slightly. Her eyes narrowed to match.

"Why, Baloth, when did you become so pensive?"

"Age brings many things, Selene. Not all of them unpleasant."

"I sincerely doubt that." Selene chuckled.

"You'd be surprised."

"Pish." The princess waved away Baloth's words. "A matter for another day. Today, I want to know what has you so thoughtful."

"Three things," Baloth said, leaning forward in his chair to count them on his fingers.

"The gobli, the Dûhrani, and winter. The Gobli Horde will move south very soon. As it does, it will destroy the northern farmlands. That's one blow to the realm."

He folded down his middle finger, leaving his thumb and forefinger extended.

"Dûhr's myriadi will organize to intercept the Horde. They will meet in the middle regions, and their confrontation will destroy most of the orchards and ranches there. That's the second blow to the realm."

He retracted his forefinger.

"Add to that a Wyrmsweep gone awry"—he drew in his thumb—"and… well…"

He looked at his closed fist a moment, then locked his dark eyes on Selene's. "Winter won't wait. Too many will starve. The realm will collapse into anarchy."

Baloth held Selene's gaze for a long moment, then reached for a goblet on the table.

"That," he said, picking it up, "is what has me so thoughtful."

Selene watched intently as he sat back in his chair. Her mind fragmented as he brought the cup to his lips, resolved into two bright mosaics as he drained it in three great gulps, and reintegrated into a seamless whole as he wiped his mouth clean with the back of his hand. By the time Baloth returned his cup to the table, her smile had returned. She knew exactly what to say to win him over.

"I'm willing to gamble," Selene said pluckily. "I'm willing to throw Xoltith's Bones and face the roll."

She smiled then, and her eyes twinkled. "To be honest, I find the whole thing delightfully irresistible."

She leaned in closer, ran her tongue over smirking lips, and whispered, "And you, Baloth—you've been cooped up in this mountain for far too long. We both know you thrive on destruction. You ache for a Wyrmsweep. And you desperately crave the reward I offer. So, tell me—what is it that *really* concerns you?"

Baloth frowned. His brow tightened and jaw tensed.

"*You* are what bothers me, Selene," he said coolly.

"Me?"

"Don't be coy," Baloth said flatly. "We both know you've been happily in league with Blaythe from the beginning. Now you want my help to bring him down. How long, I wonder, until you turn against me?"

Selene raised an eyebrow and tilted her head.

Baloth opened his hands and looked around. "Surely you don't think my agency limited to these cold mountains?"

Selene leaned back on the divan with a pout and a half-hearted shrug.

"Fine," she said indignantly. "It's true. I cast my lot with Blaythe and his Black Church. But no more. As it happens, Blaythe intends to betray me once he disposes of Melkor. So, I must orchestrate his undoing before he can arrange mine."

"You have proof of this?"

"Proof? No. Foundation? Yes." Selene smiled and tapped her temple with a slim forefinger. "I have given this matter a great deal of thought, Baloth. Of that, you can be assured."

Baloth did not trust the princess. Over the years of their association, she'd proved to be opportunistic and deceptive, and too often favored pragmatism over loyalty. Still, whatever else she might be, he could not dismiss her political genius. Nor her remarkable guile.

"Tell me," he said, "and I will draw my own conclusions."

"Fair enough," Selene agreed. "I'll start with the gobli."

"The gobli?"

Selene nodded. "What is their greatest strength?"

"Numbers."

"Exactly. The Horde possesses inferior weapons and mediocre leadership—numbers are their only real advantage.

While they are extremely hard to kill and ungodly prolific, their attacks on the Aenin settlements imply that they've reached a critical population in the Borowood. They can't expand north because of the Cursed Earth. The Sea of Uli constrains their expansion west, and east is blocked by the Mountains Icetop. Only the south remains—the Realms Humani. But, and here's where it gets interesting, the obvious threat is to Dûhr, yet the actual damage was done to Wirith. Why?"

"Maybe they want the western Aenin. It's more fertile."

"Nonsense. The gobli aren't planters. What do they care if land is good for growing things? If they wanted land, it would be to hunt, not farm. No, there's another reason the Horde moved against Wirith rather than Dûhr. The same reason that restrains the mir."

"The mir?" Baloth raised an eyebrow. "What have the mir to do with the gobli?"

"The gobli have effectively halted traffic across the Aenin, so trade between Dûhr and the western realms is restricted to the Fwaer. The mir would find the pickings clean and easy. Yet the level of piracy is suspiciously low. We must account for that, just as we must account for the Horde moving against Wirith rather than Dûhr."

"Perhaps the merchants hired better guards," Baloth suggested.

Selene shrugged. "Perhaps. Houses Mercenary have seen increased activity and patronage from several independent weaver factions. But that would only account for a few of the more powerful Houses Mercantile, a very small number of vessels compared to the total trade along the river. What of the rest?"

Baloth tore off a chunk of heavy black bread.

"Mir guards," he said, popping it into his mouth and leaning back. "Mir guards to foil mir attacks. Problem solved."

"If you can pay in steel, drugs, slaves… but silver?" Selene shook her head. "No. The mir would turn to piracy before selling off their warriors as escorts for mere silver."

"Surely that depends on the amount?"

"Merchants won't pay more to guard a cargo than it's worth. The mir would benefit more from stealing than guarding."

"Then how do you explain the lack of piracy?" Baloth asked, reaching for a pitcher of wine. "And the Horde targeting Wirith?"

"Blaythe."

Baloth chuckled. "Blaythe?"

He poured himself wine, offered some to Selene. She nodded, sliding her cup forward.

"I think you give this priest too much credit, Selene," he said, pouring.

"And I don't think you give him enough," the princess countered. "The Black Church is larger and more pervasive than even the Great Houses realize. They have operatives *everywhere*. I believe that Blaythe has persuaded the mir to moderate their piracy along the Fwaer. He wants that trade lane open. There's a high incidence of robbery, to be certain, and the Black Church has lost vessels as well—but only enough to allay suspicion."

"And how would Blaythe manage that?"

"Simple," Selene answered. "He offered the mir something they wanted but couldn't buy. A new poison, perhaps, or some secret weave. It really doesn't matter. Whatever he gave them, they're far more likely to use it against other clans than we humani."

"And the gobli?"

"The gobli are dim witted and easily manipulated." Selene picked up her cup, took a sip. "And *they* like silver," she said, tilting the cup to Baloth to emphasize his earlier point. "With enough silver to buy weapons and armor, and enough mystical chicanery to befuddle their shamans, the Sathiians could have easily duped them into becoming unwitting lackeys."

Baloth thought a moment.

"There have been reports of gobli with steel weapons," he admitted. "And they've shown uncharacteristic restraint in the upper Aenin."

He took a deep breath, let it out slowly.

"Suppose you are right about the mir and the gobli, Selene. What of it? How does any of it imply that Blaythe will betray you?"

Selene smirked. She'd contemplated many mosaics once she realized that Calista and Mordavo were working to undermine her gambit in Dûhr. In so doing, she came to understand that she was but a pawn in Blaythe's game.

"Blaythe is clever and subtle," Selene replied. "Here's what I believe. The Black Church armed the gobli and loosed them upon the Aenin. Why? First, to isolate Wirith so the Sathiians could more easily usurp control of the realm from

House Balistrahd. Second, to weaken Dûhr economically so that they could more easily gain influence.

"However, in doing so, they created a powerful force in the Gobli Horde. A force they now need to dispel. That's where Dûhr's recent buildup of the Houses Mercenary comes in. I believe Blaythe intends to call down a full-scale gobli invasion, then use Dûhr's myriadi and Wirith's forces along the River Glider to destroy them, simultaneously weakening the Houses Mercenary while appearing to save Dûhr and liberate the Aenin."

"As I've said, that path leads to famine," Baloth reminded her. "Even if Blaythe could command the Horde, what would he gain from starving a nation?"

"Popularity."

"Popularity?" Baloth laughed. "You must be joking!"

"No," Selene said flatly. "I'm quite serious. And it all comes back to the mir."

Baloth's smile froze.

Selene continued, unperturbed. "Until land trade across the Aenin can be reestablished, the Fwaer will remain the only viable western trade lane into Dûhr. With mir support, Blaythe can bring in enough food from Sathiian strongholds in Isitar and Rha to save the people from starvation. By the end of the winter, he will be the most popular man in Dûhr. I and my Family will be completely overshadowed. I will hold the throne, but he will hold the people. Thus, I am betrayed."

"So, your solution is a Wyrmsweep on the Gobli Horde," Baloth said, "to lend aid to Dûhr's myriadi and ingratiate yourself to the people."

"Exactly!" Selene said brightly. "After the battle is engaged, of course—but not too long after. I'd also like the Houses Mercenary weakened a bit; not so much as Blaythe, but enough to give me some room to maneuver. And it would be nice to have the people think that I care about them. That never hurts."

She threw Baloth an impish smile.

"We both benefit, Baloth. By recruiting your azûne against the Horde and securing sufficient provisions for the winter months to compensate for the ruined croplands—unwittingly provided by Blaythe himself, I might add—I get credit for saving Dûhr from ruin and you gain your heart's desire. After the battle, you and your azûne will be heroes and the Family Royal will have no choice but to grant you Great House status. Between your wyrms and the swarm of recruits you will doubtless enjoy, House Kal Brathyr will stand as the strongest Great House Mercenary in all the Realms of Dûhr!"

"You've thought this all out, haven't you?"

Selene smiled. "Oh, Baloth, you have no idea."

Baloth stroked his chin and pensively eyed the princess.

"Very well. I will do as you ask."

"Wonderful!" Selene chirped, clapping her hands.

"Tonight," Baloth said, pouring himself more wine and raising his cup to Selene, "we will make plans and celebrate. Tomorrow, I will have my magickai return you to Dûhr."

"An excellent agenda." Selene returned Baloth's toast, then placed her cup lightly on the table and leaned back on the divan. "But I will not be returning to Dûhr. Not right away."

"Oh?"

"I'd like your weavers to send me back to Sulbriar," she said.

"Rowayan?"

Selene smiled coldly and winked. "I think he's due for a lesson in manners."

Baloth chuckled.

"After that," she continued, "I've a few loose ends to tie up in Khâlir before going home—shipments to arrange, allies to coddle, agents to position… but first…"

Selene leaned forward, humor gone.

"First, we must talk about my brother."

CHAPTER 67

GUILT

Lord Priest Kargan Teahl sat in a plain wooden chair at a plain wooden desk and watched Arael Laran pace back and forth across his office as she recounted her experiences since leaving Aerkon's temple. She told him of the Sathiian attack in the sewers, their passage through the earth, their encounter with Sadrahehn, and their dilemma over Fedahi. Her account was clear and comprehensive, and her voice was strong and steady—until they reached Dûhr.

Arael stopped pacing and fell into one of the plain wooden chairs by Kargan's desk.

"When I saw Gabrael lying there at my feet, my hopes just… sank. I lost all feeling, all sense of attachment. I wasn't even concerned with her condition—I just assumed she was dead. And I felt… nothing. All I could think was, How am I going to get us out of these sewers?"

"Your response was natural," Kargan replied. His voice was hard and craggy despite his attempt to soften it. "Concern for the living, not disregard for the dead."

Kargan Teahl was a short man, solid and stocky, almost as wide in the shoulder as he was tall, with a broad nose, heavy brow, and a mouth as expressive as a scrape across a clay tablet. What was left of his hair was dull red and closely cropped against his head and his jaw. His hands and feet were almost disproportionately large. His eyes were amber. His flesh was dark, almost black, and testament to dwarfin blood on his father's side.

Arael gave a weak shrug with her good shoulder.

"Maybe so. In any event, Gabrael wasn't dead, which didn't help matters."

"Why not?"

"It was difficult enough to move through the sewers with Gabrael and Fedahi as guides. Without them? And lugging her unconscious body besides? There was little chance we'd survive."

"But you went on."

"Yes."

"With Gabrael."

A pause.

A tight-lipped nod of the head.

"We had to," Arael said softly. "We couldn't... I couldn't leave her behind."

"No," he agreed. "Of course you couldn't."

"I ordered Rahne to stretch a stone skin over the passageway and separate us from the rest of the sewers. Then Pendaro and I tended her wounds. I'd never seen Pendaro so stricken, so fearful. He was pale, shaking..."

She looked up, caught the lord priest's eyes.

"They'd been close a long time ago. Did you know? I'd assumed they'd had a falling out—they barely spoke two words to each other throughout our entire journey. I know better now… oh, the poor man…"

The priestess sniffled, sobbed.

Kargan waited quietly.

Arael blew a heavy breath and wiped her face with her arm.

"I don't know what I expected to see," she said. "Sucker scars? Claw marks? I don't know…"

She took another breath, regained her composure.

"She'd been stabbed in the back, just below the ribs. The blade had broken off in the wound. I couldn't understand it at first—I mean, not only had she survived a fatal blow, but the knife blade had broken off? It made no sense. Until we examined her properly. It turns out that she was wearing thin chitin armor beneath her cloaks. The armor saved her."

"Fedahi?"

Arael made a small, plaintive shrug.

"I don't know," she said, "but I think so. In any event, he either stabbed Gabrael, was himself killed by whoever wounded her, or fled when she was attacked. I didn't care at that point—all I cared about was keeping her alive. We managed to stabilize her. I… I don't know how. Rahne bound her for transport while Pendaro and I rested. Pendaro was tight lipped and stone faced when we finally set out. North, I think."

"To find an exit?"

Arael nodded. "I wanted to reach clean air as quickly as possible. I didn't care whether we were close to your temple. I just wanted to get us to safety."

"Is that when…?"

Arael nodded again.

"We must have passed over a hidden glyph. Nothing happened at first; then the whole tunnel lit up. Two lines of green light cut across the span of the passage, one in front of us, one behind. They started to sweep in toward us, stretching higher as they closed in, like walls of light growing out of the passage floor. There was nowhere to go. We were trapped between them."

"Yet you escaped."

"Rahne shouted that we should go under the barrier and dove into the water at the base of the light wall. We moved to follow, but when the water started frothing, we knew we couldn't."

She took a slow, deep breath. "What happened next is a blur. Pendaro dropped Gabrael's body and grabbed me with both arms. He… he kissed me on the forehead. It was so gentle. Then he said 'For Gab' and lifted me into the air like I was a doll. Wargrum, what strength! I remember… I remember his skin cracking… breaking apart…"

Then, the truth of it struck.

"Pendaro couldn't weave," she realized. "There wasn't time. He must have used his body as an Aethic conduit without shaping the flow! Oh Wargrum, that's how he had the strength…"

"To do what?"

"He threw me over the top of the light wall before it reached the ceiling."

"Ahh."

"His body couldn't contain the unshaped energy."

Arael wiped her eyes, sniffled again.

"I hit the ceiling… I remember that… and fell to the ground. Landed on my arm." She ran her fingers lightly over the sling holding her right arm immobile. "I remember hearing it break. And the pain. But I could only see a wall of green light. It was so bright! It flared and everything went dark. I used my sunstone to look for the others when my sight returned. There was nothing but ash. Pendaro was gone. Gabrael was gone."

"And Rahne?"

"Dead. Half of him was floating in the canal, the other half was missing. Disintegrated. I gathered some rocks and flotsam, built a cairn to cover what pieces I could find. I held a small service. I don't know how long I prayed, but it must have been a long time. I was famished by the time I was done."

"That's when the patrol found you?"

Arael shook her head. "No. I headed off down the tunnel looking for an exit. A patrol found me about fifteen minutes later—two assassins, a warrior royal, and a Sathiian priest. I think we were all surprised to run into each other. Unfortunately, they recovered first. At least one of the assassins did."

The high priest touched her left hand lightly to her left cheek.

"I was hit in the face with a dart as I started a StoneSkin weave. I remember a sharp pain… and heat. There was a lot of heat."

She paused, scowled.

"Then there was a flare… red—yes, bright red. A Sathiian spell? I felt a terrible pain in my bones, like they were all breaking at once—and I… I…"

She shook her head and looked at the lord priest abjectly.

"I'm sorry. That's all I can remember."

Kargan nodded and sat back in his chair.

"My high priest Vayen and two of his adepts happened upon the scene as you fell," he said. "Vayen's adepts engaged the patrol. He petrified the Sathiian and caused her spell to miscarry. That alone saved you. Had they arrived even one second later, Wargrum would have lost a dedicated servitor and Sathiis would have gained another serpent."

Images of her own lost adepts slithered through Arael's mind. She closed her eyes and tried to make them go away.

"You did the right thing, you know," Kargan said.

Arael opened her eyes, looked quizzically at the lord priest.

"Coming here the way you did," he explained. "By way of the Underwet. That was a good move. Blaythe contracted House Loquay to slay your band once you reached the city. That's how we learned of your coming and what prompted us to send scouts to search for you. Whatever his intent, Fedahi seems to have saved you from at least one assassin's knife."

"Beya," Arael cursed. "Better to have faced the assassins than those sewers. Rahne, Pendaro, and Gabrael would still be alive."

Kargan shrugged. "Maybe."

"Maybe?" Arael's eyes widened in disbelief. "How can you—"

"Loquay is crafty and brutal," Kargan said bluntly. "It is as likely as not that you would have all died. And these—"

He patted a pile of papers on his desk.

"—would be in Loquay's hands."

Arael started to speak.

Kargan raised a hand to silence her.

"Gabrael fulfilled her mission, Arael," he said. "She died with honor. Rahne and Pendaro perished in the service of Wargrum. They died with grace. None of them died by any fault of yours. You know that, but you haven't accepted it. So, you suffer. No doubt, you constantly review the events leading to each death and ask yourself, again and again, what you could have done differently. Who knows how long it will take before you accept that you bear no blame? An hour? A day? A week?"

He shrugged and sighed.

"If you continue to leave your emote unchecked, it may take you the rest of your life."

Arael tightened her lips. She lowered her eyes. "My apologies, my lord."

"Don't apologize for your feelings, Arael. Just don't let them define you."

Arael nodded and rose from her chair, bowed, and turned to leave. Kargan watched her cross to the door, then looked at the papers on his desk.

"Before you go, Arael, do you know what it is that Aerkon has sent me?"

Arael turned back to face him. "No, my lord."

"Really? No idea?"

She shook her head. "Clearly, it must relate to the Black Church. But as to the specifics, well… it never occurred to me to look."

"Never occurred to you to look." Kargan chuckled. "Well, I suppose I can't fault you for that." He moved a few papers aside and picked up a small object. He held it up for her to see.

"This was hidden in the bundle you carried," he said. "Do you know what it is?"

"No, my lord."

"It is Nimwe's Ring of Stone."

Arael's eyes widened. Her jaw dropped.

Kargan turned the plain stone ring slowly between his fingers, then looked through it at Arael.

"Walk out the door, Arael," he said. "Suffer your pain, lament the loss of your fellows, pray for their souls. But tomorrow morning, one of two things must happen: either you will accept that you made no missteps and return here, or you will send Vayen to me."

CHAPTER 68

GRAY COUNSEL

Calista leaned against a marble column in a far corner of Ufwin's Hall of Gray Counsel, well removed from the throng of delegates that had assembled to hear her mother speak. She was exhausted and anxious. After a week deliberating with her mother and her advisers on Ufwin's best course in the shadow of the Snake, Calista's tolerance for political bandying was depleted. If her presence went unnoticed until seats were taken, she would be very happy.

Calista yawned and rubbed the back of her neck, closed her eyes, and sighed.

My part is coming to an end. It's up to Mother now.

The Counsel members began to take their seats among five groups of chairs symmetrically arranged about a raised pentagonal dais in the center of the hall.

Each group of chairs was a different color and reserved for a particular group of conseli. The seats of the Anzu were gold and reserved for representatives of Ufwin's Houses Mercantile; those of the Brand were red and held for envoys of the Houses Mercenary. The seats of the Uberan and the Elahan were green and blue, allocated to delegates of the Freefolk of Ufwin and members of the College of Art. The fifth and last group of chairs were white and held for the Corum, the members of Ufwin's Family Royal.

In accordance with the Code of Udox, no seats were included for ecclesiastic legates. Religious groups were prohibited from directly influencing Ufwinian law and policy.

Calista watched the delegates take their seats. When the din dropped to murmurs, she looked to the far end of the hall. The great bronze doors swung slowly open, and her mother, Lady Talaya Deluras, queen of the Realm of Ufwin, stepped imperiously into the chamber. She stood in the entryway until the more persistent susurrations faded to silence, then walked slowly to the raised dais. Conseli, messengers, retainers, and servants bowed respectfully as she passed, then hurried to their seats or scurried from the hall.

Talaya Deluras was an imposing humani woman. She was tall and lean and moved with the measured step of a fighter. Her features were neither homely nor handsome. She had light eyes speckled with blue and fair hair flecked with gray. Her attire reflected the simplicity of her tastes: she wore a long gown of green satin and black velvet, asymmetric in traditional Ufwinian style, embossed with geometric embroidery in silver thread, and matching shoes barely noticeable where they peeked out below the hem. She wore just two pieces of jewelry: a wedding band about the fourth finger of her left hand and a slim band of blue crystal on her right thumb. Simple ornamentation for strong, elegant hands. Her bearing and aspect presented a striking portrait of self-confidence and inner strength.

Calista took her seat among the Corum as Talaya stepped onto the dais. Though Calista was aware of her mother's intentions, it struck her as odd to see her stand before the Gray Counsel without the Ornaments of State. Judging by the puzzled expressions and sidelong glances around her, the assembly also found it unsettling.

Ufwinian custom held that the head of state had three symbols of power: the Crown of Wisdom, the Ring of Resolve, and the Staff of State. The rules of conseli conduct depended upon which items were worn or wielded by the sovereign at any given time.

The Crown symbolized the sovereign's obligation to act in the best interest of the people and that their counsel was solicited.

The Ring signified the supremacy of the sovereign's will and that debate would not be tolerated.

The Staff epitomized the indivisibility of the sovereign and the State.

Only once had a sovereign come before the Gray Counsel without bearing at least one of the Ornaments of State.

That sovereign had mysteriously disappeared shortly thereafter.

Gahlyfahx saw Calista as she selected her seat and quickly shouldered his way to her side. After years of separation, he wanted to lift his sister with a hug and spin her around until they both fell dizzy to the floor. As he claimed the seat to her right, he settled for taking her hand in his and whispering, "Cali! By Pheon's Fires, it's good to see you."

Calista snapped into a broad grin at the sight of her beloved brother. She squeezed his hand, whispered back: "Gahly! I was told you were off fighting the Haugwym and weren't expected for some time!"

He shrugged, grinned. "I only just arrived. But I'll tell you this, sister—had I known you were in the city, I'd have beaten through Grim Thunderer's thick hide to get here sooner!"

Calista beamed. "You would have too! Gods above, that poor horse! And to think, you used to love animals."

"I still do." He nodded toward the delegates of the Anzu, adding sarcastically, "Even those with two legs."

Then he chuckled and asked, "When did you get back?"

"Last week. Unexpectedly for all concerned. You?"

"Only this morning."

"And here you are." Calista chuckled, glanced at her mother. "Oh, Mother is about to speak."

The queen surveyed the delegates as they stood dutifully before their seats. When she had their full attention, she bade them sit. After the sounds of chairs moving and feet shuffling faded away, she spoke in a clear and resonant voice.

"Good conseli of Ufwin," she said, "not long before his disappearance, my husband addressed this body as a citizen; as I address it, today. Not as king, not as State—as a man. He knew that, no matter the depth of allegiance one affords their liege, no one should be made to embark upon a dangerous road without the conviction that the journey's end warrants the danger. Such decisions can only be made from the heart.

"Many of you were present that day and remember Gahlyfrey's words, for they were brief and germane. I cannot do justice to his eloquence or his passion, but I can repeat his message, for it was burned into my memory even as it came from his lips. 'Beware those that serve the Black Church,' he said, 'for their god is false and their convictions depraved. Grant them no heed lest their venom poison your soul, nor any accord or covenant lest you fall to their wickedness.'"

The queen paused for a slow breath. She wanted to give the assembly time to remember their beloved king. She needed that memory. It would be through their love for him that she would touch their hearts.

"For thirteen years we have kept faith with those words," she said. "We have toiled diligently to thwart Sathiian schemes, in lands near and far, and made great sacrifices to preserve the honor and dignity of our Houses."

Talaya was a passionate and rousing orator. She walked the dais as she spoke, looking the conseli directly in the eye—recognizing their contributions and reinforcing the strength of her message.

"We have shared the best and the worst of times: we have reveled in victory and commiserated in defeat; we have achieved glorious advances and suffered devastating setbacks; we have celebrated bright days of joy in the Light of Pheon, and we have endured dark nights of dread in the shadow of the Snake. But we have persevered. We did not succumb to the Serpent or its lies. We survived. It was not an easy path, but it was one that we chose to walk. And it was a path we were proud to walk together."

A murmur of assent swept through the assembly. This was not what they anticipated when they'd gathered to hear their queen speak. She'd touched their hearts through memory. Now she needed to join that memory, so they might see her in the same light they remembered her husband.

The queen raised open arms and declared, "I come to you as Gahlyfrey did, without Crown, Ring, or Staff. I stand before you stripped of royal authority, garbed only in the respect I have earned during my tenure as queen. I do this because Ufwin now stands at a perilous crossroads and both paths lead to hardship. If we are not united when we choose which path to follow, it will not matter which we take, for it will surely lead to disaster. I come to you as a sister and give you my Family as siblings, so that we might determine our road together, free from obligations of fealty and released from the bonds of political alignment."

She turned to the Family Royal and commanded, "Stand down the Corum."

Gahlyfahx shot Calista a surprised look. It was one thing for the queen to attend the Gray Counsel without the Ornaments of State, but quite another to disband the Corum. Without the House Royal as a separate voting bloc, she invited the possibility of deadlock when she stated her issue and called for votes. It would take a three-fourths majority to reach a resolution. Worse, it was a deadlock not even she could break—without the Staff of State, she would be forced to take her seat with the Elahan once she finished her address.

As the members of the Family Royal rose from their chairs and moved to join the other voting blocs according to their professions and allegiances, Calista pulled Gahlyfahx aside and whispered hastily.

"Whatever happens, find a reason to sway the Brand to vote in favor of what Mother proposes. I'll explain later. Trust me, Gahly."

Gahlyfahx scowled, then glanced at their mother.

"I hope she knows what she's doing."

"She does," Calista reassured him.

Then she moved to take her place with the Uberan.

Talaya watched the members of her House melt into the other four voting blocs, their royal status suspended for the remainder of the Counsel. After presenting her case, she would also surrender her sovereignty. While speaking, however, she remained the queen of Ufwin and intended to use all her presence and authority to garner support for her proposal.

When silence reigned again, Talaya raised her hands to shoulder height, palms out, and slowly curled her fingers.

"The Serpent has grown, and its coils have tightened," she said.

She brought her hands together and entwined her fingers.

"And they have crushed the spirit of the west. Iotia is lost. Isitar and Rha are lost. Wirith has fallen to the Snake, and Dûhr teeters on the brink. To the south, Umber's Houses Mercenary falter before the Sathiian regime in Tuli. Each day sees victory slip farther from their grasp. The blight on the Thayle heralds starvation for Umber, while Tuli grows fat on supplies from Sathiian-ruled Sador. Umber cannot hope to prevail. They will fall."

She unlocked her hands and looked at her empty palms.

"When Dûhr and Umber fall, Ufwin and Khâlir will stand alone against the Snake. The Elfin Republics may not be able to aid us; they will find it difficult to penetrate the growing Sathiian presence in the Uli. The Dwarfin Kingdoms will not be able to provide support. Their ongoing civil unrest, aggravated and perpetuated by the Sathiians, consumes the full measure of their attention and resources. Without assistance from these allies, faced with a two-pronged attack from the northwest and south, Ufwin cannot hope to survive. The Serpent will surround us, enfold us, and crush us."

Murmurs and whispers swept through the assembly. Disbelief clashed with denial, bewilderment with accusation. And beneath it all, outrage.

"Unless we act—now!" Talaya declared loudly, silencing the chamber. "Swiftly! Resolutely!"

She paused for a heartbeat, lowered her voice. "But how?"

She let the question linger while she leveled her gaze upon the Brand.

"Some have suggested," she said, "that the time for military action is long overdue, and that we must send our myriadi to Dûhr and Umber to repel the Snake before it can swallow those realms."

There were cheers from the Brand.

The queen waved them away.

"Some have suggested that military action without tactical advantage or operational superiority would be folly." She turned her gaze to the Anzu. "And that such folly would drain the wealth of the realm without producing a decisive victory."

There were grunts of assent from the Anzu.

The queen waved them away as well.

"The truth is, until now both were correct," she said, looking at each faction in turn.

"But—" She held up a finger. "That was before we learned the secret of Adderash's power."

The assembly waited, bated. Their anticipation was palpable.

"Adderash's secret is a drug," the queen said at last. "A narcotic born of a rare species of lotos known only to the Red Jungle and the Black Isle of Sador. It is through addiction to this drug that Adderash holds dominion over the west. It is through addiction that Adderash manipulates the Houses Great and Royal. It is through this oppression of the humani spirit that he carves out an empire."

Talaya looked over the stunned faces. She made no effort to hide her disgust, hoping her revulsion would heighten their own.

"Many have fallen to Adderash's drug. Once enthralled, none have escaped its grip. Those dependent upon Adderash's narcotic have no choice but to yield to his will. We cannot blame them, for it is not through weakness or improvidence they have fallen captive, nor is it by their own will that they force their realms to serve the Black Church. None of us can know the agony they must suffer, and I pray that none of our people ever do."

She looked down and shuddered, paused, and collected herself.

"Yet this drug that enslaves our brethren also offers us an opportunity. Without addiction to force compliance, Adderash cannot maintain his hold over the realms he has conquered. We have only to deny Adderash access to the lotos, and his empire will collapse. We have but to cut off his access to Sador and the Red Jungle, and he will fall."

Now came the critical moment. Talaya had drawn upon her people's memories to touch their hearts; she had touched their hearts to stir their passion; she had stirred their passion to arouse their fury. Now she would make plain her intent and pray that these forces would galvanize them to action.

"I propose," Talaya declared boldly, "that we attack the Sathiians on that front, swiftly and savagely. Let us strike at the very foundation of Adderash's empire! Let us send our myriadi to Dûhr and crush Blaythe's fledgling Church there, and from there to the Tameron to rout the gobli, secure the pass, and deny Adderash the Red Jungle. Let us send our weavers to the Mountains Moril and free the xyborgh beetles from the sand that binds them, then drive them south to Tuli. Let us send myriadi to Khâlir to join with their Houses Mercenary and sweep west to liberate Wirith, and from there to free Isitar and Rha! Let us send our fleets to unshackle Iotia and from there to the Black Isle of Sador itself, destroy its ports and ravage its lotos fields! Let us turn all our resources to the destruction of Adar Ashan and purge his Black Church from the face of the world!"

CHAPTER 69

MANNEQUIN

Arwynn's father, Celwynn Blackhand, believed that fear was the foundation of power and that mastery over life and death was the basis of fear. On that conviction, he built a House Assassin. Arwynn believed that information was the basis of true power. When he assumed control of House Blackhand, he restructured it to that end. Arwynn's agents listened, intercepted, listed, checked, reported, analyzed, filtered, disseminated, gossiped, and lied. Arwynn trafficked in information through disguised interactions with unsuspecting members of elite society, who often became prey.

Once the mir departed with their prisoner and his agents left to carry out their assignments, Arwynn hastened to his quarters to attend to the spatters of Lindrowe's poisoned blood dappling his clothes and skin. He secured the heavy door partitioning his rooms from the rest of the keep, then grabbed a lamp and slipped through a secret door by his bed to his changing room.

Arwynn's secure changing room was expansive, well appointed, and meticulously kept. The shadows thrown by his lamp gamboled along multifarious jars and bottles, flasks of cosmetics, exfoliants, and chemicals neatly arranged on three wide tables along the right wall. On the left were three sizable armoires, a large marble basin, a dressing table with stool, and two full-length mirrors on pivoting mounts. At the far end of the room, a water tank hunkered, spiderlike, on a tenebrous web of iron trusses over three alcoves containing a toilet, bath, and shower. An oval bowl of metal rested on a stone pedestal near the shower. As wide as a man's arm and half again as long, it was scarcely a hand deep. Its interior was deeply pitted, as though by spatters of acria.

Arwynn set his lamp on a table, picked up a ceramic flask, and crossed to the bowl. Placing the flask on the stone pedestal close to the shower, he removed the Uth'q Q'wahi from the folds of his tunic, carefully unfolding the damp cloth that swaddled it. Very little of his blood remained on the disk, just enough to protect him for the time it would take to disrobe and bathe.

Setting the Uth'q Q'wahi beside the flask, Arwynn undressed, carefully placing each article of clothing in the metal bowl. His ring, his sandals, the false fingernails from his hands, and the wig from his shaved head also went in the bowl. He would burn his clothing and accoutrements later.

Then, flask in hand, he stepped into the shower and pulled one of the three metal chains hanging down the wall, and cold water rained from above.

He turned slowly, allowing the cascade to douse every part of his body. When Lindrowe's blood had been washed away and the water ran clear, Arwynn released the chain and opened the flask, pouring a gritty green liquid into an open palm. He sniffed it, winced, and began to rub it over his skin. He started with his face and head and carefully worked his way down his body, using a long brush to scrub his back.

As he scoured away the last vestiges of the poisonmaster's blood, he also removed the healthy bronze color of his skin and the dark hairs on his arms, chest, and legs. When he was finished, all that remained were the lashes that rimmed his eyes, the transparent nails of his hands and feet, and hairless white skin.

Arwynn stepped out of his shower and walked to the nearest of his armoires, opening an ornate door to retrieve a fluffy towel. Blotting himself dry, he was careful not to rub or scrape. He followed his reflection in the large mirrors from all angles to make certain nothing marred his pale skin.

Looking back from the mirror was Arwynn's greatest secret—his true face.

So much like his sister's.

He had employed a strict regimen of drugs, diet, and physical conditioning since adolescence, all aiming to develop his body to be the perfect canvas upon which to paint a disguise. He was smooth, hairless, and pale; devoid of scars or birthmarks and easily decorated or dyed. His muscles were well toned but lean and smooth, allowing him to assume radically different personae and shift easily between genders.

He could be anyone.

Seated at his dressing table, Arwynn gazed into the largest of its three sunstone-rimmed mirrors. He scrutinized his body until he was satisfied there were no blemishes requiring special treatment, then applied a lotion to his face, neck, and hands. As the emollient absorbed into his skin, he relaxed, closed his eyes, and let his mind dwell on recent events.

Scarcely a week ago, Morkainen had come to him with suspicions of Lindrowe. Two days later, Malaraphi returned from the Red Jungle with word that the Black Church held the Horde's leash.

It was fortunate that Morkainen recalled Ciridan from the Mind-bender's when he first suspected Lindrowe's treachery.

Given the early stage of her training, Ciridan's weaves were sorely limited, but causing a dazed mind to misperceive sights and sounds fell easily within her abilities. Lindrowe had not seen Arwynn Blackhand accuse him of betraying his House, nor any of his associates, but a roomful of mir in a nondescript cellar accusing him of betraying its clan.

It didn't matter to Arwynn if the mir killed Lindrowe. If they killed him, they removed a threat to his House; if they didn't, he could consider arranging for a rescue and leverage the gratitude that would follow.

But Lindrowe's expulsion had come at a high cost. The only way to definitively quash all facets of the poisonmaster's treachery was to retire his closest associates, including his brewmaster, Ebra Nehan, who oversaw the manufacture and distribution of all House poisons. Arwynn could not risk those secrets falling into enemy hands. When Mad'rhaq and its attendants departed with Lindrowe, he ordered Ciridan to retire Nehan and her coterie. He left the other necessary retirements to Morkainen while Malaraphi concealed the night's events from their adversaries.

Straightening, Arwynn pulled open a small drawer at the base of one of his dressing table mirrors. He took out a vial with a black label, removed its stopper, and let fall a single drop of its contents into each of his eyes. His eyes burned for a moment, then tingled with a radiating warmth as the liquid darkened his irises.

Returning the vial, Arwynn stood and perused the markings on several squat ceramic canisters on a table. Making his selection, he removed its lid and returned to his seat before the mirrors. Inside was a nut-colored cream.

With practiced care, he spread the cream lightly over his face. As his skin bronzed, his thoughts turned to Welbley Blaythe…

What are your barges bringing into my city? Your hold of the Horde has thwarted me. Without a gobli raid to cover my hand and draw out your mir guards, my plan to capture your cargo cannot succeed.

… and Arcturi Lacosia…

What are you doing in the Gardens? You've struck a deal with Loquay to secure the Underwet beneath your temple, but where are you now? What are you scheming? How do you evade my sulari?

… and the Black Church.

When your temple is complete and you have secured your distribution network for your somphora and lotos narcotic, how long will it be before you enslave all the Great Houses of Dûhr.

As he rubbed color over his arms, he thought it ironic that, even as the Sathiians tightened their grip over Dûhr, the Clubfoot himself should unintentionally set in motion a sequence of events that would destroy his own lotos fields. Trapped in his tree form, Zaaldirn could not counteract the toxins he'd tilled into his fields as indemnity against Adderash's betrayal.

The loss of those fields will come as a heavy blow. You will have no choice but to scale back or defer your plans for Dûhr. Either will give me time to adapt my plans to Morkainen's discoveries.

His arms and chest now tinted, he turned to his abdomen.

Most curious, Morkainen's information.

The blademaster's assassinations had yielded their desired effect: Loquay and Savarat blamed each other and retaliated. Their sulari did not clash in the buffer zones between their districts, however—they battled amid a vast maze of warehouses in another quarter of the city that neither controlled. The warehouses held nonperishable foodstuffs.

By Morkainen's report, the warehouses were owned by Houses Antoresi and Greshank, Great Houses Mercantile contracted by Princess Selene under the guise of Miriam Lancashir of Khâlir. No doubt, Loquay and Savarat chose that area to coerce those Houses to pay higher prices for continued protection. But why would the Houses Mercantile employ Houses Assassin to protect food? And why would the princess stockpile it in the first place?

And what is she after in the northern wildlands?

Arwynn sighed, shook his head, and returned to his disguise. His questions did not worry him. He was confident answers would eventually reveal themselves.

They always did.

CHAPTER 70

NECESSARY EVIL

Arael sat in a small alcove adjoining Kargan's study. The alcove was sparsely furnished: two scroll racks, a shelf of books, and, beneath a window with a western exposure, three plain wooden chairs around a low wooden table. The tabletop held unrolled scrolls, old books, and a scattering of papers. Arael identified several as part of the parcel she'd brought from Wirith, recognizable by their stink and smears of filth, but there were more. Old scrolls mostly, and a few tattered parchments covered with sketches and scrawled notes.

After collecting pages from his desk, Kargan joined Arael in the alcove. She started to rise, but he motioned for her to remain seated and handed her the papers as he took a chair next to her. Arael's eyes narrowed as she flipped through the pages with increasing speed.

"Wargrum," she murmured. "He already controls Dûhr?"

"To a large extent, yes," Kargan acknowledged. "But there's more."

He took the pages from Arael and picked up two parchments from the table, handing her one with a drawing of a six-petaled water flower. Some notes were jotted beneath the drawing, so poorly penned that she could not read them easily.

"This is the lotos flower," Kargan said. "Are you familiar with it?"

"No."

Kargan grunted and shrugged. "Ah well, it was unlikely that you would be."

Arael looked at the drawing more closely.

"The flower is quite rare," Kargan said. "It grows only in warm, marshy areas—primarily the Isles of Sador and Iotia, and along the southern fringes of Evereve Marsh. Its petals are very delicate. Very pretty. They grow six to a flower and vary from light yellow to a rich golden orange. When properly prepared, the petals produce a hallucinogenic drug called palos."

"I've heard of palos," Arael said, looking up from the parchment. "It's used by cults in the southern realms as a means of augury and dietetic communion."

"That's right."

Kargan took the parchment from her and handed her the second. It also featured a drawing of a flower. Arael thought it was the same flower, but blue, then noticed its petals were longer and more furled.

"As it happens, the lotos has a cousin of a darker nature," Kargan explained. "This one's petals yield a very powerful and very addictive narcotic."

He jerked his head to the other papers scattered over the table.

"Aerkon discovered that Adderash is using that narcotic to control Houses Royal throughout the Realms Humani."

"Even Adderash is not so—"

"Opportunistic?"

"No."

"Reprehensible?"

"Powerful," Arael finished.

"Ahh."

Kargan shrugged his shoulders. "My agents in House Kythidûhr have confirmed the addiction of both Prince Melkor and his wizard royal, and the ministers of river trade, worship, and commerce. The tax adjudicator and minister of the treasury also show signs of addiction, as do several lesser members of the House Royal—mostly lesser members of the Family the Black Church wants to keep in line. That's my guess, anyway. I suspect Princess Selene is addicted as well, but I haven't been able to verify it."

"If she's not," Arael said, "we can use her as a wedge against the Sathiians. Once she discovers what Adderash has done to her brother and her Family, she will surely support us in—"

"Oh, Arael!" Kargan laughed out loud. "You are not well versed on the Dûhrani Family Royal, are you?"

Arael cocked her head—being from Wirith, she knew very little of Dûhr.

"Selene has plotted against her brother for control of the realm since she was old enough to understand the concept of power," he explained. "Against most of her Family, come to tell. If she remains free from addiction, it was not by accident. I'd wager she's in league with Blaythe."

"Beya…" Arael whispered. "Then what are we to do? What *can* we do?"

Kargan did not reply. He quietly rose and turned to the window, looking out over the Gardens of Twilight. Laborers were at work just beyond the stand of firs that bounded Wargrum's acreage, constructing a temple to a false god. Once it was complete, Adderash's foothold in Dûhr would be secure and his position would be unassailable.

Without turning from the window, Kargan said, "We must destroy Adderash's temple. Before the last block is laid."

Arael could feel astonishment on her face, felt her chest tighten, her belly twist. Never had she heard a lord priest of the Elem propose open aggression against another sect, even a false one! The very notion ran counter to the Elem's tenets…

Yet, through the shock, somehow, Kargan's words rang clear and true. Aerkon had warned her long ago that desperate measures would become necessary against the Snake.

How did he phrase it? "The results one achieves can never be used to justify one's means; but then again, there are exceptions to every rule."

She realized what disturbed her was not Kargan's exhortation of violence but that the prospect brought a strong sense of relief. After what she had endured, after the tragedies the Sathiians had precipitated, she knew too well the cast of Adderash's minions and the lengths they would go to achieve mastery over the Realms Humani. The world they would beget would be bleak and miserable. It would be a world without kih or eie, where the tides of the emote were ruled by the Snake and the fires of the soul were reduced to embers. Averting that was surely a noble goal.

And if the cost was her soul...

Then, so be it.

Arael stood and moved to stand beside Kargan. She looked out the window and listened to the sounds of distant construction. The lord priest was right—Adderash could not be allowed a defensible base of operations in Dûhr.

The priests were silent for a long time.

CHAPTER 71

THE HAUGWYM

Ominous clouds hung over the horizon, heavy and black against the belly of the sky. The sun had not yet set, though the last of its warmth and light was already lost to the rising winds, stiffening with the gathering darkness.

In the face of the coming storm, Gahlyfahx and Calista led their small company north from Ufwin along the easternmost fringe of the Tanglewood. They traveled on horseback in a rough diamond formation, prince and princess at the forward point. Warriors formed the diamond's periphery, magickai formed its interior, and half a dozen scouts were deployed in a wide arc about the main body. All were committed to Queen Talaya's cause and rode with Calista and Gahlyfahx to expel the Sathiians nesting in Dûhr.

As their pace slowed with the deepening dusk and the scouts spread out to search for a suitable place to camp, Calista found herself wondering whether the Gray Counsel had reached a decision.

They had clamored impassioned support for her mother's petition and been eager to enact her bold plan until the speaker for the Anzu, Berocha Antiduhli, argued that Ufwin lacked the resources to move against the Sathiians on such a grand scale without undermining its defenses against Haugwym raiders and leaving itself vulnerable to Sathiian incursions by sea from Iotia or Sador. Perhaps, he shrewdly submitted, there were funds of which the Houses Mercantile were unaware, and those moneys might be sufficient to support the queen's campaign without compromising Ufwin? As things stood, however, he claimed her plan would ruin the realm before victory could be achieved, and the Anzu would not sanction it.

Despite his clever framing, Calista knew that Antiduhli's dissent was motivated by greed. The Anzu profited from the continued state of heightened security.

As the debate continued and tempers flared, it became clear the alliances between several Houses Mercantile and Houses Mercenary would split the Counsel and deadlock the vote.

There were only two paths to ratify the queen's plan: certify that additional funds were available to finance the war, or prove that the dissenting Houses were traitors to the realm. Either would take days, during which the Anzu would certainly seed sedition among the other blocs.

Calista decided to take matters into her own hands. When the Gray Counsel disbanded for the night, she approached her brother with the idea of assembling an independent band to thwart Sathiian designs for Dûhr. If she could not save Melkor, perhaps she could help save the realm they both loved.

Gahlyfahx took some convincing. On one hand, he believed that Ufwin should take a more aggressive stand against the Black Church and was eager to lead a force against Adderash's minions. But on the other, he believed in the rule of law and was loath to act without the sanction of the Gray Counsel.

Calista knew her brother, though. Convincing him with matters of principle, of urgency, and of love was fairly easy.

With Gahlyfahx committed, she had little trouble mustering a small, well-equipped band. Three days later, the Gray Council retired from yet another day of debate, and the party slipped away into the open lands north of the city—sixty-three strong and eager to strike whatever blow they could against the Black Church.

A small force, but one small force can turn a battle, and one battle can win a war.

That was three days ago.

As she rode slowly on in the deepening dusk, Calista couldn't help but wonder how future historians would view her tiny army.

Would they be heroes? Renegades? Rogues?

She put the question from her mind. It would be answered by those who won.

I'm coming, my love.

Calista opened her eyes with a start, suddenly aware they'd stopped moving. In the darkness ahead, she could make out Gahlyfahx conferring with one of the scouts and rode to his side.

"What is it?" Calista asked. "Why have we stopped?"

The scout looked at the princess, then the prince. Gahlyfahx gave a curt nod.

"Haugwym," the scout replied. "At least forty, probably more."

Calista looked at Gahlyfahx, tiny spiders of fear skittering in her belly.

"Haugwym? What are the Haugwym doing this far from the Great Flat?"

Gahlyfahx shook his head. "I don't know. But they pose a problem."

He looked around, rubbing his chin with a gloved hand.

"Bad news, either way," he grumbled. "We can't go west without entering the Tanglewood. That would slow our progress by a few days at least, and chance encounters with its beast tribes. If we give way to the east, we present our flank."

He looked back to the scout. "Two score, you say?"

The scout nodded. "At least."

Gahlyfahx grimaced.

"Beya! Even two dozen would be too many. They're brutal fighters; we risk an unacceptable number of casualties."

"Are they aware of us?" Calista asked. "Perhaps with surprise—"

"No," Gahlyfahx interrupted. "In ten years, we've never been able to surprise the Haugwym."

He took a deep breath. "We'll change formation, spread a line across the plain, and ride into view. I will advance to parley. If we can trick them into thinking we're stronger than we are, they may let us pass."

"I'll go with you," the princess said.

"No. I won't jeopardize both of us. You stay here."

"Brother, *I'm* the diplomat," Calista argued. "I'm the one who should address them, not you. Not to mention that—"

"No!" Gahlyfahx repeated. His tone left no room for debate.

"You will remain here because you *are* a diplomat. I want them to think we are all warriors. From a distance, they'll see only heavily armored figures on horseback."

He turned to the scout. "Distribute patches of metal and spare armor to the weavers—anything that might glint in torchlight. Have them affix it to their heads, arms, and legs. Tell them to stuff their cloaks at the chest and shoulders so they appear to be wearing breastplates and pauldrons. Then distribute torches, one for every six, and line them up. They have ten minutes."

With his company suitably attired and lining the hillock adjacent to the Haugwym encampment, Gahlyfahx rode forward to parley. As he drew near the halfway point, he could see the Haugwym emissary sent to meet him through the darkness. At first, he could only discern that the raider was of great stature and mounted on a horse of enormous size. As the distance decreased, he noted the raider wore a full helm of black iron, styled as the muzzle of a desert wyrm, and massive gauntlets of leather and steel. The rest of the raider's body was concealed by dappled silk, though he suspected a full set of heavy plate armor beneath the colorful cloaks. No part of the Haugwym's body was uncovered.

He raised his right hand to shoulder height, then placed it flat against the center of his breastplate in the Ufwinian sign of peace.

"Hail the Haugwym," the prince said.

The raider stopped ten feet before him and made no gesture, peaceful or otherwise.

"Who are you?" the raider asked in the Trade Tongue.

The voice was rough. Guttural.

The prince straightened in his saddle. "I am Gahlyfahx Deluras," he declared, "prince of Ufwin and son of Gahlyfrey Deluras. Who are you to speak for the Haugwym?"

"Prove you are who you say," the raider returned.

Gahlyfahx reached over his shoulder to his back-mounted scabbard and drew his sword. It wasn't steel but a serrated red gemstone fused to a gilded hilt of dragon bone. Unsheathed, the blade sucked in what little ambient light there was and gave him a bloodred aura.

"The Blade Warsong," Gahlyfahx proclaimed. "True blade of the true prince of Ufwin."

"A weapon may be stolen," the raider said. "Show your hand."

Gahlyfahx scowled. He snapped his left wrist hard enough to throw off his gauntlet and raised his hand for the Haugwym to see. The small and ring finger were missing: one cut off, one bitten away.

The raider made a low rumble and lowered its head slightly in what passed as a show of respect.

"I accept that you are Gahlyfahx Halfhand," the Haugwym said. "I am Ka'an of Breed Kûm. I carry a message for you from the Calai Kûm."

The prince sheathed his weapon, the bloody radiance dissipating.

"Speak."

"The Calai Kûm says that you act without Gray sanction," the Haugwym said. "That you ride to the Realm of Dûhr to fight the Snake of Sador. Is this true?"

"It is."

"And do you swear it is so, on the honor of your House?"

"I do."

"Bloodswear."

"My word is my oath."

"Bloodswear."

Gahlyfahx glowered at the raider for a long moment, then removed his helm and dropped it to the ground. He took a knife from a sheath in his saddle and kissed its blade, then cut the thumb of his left hand and drew a line of blood down the center of his face, forehead to chin.

"I so swear upon the honor of House Deluras."

The Haugwym returned a low rumble and another slight bow.

"Then I am commanded to aid you," Ka'an said.

Gahlyfahx cocked his head.

"Aid me? Your people and mine are enemies!"

"Things are not as they appear, Gahlyfahx Eightfinger," the raider replied. "They never have been."

The prince's eyes narrowed.

The raider waited.

"Why?"

"The Haugwym have but one enemy," Ka'an said. "The Black Church. When you broke away from your House to attack the Snake, you showed yourself our ally. But you are weak. Without our aid, the Snake will crush you."

"Clever words, Ka'an, but words only. They do not undo ten years of war."

"Had you been our enemy, Gahlyfahx Halfhand, we would have killed you yesterday when you camped at Wyvrehn Rock. Or the night before, when you slept beneath the Trees of Twisted Spirit."

Gahlyfahx scowled. "You followed us."

"No. We traveled ahead of you."

"Ahead of us?"

"To clear your path of danger."

"We saw no sign."

"We left none."

Gahlyfahx's scowl deepened. He could not deny that they'd met no resistance since leaving Ufwin, nor that the places they'd camped were as the raider described.

"If what you say is true, why show yourselves at all? Why not continue ahead of us until needed, unseen and unsuspected?"

"You would have continued northward," Ka'an replied.

"That is the direction of Dûhr."

"The direction, not the path."

"And where is the path?"

"East."

"East? The mountains?"

"The ruins."

CHAPTER 72

ON THE RIVER FWAER

Welbley reclined on a cushioned divan on the upper deck of his lavish barge, the fifth to travel to Dûhr since his covenant with House Blackhand. He hummed contentedly as the vessel slipped slowly through the dark waters of the Fwaer. Belly full and thirst slaked, he delighted in the cool caress of the midnight air and the rich fragrances that drifted to him. Having concluded his preparations, he was finally able to relax and enjoy the last leg of his journey to Dûhr.

Dûhr. City of opportunity.

Welbley closed his little eyes and went over his schedule again. He would arrive at Westgate in a few days, where he would be met by four Sathiian adepts and two dozen of Blackhand's sulari. Kaleena's agent in Amsted reported that Blackhand's subjugation had proceeded without incident and she would have no difficulty securing the sulari he required.

Once his cargo was unloaded, he would proceed to the Gardens of Twilight with two adepts and assume command of the acolytes and attendants already positioned in the emergent temple. The other two adepts, escorted by Blackhand's sulari, would transport his crates to a nearby warehouse, and from there to the Underwet, where they would secure them in the vaults beneath the temple. They would then deploy the sulari to augment the temple's defenses in anticipation of attack.

The Churches of Elem had made no move against Sathiian expansion into Dûhr. Their tenets were founded on strict standards of social and religious tolerance; they could neither censure nor impugn the Church of Sathiis without hypocrisy. The only exception was the Church of Wargrum. Of the four Churches of Elem, only that renegade faction had outwardly acted against the Black Church, each time with increasing boldness. They had fanned public sentiment against the Black Church in Rha and demonstrated against Sathiian policies in Wirith. If the pattern of escalation continued, Welbley expected an outright attack on his supporters and property in Dûhr. Shortly after his arrival, no doubt, but prior to his temple's completion.

Let them come. Let them die.

Welbley smiled, confident his forces would crush whatever assault the Wargrumites might make. In addition to Blackhand's sulari and his own adepts, Welbley had secreted a full myriadi of warriors royal beneath his temple. Include the combined might of the Crimson Witch and the four mutati liches he'd brought from Evereve, and he'd have more than ample a force. If by some bizarre quirk of fate even *that* was not enough, he still held a powerful trump: Adderash's Sacred Shield. An anti-Aethic shell that no spell or force could penetrate.

Welbley sighed happily, a smile curling on his pudgy face.

Though he looked forward to assuming command of Sathiian forces in Dûhr, it was the week following that truly excited him, when he would stand before the Court Royal and reveal how a coalition of Dûhr's Houses Assassin had used elfin laef stolen from Wirith to pay the Gobli Horde to attack the settlements along the Aenin. In one masterful stroke, he would turn Dûhr's Houses Royal, Mercenary, and Mercantile against its Houses Assassin and provide justification for Wirith's House Royal to reopen trade. His evidence was erroneous, of course—the papers forged, the circumstances contrived, the facts twisted—but that was irrelevant. The people of Dûhr had suffered greatly over the last year. They wanted...

No, they need...

... someone to blame. Welbley would give them a scapegoat, and they would turn on the Houses Assassin with little concern for the quality of the evidence.

Between the gobli incursions in the northlands and a war between Dûhr's Houses, there would be more than enough activity to conceal Sathiian manipulations. By the time things settled and the city began to recover, Welbley would rule House Kythidûhr in Wirith, and his operatives would control Dûhr's most influential Houses—including the House Royal.

The realm will be ours.

Welbley's smile broadened, and a soft chuckle escaped his throat, growing steadily louder until it became a boisterous laugh.

By Sathiis's Bloody Coils, I love my work!

CHAPTER 73

FIRE, FAMILY, AND FREEDOM

I n his study, Arwynn propped his head in his manicured hand and studied the sprawling map at his feet. The tiles had shifted significantly over the past weeks. There were now more of House Kythidûhr's silver tiles outside the city than inside, neatly arranged with those of three Great Houses Mercenary between the city and the Borowood. The cluster of Sathiian purple tiles in the Gardens of Twilight was larger than before, with more of Loquay's yellow tiles among them. And there were slightly fewer of his own.

Arwynn stared at the four stacks of markers between Dûhr and the Borowood. It was a remarkable force—seven Myriadi Royal and twelve myriadi from three of Dûhr's greatest Houses Mercenary—over eleven thousand warriors.

The Sword of Pheon, he mused. *The prince has chosen an ambitious name for his army.*

He puffed at a stray ringlet of red hair that had fallen across his face and drummed his long red nails against his temple.

How did you do it, my prince?

Arwynn shifted in his chair and loosened his bodice.

He'd been intrigued by the prince's choice of regent and deployment of magickai, but it was Melkor's sudden boldness that had spurred him to exploit Glayden Kanidûhr's weakness for redheaded courtesans and penchant for trading secrets for carnal favors.

Arwynn narrowed his smoke-shadowed eyes and pursed his red-painted lips as he contemplated the things he'd inveigled from the prince's cousin.

Melkor had sent two dozen riders to the Borowood two days before he led the Sword of Pheon out of Dûhr. Arwynn now knew their mission. The riders were veteran weavers recruited from the Green Raven and the Red Mantis, powerful guilds that openly opposed the Black Church. The Ravens were to lay waste to the southern pass of Tameron; the Mantises were to split the Borowood with a massive conflagration and drive the fires toward Wirith and Dûhr.

The Ravens will cut off the Borowood from the Gobli Lands. The Mantises will split the Horde in the Borowood. Melkor's army will only have to defeat half the gobli—Balistrahd will be forced to deal with the rest.

Melkor named Cendek Tulane as his binding surrogate the day before his departure. This surprised everyone; Cendek was Melkor's third cousin, far removed from the throne. It further surprised Arwynn to learn that Cendek secretly despised Selene.

Tulane was a wise choice. His insignificance shielded him from Blaythe's machinations, and he will never trust the princess.

On the day of his departure, Melkor had the Sathiian advisers granted to him by Welbley Blaythe seized and personally cut their throats. He then formally instated Cendek, binding the wizard royal and the members of his Family to his service. Selene was absent and could not oppose.

He's freed himself. Somehow, he's broken Blaythe's hold.

Arwynn pouted.

Melkor's actions complicated things. When he recovered from incredulity, Blaythe would have to wonder if any of his other pawns had thrown off their yokes… especially pawns who might keep their liberation a secret until they were in position to strike.

Pawns like me.

Arwynn decided two things immediately: he would discover how the prince had defeated Blaythe's drug and do likewise, and he would move against Blaythe the night the priest claimed his temple.

INTERLUDE FIVE

THE SERPENT AND THE FROG

The two men faced each other across a wide table laden with food and drink in a room of lavish wealth. The young man was beautiful and reclined leisurely in his seat. His golden skin and inky hair offered elegant contrast to his stylish white tunic. The old man was hideous and sat stiffly in his chair. His patchy red hair and cadaverous skin clashed with his sumptuous blue robes.

"Think he'll survive?" Zithwathn asked.

"I don't think any of them will," Adar replied.

"Even with the shell and the moss-spitters?"

"They are both first attempts. Something will go wrong."

Adar took a piece of fruit from his plate and eyed it appreciatively, then took a small bite. Zithwathn folded his arms across his chest and sulked, white eyes narrow and craggy lips drawn in a tight frown.

"What is bothering you?" Adar asked, daintily returning the fruit to his plate.

The old man grunted. "This whole game in Dûhr has been a waste of time and money."

"Not at all. I'm getting exactly what I wanted."

"Oh? And what is that?"

Adar smiled. "Martyrs."

PART SIX

DEVASTATIONS

In which battles ensue,
nobility dies,
and spirits of valor are reborn.

CHAPTER 74

ON THE PRECIPICE

There were two levels beneath the main floor of Arwynn's stronghold: the upper and lower cellars.

The upper cellar was divided into four sections, each linked to two others by a narrow passageway. This construction allowed for the rapid isolation of any given section in the event of a breach; the compromised section could be flooded with poison gas from tanks stored on the floor above and later vented by means of a hidden bellows system. Primarily used for storage and equipment maintenance, one section of the upper cellar housed a machine shop and solid chemical laboratory—the still air ideal for fine crafting and work with resins and powders.

The lower cellar provided access to the Underwet. It consisted of a loose maze of uneven tunnels, faintly illuminated by phosphorescent lichen and studded with traps. The three points where the lower cellar joined to the Underwet were well disguised and well defended by Morghanti and Sadri.

It was at one of these points that Arwynn waited behind an illusory wall, eyes fixed on the sewer channel that stretched into the darkness to either side.

Soon Morkainen would arrive and his part would begin.

Arwynn noted his blademaster's approach, though he continued to stare into the sewers. He acknowledged the half-elfi's presence only when Morkainen gained his side.

"Have any contingencies been triggered?" Arwynn asked. He never acted without contingency plans. Unexpected circumstances and chance events might affect the way he attained his goal, but very rarely precluded its attainment.

"No," Morkainen replied. "This plan is locked until our forces gain Blaythe's temple."

There were three contingency triggers in his strike on the Black Church. By Morkainen's report, the first two had passed without the need to alter course.

Arwynn nodded.

"Have Loquay's sulari withdrawn?"

Morkainen shook his head. "No. They hold firm. They observe but take no action."

"Well enough. Loquay knows that our move against Blaythe will ultimately work to her advantage. If we succeed, we remove a thorn in her side."

"And if we fail, our House will collapse in the aftermath."

"Most likely."

"Her share of the spoils will be large."

"Very."

After a moment, Morkainen remarked, "I think you give Loquay too much credit. She's crafty, but short on prudence.

It's the prince's campaign against the Gobli Horde we have to thank for our good fortune, not Loquay's foresight."

A pause.

A shrug.

"Perhaps," Arwynn granted. "It's enough that her hands are tied for the moment. She can't advise Blaythe of our actions for fear of our reprisal should we succeed; she can't move against us with confidence without the Myriadi Royal backing her up. If Houses are cut, her House will bleed."

"And when the battle is done?"

"Loquay won't attack if we win. She'll assume we held back sufficient reserve to repel a Sathiian counterattack if we failed. That will stay her hand."

"You play a dangerous game, Arwynn," Morkainen said, "assuming that Loquay is as thoughtful as you. Either way, our best defense is a swift and decisive victory."

"That certainly cannot harm us, Rahain. How stands our force?"

"Prepared and positioned," Morkainen answered. "Modrihihl left with his shard twenty minutes ago. I'll give Ciridan's shard leave to go when we're finished here and have Tempek's follow thirty minutes later."

Thirty minutes, Arwynn thought. *Time enough.*

"Each shard is eighteen sulari, two or three Sadri, and a few elites," Morkainen continued. "Mine's smaller, but still sufficient to break into three or four splinters depending on what we encounter."

"Well done," Arwynn said. "Whispers?"

"Two. Free support."

"The Gardens?"

"Malaraphi has four Sadri in the Gardens of Twilight, one at each Elem temple. By his augury, Blaythe's forces will attack Wargrum's temple shortly after Ilia meets Glae. Once the attack starts, his Sadri will hit the Sathiians with elemental magicks. It will appear to Blaythe that the Elem have rallied to support the Wargrumites. Assuming he's monitoring the battle."

"He'll be watching."

"Then we have our distraction," Morkainen said. "On force of arms, we'll carry the battle inside the temple. Blaythe believes you incapable of turning against him. He won't be prepared for our attack."

Arwynn nodded. He touched his fingers to the slim chain he wore around his neck. Each of his splinterheads wore a similar chain. Malaraphi would destroy the master chain he wore, and all their linked chains would shatter to signal the initiation of the Sadri attack.

"You have your linkchain?" Arwynn asked.

"Yes."

"Then we're ready."

Morkainen nodded. "I'll send off Ciridan."

Arwynn watched Morkainen depart, then turned to make his way back to his keep. Thirty minutes was not a lot of time.

CHAPTER 75

OPPORTUNITY

Fedahi waited a long time before venturing from his refuge. After being waylaid by two of Loquay's sulari, it had taken him several days to heal.

During the first days of his recovery, after he'd dragged himself into a hiding place away from the ambuscade, Fedahi wondered how Gabrael had fared. Did she survive the attack? Had she rejoined Arael's company, and had they made it to the Temple of Wargrum?

Then he realized he didn't care. Not about Gabrael, not about the priests, not about their mission.

The only thing he cared about was Ciridan Lothloran. Nothing else mattered.

Only Ciridan.

Dear, sweet, lovely, dead Ciridan.

When Fedahi felt strong enough to leave his sanctuary, he did so cautiously. Despite his obsession with Ciridan, he remained lucid enough to appreciate the perils of the Underwet. The sewers beneath Dûhr were a deadly maze, and many accomplished sulari had lost their lives to the things that stalked its odious hollows. Then there were Sathiian acolytes to contend with, not to mention Loquay's sulari, the occasional cadre of Myriadi Royal, and Blackhand's splinters.

Ironically, Blackhand's agents posed Fedahi the greatest threat. House protocol marked missing sulari as defectors after two weeks without contact. His sudden appearance in the sewers after so long would be cause enough for his death. So it was with great care that he skulked about the dark tunnels—looking here, listening there, avoiding this patrol, spying on that one—all the while observant for any information on the woman who ruined his life.

A picture soon emerged. The changes in Blackhand's patrol patterns, the increased security along the points where the Underwet met his cellars, and the whispers of recalls and transfers among Morghanti and Vehem implied that House Blackhand was preparing to launch an attack. A big one.

Fedahi knew what he had to do.

By the time the Myriadi Royal were recalled from the sewers, Fehadi had obtained what he needed to disguise himself as one of Morkainen's Shadows.

By the time the first of Arwynn's shards reached Blaythe's temple, he'd positioned himself to slip into the force.

CHAPTER 76

MOSS

Ciridan led her shard through the Underwet toward the Sathiian temple. They moved swiftly and silently, silhouettes in the near dark, and left no trace of their passage beyond faint footprints and smudges on slimy stones.

Modrihihl's mission with the first shard had been to clear the way from Arwynn's lower cellar to the Sathiian temple and breach its base. Ciridan's mission with the second shard was to infiltrate the temple and prepare to confront the Sathiians from within. Once inside, Ciridan would break her shard into independent splinters and send them deeper into the temple to prepare for their attack. Her responsibility would be limited to the three sulari in her own splinter. She was confident that she could deal with them, if it became necessary.

Confident, but not certain.

Ciridan halted their advance as they neared the temple's foundation. She could not discriminate which of her senses triggered an alert, but she heeded the warning.

The Sahadi squinted her eyes and peered through the gloom. Even with her heightened vision and the cold glow of the ubiquitous lichen, she saw nothing that bespoke danger. When she strained her ears against the heavy stillness, she heard only the natural sounds of the Underwet: water and vermin and insects engaged in an orchestra of decomposition. A gentle touch brought no sense of vibration from the walls or the floor. A tempered sniff—

?

—brought an anomaly. Beneath the pong of decay, she could make out a strangely sweet tint to the air. Like a sweet herb. Or a flower.

Then it was gone.

Ciridan took a step toward the corridor that cut across the passageway ahead. She signaled her sulari to remain still and smelled the air quizzically.

Nothing.

Another step.

A third.

She found the scent again. Sweet and somehow sickly, like the dying breath of a fragrant blossom. Then it disappeared again, lost to the drifting currents of the Underwet.

Ciridan frowned and eyed the cross passage carefully. Their goal was thirty yards to the right. If Modrihihl had been successful, the rock that cradled the temple's foundation would be riddled with holes large enough to crawl through. But what of the path to the left? That way led deeper into the Underwet.

Ciridan took a last whiff, detected nothing.

She motioned her troops ahead.

They entered the corridor and turned right. Moments later, they reached their destination.

There was no one there.

No sulari met them, no priest attacked. There was no sentry, no ambush, no sign of battle. The area was silent and still, littered with thick piles of dull green moss about and between several large tunnels that perforated the rock where the passageway ended.

The tunnels were the work of xyborgh beetles. Modrihihl had brought four with him. The Sadri in his shard had kept the beetles miniaturized until they reached this place, then allowed them to regain their true size before casting a spell of hunger. The ravenous creatures would eat through the rock, opening tunnels the size of a man as they passed.

They got this far, at least. But there should be sulari here. Where are they?

She took a deep breath. The smell of rotting flowers was strong here. The moss was the likely source, or something inside the beetleways...

Ciridan signaled her sulari to hold their position and moved closer to the tunnels. As she approached, the mounds of moss grew more distinct, and it became clear they were the source of the odor. They were misshapen, lumpy masses—a hodgepodge of moss and lichen and vine and peat, interspersed with tatters of cloth and bits of metal and scraps of leather without order—some singly, some wed into larger piles.

The beetleways seemed clear of the curious green, and it grew nowhere else on the walls or floor of the passage that

Ciridan could tell. It didn't appear to grow naturally on the tunnel floor, and what was present moved easily when she pushed it with her blade. It was as if whatever the green had grown upon was not a part of the tunnel at all, but…

Gods below…

"Savishi," Ciridan whispered, signaling the Sadri to join her. She waved her hand at the nearest mossy heap. "What do you make of this?"

Savishi squatted and studied the strange pile. She muttered and whispered, then poked the vegetal pile with a dagger. Silver sparks skittered down the blade as it sank into the tangle. When she retracted the blade, it was bloodied.

The Sadri showed the blade to Ciridan.

"Animalia," she said quietly. "Do you want more?"

"No, that's enough."

Features grim, Ciridan looked around and, just loud enough for all to hear, said, "These are the remains of Modrihihl's sulari."

The sulari looked about as her words registered. They could now see that the larger masses were clusters of smaller mounds, and that the smaller mounds were roughly humani in shape and size. The tatters of leather and cloth were the remnants of armor and apparel. There were also shreds of purple cloth amid the moss. Whatever had done this had consumed sulari and Sathiian alike.

"Tendak, Seifa," Ciridan called softly.

The two Shadows moved swiftly to her side.

She waved her hand about the area: "Look for glyphs."

They nodded and bent to the task.

Ciridan charged four Morghanti to reconnoiter the area and determine how many had fallen to moss. She ordered the others to remain still and touch nothing, then turned a quizzical eye to her two Sadri.

Savishi shook her head. Agraxix shrugged.

Ciridan furrowed her brow and looked around. The mossy clumps appeared to be in defensive clusters, and the beetle tunnels were wide and evenly spaced. That suggested that Modrihihl's group was attacked after they'd set the beetles to bore.

"Do you think anyone survived?" Savishi asked.

Ciridan thought a moment. "If the tunnels pierced the temple, some may have made it inside."

"Perhaps," Savishi said. "And possibly their attacker."

Ciridan nodded. "Agraxix, what can you tell us?"

The second Sadri closed his eyes and steepled his fingers before his nose and mouth. He inhaled deeply before releasing a long, even breath. He opened his eyes and looked at her.

"There is nothing living here other than us and the green," he said, indicating the moss heaps. "No vermin, no insects. If the green itself did not do this, whatever did is no longer here."

"It's inside the temple," Ciridan said.

"It stands to reason," Agraxix affirmed.

"Beya."

Ciridan looked at the boreholes in the wall, then at her sulari, then at Agraxix and Savishi. Behind the Sadri, she noted a Shadow and a Blade standing ready to report.

"Seifa," she said. "What have you found?"

"There were three glyphs," the Shadow reported. "All dead. I can't say whether they were deactivated or triggered."

Ciridan nodded. "Tendak?"

"Between eight and twelve dead," the Blade replied. "A few masses appear to be multiple bodies. Mostly sulari by the clothing fragments: Loquay's and ours. A few Sathiians as well. There are several smaller clumps here and there, about the size of rats, and many tiny tufts scattered about randomly on the floor, walls, and overheads."

Vermin and insects. An indiscriminate attack; a blanket weave.

Ciridan gave a curt nod and gestured with her left hand. Seifa and Tendak waited where they stood. Ciridan leveled her violet eyes at the Sadri.

"Agraxix, form your killing fog," she commanded. "Savishi, coax it into the temple through the beetleways."

"You three," she said, turning and pointing. "Follow the fog with me. Everyone else, stand sly till I say fly."

CHAPTER 77

ICE AMID FIRE

The Flat of Obruhk was a wide, level expanse of ground that stretched out a mile from the southeastern fringe of the Borowood in a broad swath several miles across. Prior to setting the centerline of the Borowood aflame, Melkor's wizards had razed the flat for the benefit of his archers, so the advantage would be theirs when the fires drove the gobli from their warrens. Once verdant with tall grasses and scrub, it was now a blasted wasteland, dotted with the skeletal remains of a few obstinate trees and deep drifts of ash.

Melkor sat atop his mount at the edge of the flat and looked out over the charred landscape with calm detachment. There was a time when the sight of such devastation would have caused him terrible grief. For a moment, he wondered what it would have been like to stand upon the scrub as it burned, to stand amid fires as voracious as those that now consumed the Tameron and the Borowood. What would it be like to feel that awful heat, so pure and cleansing?

He felt nothing.

Not sadness.

Not remorse.

Not even curiosity.

What little emotion remained was muted and irresolute. Distant. Like a subtle taste for which he had to search. His was an existence rapidly dwindling to one of intellect alone, an existence without feeling or passion. But it was an existence that freed him from Blaythe's drug, and it would soon liberate his realm from Adderash's clutch.

The prince lifted his gaze from the blackened landscape. Between the craggy peaks that lined the Tameron to his right and where the Borowood's dark contour met the backdrop of the night sky to the left, he could see a long orange glow. The light of a hundred conflagrations. Half of which were being driven inexorably toward the blasted flatlands before him by a dozen distant wizards.

CHAPTER 78

BLUE PLUS

The beetleways all led to the same large subterranean chamber: one entered on its west wall, one near its center, and the third by the base of the north wall. There were two additional beetle tunnels in the north wall. Near the west wall were the remains of four large crates that appeared to have been damaged or destroyed by the beetles' emergence.

Six vegetal heaps lay on the earthen floor, three near the easternmost beetleway in the north wall and three scattered about the chamber's eastern half. One particularly large and gruesome mass lay amid the broken crates. The entire scene was lent a surreal quality by the eerie blue effulgence that filtered from Agraxix's killing fog as it undulated along the ceiling.

Ciridan, Agraxix, Savishi, and three Blades entered the chamber first, to vet the area. Agraxix crouched near the broken crates with two Blades, sifting through the pulverized rock that rimmed the beetles' points of entry. Savishi stood near the north wall, swaying gently to the tune she hummed to keep the killing fog roiling along the ceiling. The third Blade stood guard at the east wall, by the chamber's only door.

Ciridan moved to examine the crates with Agraxix. As she drew near, she saw not one mass between the crates but two. One appeared humanish, though clearly not a being of flesh and blood. Its limbs and extremities had lengthened and taken root in the floor. Umbilicals and pale tendrils joined it to several other vegetal masses. These originated from its ruptured chest, from what had apparently formed its intestines and major arteries. The creature's lungs were also exposed, though they looked more like swollen bladders than lungs. They quivered now and again and discharged a faint floral odor. Near the creature was a monstrous mossy mound, much larger than the others, insectile in aspect. The transmuted remains of one of the xyborgh beetles.

Ciridan drew up her face in disgust. "What is that?"

Agraxix looked up and followed Ciridan's gaze.

"A mystery," he said, standing and clapping his hands clean.

"Man turned creature?" Ciridan asked. "Or a creature shaped as man?"

"Man turned creature."

"You're certain?"

Agraxix nodded and pointed at the bloated organs in the creature's torso. "The innards tell the tale. Were this a creature shaped to appear humani, its creator would not have wasted the energy to shape the internal organs. A humani transmuted into a creature, however, would—"

"—hold their organs," Ciridan finished, then nodded and sucked at her lip in thought.

"Is this the creature that killed Modrihihl's sulari? Or a victim itself?"

"Now that is difficult to say," the Sadri admitted. Then he smiled. "But it does lend excitement to the night."

Ciridan grunted and shook her head. She turned from the Sadri and dilated the iris on her new ring. In the light that spilled from the small sunstone within, she examined the ampoule of liquid affixed to a metal bracelet on her wrist. A chemical reaction within the liquid had been initiated when she left Arwynn's keep. The liquid was now deep blue.

Blue plus. Maybe ten minutes to violet. Then twenty to black, when Tempek's shard will enter the beetleways. We must be positioned by then.

Ciridan considered burning the gruesome thing on the floor before calling her remaining sulari up from the sewers—but quickly dismissed the idea. She would need Savishi to guide the smoke into the sewers to keep it from wafting into the temple and alerting the Sathiians inside. That would limit her sulari to two tunnels and force Savishi to relinquish control of Agraxix's fog. Agraxix would have to dispel his fog, lest it affect them, then reconstitute it. At blue plus, there was no time for such doings.

Especially when she had already used so much of her power to evade detection by her own Sadri.

"Bring in the others," she said to a sulari. "We need to move."

CHAPTER 79

DOUBT

Welbley Blaythe was an astute man, but his imagination was limited by logic; he was not given to flashes of creative insight or unexplainable feelings of anxiety. Even so, three nights prior to his arrival in Dûhr, as his sumptuous barge slowly sailed on the River Fwaer, he began to experience a vague distress. The more he dwelled on it, the greater it became—but it wasn't until Dûhr loomed on the horizon that he began to settle on a cause.

Ever since his embrace of Sathiis, Welbley had maintained unswerving confidence in his role as an instrument of the Serpent of Heaven. Never once had he disputed the Black Church's doctrine, doubted its destiny to rule over the entirety of the Realms Humani, or questioned the leadership of Adar Ashan. But now… recent events rattled his convictions.

Like the mysterious Malaraphi.

The lord sovereign had waved aside Welbley's concerns over an elfi named Malaraphi within House Blackhand. Adar had insisted that it could not possibly be the same mage that felled Zithwathn the Blue, arguing that it must be some opportunist seeking to draw power from the name. But Welbley had detected a hint of unease in his tone.

Could it be the same elfi? Did my lord lie?

Then there was the matter of Wirith. Welbley hadn't learned the fate of Aerkon's temple before leaving for Dûhr. Lacosia's success or failure would affect Adar's plans for the Realm of Wirith. Welbley knew Wirith better than anyone in the Black Church, yet Adar had ordered him to Dûhr.

Is the outcome being kept from me?

Even if Welbley agreed with his lord's reasons for sending him to Dûhr, he could not overlook the strain on the lotos supply. His agents desperately needed their consignment of Zaaldirn's lotos to tighten their hold over the northern realms. No deliveries had yet arrived. Unless they had... through distribution networks outside Welbley's.

As his barge drifted closer to Dûhr, Welbley began to feel that he was no longer part of the great Sathiian juggernaut, but perhaps an obstacle in its path.

Kaleena delivered the assassins she'd promised. When he arrived in Dûhr, Welbley was greeted by a delegation of four adepts, two dozen of Blackhand's sulari disguised as acolytes, and his new steward, Uthmahr Tecco. They exchanged superficial pleasantries; the area was too open to speak plainly.

They stowed Welbley's personal effects in Tecco's carriage and securely lashed the four large crates he'd brought from Evereve to carts. Welbley proceeded with Tecco and two adepts to his new temple, while the others took his cargo to the warehouse.

Comfortably seated in the carriage, Welbley went over his assets: Tecco, four adepts, two dozen sulari, eight more adepts and four times that many acolytes at the temple, Loquay's agents in the Underwet, four mutati liches, and Kaleena's magickal wards. He smiled. His temple was impenetrable, even if its physical structure was lacking.

It was not until they were secure in his sumptuous office with privacy enchantments woven that Tecco informed him of Melkor's strange behavior.

And the deaths.

Welbley stared at the door after it closed behind Tecco, then rose from his desk and began to pace back and forth before it. His steward had been right to wait until they reached his office to tell him of the prince's actions—his surprise and concern would have been apparent to anyone watching. His confederates and adversaries saw him as a man of composure and confidence. They would assume he knew of Melkor's deeds and that his actions were of no concern to the Black Church. That would inspire his allies and give his enemies pause. And it would give Welbley time to solidify his position.

But now, in the privacy of his new office, where the walls were blind and deaf, Blaythe let his worry show. A frown bit deep into his chubby face, and his little eyes smoldered with outrage. It was bad enough that one of the Black Church's most valuable pawns had freed themselves from control, but the prince had not stopped there. He had killed his priests and now led an army against the Gobli Horde.

The loss of one pawn might very well rob him of another.

Damn. Damn, damn, damn…

Welbley stopped and rubbed his face with his hands. He took a deep breath, expelled it loudly, and crossed the room to flop onto a stuffed divan. He stared blankly into space, hands rubbing back and forth on his thighs, as his thoughts slithered around his problems.

Then it struck him, and a smile slowly crept over his fleshy lips.

A cure is more valuable than a curse.

If he could determine how the prince had defeated the lotos, he could use that knowledge to secure inviolable prominence in the Black Church.

Adar Ashan already held the power to subjugate through addiction; Welbley could give him the power to offer surcease from that addiction in exchange for otherwise unattainable favors. The loss of the Gobli Horde seemed a paltry price to pay for that opportunity.

But the smile collapsed as another thought struck.

If Melkor could defeat the drug, then who else? Balistrahd? Mordavo?

His brow tightened.

Blackhand?

Without another thought, Welbley leaped from the divan and rushed to order the immediate termination of Arwynn's sulari.

CHAPTER 80

IMPATIENT SPIRIT

Fedahi grumbled at the luckless turn that separated him from his quarry. Until moments ago, fortune had been with him. He'd disguised himself completely—in form, feature, and scent—and managed to insinuate himself into first Ciridan's shard and then her splinter.

It should have been a simple matter to waylay her, drag her away, and slowly dismember her. But the spirit of fortune had abandoned him as suddenly as it favored him.

From her splinter, Ciridan selected him to remain behind to secure the chamber and brief the next shard. That wouldn't have been so bad—once her splinter departed, he could have deserted his post and shadowed her until he could steal her away. But Ciridan posted a second sentry. A Blood.

That complicated things.

I should have killed her when I had the chance.

Fedahi felt angry. Forsaken. He'd bided his time so judiciously, met each opportunity to slay the Sahadi with prudent restraint so he could prolong her agony. Make her suffer for an appropriate duration…

Now, he leaned against the wall by the chamber's only door and waited, eyes touching briefly in turn on the grotesque thing sprawled on the floor, the two beetleways that led out of the chamber, and the Blood that stood silently between.

Curse you, spirit! Curse your false promise of aid, your impatience, your—

Fedahi's scowl lightened.

Your impatience…

Suddenly, he understood. The spirit had not abandoned him; it merely withheld its aid when he withheld his hand! The spirit had already provided him with two opportunities to kill his betrayer, both of which he'd let slip away. Their desires were aligned, the assassin's and the spirit's, but only to a point: while Fedahi actively sought Ciridan's death, the spirit was with him; when he restrained himself, so too did the spirit.

Is that it, spirit? Swift and certain, is that what you want? Kill her and be done with it? Finish the task quickly so that you might move on, eh? Lend your aid to another's vengeance? Hmm? Is that it? To gain your blessing, I must forgo my own satisfaction?

Silence.

Stillness.

The spirit did not answer.

CHAPTER 81

DECEITFUL WRATH

Kaleena stormed down the corridor to Welbley's office, her misty cloaks a deep crimson swirl.

Her role in the unfolding drama had changed. Where it had been her task to clandestinely sabotage Welbley's defenses during his temple's construction, her new goal was to keep the priest off balance until Arwynn's forces initiated their attack. A few days ago, that sounded simple enough. But that was before Melkor executed three of Welbley's priests.

Welbley must be beside himself. If Melkor could throw off his control, who else? Arwynn is a logical suspect—his cunning is formidable; his resources, great; and his spies, pervasive. What the prince could learn, Arwynn could steal. Blaythe must suspect him.

Kaleena quickened her pace.

If Welbley believed that Arwynn was no longer under her control, he would immediately dispose of the sulari stationed throughout the temple. Without them, the odds of Arwynn's victory in the coming battle diminished considerably. She could not allow that.

Kaleena knit her brow into an angry scowl and let a deep growl curdle in her throat as she approached Welbley's office.

She wanted to appear as angry as he expected her to be, or her ploy would never succeed.

She raised a tight fist and beat upon the door.

Welbley stopped, startled. He was reaching for the door when someone beat on it from the hall.

"Who is it?" he demanded.

No one answered.

Blaythe scowled. "Open!"

The heavy wooden door swung inward. In the threshold stood the Crimson Witch, red cloaks writhing about her body like waves of blood. Welbley's little eyes narrowed, his thick lips falling at the corners. This was an untimely nuisance. He had neither time nor penchant to placate so fickle an anger as that of the witch.

With an exasperated grunt, Welbley dispelled the glyph that warded his door and moved beside his desk as the witch entered. Kaleena did not take her eyes from the priest as she strode in.

Welbley motioned for her to sit.

She ignored him.

"I," she said angrily, "am not happy!"

"Oh?" Welbley's tone was as sarcastic as the witch's was caustic. "Really, now? We can discuss it later. Right now, I have sulari to kill."

"That can wait," Kaleena hissed. "Sit!"

Her hair writhed without wind, her cloaks churned like gory storm clouds, her eyes bled thick red light.

Welbley took an involuntary step back. He looked at the door, then at the witch. Never before had he seen the Crimson Witch enraged, nor had he felt such alarm.

Sulari forgotten, he backed away and sat at his desk.

She followed with her eyes and placed her hands flat on his desktop, leaning into his face. Her nails seemed longer, sharper than he remembered. The tattoos on her hands pulsed.

Tattoos?

"You swore to me—*swore to me*—that Arwynn Blackhand would be mine!" she seethed. "Mine! Mine! Forever! You assured me that there was no escape from your drug. And I believed you! I believed you! And now this…"

She growled loudly and pulled back her lips in a snarl. Her teeth seemed sharper.

Welbley tried to regain the aura of dispassionate calm that was his strength.

"Kythidûhr has slipped through your fingers, Welbley. Like so much water through a sieve. Is Blackhand to slip through mine as well?"

He failed.

"Hold your tongue, witch!" he snapped.

Indignation overwhelmed fear. He rose from his chair and thrust his face close to Kaleena's.

"I will not be spoken to in such a manner!" he hissed. "Not by you. Not by anyone. Is that clear?"

Kaleena's eyes narrowed. The red of her cloaks grew deeper, darker.

"Do you think me unconcerned?" Welbley demanded loudly, throwing aside his chair. "Do you think me undistressed? Hmm? Do you think I've not wondered about these very things?"

Kaleena's lips slowly parted in an acrimonious sneer.

Her teeth seemed longer still. Pointed.

"I don't care what you feel or think," the witch snarled, "I care about my interests! Mine, and mine alone. What I want from you are explanations. How did Kythidûhr break free from your drug? And will Blackhand do the same?"

As she spoke, he watched her nails grow long and curved, like the talons of a hunting bird. Two cut into the polished surface of his desk. He wondered whether Adderash's Sacred Shield could nullify Kaleena's enchantment before her talons could rip him apart.

He decided not to take the risk.

Not yet.

CHAPTER 82

VISIONS OF BEFORE

After conferring with Morkainen, Arwynn returned to his keep and did three things. First, he set a series of failsafe wards. Second, he retrieved a cilice and his slaygear, preparing himself for combat. Third, he retired Tempek Mikahr and assumed his identity. Posing as the Shade, he would use Tempek's splinter to search Blaythe's temple for the lotos drug under cover of the attack. He didn't expect Kaleena to fail, but he couldn't be too careful. The cilice was a necessary hedge.

Arwynn eased open the door and scanned the hallway beyond. It was empty. And dark, save for a dim glow of silver somewhere beyond a distant bend.

He listened carefully… nothing.

He sniffed the air… stale.

The faint scent of flowers permeating the chamber did not extend into the hall.

I cannot dally about these cellars. The drug will not be here. He's a crafty one, this priest. His treasure will be well hidden.

Arwynn closed the door and turned. Two Bloods were inspecting the beetle tunnels in the chamber's north wall while a Blade continued to search for signs of Ciridan's missing sentries. At the far end of the room, Mahala examined the thing that lay sprawled between broken crates. The sulari Ciridan posted in the sewer below had informed them that the mossy lumps were transmuted humani remains. The thing on the floor, however, was a mystery.

The Blade approached. She held up a curled hand, trailing a fine powder from her palm.

"There's a layer of pulverized rock from the xyborgh sprinkled over most of the floor," she said. "Ciridan's work. Has to be."

"And the sentries?"

"There were two."

"What happened?"

The Blade pointed to the western of the two tunnels in the north wall.

"There's disturbance in the dust at the mouth of that tunnel."

She traced a path through the air from the tunnel to the chamber's only door.

"Something entered, shuffled about just inside the room, then moved across and out the door. Two legged. No attempt to avoid the vines and runners—stepped on some, kicked aside others. Other than that, the dusting hasn't been disturbed."

"That heap of moss nearest the west tunnel?"

"It formed after the room was dusted."

"And the others?"

"Before."

So, it's mobile.

Tempek nodded. "That accounts for one of Ciridan's sentries. The second must have fled."

The Blade nodded. "Down the hall."

Tempek thought a moment, then called his Sadri. "Mahala."

The woman looked up from where she crouched. "Yes?"

"Tell me what happened."

Mahala (*Time*) hesitated a moment, then straightened and said smugly, "You realize, Tempek, that the PastVision exacts a random toll. It may weaken me to where I cannot continue with your splinter."

Only the Sadri had the authority to second-guess their splinterhead. It was one of the few conditions that Malaraphi demanded in exchange for his services. Arwynn regretted giving in to the old elfi. And he had never liked Mahala.

"I know," he said.

"Will you assign a surrogate?"

"No. Weave your magick. Your family will be compensated."

Mahala glared at Tempek for a long second before stepping carefully to the center of the room. She raised her arms and focused her thoughts, then started mumbling as her fingertips danced in the air. Red flickers of light began to prance about her extended fingers, darting from her hands to random points in the chamber and back.

The sparks grew more numerous and more chaotic. They began to fly madly, ricocheting about the chamber as Mahala's consciousness slipped backward in time. The whizzing motes passed through all things of the temporal present and rebounded off the ghost images of what had occupied space in the past. Soon, the near present was consumed by the red motes, and the near past revealed itself.

A shadow flitted past.

A slower darkness followed.

Three voids took shape, then became two as the darkness flew from a beetleway in the north wall. Soon, the echoes of Ciridan's splinters disturbed the radiance as they gained the chamber from the temple beyond through the twin exit tunnels.

Mahala slipped farther back along the timeline.

The ghostly silhouettes made plain the manner of Ciridan's entry into the chamber, and finally the chaotic tumult that preceded her arrival. Then two humanoid figures emerged from the beetle's entry shafts, as though coughed up from the sewers below, while another backed toward them from across the chamber, leading the dark forms of gigantic beetles back toward their points of entry. Then the scene went wild, with a visual cacophony of scarlet bursts until hollow, lightless spaces took humanoid shape where the lumpy masses now occupied the chamber.

Then, the spell was over and the few remaining bloody sparks faded from sight.

The PastVision imposed enormous physical and mental tolls on a weaver. Unlike shaping the physical world, the energy required to manipulate Aethic threads across time was extracted directly from the caster, consuming their memories and aging them in an unfair ratio to what they glimpsed. Mahala had found a way to circumvent the spell's aging effect through the consumption of surrogates, but memory wasting could not be avoided.

But now, without a surrogate…

Mahala swayed listlessly, eyes open and glassy. Her face was deeply lined by decades of unlived years, her hair streaked with brittle gray. Her fingernails were longer by inches, yellowed and cracked by stolen time.

She teetered, then fell to her knees with a loud crack. She did not appear to notice.

Arwynn moved to the Sadri's side and crouched beside her. "What happened?" he asked softly.

"Four," she said. "There were four."

"Four," Arwynn repeated. His voice was low, measured. He took gentle hold of her…

"Men," the Sadri said. "But not men."

… eased her down to lie on her side…

"Not alive," she mumbled. "Not dead. Between."

… and cradled her head in his lap.

"Liches," he said.

"Yes…"

Mahala suddenly locked eyes with him—she was present and clear.

"There were four," she said hurriedly. "Locked in the crates. The beetles smashed the crates when they ate through the walls. That freed them. One… one was gored… by a beetle… its body…"

She began to falter.

"Its body…" Arwynn pressed gently.

"Exploded. A great spray. Not blood. Not blood." She fought to hold the moment. "They all died," she whispered. "Six of them. People."

Lucidity slipped away.

"Six people died," Arwynn whispered. He moved a lock of hair from her face.

"Gas... their breath..."

She slipped a little further out of the present.

"And then?" Arwynn asked.

"They left."

"Through the doorway?"

Mahala paused, slipped a little further away. "One. Only one. Others went... sewers..."

And she was gone.

CHAPTER 83

ROYALTY AND RAIDERS

The Haugwym proved to be far more organized and knowledgeable than the barbaric nomadic raiders the Ufwinians had branded them. They held knowledge of a network of primeval ruins that undercut the Realms Humani and mastery of the keys to the interdimensional portals and World Gates hidden throughout those ruins.

Haugwym expertise with the World Gates reduced the Ufwinians' journey from ten days to one. They moved from ruin to ruin without ever leaving the innards of the earth, through dark and ancient realms by passageways natural and not, through shadowy spaces where the air was laced with malice and ululant cries echoed in thick gloom. The Ufwinians realized that they were moving through ageless and magickal places. Had they known the nature and extent of those magicks, they would have been terrified.

Through it all, their numbers grew. More Haugwym joined the party with each new tunnel between World Gates, with each step across dimensions. For every raider that died or disappeared on their surreal journey, a dozen more joined. By the time they reached the ruins of Ûthmir in the Mountains Icetop at the eastern edge of the Borowood, their small band of sixty-three had grown to nearly twelve times that number.

It was there that the Haugwym received word that Melkor's army had reached the Flat of Obruhk.

They did not tell the Ufwinians.

Gahlyfahx and the Haugwym raider called Ka'an looked out over the stones that ensconced their position. Neither had words to describe the scope of the conflagration that met their eyes, so immense was the sea of flame that consumed the lands below. Even from their vantage in the Icetops miles to the east, they could feel the heat carried on the dark smoke.

"By my soul…" Gahlyfahx whispered. "The entire Borowood is burning!"

"And the Tameron," said Ka'an.

"What caused this?"

"Melkor's magickai."

"Melkor?"

"He calls the gobli to war. Look upon the flat."

Distracted by the scale of destruction before him, Gahlyfahx had not noticed the army lining the Flat of Obruhk below their position. Through the smoke and distance, he could just make out the silver-and-black regalia of House Kythidûhr.

"He must have ten thousand soldiers," Gahlyfahx said.

"Eleven thousand six hundred and twelve," Ka'an said. "It will not be enough."

"Almost twelve thousand? Not enough?"

Ka'an shook his head.

He pointed at the burning landscape and said, "You look at the burning forests and think, 'It is but a small fraction of the Gobli Lands, there cannot be many of the creatures within.' You cannot imagine the number of gobli that will soon emerge."

Gahlyfahx looked at the distant fires. He was silent for a moment, then said, "This is why you brought us here instead of Dûhr, isn't it? To join in this battle against the gobli."

"Yes."

"Then you should not have. We will not fight for Kythidûhr."

Ka'an tilted his head.

"House Kythidûhr serves the Black Church," Gahlyfahx said. "To aid him is to serve the Snake. We will hold our position here, allow Kythidûhr's army and the Gobli Horde to destroy each other, and then rout any that remain."

Ka'an shook his head slowly from side to side. "You do not understand, Prince Halfhand. It is the Gobli Horde that serves the Snake, not the prince of Dûhr."

"That is not so. Melkor—"

"Melkor freed himself and his city before leading his army to this place. Cendek Tulane now rules Dûhr. This was proven to us."

"When?"

"Two days before you left Ufwin."

"Why didn't you tell us?"

"It was not time."

CHAPTER 84

FINGERS OF A BLACK HAND

Morkainen brought his shard out of the sewers some distance away from the Gardens of Twilight, then doubled back through alleyways. When they reached the Gardens' eastern periphery, he opened a breach in its boundary wall with a powerful acid. As the mortar between the stones popped and fizzled, Morkainen broke his shard into three large splinters.

He sent the first splinter back into the sewers, to enter the walled Gardens through a secret passage near the crypts beneath the Temple of Anwin. He sent the second south through the city's back streets, to scale the wall in a place thick with kalypshia. (Because the kalypshia provided an effective deterrent against trespassers, the area was seldom surveilled; with a Sadri's weave to hide their heat, they would slip easily past the deadly vines.) The third would enter the Gardens with him, through the hole he now opened in the wall. Once inside, they would wait in the orchard between the temples of Anwin and Sheeshee until Malaraphi signaled the attack.

As he watched the wall disintegrate, Morkainen touched one of the daggers sheathed at his shoulder. It had been a long time since he'd worn his c'thuto knives. Not since Gehn. Tonight, however, he found great comfort having them at hand. Compared to the acid within their crystal blades, the chemical that ate the stone wall before him was little more than water. Although he was confident his sulari could dispatch any soldiers Blaythe could muster, he was certain one of his c'thuto knives could slay any creature the priest could summon.

As mortar sputtered and foamed, Morkainen began to feel strangely connected to the disintegrating wall. The pops and splutters resonated within him, and he found himself wondering what it would feel like to break apart.

Would it be a painless thing? More a dissolution of existence than a deterioration of physical form? Or would it—

A stone fell from the wall with a heavy thud.

Then another.

Two more.

Morkainen scowled, shaking his head. The Emptiness wouldn't overcome him tonight.

The way was open. It was time to enter the Gardens.

Arwynn assigned two Blades to return Mahala to the keep, then divided his shard into three splinters. He ordered the two larger splinters to follow the beetleways deeper into Blaythe's temple, then led the third out the chamber door into the hall. He was confident that Blaythe would not store important items in the cellars, but prudence demanded that he give them at least a cursory inspection.

They encountered several more mossy heaps as they crept through the cellars.

The faint scent of flowers waxed and waned but never failed to maintain an unhealthy presence.

Malaraphi and Elyssa Covaine (*Heat, Pyrotechnica*) sat on the lip of the highest of seven spires that crowned the Temple of Pheon and waited for Blaythe's forces to attack Teahl's temple. Except for Elyssa, to whom he could speak directly, Malaraphi maintained mental contact with the Sadri deployed to the other Elemian temples: Zehedros (*Storm, Song*), atop the great arch of Anwin's temple; Grithsdane (*Lightning, Bending*), between the minarets that rimmed the Temple of Sheeshee; and Zina Atay (*Stone, Animus*), atop the southeast annex of the Temple of Wargrum.

Once Blaythe's forces attacked, the four Sadri would assail them with magicks appropriate to the Church where they were stationed: Anwin, water; Pheon, fire; Sheeshee, air; Wargrum, earth—the goal being to make Blaythe believe he was under a combined Elemian attack. If he chose to attack the Elemians and draw them into the fray… well, that would simply be good fortune.

Malaraphi's only concern was that he did not know the hour of the Sathiian attack. He'd been able to augur the attack itself with relative ease; determining the day required substantially greater effort, while pinpointing the precise time proved impossible. He was only able to determine that it would happen when Glae and Ilia shared the same space in the sky.

He looked to the heavens.

Glae and Ilia just touched.

It cannot be much longer. After the sisters kiss, they—

Morkainen eased his sulari through the hedgerow that marked the boundary between the Temples of Sheeshee and Anwin, then turned north toward a brushwood of trees and signaled his sulari to cover. They disappeared into the shadows.

A soft breeze shook loose some leaves. As they drifted silently to the earth, the crumbling sensation returned. This time, accompanied by a vague impression of warmth.

Morkainen ignored it.

He focused on the Sathiian temple that loomed a short distance away. Scaffolding clung to its facade in several places, but he knew it belied the integrity of the structure. The temple was a fortress, and its inhabitants were every bit as ruthless as his sulari.

Creeeeeak…

Morkainen froze. He cocked his head to listen but caught no sound beyond the breeze rustling the leaves. The frogs had grown silent. The crickets, still.

A long moment passed.

Another.

Then the sound returned, louder and fuller.

eeeaaaagggggghhhhhhhhhhhkkkkkkkkkkkkkkkk

Morkainen twisted around.

That's coming from—

Malaraphi stiffened as the Aethic link with his Sadri abruptly failed and his world went black.

His linkchain caught and snapped as he collapsed.

CHAPTER 85

DEEP INTO VIOLET

Ciridan and three sulari huddled in a storage closet off a clerical office on the ground level of Blaythe's temple. The body of the attendant clerk lay naked at their feet, his clothing stuffed between the door and its jamb to minimize sound and light. Even so, Ciridan used her ring's glowstone sparingly and spoke in hushed tones.

"We're here," she whispered, sketching out the surrounding hallways and chambers on a scrap of paper. "Two corridors removed from these cells, where Blaythe's acolytes sleep and pray. When the attack begins, we'll wait for the battle to slip past this office. Then we'll move out and attack from behind. Our attack will be staged. First, spraydarts—who's primed?"

Two Blades raised their eyes to hers and nodded.

"Succuya," said one.

"Iko sarate," said the other.

Ciridan nodded; both had deadly poisons. "Good."

She turned back to the map, traced a corridor with her finger. "After the spraydarts, we'll fall back and circle around to this area, through this corridor, and engage the survivors hand to hand. I suspect—"

She froze midsentence, eyes on the door. The sound was faint, possibly inaudible to the others. She glanced at the sulari and quickly covered her ring.

The room went dark. Five hands reached for weapons.

Ciridan put an open hand on the door and pressed her ear lightly against the smooth wood. She felt nothing unusual but could hear movement on the other side. Soft. Shuffling. It was aimless motion, as though the newcomer had forgotten where they were going, remembered, then forgotten again.

The sound drew closer…

She held her breath and—

… closer…

—tightened her grip on the contoured hilt of her shortblade.

… then away.

Ciridan let her breath out slowly but maintained her grip on her weapon. It was the only defense she possessed. She could not rely on magick; she didn't have the power.

For a moment, she thought she detected a subtle flowery scent.

Then it was gone.

CHAPTER 86

OMIUM

Arael safeguarded her individuality. She constructed a vault of pure will about the core of her identity as she let slip the psychic barriers that protected her link with the Aethios. Raw energy began to seep, then flow, then surge into her as her physical defenses weakened, crumbled, and collapsed.

Her body began to shudder.

Her flesh began to crack.

The vessel of her body could barely contain the unshaped energy she had opened herself to channel into the gholem.

An hour before Ilia and Glae kissed in the night sky, Kargan Teahl evacuated his temple of all but Arael Laran and four high priests. Arael he assigned to the temple's central annex; Vayen and Breman, the east and west wings; Martara and Alira, the east and west sections of the cellar. Then he withdrew to the temple's observatory.

In his heart, Kargan carried desperate hope. In his hand, he carried Nimwe's Ring of Stone.

In their positions throughout the temple, Wargrum's priests gave themselves freely to the emerging whole, that in union they might accomplish what none could alone. Without fear, each tucked away the seed of their separate identity, let fall their personal protections, and reached out to the other five with complete openness of spirit. Their minds touched, connected, and merged into a burgeoning collective awareness.

Each contribution was amplified by their union, until awareness blossomed into wakefulness and the onslaught of Aethic energy that tore at their bodies lost its violence and softened into a surging rhythm, like the pulse of a great creature a thousand times more powerful than the imagination that spawned it.

To the Wargrumites, the Ceremony of Omium represented the ultimate intimacy that mortals could attain. It was an act those of dark heart could neither comprehend nor imitate, for their mistrust prohibited them from openly joining. They could never rejoice in the rapture that Arael now felt as she merged her soul with those of her brethren.

Neither could they harness the unimaginable power that came with the Omium.

Through the Ceremony of Omium, each of the six priests became first a conduit for the Aethios, then part of a greater whole as their essences merged until all that remained was a shared sense of oneness.

Less than consciousness.

More than awareness.

Gradually, the collective whole became aware of a sense of purpose as Kargan's gentle influence manifested. With that sense of purpose came intent, and the power to shape. With the power to shape came the desire for form. And the beginnings of control.

A resounding rumbling filled the air as the Temple of Wargrum rose out of the earth. The power of the Aethios, channeled through the matrix of Nimwe's Ring of Stone, simultaneously destroyed and remade Wargrum's temple.

Masonry popped and crumbled.

Iron reinforcements twisted and realigned.

Stone and brick and wood merged and melded.

As the building rose slowly up and out of the ground, the two annexes contracted and slid into bilateral symmetry about the temple's central chamber. The upper tiers contorted, collapsed, and sank into the central dome to form a rough approximation of a head atop the bulk of the primary structure. The north wing lengthened, curved, and slid easily into the earth, connecting the restructuring stone of the temple's upper levels to the substance of its lower halls.

In the space of minutes, the transformation was complete, and the temple was gone. In its place stood a gargantuan creature composed of its essence.

A creature that turned its head in the direction of Blaythe's temple.

CHAPTER 87

MISDIRECTION

Welbley moved to a nearby window. He let his fingers linger on the heavy curtain but did not draw it aside.

"I was en route to Dûhr when my priests were murdered," he said. "I learned of Melkor's contumacy only this evening, upon my arrival. I've not yet determined how he freed himself from the lotos."

Very slowly, Kaleena withdrew her talons. And her teeth. Her cloaks settled to ruby as her rage cooled to displeasure.

"Tell me then," she said with quiet intensity, "what you suspect."

"Suspect?" Welbley chuckled. "I suspect nothing. Why should I? Somphora and lotos are the perfect tandem. Only death can break their grip."

"Yet the prince has obviously done so."

A pause.

Uncomfortable and still.

"Perhaps," said the priest.

Kaleena scowled. "Perhaps? How else can you explain his daring? He killed three Sathiian priests in open Court! The political damage is not yet calculable. What more will he levy using his coalition with Great Houses Mercenary?"

"It could be a ruse."

Kaleena's expression changed from irritated to incredulous. "A ruse?"

Welbley turned to face her. He nodded.

"You cannot be serious," the witch sneered.

He nodded again.

Kaleena threw back her head and laughed.

Welbley spoke in an even voice, sounding braver than he felt. "Think about it, Kaleena. There is no way to defeat the tandem. No way at all. Even dwarfin physiology is susceptible. That is *fact*. But there are ways to delay its effects, to make it appear as though the drug has been defeated. It's more likely that Melkor has found respite, not release."

Kaleena stopped laughing.

Welbley shook his head and sighed. "But the means for such an illusion would certainly be fatal. Slow death of the brain. Surely Melkor would never accept such a fate simply to disserve me. That would be irrational."

"So is hatred, Welbley."

The Crimson Witch smiled.

"And Melkor Kythidûhr hates you. Very, very much."

Kaleena's hopes for Arwynn drained as she listened to Welbley. She began to believe that Melkor's deliverance was illusory and meant to provoke the Black Church into acting prematurely. That he led his army northward more to die beyond

Dûhr's scrutiny than defeat the Gobli Horde. Nevertheless, her indignation had served its purpose and turned Welbley's suspicion from her brother. The priest could understand how hatred could impel Melkor to act as he had; Melkor was a fundamentally noble man. But Arwynn was an assassin. For him, only vengeance could heal the wound Welbley inflicted, and vengeance required a true cure, not the illusion of one.

"You realize, Welbley," Kaleena said, "that I came here to kill you."

"I'd gotten that impression."

"I was certain that you'd delivered Blackhand to me under false pretense. I must admit, however, that there is merit in what you say."

Welbley nodded halfheartedly. "Though I fail to see what Melkor gains by his artifice."

"That's because you look too deeply," the witch chided. "The answer is plain; with his death, Melkor turns his city against you."

"How so?"

"Ask yourself," Kaleena said, "why does the prince lead an army against the Gobli Horde? Why not just send the Houses Mercenary off to fight? Why join them? Why lead them? To hurt you. True, he has made his life forfeit with his ruse, but once he engages the Horde, it will make no difference how he dies. If his campaign fails, the people will think you sabotaged his efforts in retaliation for the death of your priests. He will die a martyr, and his death will galvanize the people against you. If his army is victorious, he will die a hero and his subjects will take up his battle against you in his memory."

"A shrewd move," Blaythe grumbled. "But whose idea, I wonder? Not Melkor's. He was predictable in his best moments, and too addled by the lotos to outwit me, even accidentally. It must have been one of his advisers… or could it be that Selene has—"

Bang! Bang! Bang!

"—eh?" Welbley wheeled, commanding the chamber door to open.

Tecco sprang into the office and dashed to the window nearest the lord priest's desk.

"What is it, Tecco?" Welbley demanded.

Tecco threw aside the window's heavy curtain and thrust a wavering finger out over the Gardens below.

"There!" he cried. "You can't see it yet, but listen! Listen!"

Welbley moved to the window and suspended the Sound-Killing enchantment on its frame. They were met with a grinding noise from some distance away as the wall of silence collapsed.

"Listen!" urged Tecco. "Do you hear it? Do you hear it? It's the Temple of Wargrum!"

"The Temple of Wargrum?"

"Yes! It's moving!"

CHAPTER 88

COMPROMISE

Fedahi's eagerness to locate Ciridan was tempered by his fear of the creature that wandered the temple halls. Twenty minutes ago, as he contemplated how best to slip away from his post, a lanky humani had stepped out of the beetleway near his fellow sentry. As the Blood turned to dispatch the intruder, the humani expelled a great breath upon her. She fell to the ground in convulsions, her flesh simultaneously exploding and transmuting into plant. By the time it was over, Fedahi was fleeing down the second beetleway, afraid to breathe.

From the beetleway, Fedahi gained an acolyte's cell, and from there a hallway. A few moments later, he came to a wide serpentine corridor lined with tapestries depicting scenes from Sathiian scripture. As he prowled on, his fear ebbed and his thoughts turned once more to the object of his pursuit. Somewhere nearby, the flaxen-haired Sahadi awaited his blade. He had but to find her.

Isolate her.

Kill her.

A shudder went through him at the thought. It was quite pleasant.

Slowly, Fedahi's reason again gave way to his obsession, and his subconscious mind twisted reality to accommodate his fantasy. He came to believe that his encounter with the creature in the cellar had been engineered for his benefit. Had it not freed him to carry on his search for Ciridan? Had not the only witness to his desertion been removed? Did not the unnatural nature of the creature imply the workings of a supernatural hand?

This was your work, wasn't it, spirit? It was your hand that sent the fiend.

Fedahi quickened his pace as his delusion coalesced.

Yes, it was! I see that now. You wanted to speed me on my way, to end this affair quickly. You used fear to drive me forward, fear to bring me so quickly to—

A smile tugged at his lips. Again, it was a matter of speed. Speed was greed.

It never occurred to Fedahi that a spirit powerful enough to orchestrate his escape would be capable of destroying the Sahadi without his help. That a spirit should send him aid in a form that would incite him to greater speed, however, was right and true.

Fedahi's smile widened.

Yes, spirit, yes. Quicker, I agree. Faster, I agree. But not too fast for my own pleasure. We must both be satisfied. You and me both.

In his head, he sang a song of compromise as he crept along the corridor.

Swift to find the woman,
and carry her away;
slow to kill the woman,
by my hand, my way.

His smile broadened into a toothy grin.

By my hand, my way.
By my hand, my way.

CHAPTER 89

Inaccessible Assets

Welbley turned to Tecco. "What's happening?" he demanded. "Is this an attack?"

Tecco shook his head, sputtered: "I don't know, my lord."

"Beya!" Welbley shoved him aside. "What else could it be?"

He fired a fierce glance at Kaleena. "What do you see?"

The witch stepped to the window and leaned against the ledge. She looked toward the area of the Wargrumite temple and focused her will. Her scarlet cloaks grew darker and deeper red, and her eyes grew bright and bloody. Then twin beams of ruby light burst forth from their sockets and lanced through the night.

The hellish light rendered transparent all flesh and blood and bone upon which it fell and made translucent all things of leaf and stem and trunk. Only objects of earth and stone stood out boldly for all to see, brilliantly embossed in a crimson sheen. By the witch's eyes, they watched Wargrum's temple pull itself out of the ground and assume a humanish form.

"Sathiis's Bloody Coils!" Welbley whispered. "A gholem! And of such a scale as I've never imagined!"

"It will crush us!" Tecco cried. "It will destroy this temple and everyone inside!"

"Nonsense!" Blaythe hissed, silencing his henchman.

"It would appear, Welbley," Kaleena said, eyes fading, "that Teahl intends to give you no time to consolidate your power in Dûhr. An interesting approach, don't you think? Attacking you with his very temple transformed—it certainly lends itself to interpretation as divine intervention."

"Bah!" Welbley spat. "So he believes! But you forget that we've long been aware of the Wargrumites' animosity. We are well prepared for an attack of stone and earth."

He turned to Tecco, commanded brusquely: "Sound the alarm. Then fetch the staves. I will join you shortly."

Tecco turned to leave, but Welbley spoke again.

"Has Dorumo left yet?"

"No."

"Send her to secure the upper halls."

"The upper—?"

"Just do it!"

Tecco nodded and ran from the room.

"Staves?" Kaleena asked. "What staves?"

"Focused disintegrative charges," Welbley answered.

Tecco rejoined Welbley and Kaleena as they reached the temple's ground floor. His expression was one of fear battling confusion.

"What is it?" Welbley growled.

"Your cargo, Lord," Tecco managed.

A sudden frown cut across Welbley's pudgy face. "What of it?"

"Containment has been compromised."

"Beya! Where are the staves?"

Tecco pointed to the stairs leading to the lower levels. Two acolytes were sealing them off.

"What? Why weren't they in the vault?" Blaythe snarled.

"There wasn't time," Tecco sputtered. "Your cargo required —eckkh!"

Kaleena grabbed Tecco by the throat and slammed him against the wall with surprising ease.

"What's going on?" she demanded, eyes red with malice.

When Tecco looked helplessly to Welbley, the witch turned her angry gaze upon the lord priest, still holding his servant pinned to the wall.

"What is this cargo, Welbley? And why does it require containment? Has it—"

Kaleena's eyes constricted to menacing slits, and her voice dropped to a whisper.

"Gods below—have you brought plague to Dûhr?"

"No!" Welbley assured her. "Nothing so mundane."

"Then what?" the witch demanded. "Why does your man look so fearful? Why do your lackeys seal the stairs to the halls below?"

"Liches."

Kaleena released her grip on Tecco. He gasped for breath as he slid down the wall, cradling his throat.

"How many?" she demanded.

"Four."

Kaleena's eyes widened. "Four?"

Blaythe nodded. "Four very unique liches." He turned to Tecco. "Where are they now?"

"Lower… levels…" Tecco wheezed. "So… far…"

"So far?"

"Foundation… has… been breached…"

"What?" Welbley cried.

"B-beetles," Tecco stammered. "Giant b-beetles. Bored through the s-stone… ate right through the walls… into the lower storage level… the holding area."

"Blast!" Welbley exclaimed. "When?"

"An hour ago. Maybe two."

"Beetles of this type are not indigenous to Dûhr," Kaleena said. "They were placed there deliberately. By the Wargrumites, no doubt. To distract you. They are crafty, these priests, to draw your attention inward while they attack."

Welbley threw Kaleena a venomous sneer, then glared at Tecco and ordered, "Unseal those stairs and send adepts to the lower levels. Contain the liches; kill Blackhand's sulari. And get me those staves! Now!"

CHAPTER 90

THE SWORD OF PHEON

A torrent of gobli erupted from the burning forest and surged onto the Flat of Obruhk like a tsunami. Many had covered themselves in blood for war; others had woven animal entrails about their bodies and wore the heads of beasts upon their own. More simply charged into battle aflame, their wiry hair ignited by the magickal fires.

The flat responded with a sharp blare of horns. Sentries sounded; commanders ordered; warriors mounted; archers bent bows; infantrymen hefted pole arms and shields, locking their lines. With martial discipline and seasoned efficiency, the prince's forces snapped into an arrow formation. Melkor took the point.

Melkor held a hand above his head as he watched the Horde spew from the burning Borowood. When the gobli crossed into range, he dropped his hand. The air filled with black clouds of arrows, silver points like shooting stars as they streaked through the night to find targets.

The Horde ignored the arrows and trampled the fallen, not slowing.

Three more volleys followed before the horns sounded again. The Dûhrani army charged onto the Flat of Obruhk, and clouds of ash took to wind over the charred plain.

Horsemen pulled away from the infantry and split into wedges.

Then the two great armies met with an explosive crash.

The Horde tore into the Dûhrani like wild dogs savaging a carcass. They wielded their weapons with artless barbarity and hurled whole corpses over the battlefield like gibber stones, or used them as rams. When their weapons broke, they seized a limb of the nearest creature and tore it free to use as a gruesome club.

The humani responded with accomplished precision but could not withstand the staggering force of the gobli tsunami. The crushing tide of creatures flattened their ranks and demolished formations all along the battle line. Whole companies of cavaliers and infantry were tossed aside like flotsam, warriors swept away like spume.

And still the brutes spewed from the burning forest.

Overwhelmed by the sheer number of creatures, the humani fell into disarray—except the prince. Melkor Kythidûhr held his ground at the forefront of the melee, his silver sword gleaming through great arcs of blood.

It was as though Pheon had infused the prince with the fire of the gods. Here a bolt pierced his chest, there a wild blow ripped the armor from his shoulder, but he fought on, focused on his enemies and immune to pain. He stood imperiously upon the corpse of his steed atop a mound of dead fighters, meting out death with supernatural fervor. His resplendent silver armor, battered and bloodied as it was, shone like a beacon across the sooty battlefield.

Rallied by the vision of their prince, the Dûhrani rejoined the battle with renewed vigor. Such pride filled their hearts that their eyes grew blind to all but the targets of their blows, and their ears grew deaf to all but the sharp ring of deflected metal and the wet impact of gainful strokes.

So furiously they fought, so full of fervor they were, that when the air about them glittered and split and silken-cloaked figures sprang forth, they were convinced their prince had called down the forces of heaven to smite the Gobli Horde.

The Haugwym charged from the foothills and gained the battlefield using a sequential array of teleportive fields as the gobli forced the humani back to the edge of the Obruhk. They struck the Horde's eastern flank and opened a wide hole, into which their numbers poured.

The Horde responded without thought. Like a monstrous amoeba, it sealed its wound with its own numbers and swallowed the intruders within its mass.

The Ufwinians thundered onto the battlefield in a gleaming wedge of heavily armored cavalry around a company of mounted magickai. Gahlyfahx rode point, wielding the Blade Warsong with merciless efficiency. With each blow he landed, the sword's bloody aura brightened; with each death he dealt, its radius increased. Less than a minute after the Ufwinians engaged the Horde, Warsong's cerise glow engulfed everything within thirty yards of their prince.

Then the sword began to sing.

Softly at first, to Gahlyfahx alone, then louder and louder, until it became a terrible wail that drove fear and exhaustion into his enemies while its bloody radiance brought valor and strength to his allies.

Baloth watched the Borowood burn for a long time before he pulled away from his four azûne to reconnoiter the lands below. Leaving them to circle above the clouds, he coaxed his wyrm into a slow spiral descent. The thick smoke from the fires obscured his presence, save those brief moments when he dipped low enough to glimpse the battlefield. He carried on this way for several minutes, flitting in and out of caliginous cover like a fleck of darkness dancing on the skin of a storm cloud.

Slowly, he came to understand the way of the battle. The conflagration in the Borowood had driven the gobli into the Dûhrani army on the Flat of Obruhk while a second force, not of Kythidûhr's banner but clearly an ally, attacked from the east. During battle, the humani ranks had been split into three clusters, and the second force splintered into a score of isolated fragments. Kythidûhr must have thought to drive wedges into the Horde, not realizing how quickly its numbers would turn against him.

Even with his smoke-filled view of the battlefield, Baloth was impressed by the scale of the conflict. Thousands already lay dead on both sides, and Kythidûhr's army fared far better than Baloth had expected.

Unfortunately, the humani field position thwarted Baloth's plan to kill the prince. The gobli had pushed the humani infantry to the southern rim of the flat and hemmed their horsemen into isolated pockets. The azûne could identify clear points to target the gobli without compromising the myriad, but it would be impossible for him to catch Melkor in an acria strafe without drawing suspicion.

Then a thought struck him.

Would my desires not be served as well by the prince as the princess?

Baloth's azûne were unaware of Selene's agenda—it was his charge to kill Melkor in a manner that would seem accidental. The Dûhrani had fared remarkably well against the Horde; with Baloth's support, they might carry the battle. Should that come to pass, Melkor would certainly reward him Great House status, as his sister had promised. If confronted by the princess, he could simply claim that the opportunity to kill her brother had not presented itself.

Baloth smiled. The princess of Dûhr had taught him much.

Decision made, Baloth rejoined his circling azûne. With a series of hand signals, he issued commands—one azûne would attack the gobli battling the unknown faction to the east, two would bear down upon those attacking the main Dûhrani force, and the fourth would join him to strafe the creatures still streaming from the Borowood.

Calista watched the battle from the foothills with fear in her heart and a prayer on her lips. Beside her stood Ka'an.

Gahlyfahx had charged her to monitor the battle and send word to Dûhr if the Horde overwhelmed Melkor's army. Ka'an remained behind to guide her to Dûhr through the World Gates should the need arise. Though both would have gladly given their lives to land a blow against the Snake, each appreciated the importance of their mission.

Calista, to protect a realm.

Ka'an, to protect the daughter of the Calai.

The Haugwym split into dozens of small bands after they attacked, each pushing deep into the tide of gobli that still flowed from the Borowood. These bands quickly lost their momentum and became mired within the Horde's mass.

Then the shrieking began.

With horrifying cries that sliced through the din of battle, the Haugwym tore away their cloaks and armor and launched themselves at the gobli with renewed fury. This time, they attacked not only with blade and spear and hammer but with claw and tooth and tail. For the Haugwym were not humani; they were sauri.

In the shock of that revelation, the silhouettes of wyrms against the sky went unnoticed.

CHAPTER 91

FALLING TO BEDLAM

When Malaraphi's linkchain broke, the other necklaces followed in rapid succession, and Arwynn's splinters leaped into action. They sprang from behind screens and partitions, around pillars and supports, atop cabinetry, beneath furniture, from doors and curtains and staircases. They appeared without warning, without sound, their presence heralded only by the soft whistle of poisoned darts or a sudden mist of acid or poison gas. Though their numbers were diminished by the loss of Modrihihl's shard, the synchronicity and ferocity of their attack caught the Sathiians by surprise and wreaked havoc among their ranks.

Already scrambling to mount a defense against Teahl's rising temple and lacking the glyphs and alarms covertly dismantled by the Crimson Witch, the Sathiians barely succeeded in disengaging from combat to regroup.

In a few cases, however, seasoned priests fell back not from surprise but to work the Strand of Flesh upon the fallen between them and their enemies.

Corpses, Sathiian and sulari alike, began to soften.

Intertwine.

Fuse.

Like wet cloth, the flesh of the dead rose in great sheets between clusters of priests and assassins. Assuming these walls to be cover for the Sathiians' retreat, the sulari pressed forward, intent on hacking open a path to their enemy.

But the sheets of flesh proved too yielding to be more than superficially cut by their weapons. The walls collapsed upon their attackers, enveloping them like cocoons. The trapped assassins struggled to free themselves, but their cries and curses were almost immediately crushed from their throats as their bodies melted into the mass of flesh.

As the sheets of flesh absorbed the sulari, the Sathiians plied the Strands of Motion and Dominion. Like puppeteers, they moved the hungry flesh toward the assassins, whose turn it was to fall back against a very different kind of savagery.

Zina Atay was so shocked at the metamorphosis of Wargrum's temple, she lost control of her Aethic channel. The backlash of its collapse swept through the link, pummeling her and her fellow Sadri into unconsciousness.

She never realized she was falling.

She never felt herself hit the ground.

She never felt the great foot of Wargrum's temple crush her.

Ciridan's splinter appeared from the corridor to see a group of six Sathiians directing what looked like a wall of flesh against one of House Blackhand's splinters. Her sulari filled the air with a burst of spraydarts. Two of the priests died, along with their control over the fleshy wall. A large section folded and collapsed on two nearby acolytes. Their cries were promptly squelched, and their mass was added to the fleshy heap.

Two of the four remaining priests regained control of the hungry mass, halving it and rotating a portion to intercept Ciridan's splinter. The other two wove supporting spells as the flesh slowly came about.

There was a spray of acid.

There was a flash of light.

Elyssa was not connected to the Sadri link and unaffected when it failed. She worked quickly to revive Malaraphi. Within moments, the old elfi was awake and returning to strength and vigor. He was reestablishing weaves within moments, restoring the severed link with his distant Sadri and calling them to consciousness. Then he rose to survey the scene before him.

The Wargrumite temple moved toward the Sathiian stronghold with deliberate, thundering steps. Its form gained definition with each footfall. Portions of it continued to break apart or transmute in shape and substance as it walked. Masonry and tile and brick, wood and stone and mortar, crumbled and joined and mixed as its form refined, hardening into stone and sprouting protective vegetation. Over just seven steps, the immense gholem lost its rough approximation of humani shape and became an effigy of Wargrum, with a body of sculpted rock and tangled locks of ivy.

Then Malaraphi understood.

It was no wonder his auguries had seemed insubstantial; he'd embedded an invalid assumption in his query! He'd assumed that Blaythe's forces would overrun the Temple of Wargrum and had been focused on divining the time of that event. He'd not considered that the situation might be reversed, that the Wargrumites might initiate the conflict. Nor did he imagine that the Sathiian attack on Teahl's temple would be directed against the very temple itself. Now he understood and realized that the portents had always been there—he'd simply failed to interpret them correctly.

Malaraphi cursed beneath his breath and turned to address Elyssa, but the faint sound of metal on ceramic caught his attention. He looked down.

Fragments of a broken chain lay at his feet.

He touched his fingers to his neck and found only flesh.

Broken.

Malaraphi cursed, aloud and imaginatively.

When he lost consciousness, he had inadvertently signaled that the battle between the Sathiians and the Wargrumites had begun, that the time had come for Blackhand's sulari to initiate their attack inside the temple. By now, the halls would be red with blood.

And Arwynn… If he should die, who do I have left? Will it all… end? Here?

The wizened elfi stared at the remnants of the broken chain. He'd been so careful, so deliberate in his actions, his plans…

Has it all been for naught?

A glimmer of an idea surfaced.

Of course!

Malaraphi fixed his gaze on Elyssa.

"Our strategy has changed," he said quickly. "We will no longer provide a diversion to cover Arwynn's actions. We must focus Blaythe's attention away from them."

"The gholem?" Elyssa asked.

Malaraphi nodded. "The Wargrumites have circumvented Sathiian mastery over flesh by attacking in a vehicle immune to that Strand. But their vessel is not invulnerable. Blaythe's adepts will try to destroy it before it reaches their temple. We will protect it and keep Blaythe's attention divided."

"When the gholem reaches the temple, it will destroy it," Elyssa said. "The sulari inside…"

"Are not our concern."

The Sathiians fell to the ground screaming as acid burned away their clothing and dissolved their flesh. Their spells misfired, blasting wide holes in the ceiling above their intended targets.

Ciridan wasted no time. She rushed her splinter out of the passage under cover of the falling debris and ordered them to continue their attacks independently. Then she turned to face the two remaining priests, a poisoned blade in each hand. This was her opportunity to kill herself and move on to more important matters.

Ciridan plunged headlong into the Sathiians as they struggled to bring their fleshy walls forward and used her momentum to bury her poisoned blades deep in their bellies.

Both walls of flesh spasmed as the poison burned through their controllers…

Ciridan rolled free of her victims—

… collapsing into a single mass as they died.

—and began opening a channel to the Aethios as she clambered to her feet.

Pseudopods erupted from the writhing mass of flesh and began to lash out in all directions. Without Sathiian controllers providing direction, the senseless bulk struck blindly to feed its unnatural hunger.

Ciridan spun to flee but slipped on tile slickened by liquefied flesh.

She fell to the ground. Her burgeoning Aethic channel slammed shut as the shock of her landing rocketed up her spine. Dazed, she scrambled to gather her wits and distance herself from the flailing lengths of flesh.

A pseudopod landed to Ciridan's left; another found a dead priest to her right. Instinctively, the mindless mass ceased flailing to draw the Sathiian's body into itself, affording her precious seconds to gain her feet and escape.

Adrenaline surging, heart pounding, she dashed into an adjoining passageway—

Whump!

—slammed into two Sathiian adepts. She tried to roll with her fall, but her left leg twisted painfully under a toppling priest.

Her head struck the tile with a dull crack.

Welbley, the Crimson Witch, and four purple-robed adepts looked across the Gardens of Twilight from a balcony on the second level of the Sathiian temple. Word had just reached them of battles in the lower halls, but they had no specifics.

Between the mammoth gholem plodding toward his temple and the stone-eating beetles in the cellars, Welbley assumed his acolytes battled Wargrumite priests and focused his efforts on destroying the gholem. When it fell, the Wargrumites would lose hope and flee.

When the massive gholem cleared the tree line, some two hundred yards away, Welbley raised a serpentine staff high in the air. Icy silver light flared from its head. Four more flares of colored light burst into being at his behest, invoked by adepts on his left and right. When the gholem was a hundred yards away, Welbley threw his arm down. The cold ball of light stretched long and jagged, like a bolt of lightning frozen in time, then streaked toward the plodding giant—quickly joined by four others of varying colors.

Welbley grinned as he watched the radiant bolts of energy streak toward their target.

These were not disintegrative charges; that power was bound to staves locked in the battle-filled lower halls. These were only Aethic fire. Though the energy could not dissipate the substance of stone, Welbley was convinced it could shatter it.

His expression turned from glee to bewilderment when the Aethic blasts were deflected.

And from bewilderment to shock when one bounced directly back at them.

CHAPTER 92

WYRMSWEEP

The silken vestments that cloaked the Haugwym, the heavy helms that obscured their faces, the leather harnesses that bound their great tails to their backs—all were torn away in seconds, left to litter the flat. Deception was no longer required. Each sauri drew to its full height of seven feet (or more) and sprang to battle with a great leap and terrifying cry.

The sauri were humanoid in form but reptilian in nature. Their heads were oblong and wyrmlike, squat muzzles lined with sharp teeth and slit-pupiled eyes. A bony ridge crested each head, lessened at the neck, and rose high again about the upper back before fading over the rump. Midway along the length of a great and heavy tail, the ridge grew tall again before disappearing near the tip. Though their arms were jointed like humani's, their thickly muscled legs showed an extra joint between the knee and ankle. Their hands and feet were bare, armed with powerful claws sharpened for battle. The wide scales of their bodies glittered, green and blue and red.

The scant armor the sauri wore beneath their discarded apparel was comprised entirely of bone. Their arsenal of weaponry ranged from familiar to bizarre: from swords and axes, to pole arms and barbed whips, to steel spikes affixed to their shoulders, elbows, and knees. Many had sheathed their tails with harnesses of tethered chains laced with sharp blades.

The sauri moved through the gobli like scythes through dry grass, mowing them down with claws and weapons and blades that sliced cleanly through anything within the arc of their massive tails.

Melkor heard the startled cries of his warriors. Angels, it seemed, had joined the fray, descending from the heavens to aid them in their struggle against the Horde. He wanted to look to the east, to the source of the cries, but dared not turn his attention from the battle at hand. He had to maintain the image he'd labored to create until the time came to abandon his body.

A crossbow bolt pierced his left thigh. He faked a reaction.

A club cracked his ribs. He pretended to feel it.

But Melkor felt nothing. Not the bolt, not the club. Through the Crucix, he controlled his body, but the sensory bonds were limited. He still perceived sight and sound, and smell to a lesser extent; taste and touch were completely disconnected from his awareness—as were all bodily limitations imposed by physiology. He felt no pain, no fatigue, no physical constraints.

He would let his body expire when the battle was won.

But now, amid its furor, he needed to fight without distraction. If his troops knew that it was magick that bound him to life, they would fear for their own. If he remained fixated on the enemy, they would seek to emulate his passion, and his legend would inspire them and their progeny for generations. So he focused on his enemies and climbed higher on the growing mountain of their corpses, cutting down any gobli that dared clamber up to reach him.

When the sky darkened with the great shadows of flying things, he maintained his concentration. Nor did it slip when the gobli throng before him exploded in a wall of flame and blood and vapor.

Bolstered by Warsong's bloody light, Gahlyfahx pushed his wedge of warriors and wizards deeper into the Horde. Their strategy was to penetrate as far as possible before forward progress was stymied; then the wizards would form teleportive fields to remove them from the battle to a place where they could regroup and charge back into the fray from a different point.

Of the wizards in their band, three held teleportive fields at the ready while the other fifteen plied their Strands against the Horde. With each new charge into battle, they attacked the gobli with elemental magicks—turning the earth and air against them, throwing fire, and transmuting sweat and blood into acid. As forward momentum waned, seven forewent their offensive spells in favor of defensive magicks.

Three distorted the air with spells of reflection that bounced randomly from warrior to warrior along the wedge's periphery. Where the spell landed, the warrior was distorted in size and location, so gobli blows were improperly placed.

Four others encircled the band with spells of thickening, which slowed all objects surrounded by air, so that hurled objects and projectiles fell to the ground before striking their targets. The remaining magickai employed more gruesome spells, so that they might dishearten those gobli they could not directly affect.

The wizards of the Guild of the Red Mantis stole the lives of gobli as they approached and transferred them to nearby warriors, healing wounds and replenishing vigor as the hapless gobli grayed and shriveled and died.

The mages of the Green Raven caught the death cries of the gobli from all around, amplified them, and concentrated them into ghastly shrieks, which they projected forward like battering rams, powdering bone and liquefying organs.

The casters of the College targeted the gobli to the rear of the Ufwinian wedge and placed upon them the images of humani warriors, so that their own kind might cut them down.

And through it all, the warriors of Ufwin fought.

And fought.

And fought.

Baloth's azûne dove from the black sea of smoke over the Obruhk, the roar of air over scaled wings the only herald of their coming. Six hundred feet above the battlefield, the sound became audible to the warring parties below, though few recognized it for what it was—the onrush of five humani warriors mounted on winged dragons.

At five hundred feet, the wyrms snapped their monstrous wings forward with such thunderous force that hundreds on the battlefield were thrown to the ground from concussive bursts of displaced air.

Four hundred feet.

Muscles coiled.

Three hundred feet.

Jaws dropped.

Two hundred and fifty feet.

Gullets flexed—

Two hundred feet.

—and purged.

Panic broke over the crowded battlefield, but none could flee: their numbers were too great. There was no escape from the torrents of acria that spewed from the throats of the onrushing wyrms. Once disgorged, the streams of thick bile began to break apart into loose globules interspersed with heavy spray. Moisture in the air fizzled away from the viscous substance as it fell, giving each globule a sizzling tail of steam. Earth and rock and metal exploded instantly upon contact with the wyrms' bile; flesh and bone were vaporized, and fringe areas of contact burst into flame.

The azûne continued their deadly strafe until they reached the outer periphery of the battlefield, then arced up and away, back to the dark clouds that had concealed their coming, positioning themselves for another pass.

CHAPTER 93

TWISTED FATE

Fedahi could not believe his good fortune when he caught sight of Ciridan struggling with two Sathiian adepts. He cracked a toothy grin; the spirit had accepted his compromise.

Swift to find, slow to kill.

Elated, he sprinted down the corridor to dive into the fray—

—and dropped to the floor at the sound of the familiar click, scraping away the skin of his left cheek and jaw as he slid the rest of the way across the tile.

PfftPfftPfftPfftPfftPfft

Ciridan managed to prime her spraydarts as she kicked herself free of the Sathiians, but one of the priests gained his feet before she was in position to release the darts. She rolled to her side and tried to bring her chest forward to aim—

The priest's kick landed solidly in her kidney and knocked her onto her back.

Ciridan's sight went white, and her body stiffened with a sudden rush of pain.

The darts released.

A spray of tiny poisoned darts blasted from hidden hous-ings beneath Ciridan's tunic. A dozen lodged in the Sathiian's extended leg, and several more caught him in the groin and belly. He screamed in shock as the darts hit, then in agony as he fell to the floor in a spasmodic seizure.

Ciridan didn't care.

In her instant of pain, she'd lost hold of all her magicks.

Fedahi's attack was neither sudden nor furious. He stepped behind the surviving Sathiian, cupped his left hand over the man's mouth, and forced back his head. The dagger he'd strapped to his stump dragged across the priest's throat. It was over quickly. Fedahi let the man slip to the ground so he could attend to his prize.

Ciridan Lothloran.

Fedahi shuddered.

He could imagine no sweeter moment, no greater instant of satisfaction. This was the epiphany of his entire existence. The woman that had sent him to die in Evereve now lay dazed at his feet, wavering in and out of lucidity.

But she was alive.

Alive.

His body tingled with delight. He tittered giddily.

"You… oh, you—ho ho ho—oh, Ciridan, Ciridan! How I have longed for this moment."

He laughed, nudged her with the tip of his boot.

"You have no idea what our time together will mean to me. No idea."

Fedahi's dark eyes glittered with malice as he straddled Ciridan's body and lowered himself into a crouch. He bent his face to hers, so that he might taste her breath before he spirited her away…

… and chanced to notice a drop of blood.

It was a small thing, a single drop, but the sight froze his heart. He moved her cloak and looked below her right breast.

More blood on her tunic.

"No."

Not all the spraydarts had cleared their housings.

"No!" he cried. "No! No! No!"

Fedahi snarled like an animal and dropped his full weight on Ciridan's pelvis. He grabbed her face roughly with his good hand and jerked it forward.

"I will not be cheated!" he spat. "You will not die by poison—you will die by my hand! My hand, my hand!"

Ciridan's eyes widened in a moment of clarity as Fedahi raised his right arm to strike. Her body went rigid with fear. Her muffled gasp slipped through her captor's fingers.

"Yes! Yes, you see me now!" Fedahi ranted. "You see the face of your death! You see now that it is Fedahi Hasraheed that ends your miserable life! You would dispose of me? Ha ha! It is *I* who will dispose of *you!*"

He brought down his blade—

—and his arm was stilled by a thick pseudopod of flesh that wrapped tighter than kalypshia. Another caught him, held. A third. A fourth.

It was not Fedahi that frightened her. It was the writhing mass behind him.

"No! No! Noooooooooooo—"

His wail was cut by a fifth, then sixth, offshoot of flesh.

Images of Evereve Marsh rushed through his head.

But only for a second.

CHAPTER 94

DARKNESS

Arwynn had broken away from his splinter by the time the alarms sounded. He slipped unnoticed into a dark alcove and watched the Sathiians mobilize for combat. Most ran to the main halls or downward stairs, but several dashed to stairways leading upward. He thought that odd.

The promenades.

Blaythe's adepts must have detected Morkainen's approach and scrambled to launch a magickal counteroffensive from the promenades—wide walkways circling the second and third levels of the temple's towers, providing access to grand balconies that jutted out over the Gardens of Twilight.

Good. There will be fewer inside.

Arwynn followed the priests to the third floor, then snuck into the temple's central tower. When he gained the fourth level, he began to move more cautiously. If Blaythe had a guardian anywhere, it would be here, on the level where he slept.

The fourth floor of the temple's central tower consisted of six large rooms ringed by two circular corridors. The rooms were divided into three sets of two by narrow passageways radiating from the landing, where a spiral staircase joined to the level below. There was a large, heavily shuttered window where each passageway opened into the outer corridor. Two large metal doors were set into opposing walls of the inner corridor ring, bedecked with images from Sathiian scriptures.

Arwynn crept along the inner hallway, eyes sharp and ears alert for hints of movement or the telltale click of a mechanical device. He ran his fingers lightly along the metal doors and sniffed. Nothing. He peeked behind the tapestries decorating the corridor. Again, nothing. He looked down the three passageways that led to the outer ring of the corridor. Two were gloomy and quiet.

Down the third, he saw flickers of light. Yellow. Green. Blue.

Removing a short knife from a sheath on his thigh, he moved slowly down the passage. He chose a silvered knife rather than a nonreflecting blade; its mirrored surface would allow him to survey the outer corridor before entering. As he neared the passageway's end, he became aware of hissing sounds accompanying the flashes of light, and a distant booming. He paused and sniffed the air.

Boom!

It was fresh, cool—

sssss(blue flare)sssssboom

—laced with a trace of… burning? Sparks?

sssss(green flash)sssssscrack

Reaching the end of the passage, Arwynn examined the outer corridor reflected in his blade. It was empty. Tile floor, gilded ceiling. The smell was stronger. It came from outside and below. As did the staccato bursts of light and hissing sounds. And voices—garbled and pained.

sssss(yellow flash)sssssss(blue flash)sssssscracksssss(green flash)(yellow flash)sssss

Boom!

Arwynn crept up to the window and slid the metal screen aside. Bursts of bright color flooded the corridor and passageway behind him from the jagged arcs of yellow, green, and blue lightning that seared through the night outside the temple.

The source was eclipsed by the promenade a dozen feet below, but the target was easily seen.

It was a gargantuan effigy of Wargrum.

Beya—it's moving!

Easily forty feet wide and twice as tall, the massive figure was made of earth and stone and plant. It lumbered implacably toward the temple with thunderous footfalls. Most of the Sathiian magicks deflected off shields that flitted about the construct like shimmering gnats. Attacks that made it past the shields blasted away large chunks of rock and earth.

They must be on the first promenade.

A stray glance.

An image reflected in the blade of a knife.

A glimpse of a misplaced shadow down the passageway behind him.

A Prowler?

Arwynn felt his belly tighten and the hairs of his nape stiffen. He couldn't survive a Prowler—the grisly things were not of this world... shapeless horrors, bound to servitude by profane magick, as silent as nightfall and visible only as reflections.

Arwynn glanced out the window. The promenade was a long drop.

He looked back at his blade.

Closer.

He unstrapped his grappler, not taking his eyes from his knife. As he freed the barbed hook, something struck his shoulder and knocked the grappler from his hand.

It was a tendril of solid darkness, and it had punctured his left shoulder. Arwynn had never felt anything so cold. He lost sensation as the inky strand writhed and burrowed into shoulder muscle.

Arwynn slashed at it with his knife and pivoted to face the source.

His knife met no resistance. He saw no source.

The tendril seemed to originate in the gloom and darkness of the passageway behind him.

It must be that shadow.

A numbing cold spread over his left arm. The tendril had impaled his shoulder and was twining down his arm toward his hand.

Another salvo of lightning brightened the night. In the brief flash of blue, Arwynn could clearly see a shape in the passageway, monstrous and tentacled. When the flashes dimmed, he could still see it. It was so perfectly black that it was visible against the darkness. As the thing drew nearer, he could discern tendrils amid the tentacles and saw the strand that tethered him and deadened his left arm.

An amused chuckle came from the blackness.

A woman?

Another.

Not a Prowler, a priest.

Arwynn flipped the knife in his right hand and threw it at the inky mass—

A fat tentacle of thickened gloom swatted it away, then stretched and tapered into a tendril that writhed toward him.

Arwynn straightened his shoulders—

The tendril struck before he could trigger his spraydarts, impaling his other shoulder.

He fell to one knee as the strand of blackness wormed through the wound and snaked down his right arm, freezing away all feeling as it went.

Myrissa Dorumo stepped from the passageway as her quarry struggled to his feet. Syrupy blackness slid over and around her like a gelatinous octopod, arms thinning and thickening, twisting and swaying. Two held her victim's arms immobile. Two swayed in the air by her shoulders. Several writhed over her body and caressed her in ways both terrifying and erotic.

"What have we here?" She smirked.

She made a subtle hand motion as she approached, and the black strands lifted the man to his feet.

"One of Blackhand's little villains? Come to steal?"

She stopped a dozen paces from her victim and sent a third tendril to worm over his cheek.

"Why are you here?" Myrissa asked.

The tendril slid from the man's cheek to his lips. He clamped his jaw.

She chuckled.

The tendril slithered between his lips.

"No matter. You will talk soon enough."

The man glared at her but made no sound. He balled his hands into fists and bent his wrists sharply. Stilettos sprang from hidden sheaths on the backs of his arms.

Myrissa laughed.

"And what will you do with those, my puppet?"

She gently fluttered her fingers. The black bands that bound the man tightened and shook his arms. The veins in his neck stood out as he strained to bring his arms forward and aim the stilettos at her.

"Oh, I see! They shoot out, do they? How clever."

Myrissa held up her hands and smiled.

"But not today."

She slid her hands along the strands of blackness that bound the man, wrapped them twice around her forearms, and threw her arms wide. Her tethers snapped tight around the man's arms and jerked outward, thrusting his chest forward and his shoulder blades together.

She heard a rapid cascade of clicks, released the tendrils, and—

A torrent of tiny projectiles fired through the man's tunic.

—brought her hands together in a great sweeping arc. The shadows and darkness gelled into a viscid black curtain that caught and held the spraydarts.

She lowered her arms. The curtain melted into darkness, and the darts clattered to the floor.

Myrissa glared at her prisoner, then smirked and gathered her tethers again.

She flicked her wrists and slammed the man into the floor, then raised him to his feet and dashed him down. She was smiling broadly when she lifted him again.

"I am really enjoying this, my puppet," she said, and threw him to the floor.

She licked her lips as she watched him struggle to move, and the inky blackness that swaddled and stroked her began to congeal.

"But I have something more fun in—"

The wall behind the man exploded.

When the quaking stopped, Arwynn raised himself to his knees and looked around. The pall of dust diffused the intermittent flashes of lightning, lending a dreamlike aspect to the scene.

A large portion of the wall behind him was gone. The area was covered with powdered masonry and small bits of debris, but the larger pieces of the wall had landed farther into the passageway or bounced off the corridor's opposing wall. He could make out a woman's body in the rubble ahead, though he couldn't tell if she was alive. There was no trace of the blackness.

Hands and arms still numb, he struggled to his feet.

The debris flew over me. I'd be dead if I'd been standing.

He lumbered to the gaping hole. The night breeze quickly cleared most of the dust, affording him a view of the Gardens. A steady cannonade of lightning continued to bombard the gholem.

Must have been a ricochet.

He felt a tingling in his fingers.

He looked at his hands; they appeared unscathed. He opened and closed his fists. More sensation returned as he flexed and relaxed his muscles. Prepared for the worst, Arwynn checked his shoulders but found no wounds. The cilice on his wrist was undamaged. All that remained of the horrible tendrils was a fading numbness... and nightmares to come.

Outside, the gholem was battered and damaged but showed no sign of slowing.

No more time.

Arwynn scanned the rubble for his grappler. When he found it, he set the barbed hook against a portion of stonework he hoped would hold and threw the line out the breach.

As he took hold and prepared to lower himself to the promenade, he thought about making sure the woman was dead, but decided to let the gholem have her.

CHAPTER 95

SACRIFICE

The relentless azûne bombardments decimated the gobli pouring out of the Borowood and onto the Obruhk. Without the constant flow of mass to sustain their momentum, the gobli began to lose ground.

The Dûhrani rallied as the battle turned, reforming their lines and attacking with renewed fervor. The sauri were whirlwinds of chaos and death, leaping and spinning and clawing with savage finesse. The Ufwinians cut wide swathes through the gobli lines and deep into the belly of the Horde, opening paths for the infantry.

Gobli on the periphery began to flee—first in handfuls, then droves. With fire and acria behind them, and steel and magick in front of them, they fled how they could: north into the charred remains of the Tameron or southwest to the Aenin.

The prince watched the gobli flee with vacant satisfaction. The Crucix had robbed him of emotion. It took effort to draw pleasure from the rout.

Melkor looked out over the battered and bloody flat from atop his hill of corpses. The gobli had gutted his army. Of the Great Houses that had joined his army, Melkor estimated only a few hundred cavaliers and half as many infantry survived. Of his own Myriadi Royal, perhaps two remained.

The gobli had killed three-quarters of his force.

But we won.

Melkor managed enough emotion for one last smile.

Now was the time to release his body and free his soul.

He raised his battered sword to the heavens and cried loudly, proudly, regally—"Long live the Realms of Dûhr! May Pheon forever fire our noble hearts!"

As he prepared to destroy the Crucix, he realized he no longer held the jewel.

CHAPTER 96

EIE AND EMOTE

A bolt of lightning bounced off the gholem and struck the Sathiian temple below Arwynn and several yards to his right. The concussion upset the broken stonework around the breach and dislodged his grappler. He fell to the promenade amid a shower of dust and masonry and wood, but managed to control his landing and roll against the parapet as more debris clattered onto the walkway.

Loud crackles of energy and bright flares of color ripped through the night as the Sathiians continued their attack. Then a familiar voice caught his attention over the din. It was his sister, below and behind him on the balcony.

Arwynn focused on her voice, tried to catch a few phrases of her dialogue with…

Blaythe!

They were yelling, arguing. They were—

sssss(green flash)(yellow flash)sssssssssssktang(green flash)(blue flash)sssssssssss

—leaving?

Blaythe must be desperate. He'll try to escape before the giant destroys his temple. No doubt, by way of his vault…

Blaythe's adepts were focused on the gholem and didn't notice the bits of rubble falling from the walkway above their heads as Arwynn moved above them and withdrew three dark vials from his kit. He held his breath, leaned over the edge of the parapet, and hurled them one at a time, in rapid succession, down onto the balcony below.

Three sharp pops.

Then the poison went to work.

Malaraphi watched as the lightning barrage abruptly ended with haphazard flares and flashes of failed spells.

For a moment, the wizard considered turning his Sadri against the Wargrumite colossus, then decided against it. Allowing the gholem to destroy the Sathiian temple would lend a pleasingly divine aspect to the evening's events.

As the gholem raised a giant fist, Malaraphi had a flicker of concern for the sulari inside the temple.

Those worthy to serve House Blackhand will survive. The fallen are expendable.

He ordered his Sadri to stand down.

Morkainen's vague impression of warmth returned when he entered Blaythe's temple. It was stronger than it had been in the Gardens, steadily mounting as he battled his way deeper into the stronghold. Fleeting inklings of memories and emotions taunted him, at once alien and familiar. He began to follow the warmth, moving in directions that increased its intensity, robotically dispatching adversaries he encountered without technique or style.

He came to a narrow passage that opened into a larger hallway studded with statuary and heraldic wall hangings. He stopped. At his feet lay a single spraydart, one of House Blackhand's. Ahead, another, then several more scattered further down.

Morkainen followed the spraydarts to the end of the hallway. They littered the floor amid wide streaks of blood that trailed down an adjacent corridor. A few blood drops at the fringe of the scene were brighter than the others. Their golden sparkle caught his eye, and a faint heat rose from them to add to his inkling of warmth—it became a hazy sensation.

He followed the droplets down the hall and up a flight of stairs to a closed door. The sensation of warmth grew fuller, richer.

He kicked the door open.

The chamber was small: an office or a place of study. There were two small desks, several shelves littered with books and papers, and four chairs arranged about a long table equipped with inkpots and writing implements. There were also two bodies just inside the doorway—neither dead yet. The male was a Sathiian scribe. He was hunched on the floor, four feet from a prone woman, lips quivering and eyes blank. Saliva dribbled down the front of his tunic. Now and again, his fingers twitched and a faint whimper escaped his throat.

Morkainen paid him less than a passing glance. The woman was the source of the heat. The woman was...

"Ciridan?"

The blademaster crouched beside his Sahadi and placed his hand gently on her shoulder. The warmth within him surged, radiating to his limbs and loins. Ciridan did not respond.

He rolled her gently to her back.

Pieces of her face fell away.

She made a small sound. Her eyelids fluttered. The last of her face cracked and slid away, her true identity becoming clear.

"Mirithwin…?"

Morkainen felt disoriented. Shaken. He tried to steady himself, but his limbs would not comply. He fell where he crouched, the heat within him surging, receding, then surging again.

Mirithwin narrowed her eye, forced it to focus. She wanted to look upon the face of the only man she'd ever loved. Still loved.

His flesh tingled, his muscles twitched, his body hair stood on end. Bits of a past he'd never had pelted his mind. Tiny memories at first, strung together by a warm thread of affection. Pieces. Scraps. Mere driblets of the sea of recollection and sensation dammed beyond his perception.

A dam that was now failing.

Mirithwin's weave had not simply excised her existence from Morkainen's knowledge and memories, as was the case for all others she severed; it had completely sundered all portions of his eie and emote that touched upon or flowed from the only love he'd ever known. With his Severing, she'd inadvertently condemned Morkainen to a life without love and all the feelings it engendered. It was only now, as her life ebbed, that the threads of eie and emote she had cut began to reconnect…

"Gods above! Mirithwin!"

Mirithwin looked into Morkainen's welling eyes and smiled.

"I have never loved as I love you," she whispered.

Then she was gone. And the Severing was undone.

The dam broke.

A torrential onslaught of eie and emote overwhelmed Morkainen.

Mental images exploded with stunning intensity, amid banners of faces and thoughts atop streamers of emotions and experiences. Love, joy, care, tenderness, ardor, passion, affection, empathy, gladness, delight, sympathy, rapture, exhilaration, happiness, ecstasy, bliss, rhapsody—all and more flooded into the empty vessel of his spirit.

The sweet and good he had never known now surged into him in a single instant.

He could not stop it.

He could not control it.

He could not contain it.

The warmth intensified into heat, sharpened into burning pain, then flared into searing agony.

Morkainen's mind and body went numb; his senses failed; lesser vessels throughout his body ruptured. Blood flowed from his eyes and ears. His flesh split in patchwork patterns about his chest and face and limbs, spilling blood and yellow light as lost memories shuffled randomly into his mind like new cards into an old deck.

Then the torrent lessened.

Agony faded to simple pain.

The deck of his mind began to fall into a new order—gaps bridged, holes filled.

And for the first time in so many dark and loveless years, Rahain Morkainen was whole.

"Miri!" he screamed. "Miri! Mirithwin!"

CHAPTER 97

A SERPENT UNCOILED

Welbley and Kaleena hastened down a long stretch of curved corridor, skirting corpses and open pits as they hurried to the second level and Welbley's vault. So intent were they on reaching the strong room, and so loud was the clamor of combat from the floor below, they did not notice the cries echoing in the hallway ahead of them.

When the mutati liche that had once been Tehru Shaddoht emerged from a stairway between them and their destination, they were taken completely by surprise.

Realizing that vials of compressed gas had been thrown from above, two of Welbley's adepts immediately angled their lightning upward. The first missed Arwynn but passed close enough to force him off the parapet, burning his face and hand. The second blasted away the parapet and a portion of the promenade.

Arwynn held his breath as he fell into a red cloud of poison gas with the wreckage of the promenade. Two of the four adepts were already choking as he regained his feet. The other two had moved to the edge of the balcony, trying to stifle their coughs enough to weave.

Arwynn clenched his fists and snapped his wrists to release the poisoned stilettos. With a second wrist snap, he fired them into the choking adepts.

He was bolting down the corridor after Welbley and Kaleena before their bodies hit the ground.

The phantasmic Kuluth Brame had descended upon Morkainen unnoticed amid the deluge of eie and emote, attaching themselves to his psyche with tendrils and spines and tentacles and hooks. Even so, they remained hard pressed to keep their grasp, so turbulent was the flood of sensations that still battered the half-elfi.

To pervert him to their master's service, they needed to strengthen their grip on his mind. For that, they required stability.

Or a single dominant emotion.

"Scales of Mayhem!" Blaythe exclaimed.

"Beya!" Kaleena cried.

The thing that had been Tehru stepped from the landing and turned to face them. Had he not known better, Welbley would have sworn that a smile passed its lips as it locked its dead eyes upon him and shambled closer.

Somewhere behind the liche, a terrible wail sounded through the hall. Then a long shadow fell across the curved wall behind it.

Shouting erupted from the stairway—

Morkainen stepped into the corridor. He was carrying a body.

—and grew louder, chased by the thunder of running feet—

The mutati liche stopped and its chest began to swell, as though taking in a great breath of air.

The Kuluth Brame tittered when Morkainen came upon Blaythe and Kaleena. The lines of hatred that linked them were as dark and hostile as they were vibrant. Easily amplified. Easily focused. Easily made dominant.

Blaythe!

The name echoed through Morkainen's head like a thunderclap. As cold as his heart had been for too many years, it grew colder. This time not from lack of emotion but from the intensity of his hatred.

Blaythe was the cause of his misery. It was because of Blaythe that he'd been reunited with his truest love only to watch her die. It was because of Blaythe that he'd been made whole again only to suffer the deepest of sorrows. It was all because of Blaythe.

Morkainen was scarcely aware that he'd put down Mirithwin's body and was advancing on the priest.

Kaleena recognized Morkainen immediately. Despite her loyalty to her brother, she could not stay her hand—in Morkainen's eyes she was as much an enemy as Blaythe. Perhaps even greater. She had no choice but to attack.

In a twinkling of crimson, the air before Kaleena collapsed, compressed, and shaped itself into a shimmering red blade. It wavered in the air for a heartbeat, then shot toward Arwynn's blademaster faster than any arrow ever loosed.

Three Sathiian acolytes burst from the stairwell. Their faces were blanched, their eyes wild. Spittle frothed on their lips with each gasping breath. They saw the liche and—

The witch's blade grazed one of the acolytes' shoulders as it streaked toward Morkainen. Instantly, it doubled back on its path. Kaleena's intent no longer mattered; the acolyte's blood now bound him to the blade. It struck the man again, neatly slicing away a large piece of his scalp, then reversed itself with impossible speed.

Unencumbered by physical constraints, the Aethic blade struck again and again, whizzing about the terrified man in impossibly tight orbits until he was sliced to pieces.

—fled screaming down the hall.

The liche expelled a great green cloud from its bellows-like lungs.

A resplendent burst of silver light exploded from Welbley's staff and coalesced into a shimmering globe around around him. The silvery field neutralized the magickal essence of the spore cloud as it passed. Welbley gagged on the sickly sweetness that remained, untransformed.

Welbley's gags became laughter as he channeled more power into the shimmering field. It expanded from his body like a growing bubble of iridescent air.

It intercepted the liche's outstretched hands. They withered instantly.

Welbley took a step forward and caught the liche's still-outstretched arms within the field. They too withered away, as did the creature itself as the lord priest stepped imperiously before it.

Kaleena was unprepared for Welbley's spell. Her cloaks were instantly blasted away when the priest's field enveloped her, screaming horribly as they died. Her defensive shields shattered. Her jewelry exploded. The inkvanes on her arms and hands boiled away. She stood naked and defenseless and wounded as the priest brought down his liche.

But only for a moment. A heartbeat after her magicks were obliterated, she was pummeled unconscious by the backlash from their severed links and bindings.

She never heard the deafening thunder.

She never felt the temple shake.

CHAPTER 98

WARGRUM'S FIST

Kaboom!

The whole temple shook when a mammoth fist landed against the central tower, and a deafening crash rolled over the Gardens of Twilight. Streams of dust and pulverized masonry fell from the point of impact like powdery waterfalls as the Wargrumite gholem raised its colossal fist for another blow.

Kaboom!

Cracks radiated through the stone in a jagged filigree, loosening the stone blocks that did not split.

Kaboom!

The massive fist penetrated the structure in a deadly cascade of broken timber and masonry. The shock wave from the first blow had distracted the combatants inside, and the concussive force of the second had broken their ranks, but there was no escape from the collapsing structure. The falling debris crushed them indiscriminately, splattering the temple's crumbling interior with the blood of Sathiian and sulari alike.

Wargrum's avatar widened the hole with two more powerful blows, then reached in with both hands to grip the sides of the opening and tear the temple asunder.

Morkainen's pace quickened with each footfall until he was charging headlong at the priest.

"Blaythe!" he bellowed. "Blaythe! You are the one! You! You, Blaythe! You!"

He ignored the adepts that fled past him and paid no heed to the hail of masonry that crashed down around him or the rifts that widened in the floor. All that mattered was the priest.

"You are responsible!" the blademaster screamed. "You are the one! You! You, Blaythe! You!"

As the lord priest turned his attention from the withered remains at his feet to the onrushing assassin, Morkainen drew a gleaming slender blue knife from a sheath at his shoulder.

Arwynn's desire for stealth gave way to the need for speed. Having witnessed the approach of the monstrous gholem, and having slain those that would have destroyed it, he knew the creature would level the structure in a matter of minutes. His only chance was to follow Blaythe in his escape.

Arwynn dodged wreckage and falling debris as he raced down the twisting corridor in pursuit of his enemy/savior when the world around him exploded in a brilliant burst of silver light followed by an immense wave of fatigue.

He lost his footing and fell hard, skidded on his left thigh, then half slid and half tumbled through another yard of rubble.

He stopped five feet short of his sister's naked body.

Kaleena!

She was unconscious, but alive.

Welbley Blaythe stood just beyond her, facing away. The priest's staff and robes were lightly dusted with powdered rock. At his feet lay the withered remains of something indistinguishable. Pieces of debris from the ceiling were scattered in a wide ring around him, the same diameter as the silvery globe that surrounded him.

The field must protect him.

Arwynn tried to stand, managed to gain a knee, when another wave of exhaustion overwhelmed him. He fell heavily to the floor.

He looked at his sister. Whatever felled her must have unwoven the Enchantment of Vitality. He could barely move. Another wave of fatigue would leave him helpless.

Arwynn struggled to take hold of the cilice on his wrist and squeeze. When he felt its needles prick skin, he used the last of his strength to twist it sharply. He felt the needles bite deep into his wrist and the ampoules break. Fire exploded up his arm.

Kaboom!

The temple quaked.

The stimulants burned through Arwynn's body.

Statuary along the hall toppled; pillars collapsed; sections of masonry and splintered framing crashed down from above.

His muscles spasmed. His heart raced.

Two large pieces of the floor above broke free: one above Blaythe, one further down the hall. The closer fragment missed the lord priest and crashed several feet to his left. The more distant fragment was longer and spun as it fell. It punched a hole in the floor and lodged there.

Welbley did not flinch.

A shower of dust and stone rained on the lord priest. The larger stones bounced off his glittering shell, but the smaller stones and dust passed through the barrier and settled on his head and shoulders. He didn't notice. His attention was fixed on something further down the hall.

Then Morkainen came into view.

The half-elfi looked like a daemon in the dusty gloom: hair wild, flesh cracked like sunbaked mud, face contorted in a grimace of rage. Blood flowed from his mouth and nose, trickled from his eyes, oozed from his ruined skin. He was screaming at the priest and brandishing a weapon Arwynn had only seen once before, in the Ruins of Gehn. It had been wielded then by a thing from a nightmare.

Morkainen let fly his weapon. It whistled through the air toward Welbley, ricocheted off his shimmering field, and struck the wall to his left. The crystal blade shattered, and the otherworldly acid contained within instantly decomposed the stone. The spatters that struck Welbley's barrier fizzled into nothingness.

Arwynn rose to his feet and shook off his tremors. He was still weak, but the drugs would allow him to function. For a short time.

He looked at Kaleena, then at Welbley. As much as he hated the priest, his choice was clear. Arwynn gathered his sister into his arms and staggered to the sizzling hole Morkainen's blade had burned through the temple wall.

The last thing he saw as he jumped was a bright flash of green.

"You cannot kill me, drossi skok!" Welbley bellowed. "This Sacred Shield destroys magick, deflects matter!" he roared. "I am invincible! You cannot harm me!"

Morkainen howled like an animal. He threw aside his cloaks and weapons and charged the lord priest empty handed. Welbley grinned, enraptured as much by the stockpiled Aethic energy from his staff as his own sense of invulnerability. He embraced the energy, shaped it, fed it back into his staff. The staff began to glow. A hideous, venomous green.

"Come! Come to me, skok!" Welbley shouted. "Come and die, drossi!" He thrust forth his staff with a rigid arm and vomited painful words. The sickly green radiance coalesced into a torrent of green fire.

"Do you think I would hamper my own magicks?" he roared. "The Aethios cannot flow in, but it can flow out!"

Morkainen dove beneath a stream of green fire. He hit the floor with his right shoulder and collapsed into a tight ball, then rolled forward until his feet found purchase. He used his momentum to leap as Welbley discharged a second Aethic torrent.

The second stream missed Morkainen by inches, blistering the flesh of his left thigh as it passed. Morkainen hit the ground hands first, tucked and rolled, and gained his feet running. He closed the distance before the lord priest could launch a third attack.

And bounced off the glittering barrier.

Welbley laughed.

Morkainen snarled and began to pummel the barrier, his fists bouncing off without effect.

Welbley leveled his staff at Morkainen—

The blademaster screamed and cursed like a madman. He pressed his hands flat against the barrier and pushed mightily, as though he could shove it away.

—and noticed the dust and small fragments of masonry on his arm. He glanced at the floor. Small fragments of wood and stone lay scattered at his feet.

No…

As Morkainen's pushing hands began to penetrate the barrier, Welbley realized Adar Ashan's weave had a limitation.

No!

Slow-moving natural objects could pass through the field.

Morkainen pushed his left hand through the glimmering wall of force and took hold of Welbley's staff. Aethic energy pulsed through the serpentine rod and burned his hand like fire, but he did not let go. He was beyond such pain. He barely registered the stink of his burning skin as he forced his body through the priest's barrier and reached out with his right hand, fingers rigid in two sets of two.

The Kuluth Brame shrieked horribly when Morkainen met Welbley's nullifying field. They lost their hold as he pushed through the priest's barrier—tentacles and tendrils slackened and withered, hooks and spines detached and wasted.

In the space of a heartbeat, the Kuluth Brame shriveled from phantasm to hallucination, then to random thought, and finally to oblivion. All that remained was the painful memory of their dying screams echoing aimlessly along the lines of eie and emote.

Welbley screamed as Morkainen's fingers pushed through his eyes and curled closed. The glittering field that surrounded them shimmered, then wavered, then shattered like a glass bubble.

Morkainen pushed Welbley back and slammed his head against the wall, holding it firmly with his fingers in the priest's eye sockets and his thumb in his mouth.

"YOU—"

Wham!

"ARE—"

Wham!

"TO BLAME!"

Wham!

Again and again, Morkainen bashed Welbley's head into the wall, until there remained little to hold. He let the remains fall to the ground.

Then the ceiling collapsed, and Morkainen's world went black.

CHAPTER 99

THE ASHES OF DAWN

Arwynn sat alone in a tavern on the outskirts of Dûhr, in a simple wooden chair before a dying fire, the fingers of his left hand tapping restlessly against his thigh. Outside, the first light of dawn began to brighten the world. Soon, word of the night's events would spread.

The tavern door opened. Two cloaked figures entered: one tall and thin, the other short and squat. They bolted the door behind them and crossed the room to Arwynn. Without a word, they settled into neighboring chairs by the fire.

The squat one pulled back the hood of his cloak while the other waved a gnarled hand and rekindled the fire.

"Old bones," Malaraphi muttered as he, too, drew aside his hood. "You'll understand one day."

Arwynn eyed Malaraphi's companion. The lord priest looked no less exhausted than Arwynn himself.

"You've looked better," Arwynn said.

"So have you," Kargan grunted. "Beya, you look awful."

Arwynn smiled weakly.

"Let's forgo the posturing and get down to business, shall we?" Kargan suggested.

"Fair enough," Arwynn said. "Speak as you will."

Kargan took a deep breath, said: "The Sathiian temple is destroyed. Blaythe is dead. My adepts have recovered seventy-two survivors, including your lieutenant, the half-elfi. He's alive. Barely."

"And you've come to negotiate for their safe return?" Arwynn asked.

"Hardly," Kargan scoffed. "I run a Church, not a House Mercantile. Despite their motivation, your people suffered in Wargrum's service. The least they deserve is to have their wounds tended. Whether or not they return to your service is up to them. And you, I suppose."

"Then why have you come?"

"For the future."

"The future?"

The priest nodded. "Yours is a Great House Assassin; mine, a powerful Church of Elem. But it took our combined efforts to topple Blaythe. And his was but one temple. Just imagine the forces Adderash will mobilize when he retaliates."

"That's not my concern."

"Beya," Kargan scoffed. "Of course it is! The more power the Black Church accumulates, the more freedom you lose, and the weaker your organization becomes. Same for me."

Arwynn frowned, said nothing.

"Right now, we have an opportunity to capitalize on Blaythe's defeat," Kargan continued, "and spark a larger movement against the Black Church—one with the potential to put them on the defensive."

"A noble goal. I wish you luck."

"Thank you. Unfortunately, I lack the resources required…"

"So, you came to me for financing?"

"Not quite."

Arwynn thought a moment, then smiled. "Surely, Kargan, you're not suggesting that I become a champion of your cause?"

"Why not?"

Arwynn chuckled softly. "Do you seriously expect me to squander my remaining resources on so profitless a venture?"

"The choice is yours, of course," Kargan acceded. "But before you dismiss the idea entirely, think on this. Several days ago, Melkor did two things of great significance. First, he positioned his Family against the Black Church by killing Blaythe's priests. Second, he led an army northward to drive the Gobli Horde from the Borowood."

"A fool's quest."

"Yes…"

Arwynn raised an eyebrow. "But?"

"What if he succeeds?"

"He won't."

"But what if he does?"

Arwynn's frown returned.

"Ahh, you're thinking." Kargan chuckled. "Good. Let me tell you what I think. If Melkor's army returns victorious, not only will they enjoy the full measure of gratitude and confidence of all Dûhrani, but the Family Royal will support any House that aligns itself against the Black Church. That will certainly entail valuable dispensations: materials, contracts, information—what have you. For a Great House that has already demonstrated not only the willingness but the wherewithal to strike a substantive blow against Adderash, the allotment would be very, very large."

"Tempting," Arwynn granted. "But even then, such a disbursement would scarcely compensate me for opportunities lost. The House Royal may close the realm to the Sathiians, but they can't squelch their influence. Or the market for my services. And we both know that as risk increases, so do profits."

"Profits?" Kargan looked at Arwynn for a long moment. "After what the Sathiians did—to your people, your House, your realm—you would use your talents to further their ends?"

Arwynn smiled coldly. "Now, Kargan, I never said that."

Kargan looked curiously at the assassin; then a shallow smile slowly spread across his face. "Ahh, I understand."

"Yes, I think you do."

"Professional distance."

"And appropriate payment."

Kargan stood and nodded his head deferentially, then turned to leave. Without turning, he paused and said: "I suspect, Arwynn Blackhand, that the market will treat you well."

EPILOGUE

THE MASTER AND THE MAGICKAN

After Kargan left, Malaraphi reached into his robes and withdrew an ornately carved scroll case.

"It appears the Church of Wargrum will be a patron of your House going forward," he said, handing Arwynn the scroll case.

"And a very lucrative one, I suspect," Arwynn said. "What's this?"

"A gift from Teahl," Malaraphi said. "Reward for our aid in destroying the Sathiian temple. He asked me not to give it to you until he left."

"What is it?"

"Scrolls."

"Magickal?"

"Yes. Enchantments. Vitality and World Gate."

Arwynn's body tensed, and he locked eyes on the wizard's. "Vitality? How could Kargan know about—"

"He doesn't. He insisted on a token of gratitude. I requested these enchantments."

Arwynn relaxed. "How long will his Enchantment of Vitality last?"

"Twelve weeks."

"Who will provide the Aethic conduit?"

Malaraphi shook his head. "No one. This magick is regenerative for its duration. But I warn you, there is still grave danger. The Enchantment of Vitality *staves off* needs—it does not eliminate them. You were barely alive when my Sadri found you; your debt will be far greater when this enchantment fails. If you have not purged your body of the somphora by that time, you will die."

Arwynn managed a nervous chuckle. "What choice have I, wizard? Hmm? The lotos? I'll not be its slave. Besides, if you are successful, we will have the Clubfoot's cure soon enough."

"If he has a cure."

"He does. Zaaldirn never does anything he can't undo."

"And if he doesn't?"

"Then you will inherit a Great House Assassin. And a few…surprises."

They were silent for a time, the master and the magickan; then Arwynn asked: "Why World Gate?"

"Hmm? Oh. To provide a shunt between the Icetops and the Red Jungle."

"To expedite passage?"

"And bypass Xotl."

"Xotl? What is it about that place that bedevils you, Vanir?"

"If fate is kind," Malaraphi said, "you'll never know."

END

ACKNOWLEDGMENTS

First and foremost, this book would not exist without my children's unwavering support and constant haranguing. Without Kate, Zara, and Chris incessantly bugging me to finish, this story would still be languishing on a hard drive somewhere.

Thanks, kids. I owe you one.

I am indebted to Jane Turner, my developmental editor, and Elyse Lyon, my copyeditor and publishing mentor. Jane's guidance helped refine my original manuscript into a fluid and engaging tale, while Elyse's editing and continuity corrections honed both its readability and its credibility. My appreciation also goes to Elyse for the grace and kindness she showed me as she ushered me through the publishing process. Additionally, I must express my sincere gratitude to Anna Barnes for her copy review and exceptional work crafting clever and engaging promotional materials for my novel, including an author biography that makes me seem far more interesting than I actually am.

I would also like to take this opportunity to extend my heartfelt thanks to Frank Frazetta, for artwork that never failed to excite my imagination; Jim Duffy, who introduced me to Dungeons & Dragons and set in motion more stories than I will ever be able to write; Frank Herbert, for sparking my desire to not simply weave stories but create whole worlds;

and Gary Earl Ross, for first fostering in me the belief that I could actually do it.

And special thanks go to my parents, A. James and Gaile, and my brother, Jay. Without them, I would never have found the footing to take this leap.

ABOUT THE AUTHOR

Jenna Kinkade is a mathematician, engineer, scientist, dungeon master, and designer of unique and eccentric board games. Despite the analytic training from her two masters' degrees and her doctorate, her fiction is vivid and twisted in a way that engages the fringes of the imagination and breathes new life into tired tropes. Jenna began writing stories as a teenager, inspired by her passion for visual art and her love of '70s comic books and sci-fi. Now she creates intricate worlds and devises innovative magical technologies for her stories and Dungeons & Dragons campaigns, aiming always to tell a tale that is fresh and new. *Serpent Ascending* is her first novel.

Jenna lives in Indianapolis, Indiana, with two dogs that adore her and three cats that tolerate her. There, she continues her scientific endeavors and designs board games as a hobby. You can check out her games at deviousweasel.com.